Can't
Resist
Her

The Southern Gentlemen

Back to Your Love
Couldn't Ask for More
Never Let Me Go

The Roses of Ridgeway

Kissing the Captain
The Preacher's Paramour
Loving the Lawman
The Roses of Ridgeway: The Complete Collection
Electing to Love

PHOENIX Files

Darkness Rising
Embrace the Night
Midnight's Serenade
The Phoenix Files Trilogy
Love's Holiday

Climax Creek

A Passion for Paulina
Seducing Sheri
Vying for Vivian
Adoring Ava
Persuading Patrice
Love and Life in Climax Creek: Volume One

Can't Resist Her

KIANNA ALEXANDER

 Montlake

Text copyright © 2022 by Eboni Manning
All rights reserved.

Published by Montlake, Seattle

www.apub.com

Amazon, the Amazon logo, and Montlake are trademarks of Amazon.com, Inc., or its affiliates.

ISBN-13: 9781542034098
ISBN-10: 1542034094

Cover design by Faceout Studio, Molly von Borstel

Cover illustration by Louisa Cannell

Printed in the United States of America

For every little Black girl who ever felt crushed by the weight of the expectations of others, be they familial, cultural, or societal. I see you, and I value you. Sending you love and strength.

CHAPTER ONE

Setting yet another empty box near the pile sitting by her front door, Summer Graves blew out a breath. Snatching off the bandana that had been covering her dark brown curls for the better part of the last three days, she swiped at the perspiration on her forehead, then tossed the cloth into a nearby laundry basket.

The pile of boxes she'd have to take to the recycling area of her complex was nearly as tall as her, but there was no way she was dealing with it now. Instead, she flopped on the black sofa she'd positioned beneath her window for now. She planned to reposition it later, but this kept it out of the way until she got things in place. Sitting sideways, she threw her legs over the armrest and stared through the open blinds.

She'd chosen one of the more established complexes in downtown Austin—a place not too far from her beloved childhood neighborhood, Ivy—as her new home. It had been nearly fifteen years since she'd left to pursue her education and to experience life outside her comfortable little Texas hamlet. But life had brought her right back here, back to where she began, to the only place she'd ever truly felt at home.

She touched the braided silver chain around her neck, sliding her fingertips around until she grasped her unconventional pendant. It was an antique turquoise earring—one she'd lost the mate to years ago. The leverback style allowed her to secure it to the necklace without worrying that she'd lose it too. It reminded her to be brave, face her fears, and live a life she could be proud of.

She slipped her phone out of the pocket of her denim shorts to check the time. It was well past four o'clock, and she'd been unpacking all day. Her gaze swept over the room. Though she hadn't yet hung her art collection or family photos, most of the essentials were in place.

The phone vibrated, and her sister's face appeared on-screen. Swiping, she answered the call. "Hey, Crystal."

"Hey, Summer. Still waist deep in boxes?"

She chuckled. "Yes, ma'am. You know, you're welcome to come over and help me sort through all this stuff."

"Nah. You know I hate that kind of thing."

"Fair enough."

"Have you even eaten today?"

As if on cue, Summer's stomach rumbled. The sound seemed to echo in the room, bouncing off the bare walls to reverberate in her ears.

"Damn, sis. Even I could hear that."

"Yikes." Summer blew out a breath. "I had a banana and some oatmeal this morning, but nothing else."

"I knew it. You get so wrapped up in things that you forget the basics." Crystal popped her lips. "Listen, Dad cooked dinner. Why don't you just let us come over there? That way we know you're going to eat, and we'll get to see your new place. Two birds."

She looked at her attire: the raggedy shorts that had seen better days and the faded T-shirt from the merch table at a show from the *Anger Management 3* tour. *Yikes. I'm not dressed for company. But I'm starving.* "What did Dad make?"

"Chicken and dumplings and greens."

Her stomach rumbled again. "In that case, I'll text you my address. I just need to take a shower and get into some better clothes." She typed a quick message and sent it to her sister.

"Okay, I got your addy. And don't worry, it'll just be Dad and me." Crystal paused. "We wouldn't subject you to Mom's foolishness."

She swallowed. "I know, Crystal." She couldn't ask for a better big sister or a more understanding father. But her relationship with her mother had been strained ever since she'd come out to her on her last trip home. "Tell you what. Why don't I grab a pound cake from Swingin' Sweets for dessert?"

Crystal sighed. "Oh, yes. I haven't had cake from there in ages. See if they have the marble one, will ya?"

"I'll check. But you know they usually sell out by this time of day."

"Doesn't hurt to ask. See you soon." Crystal disconnected the call.

Summer stretched and headed for her room. Leaving her phone on the dresser, she went into the bathroom for a hot shower. Beneath the powerful spray, she scrubbed away all the sweat and grime from a day spent hauling everything she owned around her two-bedroom apartment.

Once she was clean and dressed in a pair of white jeans and a clean, solid black tunic, she wrestled her unruly curls into a ponytail on top of her head, put on a pair of sneakers, and grabbed her keys.

Outside, the early July air assaulted her, reminding her that she needed to buy more summer clothes. Her years spent in California had trained her for a drier heat, but since she'd been home, the Texas sun had reacquainted her with the humid, sweaty days of her youth.

The drive to the bakery, inside the Shoppes at Ivy shopping center, proved both short and scenic. A frown tugged her lips. *Where's Mary Ellen's Tea Room? Or Wong's Chinese restaurant?* Most of the small, family-owned businesses she'd patronized during her youth were gone. They'd been replaced by the big chains, or in the case of the tearoom, parking spaces. She sighed. Progress had its place, but there was something so impersonal about the way things looked now. The character and charm of those mom-and-pop enterprises, the way the proprietors knew your name and order as soon as you walked in, the way they asked about your family and your well-being—there just wasn't any good replacement for that kind of personal service.

A few doors down from where Mary Ellen's had once stood, she pulled up to the familiar pink-and-orange painted brick exterior of Swingin' Sweets. The one-story storefront was dwarfed by the newer five-story office complex next to it, but to Summer, the bakery still loomed large in her memory. Swingin' Sweets had opened in the mid-'90s, and she could clearly remember the excitement among Ivy's residents. Finally, they had another option for their birthday and wedding cakes. Her father had been patronizing the place since opening day, having gone to high school with one of the owners. She smiled as she parked, cut her engine, and left her car to seek out Ivy's most delicious baked goods.

She swung open the door, triggering the tinkling sound of the bell hanging above it. "Hey, Nellie."

"Summer! Long time no see, sugar!" Nellie Jackson, her father's former classmate, was stationed behind the glass-fronted counter, wearing her bright orange apron over jeans and a black T-shirt. Her dreadlocks, piled atop her head in a messy bun, were dusted with gray at the roots. "When did you get in town?"

"A couple of days ago, and I'm here to stay this time." She smiled as she walked closer to the counter. "Where's Kat?"

"Somewhere in the back." Nellie's head swiveled as she called out. "Kat! Come here right quick!"

Kat Talbert emerged through the swinging door adjacent to the counter. Her attire mimicked that of her partner in business and in life, except her apron was pink. A pink rosebud headband surrounded her short Afro like a pastel halo. As soon as she saw Summer, a smile spread over her face. "Well, hey, darling!"

Summer fist-bumped the two store owners. "Good to see you again, Kat."

"Likewise. Haven't seen you in a month of Sundays." Kat slipped behind the counter and draped her arm around Nellie's waist, pecking her on the cheek. "I'm done with inventory, Nel."

Nellie blushed. "Thanks."

Summer could only smile as she watched the two of them. Growing up, she hadn't seen many loving couples around town—not that looked like them. And even though she hadn't fully known herself as an awkward, shy teen, she'd felt a certain lightness, a peace, whenever she saw the two bakers together.

Now that she was home again, a larger queer community was available to her. But considering the absolute lack of time and mental space she had right now, Summer had chosen to return to the first true queer role models she'd had, knowing they'd still be there, still steeped in that beautiful love they shared.

"I was hoping to get a marble pound cake. Any left for the day?"

Kat winked. "It's your lucky day. I've got two in the oven right now—one's for an order, but the other's all yours—if you can hang around for about fifteen minutes."

"Awesome." Summer grinned. "While I'm waiting, let me ask you something. What happened to Wong's and Mary Ellen's places?"

Nellie answered that query. "Well, Mary Ellen retired, and since she didn't have any kids, she sold the place to those new-age folks. They planned on opening up a yoga studio, last I heard. I think they may have changed their minds and resold it; now, it's just parking."

Hmmm. I'm not sure how I feel about that. Mary Ellen was certainly entitled to her retirement, but Summer would miss the high teas at her establishment.

"As for Wong's," Kat joined in, "place caught fire about seven months ago. Faulty wiring, I think. Anyway, they decided not to rebuild and left town."

Summer's brow furrowed. "Really? Nobody in town could match their egg foo young."

"True. But when I talked to Mrs. Wong, she said she didn't feel like it was worth it to rebuild." Kat shook her head. "Damn shame, too. Nothing but chains going in around here now."

"Said their place wasn't a good fit for the new Ivy." Nellie pursed her lips. "But we're too stubborn to go anywhere. Ivy's our home, and ain't nothing gonna change that."

Kat's answering nod was as resolute as her partner's words.

"I'm glad to hear that." Summer understood that life meant change. But there were some things that were sacred, like the bond of community and friendship she'd always found in her little hometown.

She enjoyed the conversation and laughs with her two favorite bakers, and before she knew it, Kat had boxed up her marble cake. After paying, she took the ribbon-wrapped box from Nellie. "Thanks, y'all."

"Don't be a stranger," Kat called as she left.

"I won't." She waved and stepped back out into the sunshine. Tucking the still-warm cake underneath the passenger seat, she headed back to her apartment, hoping she'd get back before her family arrived.

She arrived at her apartment, relieved to see they hadn't beaten her there. She set the cake on the kitchen counter, opening the box with a dual purpose in mind—the cake would cool, and the place would smell great when her family walked in. She straightened up the room a bit, breaking down boxes and ferrying them to the recycling bin adjacent to her building. After that, she cleared the clutter from her small four-person dining table.

The buzzer sounded as she shoved a pile of receipts into a kitchen drawer. She answered it, then buzzed her sister upstairs. A few minutes later, she smiled as she opened the door.

Crystal stood on the doorstep, smiling. Dressed in a royal-blue halter maxi dress and a pair of bejeweled, flat sandals, she looked both cute and comfortable. "Hey, Lil' Sis."

"Hey, Crys." Summer let herself be gently tugged into her sister's embrace, inhaling the familiar scent of her citrus body spray. When the hug ended, she waved Crystal into the apartment. "Where's Dad?"

She pointed toward the parking lot. "At the car. I buzzed so you could open the door and we could bring the food in."

"Let me help."

She followed Crystal down to the parking garage. They arrived at her black Mustang, where their father, Rodney, stood by the open trunk. Wearing a Fisk University sweatshirt and a pair of khakis, he was already holding the big stockpot he cooked his greens in. "Hey, Summer. Hope you're hungry."

"Starved." She eased herself beside him and hugged his shoulder, placing a quick peck on his cheek. "Need help bringing in the food?"

"Yeah, that'll make it a little faster." He gestured into the trunk. "Grab that casserole dish there."

The three of them ferried the food through the cavernous lobby, with its minimalist gray-and-white décor, to the bank of elevators. Summer let them into her unit and they carried the dishes in, setting them on the table. Once that was done, Summer pulled paper plates and plastic utensils from the cabinet, along with three of the amber glasses she'd unpacked earlier. With the table set, they sat for the meal.

The covered containers were opened, revealing Rodney's legendary chicken and dumplings, turnip greens, and homemade yeast rolls.

He smiled. "I hope you brought your appetite."

Crystal eased her chair closer to the table. "I guarantee she did, Pop. She hasn't eaten since breakfast. You know how she is."

"Do I ever." He shook his head, even as a smile tipped his lips.

Summer gave him a sheepish look. "You know I never turn down your dumplings, Pop."

He chuckled. "That's my girl. Looks like your new place is coming together. Are you finished setting it up the way you want it?"

"Mostly. But I was overdue for a break when Crys called."

"I'm glad you realized that." He heaped some greens on her plate.

"I never thought I'd see you living in a place like this," Crystal commented. "Seems too modern for your tastes."

Summer chuckled. "You're right, it's not my usual style. Still, it's close to work, it's clean, and they had a great discount on rent for anyone signing a new one-year lease."

The three of them sat around the kitchen table enjoying their food, Summer and Crystal listening as Rodney spun tales from his last poker game.

Crystal laughed. "It's a trip, Pop. All these years you've been talking to us about poker and trying to teach us how to play, and I still don't get it."

"I don't know why. Summer picked it up, no problem." He snapped his fingers. "You want to try it again after dinner?"

Crystal shook her head. "Come on, Pop. We don't have any playing cards."

Summer giggled. "Yes, we do. I own three decks, and I unpacked one of them this morning. It's in my nightstand."

"Dang. I guess I can't dodge the lesson, then." Crystal sighed, making the same twisty-lipped expression she always did when frustrated.

Rodney chuckled. "It's not as hard as you make it out to be. I'll school you for an hour, tops."

Crystal nodded around a mouthful of dumplings.

Rodney went back to chatting his daughters up about his poker game, then about a discussion he and his buddies had about the rising property taxes in Ivy.

When he settled into silence for a few moments, Crystal spoke up. "What day did you say you're starting at Young Scholars?"

Summer smiled as the genuine excitement for her new job returned. "Classes start in a few weeks on a Wednesday, but we'll do an orientation that Monday. I can't wait to meet my students."

"What class did they put you with?" Crystal leaned forward, clearly anticipating her answer.

"The two-year-old class. They're rambunctious at that age, but so dang cute." The lure of guiding young children, with their innocence, boundless curiosity, and those cherubic faces, was what had drawn her to study early childhood education.

"Good, good." Rodney offered a genuine smile. "And those little ones will be lucky to have you."

"Grandma would be so proud of you, following in her footsteps and becoming an educator." Crystal chewed a mouthful of greens. "I just wish I'd had more luck stopping the city from tearing down Sojourner Truth."

Summer nodded, feeling the weight of her sister's sadness—a weight she shared. "Don't beat yourself up, sis. You wrote letters and went to a bunch of council meetings to voice this family's disapproval."

"Started a petition, too." Crystal sighed. "I collected 719 of the required 750 minimum signatures, and most of them are former Sojourner Truth students and their families still living locally. Nothing came of it, though."

They finished up dinner in silence, Summer's mind wandering to memories of her days at Sojourner Truth, as well as the special times she'd spent with her grandmother. The pictures flashed in her mind like scenes from a movie, bringing with them a bittersweet mixture of joy and grief. She shepherded her thoughts, concentrating on her last few bites of food, letting the rich flavors guide her back to the present moment.

As usual, the meal was delicious. Since she was young, her father cooked, and her mother cleaned (after her dad complained once that his wife wasn't suited to boil water, let alone handle the meals). She and her sister did their assigned chores, and the household ran like the proverbial well-oiled machine.

After dinner, she sat on the sofa and watched as her father and sister worked through the finer points of poker. From what she could tell, Crystal was finally picking it up.

Rodney laid out a hand in front of his daughter. "Okay, Crys. Let's see if you've been paying attention. Identify this."

Summer peeked over her sister's shoulder. A ten of hearts, a ten of spades, a three of clubs, a three of spades, and a queen of clubs.

Crystal studied the cards, lacing her fingers together in concentration. "Um, two pair . . . and a high card?"

"Right on." He fist-bumped his elder daughter. "There may be hope for you yet."

Crystal laughed, shaking her head. Turning toward Summer, she asked, "Are you going over to Sojourner Truth? You know they'll be opening up the worksite so former students and staff can take mementos."

She nodded. "I heard about that. I don't know when I'll make it over there, but I'm definitely stopping by."

"I probably won't. I'm not the sentimental type, at least not for stuff like this." Crystal shrugged. "We cleared out everything of Grandma's when she retired, so, nothing there for me."

Summer nodded. "I just wish they weren't tearing it down."

"You know that building has been sitting vacant for a long time," Rodney commented. "The school closed a decade ago. It's just a shame there was no good replacement for the students. They've all been funneled back into the public school district, and we all know they get far less individual attention there. All in the name of progress, they say."

Summer couldn't hold back her sigh. She thought of her own former students back in California. Her earliest students were middle schoolers now; some of their parents followed her on social media, allowing her a peek into their current lives. Children deserved that individual attention, that chance to be truly seen by those charged with their education. "I get it. Progress has to happen. But I wish they were building something there that benefitted the community, instead of yet another contemporary monument to capitalism, you know?"

Crystal chuckled. "Sis, you're speaking activist again."

"I know. I can't help it." She contemplated a third yeast roll but decided against it. "I know y'all think I do too much . . ."

"You do." Her sister and father spoke in unison.

She rolled her eyes. "Still. I don't know how much I can do, but the land hasn't been cleared yet. I owe it to myself, and to Ivy, to do something."

"Summer, you do understand that your grandmother's legacy remains intact, regardless of what happens to the building, right?"

"Yes, logically, I understand that. But I still feel the need to take action."

"And what are you planning to do, that your sister hasn't already done?" Her father eyed her.

She tilted her head and stared through the open window in the living room. Her gaze lingered on a particularly puffy cloud. "I'm not sure, yet. But trust me. I'm going to come up with a plan."

Rodney patted her on the back. "Well, we're always behind you, warrior woman." He stood, then returned to the table to gather their plates and utensils.

Crystal said, "Yeah, I guess we got your back. Just please, promise you won't get carried away this time, okay?"

Summer smiled. "I'll do my best."

—

Aiko Holt stifled a yawn, then stretched her arms above her head to release some of the tension in her shoulders. It was well past six o'clock, yet she was still at her desk. This had become all too common as of late because the higher-ups were pursuing their latest building project with vigor.

Transforming the old Sojourner Truth Charter Academy into a multiuse development would be quite an undertaking, and a good two-thirds of the company's staff were assigned to the project in one capacity or another. As a midlevel planner, Aiko's responsibilities at the worksite were broad and numerous—hence all the late evenings at the office.

She stood, then took the few steps to her window. Her office on the second floor provided her with a nice view of her surroundings. The sun hung low in a cloudless blue sky, and beneath that, cars streamed by on the busy lanes of US 183.

Eyeing her reflection in the glass, she idly played with the top button of her shirt. It reminded her of the climbing rose tattoo that took up most of her left side, from her hip to the base of her throat. As a company, Abernathy stayed on the cutting edge of urban redevelopment, mainly due to CEO Miriam Abernathy and her forward-thinking attitudes. Mrs. Abernathy hadn't cared about her tattoos when she'd been hired; this was Austin, after all.

She turned toward her desk and used the specialized platform to raise her monitor so she could stand. Standing after sitting for a long period always seemed to get her creative juices flowing, and she needed a little boost to carry her through this last bit of work.

She studied the finer points of the landscaping schematic on the screen. Plantings clustered around the main building ranged from white azalea bushes to fuchsia crepe myrtles to cedar elms. The bushes and crepe myrtles were mostly ornamental since they had robust blooming seasons and would produce lovely flowers. The elms would eventually grow to provide a nice canopy of shade from the hot Texas sun.

Aiko grabbed the stylus she kept tucked in her hair. The plantings were fine, but something was off. She squinted at the screen, steadily tapping the stylus against her chin . . . until the problem became clear.

Well, shit. That cluster of elms cuts off visual flow from the road and doesn't shade the parking lot well enough. She selected the cluster, then separated the individual trees and placed them in a more advantageous layout. After a few more small tweaks to shrub placement and softening the curb around the main traffic circle, she saved the file. Satisfied, she loaded the latest version into the company cloud, then logged out and shut down her computer.

As Aiko gathered her things in preparation to leave, she smiled. *I hope the boss lady is enjoying her vacation.*

Her phone buzzed, and she slipped it out of the hip pocket of her navy slacks. As she swiped, a smile came over her face. "Peaches. What's up, bro?"

Peaches' deep voice came over the line. "Nothin' much, just finishing up my last cut."

"I thought the barbershop closed at eight on Fridays?"

"We do. But I ain't staying that late. What's the benefit of owning the place if I stay here till closing? Besides, I got a hot date." Peaches chuckled. "She look too good for me to be caught lacking, know what I'm saying?"

Aiko laughed. "Yeah, I feel you." She and Peaches had been friends since their days as roommates at UT Austin. Peaches had majored in business administration, while Aiko majored in architecture. She didn't know what magic algorithm in the school's dorm assignment system had seen fit to put the two of them together, but Aiko thanked the universe for the friendship they shared. "Where'd you meet her?"

"Tinder. Where else?"

Aiko shook her head. "I told you about all that right swiping, Peaches. It's gon' get you in trouble."

"Maybe so, but it's also gonna get me laid, ya heard?" Peaches whistled, as she often did when she thought she'd said something clever. "You need to get a profile for yourself. I'm telling you, it's a bumper crop of fine-ass ladies out here."

"You know I ain't got time for that right now. It's way too much going on."

"What do you really have going on, though? Let me guess. You over there working late again?"

"Yeah, but I'm about to leave. You know this Truth project got most of us trapped at our desks way past five these days."

"Aiko, I thought you said your boss was on vacation."

"She is. She's in Seychelles."

Peaches scoffed. "All the more reason to clock out on time, then! Why you doing extra work when the HBIC ain't even there to see it?"

Aiko laughed. "You know me. I'm dedicated to a fault."

"Tragic. But you did say this is the project that's gonna get you that promotion to senior planner, right?"

"I really think so. Besides, I'm not gonna miss Truth. Going to school there, looking the way I looked and just being myself, I put up with a whole lotta shit, ya know?"

"I can imagine. You were already dressing tomboy when we met, and I was just getting started since my moms wasn't cool with me dressing like that in her house." Peaches cleared her throat. "Well, good riddance to bad rubbish then, bro."

"You said it." She swiped a hand over her hair, finally releasing it from the tight ball at her nape. The wavy length of it flowed down her back. She kept it bound during the workday to keep it out of the way when she found herself leaning over the drafting table. "That reminds me, I gotta stop by the pharmacy on my way out, grab my mom's medication, and drop it by the house before I go home."

"How is Ms. Janet doing?"

"She's doing all right. She spends most of her time in the garden now, and she seems pretty content. You know she's loc'd up now?"

"Really? How long?"

"Couple months? They're still pretty short, but since she stopped dyeing her hair, I think the style really works well with her gray."

"Damn. Can't believe it's been that long since I last saw Ms. Janet." Peaches paused. "And how about your pops? You talk to him lately?"

"Yeah, yeah. I video chatted with him yesterday." Her father, Kosuke, still lived in his native Fujisawa, Japan. "Can you believe he's talking about climbing Mount Fuji?"

Peaches chuckled the way she did when something made her nervous. "Not for nothing, but isn't Pops a little long in the tooth for that type of activity?"

"Hell yeah, he is. I told him as much, but you know how he is. Can't tell him anything." She shook her head. "He wants to paint it and says he can only do that the right way if he goes up there."

"That's how they all are at a certain age." Peaches said something to someone in the shop before returning to the line. "Hey, look, do me a favor. Give me the website for wherever you got that fly-ass purple suit from. Had you looking like a high-class pimp, and you know I got high standards."

"That suit wasn't purple. It was eggplant." Aiko grinned, unable to resist the opportunity to tease her best friend. "So, what you're saying is that I stay fresh and fly at all times? And you want the website so you can get on my level?" She knew all too well the struggle of finding just the right look for an occasion, even though she was what most would consider slender. But when she looked in the mirror and saw herself in a well-fitted suit, the benefits far outweighed the effort. "If you just admit it, I might be willing to help you out."

"Yeah, bro, whatever." Peaches' tone was playful. "Just give me the damn website."

Returning to her desk, Aiko opened the top drawer in search of the site's business card. She wanted to snap a pic rather than risk misspelling the URL. She found it right away and took the pic, but as she sent it, her eye was drawn to something else.

In the corner of her drawer, she saw a small silver object. The light coming through the window behind her desk illuminated it just enough to make it glint a little. The stones and turquoise could use a polish, but the aged piece of jewelry had held up well these past fifteen years, despite rarely being touched.

Looking at it sent her back in time to a moment she'd never forget. A mysterious yet unforgettable encounter with a young woman in a blue dress—someone she hadn't known but had longed to ever since that night.

Peaches' voice brought her back to reality. "Thanks, bro. I'm gonna check out this site as soon as I get a break. I need to order some new clothes, and I wanna try a new place. It's Black-owned, right?"

"You know it."

"Good looking out. Now I just need to see if they sell size bodacious."

Aiko snorted. "You are a mess. Let me get out of here and get Mom situated. I'll talk to you later, Peaches."

"Oh, yes. You'll be hearing from me after this date. Later, Aiko."

Ending the call, Aiko slipped the phone back into her pocket. With her suit jacket slung over her arm and her briefcase and keys in hand, she locked up and headed out.

After leaving the office, she took the drive south to Austin, then headed east into Ivy. She went through the drive-through at Putnam Pharmacy on Third Avenue, then took Carter Avenue to her mother's modest home on Desmond Place, the only cul-de-sac in the neighborhood.

The small bungalow, recently repainted in the same soft shade of beige it had worn since Aiko's childhood, sat just to the left of the center of the loop. Aiko pulled her car up the sloped driveway, then grabbed the small paper sack from the pharmacy and entered the house through the side door.

"Mama, I'm here," she called out as she closed the door behind her. The kitchen was quiet, save for the ticking of the old analog clock mounted above the door. The light was on over the stove, illuminating the white subway-tile backsplash with a yellow tint.

Janet Holt entered the kitchen through the dining room a moment later, dressed in her favorite pink sweat suit and old pink slippers, with her graying hair tucked beneath a silk bonnet. A smile lit her face. "Hey, sweetie. Did you pick up my meds?"

"Got 'em right here, Mama." Aiko handed over the small bag.

Her mother peeked inside the bag, then set it on the counter.

Aiko folded her mother's thin, petite frame into her arms and gave her a soft squeeze, followed by a kiss on the forehead. "How are you feeling today?"

"I'm all right. My back has been acting up a little bit." She shuffled to the oak table and sat. "My knees, too. But that's what I get for all those years on my feet, I suppose."

Sitting across from her mother, Aiko said, "Yeah, I guess. But you flew with Delta during the glory days of air travel. That's pretty cool."

"It was a lot of fun." A nostalgic smile came over Janet's face, only to be obscured by her hand as she covered a dry, rattling cough. "Everything except all that secondhand smoke. But you know you're the best product of my days in the air, don't you, Aiko?"

Feeling the smile tug her lips, she nodded. "Yes, Mama. I know."

CHAPTER TWO

Summer spent the better part of Thursday morning setting up her classroom at Young Scholars Academy. She'd just gotten her keys, and she was eager to make the space her own. The building, tucked into a corner just north of downtown Austin, only had room for about seventy-five students overall. And while she'd been offered a position at a larger school with slightly higher pay, she knew she'd made the right decision to teach at Young Scholars.

While she'd been impressed with the other school's facilities, it was a chain, with many rigid guidelines in place for how the students would be taught. Things were different at Young Scholars. And it was the owner, Scarlet Goodwin, and her dedication to the education of young children that had drawn Summer to the position.

She drew a deep breath and looked around at her class, from the cubbies for student belongings to the brightly decorated bulletin boards to the carefully designated learning centers. She could feel a smile stretching her lips.

Children brought a certain life to a space. The cacophony of their laughter, their small voices asking every question under the sun, the sight of their eyes lighting up as they discovered something new or found that, yes, they could do something that had seemed impossible before. It was exhausting and messy and sweet and wonderful, and she loved being a part of their young lives. *Teaching these little ones is chaos. And I love it.*

It's in my blood, I guess. Her maternal grandmother, Beulah Graves, had spent nearly forty years as an educator. Thirty of those had been spent as principal of Sojourner Truth Charter Academy, which Beulah had founded in 1976. Summer had heard tales of what her grandmother had to overcome as a Black woman in Texas during the Second World War to accomplish her dream, and she had endless respect and admiration for Beulah's sacrifices.

Summer left for her lunch break, waving to the receptionist at the front desk on her way out. Taking a short drive to Congress Avenue, she parked and surveyed the offerings. *I'm in the mood for something with a little kick.* A lot of new places had opened since she'd last been there, so she decided to give one of them a try. A little food truck called Taco 'Bout It caught her attention, and she walked toward it.

"How you doing?" the raven-haired woman in the window greeted her. "Got a taste for something specific, or do you want a recommendation?"

"I love the design of your truck," Summer said, admiring the swirling orange and pink design painted on the body. "I'm Summer, by the way. I work a few blocks down the road."

"Nice to meet you. I'm Callie. Thanks for stopping by my truck." She leaned on the counter. "Any idea what you'd like?"

Summer rested her palm on her chest, reading over the chalkboard menu. "Let me have a couple of shrimp tacos and a side of your cilantro-lime rice." She paused. "And tell me a little bit about yourself."

Callie looked surprised. "Hmm. I don't get that a lot . . . except when it's a man trying to flirt with me."

Summer chuckled. "I'm not flirting. I'm a hometown girl from Ivy, and I just moved back after living out of state for about fifteen years. So much has changed while I was gone. Now I'd like to know a personal story, something to connect to that change. If you don't mind telling me, that is."

"No problem. I'll have to tell you while I make your order, though." Callie moved toward the flat-top grill behind her. She squirted it with oil, then tossed on two scoops of shrimp and seasoned them liberally. "Let's see. My parents owned a little taco stand over in Houston, you know. For most of their lives, they worked there and used that money to support me and my little sister. Then, along came Hurricane Harvey. Destroyed the place, and badly damaged our house, only a few months before they were set to retire."

"Oh, no. That sucks."

"You bet it sucked." She laid out two tortillas, spread them with a creamy white base, and added the shrimp. "But I had to make sure they were taken care of. So I moved here. Opened this place a while back, and I use the money I earn here to take care of myself and my parents, too." She topped the tacos with cilantro, pico de gallo, and a squeeze of orange sauce. Then she set them in a box next to a small rice container, grabbed a plastic spoon, and returned to the counter. "That's my story."

"It's pretty compelling, I've gotta say. I respect your hustle."

"Thanks." Closing the box, Callie asked, "Need a drink?"

Summer shook her head, holding up her water bottle. "Nah. Trying to cut the sugar." After taking out her wallet, she slid a twenty-dollar bill over the counter. "Keep the change, Callie. And thanks for lunch."

Callie smiled as she extended the box and spoon. "I appreciate it. And I hope to see you again."

"If this food tastes as good as it smells, you'll definitely see me again." With a wink, Summer headed across the street to the park.

After reaching the grassy expanse, she sat on a bench to eat. The meal was delicious, perfectly cooked, and flavorful. While she sipped from her water bottle, she thought about Callie's story. Hers was a triumph over a bad situation, and Summer had a lot of respect for that. The conversation had given her some perspective. Not every new establishment in Austin was owned by some faceless corporation. There were real human narratives at play here, and if her hometown had to change, she'd want people like Callie to be the catalyst.

After finishing her lunch, she drove back to Ivy, to the site of her old school. She pulled into a spot near the back of the lot, determined to grab a little piece of STCA before the whole place was reduced to rubble and carted away like trash.

According to the signs posted all around the campus, the main entrance was the only one people were allowed to use. So she headed straight there and through the propped-open double doors. A wave of familiarity washed over her as she walked across the lobby toward the north hallway, where she'd taken most of her elective classes.

At the center of the lobby, she paused and lifted her gaze to the large faded rectangle on the wall facing the entrance. In her mind's eye, she could still see her grandmother's stern yet smiling portrait hanging there.

She moved down the dusty corridor, drifting in and out of a few of the open classrooms. She saw some of the same old Impressionist prints hanging on the wall in Mr. Souder's art class. The small practice stage still stood in Miss Yates' dramatic arts class. And through the streaked glass on the door of the locked chorus room, where Mrs. Leoni had led students in song, she could see the rickety risers still set up.

She looked to the end of the hall, smiling when she saw the open door there. Inside that room, she'd taken Ms. Allen's dance class for her last two years of high school. She walked over to the barre and placed her hand on it. The once-glossy wood had become rough and dusty from neglect; it had been years since anyone had been around to polish it. The room held so many memories, and they were all around her. As she stared in the dingy mirrors, she could see her younger self going through flexibility exercises with her classmates and donning her headwrap and black leotard for the African dance she'd performed at her recital.

With a sigh, she released her grip on the barre and headed for the far corner of the classroom, where Ms. Allen's desk still sat. On the bulletin board just behind it was the item she'd come for—a vintage poster of Alvin Ailey's dance company. She moved the rickety chair behind the desk as close as she could to the wall, then gingerly climbed atop it. Carefully, she removed the thumbtacks from the corners of the poster and took the memento with her as she stepped down. After rolling it up, she tucked it beneath her arm. With one last, wistful glance around the studio, she walked out and headed to the lobby, then through the west hallway toward the gymnasium.

Reaching the gym, she entered and moved toward the oakwood bleachers. Many of the banners celebrating the various sports victories of the Sojourner Truth Cavaliers still hung from the rafters overhead, and she could almost hear the roar of the student body filling the space during a pep rally. Sitting on the bottom row of the bleachers, she closed her eyes for a moment and remembered.

The lunch periods when she'd snuck away with her best friend, Gina, to catch up on the latest gossip. Gina lived in Los Angeles now and worked at a high-end salon, styling hair for A-list clientele.

The basketball games where she and her friends had cheered their team on. Kelvin Rhodes, a star center during her high school years, now played for a professional team in Japan.

Taking PE freshman year, where she'd come up with every excuse to avoid running, only to have Coach Keys double her laps. Coach Keys had retired a few years back and still lived near the school. *I should stop by there later and see how Coach Keys is doing.*

Her fingertips found the unorthodox pendant hanging at her throat as another memory loaded. This one loomed larger than the others: more intense, more profound.

Being in this space again . . . I can't help but think about her. What is she doing now? Does she still live in Austin? Summer had looked her up a few months before coming to town but found she didn't have any social media accounts. All she could find was a social profile, but by the time she saw that, Summer had felt so weird about snooping around in her life online that she'd closed the tab and stopped her search.

She opened her eyes and blew out a breath. Turning her head slightly toward the right, she could see a tall, slender figure approaching.

She blinked a few times, trying to get a clearer view of who it was. They seemed to be walking toward her with intention: as if they knew her.

Her eyes widened as recognition hit, and her heart dropped into her sneakers.

It's her.

Aiko Holt—still the biggest crush I've ever had in my life—is walking toward me right now. Shit!

She had no idea what to do. Should she stand? Should she run and hide under the bleachers? Her brain shut down, and all she could do was sit there and stare, open-mouthed, like a country rube on her first visit to the big city.

Aiko stopped walking just beyond the reach of Summer's personal bubble.

Summer looked up slowly, taking in Aiko's impeccable style along the way. She wore black suede loafers; a smart black suit, obviously tailored to her frame; and a cornflower-blue button-down shirt. The top button was loose, revealing the curve of her throat. A black-and-blue paisley pocket square added a touch of contrast to her suit jacket. Her long, wavy hair was tied in a low bun.

Aiko's lips parted. "Excuse me. Don't I know you?"

Still clutching her pendant, Summer swallowed hard. "Yes."

Aiko's brow hitched, seemingly in curiosity. "Would you mind . . . letting me see your necklace really quick?"

Summer moved her hand, revealing the earring dangling on the chain.

Aiko's expression changed to one of recognition. "The dance, right?"

Summer nodded slowly.

A smile spread across Aiko's face. "I thought so." She took a step closer and held Summer's gaze. "It's so crazy, running into you like this."

"Yeah. I agree."

"How have you been?" Aiko sat on the bleachers, leaving a bit of space between them.

"Good, good. You?"

"Can't complain." Aiko's eyes strayed to the necklace again, then back to meet Summer's eyes. "It was a hell of a night, wasn't it?"

Summer drew a deep breath. "Yeah. It was."

—

Fifteen Years Ago

Aiko yawned as she eased through the thick crowd of revelers, headed for the punch table.

She remembered her mother's words before she left. "I know you don't wanna go, Aiko. But it's probably the last time you'll ever see most of these folks, so make the best of it."

"I should be so lucky," she'd groused as she climbed into her ten-year-old Toyota for the drive to the school.

I guess I should be more excited at my graduation party, but I'm just not feeling it.

It was only her mother's absolute insistence that had brought her here for this "momentous" occasion. The compromise was that she'd get to wear what she wanted, which was a charcoal-gray suit, matching velvet loafers, a lavender button-down, and a snazzy silver paisley bow tie.

Too bad this stupid mask kinda ruins it.

In complying with the extra-corny masquerade theme of the party, she'd purchased a mask to match her outfit. Still, she felt it took something away from her look rather than adding to it. At least everyone else at the party looked just as goofy in their masks; it was a small comfort to her sense of fashion.

She used the ladle to pour herself a cup of the fizzy pink punch and downed it in one swallow. After crushing the paper cup, she tossed it into a nearby trash can as she wandered across the gym toward the equipment supply room.

Jack, one of the few guys at the school that she actually liked, waved. He was dressed in black jeans and a blue polo. "What's up, Aiko? You as bored as I am?"

Aiko chuckled. "You know I am. So, you just ignored the dress code for this, huh?"

"Hell yeah! I didn't even wanna come in the first place. Screw the dress code."

"Where's your girl? I thought you came with her?"

"I did. She's in the bathroom." Jack shook his head. "If she hadn't been so excited about this dull-ass party, I wouldn't even be here."

"Same. My mom wouldn't get off my back about it, and that's why I'm here." Aiko ran a hand over her loose, shoulder-grazing waves. "Don't know how much longer I can take it, though."

"Did she say how long you had to stay?"

Aiko nodded. "Can't come home before ten." It was one of the few times she could remember her mother telling her to stay out longer than she actually wanted to.

Jack shook his head. "Bummer."

Sarah, Jack's girlfriend, popped over and started tugging on his arm as the DJ blasted yet another 50 Cent track over the speakers. "Come on, babe. Let's dance!"

"Later, Aiko," Jack called as he was dragged away into the crowd.

Aiko shook her head and kept walking toward the equipment room, hoping it was insulated enough to give her a break from the pounding music. If nothing else, it would give her respite from the crowd.

She almost made it . . . then stopped when she saw Coach Keys hanging near the door. Pretending to dance, she kept her eye on the gym teacher until finally, engrossed in a conversation with one of the other chaperones, Coach Keys left the area.

Aiko jogged to the supply room and slipped inside as quickly and quietly as she could. Once inside, she let out a sigh. The room was dimly lit by the automatic overhead lights, but even that was a nice break from those damn strobe lights flashing across the gym.

She began easing toward the folding chairs propped against a wall of shelves filled with basketballs and volleyballs but stopped short when she heard a sound behind her.

Filled with the dread of being caught, she spun around . . .

And saw the silhouette of a shapely girl standing in the shadows, just inside the door.

Aiko squinted. "Um, hi."

The girl walked forward a step or two until the overhead lights illuminated her. She wore a particularly ornate mask, trimmed in feathers and pearls, that obscured her entire face aside from her chin and hot pink–painted lips. Her dress, closely fitted until it flared near the floor, was a soft shade of turquoise. And while it didn't reveal too much, the fit and the halter-neck style accentuated her pert, round breasts and the fullness of her hips beneath the garment.

Aiko swallowed. *Damn, she fine. And I have no clue who she is. She could be one of my classmates or a student from the nearby John Lewis Leadership Academy, since they were also participating in the party. But that mask is huge. It's almost as if she purposely chose it to hide her identity.*

"Sorry," she muttered. "I didn't know someone was in here." She turned as if to leave.

Now with a view of her ass, Aiko had to speak up. "Hold on, baby. It's the supply room, not a bathroom stall. You don't have to rush out."

Summer stopped, then turned back with a wry smile. "I see you got jokes."

Aiko chuckled. "I try. Let me guess . . . you came in for a chair?" She gestured to the stack to her right. "That seems more likely than you coming in for a basketball."

The girl laughed, something of a light, tinkling sound. "Yeah, I did come for a chair. But I didn't plan on taking it back out there." She gestured toward the gym. "It's too noisy and crowded."

"Well, looks like we're both here for the same reason." Aiko unfolded a chair, then another, placing them side by side. "Come on over, have a seat."

The mystery girl walked over, her clear acrylic heels clicking on the cement floor. Soon, the two of them were seated next to each other.

"So, what brings you to this very uncool gathering? My mom forced me to come because it's 'part of the high-school experience.'" Aiko watched her, awaiting her answer.

"Same. My parents don't think I socialize enough with my peers. Said this was my last chance to practice before I go off to college." She shook her head. "Parents."

"Right." Aiko rubbed her hands. "So, did you come with anyone?" She shook her head.

Aiko couldn't hold back her smile. "I'm amazed. As good as you look in that dress, I can't believe you weren't here on somebody's arm."

She rolled her eyes. "I got a few invites, I just said no." She tilted her head to the side. "Am I tripping, or are you flirting with me?"

"If you have to ask me that, then obviously I'm not flirting hard enough, baby."

She laughed again, and Aiko's heart swelled at the sound.

"You are something else. And what makes you think I swing that way?"

"The fact that you seem perfectly comfortable with me, even though you know I'm coming on to you." Aiko inched her chair a bit closer. "I can sense it."

"What, like, gaydar?"

"Nah. I'm just detecting a very subtle undercurrent of attraction between us." Aiko winked. "But feel free to put me in my place if you think I'm coming on too strong."

"Well, I'm not out . . . Not yet." Her brown eyes flashed with a mixture of humor and mischief. "But your game . . . so far, so good."

"Oh, word?" Aiko rubbed her hands. "In that case, I'm just getting started. I'm Aiko. And you're . . ."

She hesitated, looking at her lap. "I'm, um . . . just call me Blue."

"Okay. Blue it is." While her curiosity was high, Aiko saw no need to press her beautiful companion for information she wasn't comfortable volunteering. Blue did say she wasn't out, and maybe that was why she was being so secretive.

"Thank you for keeping me company, Aiko." She offered a small smile. "I was pretty desperate to escape the dance, and you made the escape a little more pleasant."

"No problem." Aiko reached for her hand, wondering if Blue would let her.

Blue slipped her hand into Aiko's, her smile broadening.

For a while, they chatted about how terrible the DJ was, how many of the partygoers had ignored the semiformal dress code, and just what was in that mysterious pink punch.

Blue then suddenly said, "I . . . um . . . have something to say."

"Go ahead. I'm listening."

"You didn't have to introduce yourself. I know who you are."

Aiko frowned. "Huh? Do you go here? Or, did you, since this is a graduation party?"

She gave a slow nod. "Yeah, I'm a classmate of yours."

She racked her brain, trying to think of someone who might fit this incredibly curvy form. But she couldn't come up with anything. "Have we ever had classes together? Extracurriculars?"

Blue shook her head, her springy curls dancing in time. "No. But I would see you around, in the halls, in the cafeteria, on the commons. And . . . honestly . . . I have a huge crush on you."

Aiko could feel her face getting hot. "Baby, I . . . you gotta take that mask off and let me see you. Let me find out who you are."

She shook her head. "I can't. Because after crushing on you for this long, I can't risk being rejected. I don't want the fantasy I have of you to end."

Aiko's pulse raced as she tugged Blue's hand. "Then let me live up to the fantasy. Just for a moment, okay?"

Blue nodded and didn't fight as Aiko pulled her closer.

A moment later, their lips met.

Aiko draped her arms around Blue's shoulders as Blue placed a gentle hand on Aiko's jaw. Blue's mouth fell open, and Aiko's tongue delved inside for several long, hot passes as the kiss deepened. Their masks pressed against each other, but neither of them seemed to care.

When Blue pulled away, she was breathing heavily. "Amazing."

"I agree."

Blue touched her fingertips to her lips as she stood. "I . . . uh . . . I have to go."

Aiko stood. "Wait. Why?"

"I . . . just . . . I have to go. Thanks for sitting with me, Aiko."

"Thanks for letting me."

Their eyes met, and as much as Aiko wanted her to stay, she could see the flight in Blue's eyes.

A heartbeat later, Blue disappeared through the supply room door.

Aiko waited a few seconds, then followed. For the next twenty minutes, she hunted through the crowd for Blue, even asking a few people if they'd seen a girl in a turquoise dress. Shouting the question over the banging bass didn't get her much of a response, so she gave up, returning to the supply room.

There, on the floor near the chair Blue had been sitting in, was something shiny.

Aiko picked it up. It was an ornate turquoise earring with a few diamond chips surrounding the small central stone. It was a unique design, unlike anything she'd seen before.

Slipping the earring into her pocket, Aiko returned to the gym, hoping she could find Blue, return the earring, and finally discover who she really was.

CHAPTER THREE

"I still have it, you know."

The sound of Aiko's voice broke through Summer's trancelike state, and she blinked a couple of times. *Crap, how long was I off in fantasyland?* "I'm sorry, what?"

"I said, I still have it. You know, your other earring." Aiko chuckled, rubbing her hands together. "You all right? You spaced out on me there for a minute."

Embarrassment warmed Summer's cheeks, and she nodded. "I'm fine. Sorry, it's just been a bit of a day." Clasping her hands in her lap, she said, "You really kept it all these years?"

"You held on to that one, so why not?" Aiko gestured to the necklace. "I assume that means you were hoping you'd find the match again one day."

Summer swallowed. "I was. I just never would have expected it to happen like this."

Aiko tilted her head slightly to the right. "Small world." She quieted for a moment, watching her. "So, do you want me to keep calling you Blue? Or are you gonna tell me your name?"

"My name is Summer. Summer Graves." She squirmed under the regard of the first woman who'd ever made her heartbeat race, still the finest woman she'd ever seen. Time had been very kind to Aiko, turning her from a lanky teenager into a statuesque goddess.

More people, likely former students and staff, milled around in the room now. Summer could hear folks laughing and chatting. Yet their conversations were merely a muffled backdrop around her. Aiko had her complete focus.

"Listen, do you wanna grab a cup of coffee? You know, just reminisce a little?" Aiko's gaze swept around the gymnasium before returning to her face. "Seems we're both feeling nostalgic today."

Summer smiled and nodded. "Sounds great." While she maintained a somewhat calm demeanor on the outside, the gawky teen inside her jumped up and down at the prospect of finally gaining the attention of her ultimate crush.

Aiko stood then, towering over her. "All right. Let's meet up in ten minutes, at Bean Street Brews."

"I'll be there."

Aiko smiled, revealing the most perfect pearl-white teeth, before turning and walking away. Summer could only watch in awe as Aiko's well-dressed form crossed the gym and disappeared through the double doors.

Summer sat there for a few moments longer, simply absorbing what had just occurred. Then she got up and left the school, headed for her car. Inside, she placed the rolled-up poster and her purse in the passenger seat.

On the short drive to the coffee shop, she glanced at her reflection in the rearview mirror. *All right, Summer. Get yourself together, girl.* Years ago, she would have given just about anything to have a one-on-one encounter like this with Aiko Holt. And now, even though Summer was older and wiser, Aiko's undeniable appeal remained. As of now, she had two main hopes: one, that she wouldn't say anything goofy, and two, that the fantasy she'd held of Aiko for all these years wouldn't be dashed on the jagged rocks of a reality she hadn't prepared for.

Bean Street Brews, located in a one-story cinder-block structure called the Shoppes at Ivy, was another mainstay of the community.

Situated between Maria Theresa's Beauty Salon and Lone Star Fine Cigars, the coffee shop was the oldest in the building, having been there as far back as Summer's memories extended. The coffee shop facade featured many large hand-painted coffee beans floating across a background of festive teals and blues. The green sign above the door had been specially made to look like an old-fashioned street marker.

After parking in one of the open spots near Maria Theresa's, Summer cut the engine and climbed out of her car, purse in hand. She entered the shop to the sound of the tinkling bell overhead and scanned the space. Most of the tables were empty. Two tables were occupied by people on laptops who were no doubt making use of the free wireless internet and calm atmosphere to get some things done.

Aiko appeared then, coming around the counter from the rear of the shop. "Good. You're here."

Summer approached with a smile. "Did you order yet?"

"Yep. Just waiting for it." Aiko straightened as the barista handed her a steaming mug and a ceramic plate holding a Danish. "Do you have a preference on where we sit?"

She shook her head. "Not really."

"Cool. I'll grab us a table by the window, then." With her beverage and pastry in hand, Aiko strode away.

Summer's eyes followed her, loving the way she moved. Those long legs carried her body so gracefully across a room, making it difficult to look away. She noted how Aiko's suit grazed over her frame, showing off her figure instead of hiding it. As far as Summer was concerned, Aiko wore a suit better than any man she'd ever seen. *I love the way she leans into that masculine style, without completely surrendering her femininity to it. She's gotta be a stem—best of both worlds.* The knot of hair at Aiko's nape appeared tightly wound, making Summer wonder just how long those silky dark waves actually were now.

Someone loudly cleared their throat.

Summer turned to see the two people waiting in line behind her, then snatched her wayward attentions up and brought them back to the menu board.

A few minutes later, she sat across from Aiko with her cold brew and an oatmeal-raisin cookie. "What'd you get?"

"An Americano." Aiko took another sip and smiled. "Bean Street still has the best espresso in town."

Summer chuckled. "Funny you should say that. My dad used to come here all the time when I was younger. Some Saturdays, he'd bring my sister and me here, and he'd get his espresso while we got hot chocolate." Looking to the corner table in the front, she could almost see the three of them sitting there. "We'd sit here a good hour, and he'd sip his espresso while we talked his ear off. I'm sure my mother enjoyed the break from her two little chatterboxes." She felt a twinge of sadness when she mentioned her mother but promptly pushed it away.

Aiko's brow arched. "Is she your only sibling?"

She nodded. "Yep. Her name's Crystal; she's two years older than me."

"I see. I'm an only child." Aiko bit into the Danish and chewed.

"No brothers or sisters? Sounds kind of lonely." Summer tried not to stare at the movements of Aiko's mouth and failed. Averting her gaze to avoid being caught, she chose a particularly plump raisin in her cookie to stare at instead. "Is that why you seemed to have so many friends when we were in school?"

Aiko's expression changed, her eyes squinting a bit. "What do you mean? I thought of myself as a loner."

"How? Every time I saw you, there always seemed to be a bunch of people clustered around you."

"True enough, but you could say the same thing about any other girl on the track team." Aiko tugged at her bun, appearing thoughtful. "I guess there's something about sports that people are attracted to.

Considering the way American culture glamorizes and worships professional athletes, it's not really all that surprising."

Summer's jaw fell open, and she snapped it shut. *How can she be this damn fine, and this damn intelligent all at the same time? Sweet Lord, help me.* "That's a very astute observation."

Aiko shrugged. "Just something I noticed. At any rate, I wasn't really close with any of those people who were hanging around me. I only kept up with one other girl on the team after we graduated, but she lives in Chicago now." She finished the Danish, wiping the crumbs from her mouth with a napkin from the dispenser on the table.

"I haven't kept up with many folks from those days either." Summer sucked her bottom lip. "I mean, since I moved back to town, I've seen a few folks who never left. But I can't say I've held on to any close friendships from high school." *The only thing I've held on to since high school is my attraction to you. I know better than to say that aloud.*

"It's weird," Aiko remarked, crumpling the napkin and tossing it on the table. "High school somehow seems like it happened eons ago, and also, like it only happened yesterday."

"It really does." Summer nodded. "I've got a lot of good memories of my time at Sojourner Truth, mostly connected to the classes I took, and some truly awesome teachers. It's kinda sad to see the place go, ya know?"

"I can see why you'd feel that way." Aiko tapped her index finger against the tabletop. "But that building is old, dilapidated, and hasn't been used in a decade. It's really not serving any purpose, just sitting there like it is."

Narrowing her eyes, Summer asked, "Do you know my connection to the school's founder?"

Aiko shook her head. "Not a clue."

"I guess it makes sense that you wouldn't know, since we never really talked back then." She drummed her fingers on the table. "My maternal grandmother founded the school."

Aiko leaned back in her chair. "Oh, wow. I had no idea."

"I know I may have come across as sentimental, but you need to understand it's deeper than that for me."

"I see." She appeared thoughtful. "The wheels are already in motion on the project, though."

"I know."

Silence fell between them for a few moments before Aiko asked, "Did anybody else we went to school with know about your grandmother? I mean, other than your sister?"

Summer shook her head, thinking about those days when she still wasn't even sure of who she was. "I think I was way too awkward in those days to really connect with others on a deep level."

Aiko laughed. "Come on, Summer. Most people are like that in high school, except for the wildly popular. And honestly, even they probably have their moments."

"You seemed so confident, though." She clearly remembered Aiko sitting on the edge of a table in the cafeteria, surrounded by chattering students, looking for all the world like a royal holding court over her adoring subjects.

Aiko shook her head. "Nah, baby. I just had enough bravado to cover my awkwardness, that's all."

"Well, you had me fooled."

Aiko ran her tongue over her lower lip, her golden-brown eyes locking on Summer's face. "Maybe that was because you never got close enough to really know me."

Summer stared, unable to form any coherent words. *Either I've finally lost my mind, or she's flirting with me. Please, Lord, let it be the second thing.*

"Why did you hide from me, Summer? You could have hit me up in the hallway or come to sit with me at lunch. Trust and believe, I would have sent all those sports groupies packing." She drummed her short, nude nails on the tabletop. "All you had to do was approach me."

Summer's heart climbed up into her throat like a monkey scaling a tree.

"So, why didn't you ever come over and talk to me, before that night at the dance?"

Summer swallowed. She'd dreamed about sitting across from Aiko like this, but back then, all she could think of was a list of flaws that made her unworthy to be in Aiko's company. "I . . . uh . . . I was way too shy back then."

Aiko's gaze lingered. "Oh yeah? Well, how about now? You still too shy to get to know the real me?"

Eyes widening, Summer stuck the end of her straw in her mouth and sucked up the rest of the cold brew, letting it quench her suddenly dry throat. "Um, what are you really asking me, Aiko?"

"I think I was pretty clear." She leaned forward. "That night at the dance has been burned into my memory for all these years. I still remember every moment: the way you looked in that dress, the way your lips felt." She slid her hand over the smooth surface of the table until their fingertips brushed. "That's why I kept the earring. I never wanted to forget you."

Summer felt her pulse quicken. "I gotta admit, your game is tight."

"Sho' ya right." Aiko winked, then ran her tongue over her lower lip again. "So, is that a yes, then? Because I really want to know more about the girl in the blue dress that made my night all those years ago, and the woman she's become."

Moving her hand closer until she could lace fingers with her long-held crush, Summer nodded slowly. "Yes."

A satisfied smile stretched Aiko's lips. "Good."

Summer smiled too, feeling a lot more relaxed than she had when they'd first run into each other. It looked like fate had finally given her the chance to explore who Aiko was and what they might share. "Let's hear it, then. Show me the real Aiko Holt."

~

Aiko squeezed Summer's hand, then released it. Grabbing her mug, she downed the last of her Americano and smiled. She let her gaze sweep over her companion again. *She has "femme" written all over her.*

Summer was gorgeous in an effortless way that stole Aiko's breath. She was casually dressed in cutoff denim shorts, a light-pink T-shirt, and matching sneakers. Her dark, straightened hair, highlighted with shades of auburn and chestnut, was pulled on top of her head in a high ponytail, the ends of which grazed the back of her neck. Large gold hoops dangled in her ears. "All right, what do you wanna know?" Aiko asked.

Summer appeared thoughtful, tapping one long hot-pink acrylic nail on her chin. "You said you're an only child. Tell me about your parents, then."

Aiko rubbed her hands before resting them on the table. "My mom, Janet, is a retired flight attendant. Growing up, it was just me and her; my parents never married."

"What about your dad?"

Seeing the sympathetic expression playing over Summer's face, she continued before Summer's mind came up with a thousand sad tales to explain her father's absence. "His name is Kosuke, and he's an artist living in Japan. I don't see him often, but I've always known him, and he's always been a part of my life, just from a distance."

"Oh, I see." She looked somewhat unsure of what to say next and kept quiet for a few long moments.

Aiko broke the silence. "It's cool, really. My parents didn't stay together, but they don't hate each other, either. Mom was strict sometimes, but she raised me well, and she always had my pops' support."

"That's good to know." Summer laced her fingers together. "I . . . wasn't judging you or anything. I was just surprised."

"I can understand that. I imagine it's pretty rare, living in the South, to come from unmarried parents who live on different continents."

She shook her head. "It's probably not rare at all; people just don't talk about it. You know how Southerners can be about putting on airs. So I appreciate your openness."

"That's what getting to know each other is all about, right?"

"Right." Summer's smile shone like polished gold. "My parents have been married basically forever. They get on each other's nerves sometimes, and it's kinda funny to see my dad rolling his eyes at my mom. I know they still love each other, though."

"They sound like most couples that have been married for decades." Aiko thought about Peaches' parents, who were headed toward forty years together. "When it's right, I think marriage is a beautiful thing."

Summer watched her with widened eyes as if she'd said something surprising. "You know, I'm curious, what did you do after high school?"

"You first." Aiko watched her beautiful coffee companion with genuine interest.

"Cool. I was pretty eager to get away from home back then, so I went to Cali for college. I studied child and adolescent development at Cal State Northridge and got my bachelor's there."

Aiko felt her brow furrow as she thought about what Summer had said—it didn't seem to match up with the person sitting across from her now. "If you don't mind me asking, why were you so intent on getting away from home? You seem pretty passionate about Ivy now."

"I am passionate about the town, and I always have been. It was my parents' house I needed to escape." She tilted her head to the left, her gaze shifting upward. "Back then, I was still discovering myself. I was digging deep, determined to unearth the person I was inside. Let's just say my mother wasn't too keen on that level of exploration."

There were unspoken words in Summer's story, and Aiko knew very well what she meant. "That's rough. I'm sorry she wasn't more accepting. Have things at least improved since then?"

She shrugged. "A little, but I'm content to see as little of her as possible until she evolves." She waved her hand. "Enough about that, though. Where did you end up after we graduated?"

Aiko sensed a familiar pain beneath Summer's words. While it wasn't something she'd gone through personally, she had far too many friends who'd experienced it, making it easy to recognize. Clearly, that wasn't something Summer wanted to talk about now, so Aiko answered the question at hand. "I stuck close to home. Went to UT Austin, got my bachelor's in architecture."

"Really? That sounds interesting. What was your minor?"

"Sociology. Yours?"

"English."

"Oh, word. My best friend was an English Lit minor. Business major, though." Aiko looked at her phone to check the time, then pocketed it again. "What do you do? Are you a teacher?"

She nodded. "Yes. I actually moved back home to take a teaching position; I'm going to be facilitating the two-year-old class at Young Scholars Academy."

Aiko felt the smile tugging her lips. "Wow. That sounds pretty awesome. I hear kids that age are really something."

"They absolutely are, and that's why I love teaching little ones. I can't imagine another job that would expose me to so much cuteness, other than maybe herding puppies." She laughed. "What about you? What do you do for a living?"

"I'm a supervisory planner at an architecture firm."

"Can you tell me a little about what that entails?"

"Sure. I lead a team of junior architects or interns, based on the size and scope of the project, and assist in getting it from plan to finished building." She cracked her knuckles. "It involves a lot of meetings, both with my team and with construction and city officials."

"That explains the suit, then." Summer smiled. "You wear it very well."

"Thanks." She tugged her lapels. "I try."

"You were always stylish, even back in high school." She tilted her head to the right. "Stylish, edgy, and downright intriguing."

Aiko smiled at Summer's assessment of her look. "I appreciate that." Drumming her fingers on the table, she said, "What brought you over to the school today, anyway?"

"I'll tell you in a minute. First I want to hear something you're really proud of about yourself."

Aiko scratched her head. "I would say I'm most proud of the fact that I speak five languages."

"Impressive. Which ones?"

"I speak fluent English, Japanese, and Korean. I'm conversational in French."

Summer frowned. "That's only four languages. What's the fifth?"

"Southern Mama."

She giggled. "Oh, really? Say something for me in Southern Mama."

Queueing up her best impersonation of her own mother, Aiko folded her arms over her chest. "Chile, did you hear Mable done passed. Mmhmm. I just came from over there. Left them some food so Joe and them don't have to cook."

Summer nodded vigorously while laughing. "Yep, that's pretty spot on. I think I dabble in that as well."

"So, you were gonna tell me why you were at the school today? I'm curious to know how things aligned to put us in the same place at the same time today."

"I saw on the news that the town council had opened up the building to former students and staff who wanted to have a last look around or take souvenirs." She sighed. "Nostalgia got the better of me, and I couldn't pass up the chance. I thought I'd end up with an old textbook, or maybe a chunk of the old masonry, from where it's started to crumble."

Aiko nodded. "I saw you with something under your arm."

She snapped her fingers. "Yes. It was an old Alvin Ailey poster from my dance class. I had no way of knowing if it was still there since I hadn't been inside the building in years. But I checked, and lo and behold, it was there. All I had to do was climb on a chair to get it."

"A risk-taker, I see." Aiko chuckled. "You've definitely grown since high school." She let her appreciative gaze travel over the rounded curves of Summer's body, making no effort to conceal her attentions. "In all the right places, too."

Summer's cheeks darkened, and she offered a soft smile. "You're pulling my leg."

"I would love to."

Summer looked away, as if unable to hold eye contact.

Amused by her reactions, Aiko insisted, "Go on with what you were saying."

She cleared her throat. "I, uh . . . anyway, I got the poster, rolled it up, and took it with me. It's quite a score. Way better than a brick." She popped a fallen raisin into her mouth. "What about you? Did you get any good mementos?"

Aiko shook her head. "Nah, but I'm not really into that sort of thing."

"What do you mean?"

She shrugged, gripping the base of her bun as she felt it start to unfurl. "I don't really do the nostalgia thing. At least, not like that."

Appearing genuinely confused, Summer asked, "Then what were you doing at the school? Everybody who was there today came for sentimental reasons—or at least that's what I thought."

"I think most of the people there came to grab a little piece of history," Aiko admitted.

She squinted. "That still doesn't tell me why you were there."

She swallowed, still fiddling with her hair. "I was there for work, actually."

"Huh?"

Aiko gave up on the bun, releasing her hair so that it hung in a long ponytail that grazed her hip. "I work for an architectural firm, remember? As the supervisory planner, site visits are part of my job."

Summer's eyes narrowed. "Wait a minute. You mean, you work for . . . *that* company?"

"If you mean Abernathy Creative Development, the company that's overseeing the new multiuse center being built on the Sojourner Truth site, then, yes, I do."

Summer's lips tightened. "If you're on the clock, why on earth are you sitting here with me?"

"I'm not on the clock. Abernathy allows employees flex hours on Thursdays and Fridays. I clocked out before we left the school." She ran her fingers through her ponytail, undoing the tangles that had formed from a day of confinement. "Why are you making that face?"

"What face?"

"Like you just smelled something really funky." Aiko leaned back in her seat.

"I'm just . . . surprised." Summer spoke softly, but her tone was much sharper than it had been before. "It's a little shocking that you're part of a project like that."

"I'm confused. What do you mean, a project like that?"

"Come on, Aiko. You're smart. So I'm sure you know what this project is really about."

Summer's slightly condescending tone wasn't lost on her, and her shoulders stiffened in response. "Yeah, I do. It's about revitalizing the community by replacing that raggedy old building with something newer, cleaner, and more useful."

"If only that were it. This project is about corporate greed, about replacing a historic part of our community with something more profitable." Summer leaned against the backrest of her chair, resting one hand on her hip. "It's gentrification, plain and simple."

Aiko shook her head. "Whoa, now. In my experience, people love to toss around that word, without a real understanding of what it means."

"Do you think I lack understanding, Aiko?" She pursed her lips.

"That's not what I said."

"That's what you implied." Slinging her purse strap over her shoulder, Summer stood, gathered her dishes, and walked over to the trash cans.

Aiko gathered her things and followed.

They stashed their dishes in the bus tray atop the trash can, and Summer started walking toward the door.

"You're just gonna walk out? Just like that?"

Summer pushed her way through the door, the bell tinkling as she passed through.

Aiko followed her. On the sidewalk outside, she reached for Summer's arm. Keeping her grasp gentle, Aiko stayed her. "Summer, wait. We were just starting to open up to each other. Why are you storming off like this?"

"'Were' is the operative word here, Aiko." She looked up at her, eyes flashing. "After all these years of thinking you were something special, this is hard for me to swallow."

"What? The fact that I work for a firm that's gonna bring jobs and prosperity to Ivy? What's so wrong with that?"

She shook her head. "There are better ways to do those things. You have to know that."

Gazing into her eyes and seeing the hurt there, Aiko released her arm. "I'm sorry you feel that way, Summer. But I believe in the vision my boss has for the Sojourner Truth site."

"And I believe the best way to help Ivy grow is from within."

"I don't want this to cause a problem between us." Aiko tugged the end of her ponytail, wrapping it around her fingertips in response to the stress of the moment. "I still want to get to know you. You're even more beautiful now than you were in that blue dress."

Summer's expression softened, the anger melting from her face. She looked torn, contemplative. "I owe it to myself to see if you're everything I hoped you'd be, so I can set this issue aside . . . for now. But know that I'm an advocate for this community, and I always will be. Living in other cities taught me how truly valuable a place like Ivy is."

"I respect that. And even if you can't see it now, I love this community just as much as you do." She placed her hand over her heart. "I grew up here, too."

Summer didn't look convinced, but she gave a curt nod. "See you around, Aiko."

"Bye, Summer."

Aiko watched Summer climb into her late-model sedan and, a few moments later, fire the engine and drive away.

CHAPTER FOUR

Summer spent the better part of Friday working on action items for her community group, the Sojourner Truth Preservation Society. By midafternoon, she'd finished updating the social media page that members used as a hub for conversation and strategic planning. She'd started the group the week she arrived home, after discovering the planned demolition of her former school. Currently, the group was twenty-one members strong, with new folks trickling in every day.

Leaning back in her desk chair, she stretched her arms above her head. She'd turned the second bedroom in her apartment into a cozy little office, and as she looked around at the cream-colored walls and the modular shelves full of books, magazines, and her collection of Sanrio stuffed toys, she smiled. It had taken her a couple of weeks, but now, she finally felt fully settled into the apartment. *This place has really started to feel like home.*

She drummed her fingertips on the surface of her L-shaped workstation. It was the largest desk she'd ever owned, and she'd bought it to celebrate her new teaching position. The moment she'd seen it in the store, she'd known the space would come in handy for sorting art and science supplies for her students at Young Scholars. The school's curriculum focused on hands-on learning and exploration, and she'd already filled two large plastic totes with items to facilitate their first several projects.

She took a long sip from the water bottle on the corner of her desk, then set it down and opened a blank file in her graphic design software. As she created a text box and resized it to fit the text she planned to enter, her phone rang. She grabbed the device from her jeans pocket and swiped her finger over the screen. "Hello?"

A bright, familiar voice filled her ear. "Hey, Summer. It's me."

She smiled at the sound of her sister's voice. "Hey, Crys. How are you doing?"

"I'm okay, but I'll be better if you have good news for me."

Summer sighed. "I wish I could say I did."

"Oh, boy. So, let me guess. You couldn't find any problems with the permits?"

"No, I couldn't. I checked with the City of Austin, and with Travis County."

"Were you able to find a way to run an online records search?" Crystal asked. "Or did you speak with someone?"

"I actually went down to the Permitting and Development Center myself, in person. I spoke very briefly with someone in Development Services, who directed me to the Commercial Plan Review Division." She tapped her fingertips on the desk. "All of Abernathy's permits are in order. They were submitted earlier this year and approved several weeks ago."

"So much for that approach," Crystal said dryly. "I didn't have any better luck with the Historic Preservation Office. I'm just glad I called instead of driving all the way over there."

"Damn." Summer frowned. "I was so sure you'd have a better shot than me. What happened, exactly?"

"It turns out that in order for a structure to be declared 'historically significant,' it has to be at least fifty years old. Beyond that, they say the school only meets one of the five criteria they use to determine a property's historic merit."

"Which criterion is that?"

"Community value." She scoffed. "So, they admit its importance to Ivy, but they still aren't going to step in. Can you believe it?" Her tone held a mixture of bitterness and resignation. "Just because the building is only forty-six years old, and doesn't tick all their little boxes, the city is just going to stand by and let those corporate raiders tear down the school our grandmother founded."

Summer felt the sadness tug at her heart. "This is so frustrating. The city just seems to have such disregard for what the school means to our family's legacy."

"How many people can say their ancestors are directly responsible for educating two generations of low-income students of color, for nurturing them and sending them out into the world, prepared to do amazing things?" Crystal paused. "Coach Keys isn't going to like this."

Summer couldn't fight the rising feeling of grimness as she thought of the PE teacher, who'd been the longest-serving teacher in the school's history. Melba Keys had taught at Sojourner Truth for twenty-three years. "How is Coach Keys doing? I haven't been able to get over there to see her yet."

"She's doing pretty well, considering. She's mostly recovered from the hip replacement surgery, and she's been walking around a bit with her cane." Crystal blew out a breath. "News like this is liable to land her right back in bed."

"Don't tell her. We're not giving up the ship just yet." Summer put her elbows on the desk, resting her forehead against her hand. "There has to be something else we can do."

"Well, whatever it is, we need to move fast." The sound of papers rustling filled the speaker. "I read in the newspaper this morning that Abernathy plans to move ahead with demolition in the next few weeks." She scoffed. "I've had the hardest time focusing on running the desk ever since." Crystal had been managing the front desk at the boutique Hotel Azure in north Austin for a little over six years.

Shit. Things are moving ahead much faster than I anticipated. "I didn't get a jump on this like I wanted to because I was focused on getting settled in my place and preparing for my teaching position." Summer dragged her hand over her face. "Tell you what, I think we're going to have to take more immediate measures."

"Yeah, but what do you have in mind?"

"I was actually thinking about this before you called." She glanced at her computer screen. "Right now, we have about twenty people in our social media group. Why don't we throw a wrench in their plans by showing up and protesting?" It wasn't a guaranteed solution, but in Summer's mind, it seemed like their best shot at putting the brakes on Abernathy's plans.

"I'm not sure that will do any good."

"We're not going to just lay down and let them do this, Crys." She turned back to the computer. "Think about it. If Abernathy is like every other profit-obsessed company out there, they hate negative press and will do just about anything to avoid it. All we have to do is create the kind of attention they don't want on their project."

"And you think us showing up to march and carry signs will do that?"

"Absolutely, if we do it right." She selected a bold, all-caps font that would be easy to read, even from a distance, then started typing into the text box she'd opened earlier. "Even if we can't stop them, we can at least delay them, because they'll have to navigate the public relations minefield that automatically comes with protest."

"Hmm." Crystal sounded as if she were considering Summer's words. "I'm willing to give it a shot because it's the only play we have right now. But what will we do if we can't stop them from going through with demolition?"

"I guess the next move would be to get a space secured in the new development." She sat back in her chair, chewing her lower lip as she worked it out in her mind. "Of course, that might mean bidding against the companies that want space there."

"Even with Grandma's trust, I don't think we have that kind of funding."

"Don't worry about it. For now, that's not an issue." She adjusted the wording on the screen again, making it more to her liking. "Listen. I'm making up some signs now. As soon as I finish them, I'll get them printed. I'll take a few of them over to the site, and I'll hold on to the others for our protest."

"You're not wasting any time, I see."

"We don't have time to waste, sis." Summer dragged an image onto her project, dropping it in place. "Focus on getting as many people as you can to attend a protest next Wednesday. Post in the group, and ask our friends and family."

"I will." Crystal sounded somewhat relieved. "I really appreciate how hard you're working to preserve what Grandma Beulah built."

"Don't mention it. I know I can attribute a lot of my success in life to my days at Sojourner Truth." She smiled. "Making sure the school, and the community, don't get the shaft? That's the least I can do."

"I just know she would be proud of everything you're doing." She paused. "Oh, Hector's calling me. I'll talk to you later."

She chuckled. "Bye, Crys. Tell your man I said hi."

Disconnecting the call, Summer shifted her full focus to the protest sign on her computer. She tweaked it, resizing and relocating elements until it looked right, then saved the file. Opening another file, she repeated the process until she'd designed five different protest signs. While each one had a different image and slightly varied wording, the sentiment remained the same: stop Abernathy and preserve our community.

She saved all the signs to a folder and parked them in her cloud storage. After opening a browser, she went to the Abernathy website. The site was sleek and professional, opting for a subdued look rather than a lot of splashy graphics. She clicked the "About Us" page and skimmed the story of how the company first began as a one-woman operation back in the '90s. Then she read the brief biography of Miriam Abernathy, the woman herself. The accompanying photograph showed a smiling Black woman in her early to midfifties with dark brown hair and brown eyes. Dressed in a smart tweed suit, with her arms folded over her chest, she looked like the type of woman who was polite but wasn't to be trifled with.

Summer thought back to yesterday's encounter, and curiosity got the better of her. Navigating to the "Meet Our Team" page, she scrolled until she came across Aiko's picture and bio. In the photograph, Aiko wore a soft-yellow button-down and charcoal blazer along with a matching fedora. Her expression could only be described as a Mona Lisa smile: she looked serious and somewhat unapproachable. Despite that, there was no denying Aiko's good looks or her impeccable style.

Dragging her gaze away from Aiko's face, she perused the words in the bio. Skipping over her education and credentials, which she'd already heard firsthand, Summer read her hobbies: gardening, hiking, and sketching.

Staring at Aiko's face again, Summer sighed. *She's so fine. I really wish we weren't on opposite sides of this whole thing.* But here they were, each working toward a goal that flew in the face of what the other person wanted. Knowing that fact upset her, annoyed her, and yet did little to nothing to quell her attraction.

Maybe there just wasn't any cure for what she felt other than to give in to it.

She leaned back in her chair, tapping her index finger against her chin. There was something about Aiko that had a grip on her, and whatever it was, it showed no signs of letting go.

She got up from her chair and pushed the thoughts away as she slipped into her shoes. Grabbing her purse from the doorknob, she headed out of the office and left her apartment. At a small print shop in the Shoppes at Ivy, she watched as the technician retrieved her designs from the cloud, then printed her signs on heavy-duty poster board.

The tech passed her the signs for inspection. "Is everything in order, ma'am?"

Flipping through them, she smiled. "Yes, they look great. Thank you."

She left the signs on the counter briefly to peruse the shelves lining the wall. Finding a few useful supplies, she added them to her bill. After she paid, she exited the shop, holding a small plastic bag and carrying the stack of signs tucked beneath her arm. Loading them into the car, she then drove over to the Sojourner Truth school site and parked across the street.

She walked to the plastic fence surrounding the front of the building and used the clamps she'd bought to secure her largest sign to it. Stepping back, she let her gaze sweep over the sign. It looked great, and she was certain that even people driving by would be able to see it. Her goal had been to draw attention to what Abernathy was about to do, and this sign would do just that.

As she stared, she noticed the sign was crooked, tilted too far to the right. Undoing the clamps, she inched the upper right corner upward, then stepped back slightly to check it. Still not satisfied, she adjusted it again, then clipped it in place. Taking three large steps back until she stood on the curb, she eyed the sign again, trying to determine if it was aligned.

"It's still crooked," a familiar voice announced.

Spinning around, she searched for the source of the sound. She continued to scan her surroundings until her eyes landed on the unamused face of Aiko Holt.

~

Aiko leaned against her vehicle, folding her arms over her chest. Shaking her head, she called out, "Summer, what are you doing?"

Her shouted response was accompanied by a Cheshire cat grin. "I think it's pretty obvious what I'm doing here." She tilted her head to the side. "And I'm well, thanks for asking. How are you?"

"Fine, mostly." Aiko cleared her throat. "Excuse me for not inquiring about your mood; based on your expression, you're pretty pleased with yourself right now."

She grinned even wider. "I am."

Aiko let her gaze sweep over Summer. Her hair was tied back in a low ponytail, and large silver hoops hung from her ears. She wore a fitted lime-green one-shouldered top with the word "RESIST" printed on it in white, all-caps lettering. She'd paired the rather spot-on top with white skinny jeans and silver-and-white sneakers. Aiko swallowed, unable to drag her eyes away from the generous swell of Summer's hips, accentuated so beautifully by the fitted jeans.

"So what did your corporate overlords send you here to do today, Aiko? Burn down our little schoolhouse?" Summer's words were laced with bitterness.

Aiko shifted her attention to Summer's face. Summer's smile had been replaced by a tight-lipped, unfriendly glare of annoyance and disdain. "I don't have any corporate overlords, Summer. Miriam Abernathy is about as far as one can get from that."

"Hmph." She didn't look convinced. "Whatever. Are you going to tell me why you're here?"

Aiko lifted the briefcase in her hand. "I'm surveying so I can finalize my report to the executive team. We're starting demo soon."

"I know, I do my research. That's exactly why I'm here, putting up these signs. The community needs to know what Abernathy is really up to."

I've had enough of us shouting at each other from opposite sides of the damn road. Aiko straightened, looked both ways, then crossed the narrow road to get a closer look at the sign. Reading it, she scoffed.

"You're making an awful lot of unfair and unsubstantiated claims here, Summer."

Summer propped her fists on her hips. "Based on the research we've done, I'd say it all checks out. But I'll humor you. What exactly are you disputing?"

Aiko read a line of text highlighted in orange that monopolized the space on the sign. "Corporate greed destroying Ivy? Did you stretch before making that reach?"

Summer's eyes narrowed. "We in the Sojourner Truth Preservation Society believe that this rush to dismantle and destroy a place that's so integral to our community is driven by many things, greed being the central factor."

"And what makes you say that?"

"How many local organizations and small businesses are going to get space in this fancy new development, Aiko?"

She shrugged, giving an honest answer. "I don't know, that's not my department. I do know that none have bid on a space so far."

"None have bid, or none have bid high enough?"

Aiko let her head drop back, eyes focused skyward as she blew out a breath. "Okay, you're making a lot of assumptions. Regardless, the project has been properly permitted and managed through all the appropriate channels, and it's going to go forward whether you like it or not."

Summer's expression morphed again into a smile, but this time, it lacked warmth. "We'll see, Aiko. For now, let's just agree to disagree, shall we?"

Aiko nodded. "Fine with me." Unable to resist, she raked her gaze over Summer's luscious body once more. "I can see your beauty is matched by your ferocity."

Drawing her lower lip into her mouth, she sucked it ever so slightly, her eyes taking on a hint of smolder. "Flattery will get you everywhere with me, just not when it comes to this."

"Fair enough." Aiko winked, knowing she'd live to flirt another day. She neared the fence. "For what it's worth, I do respect your commitment to your beliefs. I just hope you'll give me that same courtesy."

"I certainly will try." Summer tilted her head to one side. "I don't want to hold you since you're on the clock and I've already done what I came here to do." She turned and began to walk toward her car. "See you around, Aiko."

"See ya." Aiko watched the sway of Summer's hips with great appreciation. It was only after Summer got into her car and drove away that Aiko was able to pull her focus back to the task at hand: her final survey of the school and the land it occupied. She walked through the opening in the temporary construction fencing and stopped by an old stone bench donated by the class of 1980. There, she opened her briefcase and removed the clipboard and attached pen she'd be using.

She spent the next hour circling the property, taking photographs, and making notes. This information would be vital to the demolition team, Kirby Construction, who'd be tasked with making sure the destruction of the building happened in the safest, most controlled way possible. As a supervisory planner on the project, she'd be there to oversee the demolition as a representative of Abernathy.

As she moved around the building, she recalled the time she'd spent at the academy as a student.

In the band room, she could almost hear the sounds of her classmates playing the scales on their various instruments. She'd played the alto sax from ninth to eleventh grade. The instrument was now collecting dust in its case somewhere in her garage, and while she hadn't played it in years, she'd held on to it at her mother's insistence.

Outside, she passed the rickety, old metal bleachers and stared over the field. The crumbling track encircling the grassy plane held memories of practices where she'd hurt her foot during a bad landing while running the hurdles. The sandpit, now taken over by a mixture of soil, weeds, and dead leaves, held the triumphant recollection of when she broke the school-wide record for the long jump.

The memories lit the corners of her mind like that old Barbra Streisand tune, and part of her saw the validity in Summer's point of view. This wasn't just an old, listless building occupying an overgrown plot in the corner of Ivy, Austin's sleepy little hamlet. This building had been their school, and it held a certain unspoken place of honor in the hearts of the students who'd matriculated through it. The lunches, the pep rallies, the first kisses, and the most embarrassing moments that had occurred on these grounds hallowed them in a way. And deep inside, a tiny part of her cringed at the knowledge that tearing it down meant the end of an era. The fact that Summer's family legacy was inextricably tied to the school's history only made things more complex.

She took a deep breath and let her sensible side return to power. Despite the feelings the old place might hold, it had fallen out of use and become an eyesore many years ago. It was time for something new, something even better. It was time for the old era to give way to the new era.

I just hope that as time passes, Summer will come to see things as I do. You can love something and still know it's time to let go.

Once she'd finished her survey, Aiko returned to her car. Taking a moment to upload screenshots of her notes to the company cloud, she then used the company's app to clock out for the day. It was just after four o'clock on a Friday afternoon, and she needed to get going. *If I don't hurry up, I'll never get a chair.*

Aiko drove into South Austin and turned her car into the parking lot at Fresh Cutz Fine Grooming on William Cannon Drive. It took a minute to find a space, and when she finally snapped up one in the very back of the lot, she parked and quickly made her way inside.

The electronic bell chimed as Aiko entered and let the door swing shut behind her.

She inhaled the heady scents of disinfectant, rosemary, and citrus. The interior of the barbershop, painted in soothing shades of gray and cream, was bustling with activity. All six barber chairs were occupied, and the low buzz of several pairs of clippers was accompanied by the hum of several ongoing conversations.

As Aiko signed her name in the logbook, Peaches waved to her from her station in the rear right corner. "What's up, homie? I'll be with you shortly."

"I'm good. Take your time, Peaches." Aiko sat in the last empty chair in the lobby area and took out her phone to pass the time. She opened her browser, then typed "Sojourner Truth Preservation Society" into the search bar and tapped "Enter." The first result was a page on a social media network popular with boomers and Gen Xers. Opening the page, she scrolled through it, shaking her head. *Damn. These people really don't want this project to move forward. At least there aren't that many of them.* She checked the page's "About" section and sighed when she saw Summer's name as founder and administrator. There was a photo of her, smiling and wearing a pink plastic birthday crown. Clicking it, Aiko landed on Summer's personal profile.

Aiko spent a few minutes looking at Summer's page and the content she'd posted. After five or six recent posts, there was a gap where she'd been less active. The next images were of her college buddies and a few things she'd shared from the Cal State Northridge Alumni Association. She'd also shared articles on child development and a few recipes. Her latest posts, however, were mainly stories that highlighted the negative impact of gentrification and urban renewal.

Before long, Aiko's scrolling was interrupted. Peaches called out, "Come on back, Aiko. I'm ready for you."

Aiko pocketed her phone as she rose from her seat and made her way to Peaches' station. "Hey, Peaches. What's up with you?" She gave her friend a quick hug.

"You know me, just working and stacking this paper." Peaches chuckled. Her short Afro was tied back with a narrow red scarf, accentuating the fullness of her kind face and the ever-present mischievous sparkle in her brown eyes. She wore a red button-down shirt and black slacks beneath the barbershop's signature black-and-gold apron. While using a black towel to dust the seat of her barber chair, she asked, "What you getting done today? Finally gonnas get that undercut?"

Aiko eased into the chair, rolling her eyes at her friend's teasing. "Don't start with me. I just want that hot oil treatment, a shampoo, and a trim."

"I got you, playa." Peaches opened the cabinet above her station and took out a small tube of oil, gloves, and a plastic cap. After turning on the small electric kettle on her station, she dropped the tube inside. She undid Aiko's bun, letting her hair cascade down her back. Lifting her hair, she said, "It's grown out a lot since the last time you were in here."

"I know. But don't you go getting scissor happy. I only want you to take off an inch. Just get those split ends before they get outta hand."

"As you wish." Peaches used small tongs to retrieve the oil from the kettle, then twisted off the top and applied it to Aiko's hair. As she worked the warm oil over Aiko's scalp, she asked, "What's been up with you? Haven't heard from you in a couple of days."

She sighed, both in response to the question and the scalp massage. "I had to go over to Sojourner Truth to start my survey process, and you'll never guess who I ran into?"

"You're right, I'll never guess. So just tell me." Peaches stretched the clear plastic cap, placed it on Aiko's head, and began tucking all the ends of her hair beneath it.

"Blue."

In the mirror, Peaches' eyes widened. "You mean the thick shawty from that high-school dance? The one whose earring you've been holding on to all this time?"

"Yep." Aiko shook her head. Telling the story aloud only reminded her of how crazy the whole situation was. "Turns out her name is Summer."

Peaches tilted her head to the side as she readjusted the plastic cap to accommodate Aiko's mass of dark waves. "And how do you know this?"

Aiko briefly recapped their initial run-in and their subsequent conversation over coffee. "It was quite an illuminating conversation, to say the least."

"Wow." Peaches chuckled. "Turns out she had a crush on you in school, and she ran out that night because she was too shy and embarrassed to let you know?"

"Basically, yes."

"Look at you! Aiko Holt, the original playa from the Himalayas!" Peaches laughed, and a few nearby patrons and barbers joined in.

Aiko scoffed. "I wish. That's not all. We're basically on the opposite sides of a battle."

"It's been a few minutes, so let's continue this at the shampoo bowl." Once Aiko was settled in the ivory ceramic bowl, Peaches turned on the spray and pumped out some shampoo from the dispenser mounted above the sink. "Okay, keep going."

Aiko spoke up a bit to be heard over the running water. "You know how far Abernathy is with the Ivy First Avenue project, right? Well, turns out some of the other former students at the school, and their parents, don't want the project to proceed as planned." She paused, enjoying the relaxing feeling of having three weeks' worth of buildup scrubbed from her scalp. "I just left, and she was there hanging a sign that bashed the company and the project."

"Yikes." Peaches sprayed her head again, rinsing out the foam this time. "What are you gonna do now?"

"I have to keep seeing her. All these years, I've thought about her and about that night. Curiosity is bugging the hell outta me, just like K-Ci once said. I just can't let this go yet."

"Hmm." Peaches wrapped a towel around Aiko's head, then raised the chair's back. "You do realize that if you keep seeing her, it's gonna force you to choose."

"Choose? What?" Aiko eyed her friend.

"You're gonna have to either choose to change your stance on the project or, possibly, choose between being with her and keeping your job."

Aiko shook her head. "Nah. I've put in too many years at Abernathy for that. But I don't think it'll come to that, at least not any time soon."

Peaches scoffed. "Famous last words."

They returned to the barber station. As she used the towel to squeeze the excess water from Aiko's hair, Peaches asked, "Is she as fine now as she was back then?"

Aiko smiled. "Finer, actually. Time has blessed her. She was thick before, but now?" She paused, whistled. "She's gorgeous. Her body looks even softer, and she knows how to dress to accentuate every curve."

Peaches sucked in a breath through her teeth. "Based on that description, I can see why you're ready to risk it all."

Aiko smiled. *I still think Peaches is being a little dramatic. Even if she's not, it's well worth my time to see what might happen between Summer and me.*

CHAPTER FIVE

Saturday morning, Summer pulled her car into an empty space in the parking lot of the Austin Public Library's Ivy branch. As she opened the door and exited the cool cocoon of her car's interior, the heat of the day enveloped her in a sticky cloak of humid air. She grimaced momentarily. *It's way too early for it to be this damn hot. Gotta love that Austin weather.*

She slung the strap of her black Dooney & Bourke bucket bag over her shoulder and walked over to her father's pickup. "Ready to shop, Dad?"

Rodney Graves stepped off the running board and closed the door behind him, his favorite canvas shopping tote in hand. "I am. Did you bring a bag?"

She patted her purse. "I brought two; they're folded up in here."

He smiled. "Good girl. Then let's go, we don't want to miss the good stuff."

She followed her father across the parking lot, then through the large field behind the library and across the narrow side street beyond. There, beside the Ivy Municipal Complex, she could see the colorful tents set up. "I haven't been to the farmers market in ages. I'm glad they're still doing it." Local farmers, shopkeepers, and artisans had been setting up this market every weekend since her childhood. It was a familiar, welcome tradition, one that reminded her of the idyllic days of her youth.

Rodney nodded. "Me, too, because the produce in that chain grocery store ain't up to my standards." He chuckled. "I should warn you, though. There have been some changes, and some of them, you probably won't like."

She frowned, wondering what he meant, but decided not to ask. Moments later, they passed under the multicolored balloon arch that marked the entrance to the Ivy Community Market.

She strolled among the booths and tables, waving to a few familiar faces and some she couldn't put names to. Soon, they came to the old blue tent where Willow Grove Farms plied their goods. The table beneath the tent, loaded with a vibrant assortment of fresh veggies and fruits, had always represented the best selection of produce to be found in the entire market.

Sam Willow, the farm's proprietor, stood behind the table, wearing a green apron over his dark tee and jeans. His once raven-black hair was now gray with white at the temples, and his copper-skinned face held kind eyes and smiling lips. "Morning, Rodney! Good to see you."

Rodney shook his old friend's hand. "Good to see you, too."

"I missed you last week, you know."

"I know. I got caught up working on that old porch railing at the house and couldn't make it over here." Rodney smiled. "But I had to come today. I'm making eggplant parmesan, and I can't have that mess they sell at the grocery store ruining my dish."

Sam laughed. "Well, no, Rodney. We certainly can't have that." His eyes shifted to Summer's face. "If it isn't Summer. How have you been, honey?"

She smiled. "I've been well, and you?"

"Good, good. Can't complain." He eyed her. "We haven't seen you in so long. Are you visiting, or staying?"

"I'll be staying, Sam."

He grinned. "Wonderful. What brought you back to us, if you don't mind my asking?"

She groaned inwardly but kept her smile intact. Life in a small community in the South was dull, so dull that the only thing to keep some folks busy was minding the business of their neighbors. As much as she loved her community, she knew she'd be answering the same questions, over and over, until people got used to her being back home.

Things had been very different in California, where people were so wrapped up in their own lives, they couldn't care less about each other's personal issues. Still, Sam was a trusted family friend, and she had no problem sharing with him. "I got a teaching position here, and I've been getting my classroom in order. But the job is only part of the reason. The rest is homesickness. I really missed this place."

Her dad, busy prodding a plump eggplant, quipped, "Of course you missed Ivy. California is expensive, overcrowded, and noisy."

She glanced her father's way, shaking her head. *To him, the whole state is Los Angeles. It's kinda precious. This is one of those moments when the "old man" really jumps out.* Turning to Sam, she stage-whispered, "I also wanted to be close to Dad. He's not getting any younger, you know."

Rodney elbowed his daughter playfully in the side. "Hush your mouth, child. I'm healthy as a horse and young at heart, too."

"I'm just messing with you, Dad. We all know you're gonna live to be a hundred and ten."

"You're damn straight. Now stop clowning and let me get my eggplant."

"Yes, sir," she replied with a giggle.

While he picked out the finest eggplant he could find, along with some fresh oregano and basil, Summer filled one of Sam's wicker baskets with some goodies to fill her own fridge. She grabbed plump beefsteak tomatoes, cucumbers, sweet yellow peppers, and yellow squash. Adding small containers of figs and persimmons, she approached the cash register behind her father and waited patiently until her turn to be served.

"You'll be eating good this week, young lady," Sam said as he loaded her purchases into the shopping totes she handed him.

"I sure will. Thanks, Sam." After paying for her items, she followed her father away from the Willow Grove Farms booth.

They walked between the booths, and Summer began to see the changes her father had spoken of earlier. Yes, there were still some familiar vendors like Mary Rhodes' flower shop, a lemonade stand run by local kids from a scouting troop, and old man Heller's butchery, famous for their grass-fed beef. But there were also several new booths, and seeing some of them made Summer's head hurt. "When did we start getting all these weird vendors, Dad? Vegan leather goods? Artisan fair-trade coffee? And is that place really advertising hot yoga?"

Dad chuckled. "I'm afraid so. I knew you wouldn't be thrilled. But to answer your question, they started trickling in a couple of years ago. Every few months there would be a new booth at the market until there were all these newfangled vendors set up here."

Summer shook her head. "This is truly wild. The gentrifiers will stop at nothing to take over our neighborhood."

"I don't know. Some parts of it I don't mind." He gestured to another booth. "Let's go over there and get some ice cream."

She eyed the brightly colored truck, with its sign advertising fresh, organic treats. The vendor, Carrey Creamery, wasn't a familiar one. "Don't you think it's a little early for ice cream?"

He eyed his trusty old stainless-steel wristwatch. "It's a little after eleven, I think it's all right. Plus, it's already eighty-something degrees out here. We could both use a little cooling down, I'm betting."

In more ways than you might think, Dad. She nodded. "Okay. Hopefully, it's as good as the sign promises."

At the service window, a young woman greeted them with a bright smile. She had curly red hair, pulled up into a high ponytail secured with a blue ribbon that matched her apron, and looked no older than nineteen or twenty. "Welcome to Carrey Creamery, where all our flavors are organic and ethically sourced. I'm Amber, what can I get for you?"

Tapping his chin, Rodney eyed the menu board for a moment. "Let me get a scoop of this vanilla with the caramel sauce. In one of your waffle bowls, please."

"Sounds good." The woman jotted down the order. "And you, ma'am?"

"A scoop of strawberry in a regular cup, please." She paused, curiosity about this new business getting the better of her. "Amber, if you don't mind my asking, is this your truck?"

With a quick shake of her head, Amber giggled. "Oh, no. It belongs to my parents. I've been working this truck for the summer; I go back to school in New York next week. They have one other truck, and they're working in it at a farmers market over in Georgetown."

"I see." *Hmm. So at least there's still some element of a family business to this particular enterprise.* "Thanks for humoring me."

"No problem, ma'am." Amber bopped off to make their order while Summer grappled with both her thoughts on the changing landscape of her neighborhood and Amber's insistence on calling her "ma'am," an honorific that should be reserved for a much older woman.

A few minutes later, Summer and her father were seated across from one another at one of the red silicone-coated steel picnic tables. "You know, this ice cream is pretty good." He spooned up another bite.

"I like it. You can tell they used real strawberries." The cool, sweet concoction melted in her mouth, cooling her body just enough to provide some relief from the late-summer Texas humidity.

"What's been going on with you? Your sister came by the house the other day, said the two of you are working on a project together."

"We formed a community group to defend Sojourner Truth from this latest attempt at its destruction." She finished her ice cream, setting the small plastic spoon inside the empty paper cup. "We think the school is important not just to our family legacy, but to the neighborhood."

Rodney looked thoughtful as he broke off a small piece of his waffle bowl and chewed it. "Yes, yes. I'm sure your grandmother would be proud of you two. Even though it's been empty more than a few years now, I'm sure that land can be put to good use."

"It's not just about Sojourner Truth, Dad." She gestured around. "It's about the way Ivy as a whole is changing. This neighborhood has something special about it, a sense of community that's really hard to come by these days. If we let people come in and ruin it, we'll never be able to get it back."

He scratched his chin. "I see, and I agree, at least to an extent."

"What makes matters worse is that I just found out a few days ago that Aiko Holt works for Abernathy, the company that's going to tear down our school."

Rodney frowned, his bushy brows nearly touching. "Aiko Holt. I know that name . . . Who is that, again?"

"Remember that night I came home from the school dance senior year, and you asked me who smudged my lipstick?"

Recollection lit his face, and his brow relaxed. "Oh, yeah. You told me you'd kissed someone, and it was a girl. I was so honored you felt safe enough to be honest with me." He paused. "It was her? Aiko was the one you kissed that night?"

She nodded. "Yes. I ran into her at the school the other day when I went to reminisce and retrieve a memento, and she remembered me."

He grinned. "Well, look at that. Seems you've been lingering on her mind."

Summer couldn't help flashing a small smile. "Anyway, she asked me if I'd grab coffee with her. That's when I found out she works in a supervisory capacity at the architectural firm overseeing the project. Before she revealed that, I assumed we were both there for the same reason: nostalgia. Turns out she was working."

"So, you've got yourself a conundrum, then." He chuckled. "I don't suppose she's got enough power to put a stop to the project?"

She shrugged. "I don't know, but I doubt it. Either way, she believes the project will be good for Ivy, so I don't think she'd stop it, even if she could."

"Her job isn't really the problem, you know." He wiped his hands on a napkin and crumpled it. "The real problem is that you still have feelings for her, and you know you probably can't get her to do things your way. Not when it comes to this."

She sighed. *Why can he still read me so well, even at my big age?* "I really do think the school site can and should be put to better use. But you're right. I still want her, even more now than I did back then. And I'm annoyed that I can't just turn it off."

"That's not how the heart works, kiddo." He winked. "Seems to me like you're overthinking this whole thing."

"What do you mean?"

"You make it sound as if the situation is black and white, that one of you has to fail or give in for the other one to succeed. I think it's a little more nuanced than that." Rodney leaned forward, holding Summer's gaze. "Why don't you just give her a chance? I know you're fired up about saving the world. But your happiness is important, too."

Summer twisted her lips. "I don't know. I care about the school and what happens to it. Beyond that, I don't want to risk getting hurt, especially not by someone I've been attracted to for so long."

"That enduring attraction is exactly why you can't walk away . . . not yet. Just enjoy her company and see where it goes. No harm in that." He rose from his seat, gathering their trash.

She watched as he carried their refuse to the metal trash barrel sitting beneath a nearby willow tree and tossed it in. Letting his words echo in her mind, she considered his advice. There had been many moments in her life when she'd acted on impulse, allowing passion or excitement to drive her to do something less than practical. Somehow, though, the idea of winging it with Aiko made her feel nervous. Unsettled.

He returned and retrieved his canvas bag. "I'm going to head home before it gets any hotter out here. My herbs are liable to wilt if we stay too much longer."

She stood, gathering her own bags. "You're right. I need to get my stuff in the fridge." She walked around to his side of the table and gave him a strong hug before stepping back. "Save me a bit of eggplant parmesan, okay?"

He offered an understanding smile, the unspoken truth passing between them. Summer hadn't eaten a family dinner at her parents' home in over a year, and they both knew she wouldn't until her mother extracted her head from her rear end. "I'll have Crystal bring you some. Think about what I said, Summer."

"Thanks, Dad. I will." They exchanged their goodbyes, and she watched him walk off toward his truck. Then, she made her way back to her car, two burgeoning bags of fresh produce in hand.

Monday morning, Aiko ran through her favorite section of the Butler Trail, feeling the vibration of each impact her feet made with the pavement. The sensation, along with the steady beat of her pulse, gave her a feeling of awareness and vibrancy that would carry her through the workday—or at least through her first coffee break.

Dawn had begun to light the sky, splashing the heavens with shades of melon, lavender, and rose. Puffy white clouds obscured the sun, cooling the humid air enough to make an outdoor run bearable. This time of year, she only ran outdoors if she could manage an early trek. If not, she stuck to a treadmill in either the air-conditioned gym near her house or the fitness center inside the office building where she worked.

She'd taken her usual path this morning, parking her car in the deck at the luxury high-rise apartment building on Second Street, then walking to the trail access point at the First Street pedestrian bridge.

She'd run down to Preston Field on the shores of Barton Creek, then turned around and headed back the way she'd come.

Keeping her pace even, she tipped her imaginary hat to the statue of legendary musician and Austin native Stevie Ray Vaughan as she passed his Auditorium Shores perch, where he stood like a poncho-clad sentinel, one hand on his guitar. Behind him, sunlight sparkled on the surface of Ladybird Lake and the city beyond. Mopping her brow with the tail of her tank top, she kept going.

After finishing her run, she returned to Second Street and entered Jo's Coffee. An Austin mainstay, Jo's had four locations in the city; this one had opened in 2006.

As she took a spot in line, she glanced at the community bulletin board. A frown creased her face when she saw the flyer for Summer's preservation society. Approaching the board, she skimmed the wording and found it very similar to what had been on the sign Summer had tacked to the construction fence. The one notable difference was the small vertical strips at the bottom bearing the URL for the group's social media page . . . and Summer's phone number.

Might as well take it, since I never got her number and she's just giving it out.

Aiko tore one of the strips off and tucked it into the pocket of her athletic shorts, then headed to the counter to order her breakfast.

Seven thirty rolled around by the time she'd finished her breakfast taco and grabbed a refill on her cold brew, so she returned to her car and traveled up Texas State Highway 1 north to the Research Park Place office complex where Abernathy was headquartered. The complex was home to thirty or so firms of varying size, most of them in the technology sector. Leaving her car with her garment bag, portfolio, and coffee in hand, she entered the four-story building.

After crossing the grand lobby, with its high ceilings, lacquered concrete floors, and walls painted in modern shades of charcoal and ecru, she visited the locker room on the first floor, where she showered away the accumulated grime and sweat from her morning run. After sufficiently drying her hair and securing it in its usual low bun, she dressed in a pink button-down top, dove-gray slacks, pink argyle socks, and charcoal loafers with a silver chain across the toe box. She groomed in the mirror, applying a little tinted sunscreen and lip balm. When she was satisfied with her appearance, she gathered her things and left the locker room.

The offices of Abernathy Creative Development occupied the western half of the building's second floor, encompassing just over five thousand square feet of space enclosed by steel and colored shatterproof glass. Grasping the cool metal of the door handle, she entered the suite.

"Good morning, Miss Holt."

Aiko waved to Tricia, the office receptionist, as she passed the desk. "Good morning, Tricia. And for the hundredth time, call me Aiko."

"Sorry. Habit, I guess." The dark-haired Tricia, Miriam's twenty-something niece from Houston, offered a sheepish smile. "Have a good day."

"You, too." Aiko chuckled to herself and headed down the corridor to her small, private office. Inside, she shut the door and leaned back against it.

She looked around the office, inhaling deeply. Since moving into the office three years prior, she'd added many accents that made her space feel more personal. The cherrywood shelves lining the rightmost wall were filled with some of her favorite books, copies of architectural magazines and journals, and many collectible jade figurines of various animals and the Buddha. Her father made a habit of sending her a hand-crafted figure every year on her birthday, and she'd amassed quite a collection.

After tucking her garment bag into the lower drawer of her desk, she took her portfolio and phone and headed to the conference room for the morning's meeting. She took her seat at one end of the six-person glass-topped table and scrolled through her emails on her phone.

Logan Warner strode in then, wearing a black suit with a yellow shirt and a striped yellow tie reminiscent of a bumblebee. A senior architect with more than twelve years of experience in the business, he served as project manager on the Sojourner Truth project. Carrying the black leather briefcase he was rarely seen without, he went to the opposite end of the table, placed the case down, and flipped it open.

On his heels, junior designer Fiona Dawson entered. Her blond hair was finessed into a topknot, and she wore a navy-blue shift dress that matched the frames of her eyeglasses. Once she was seated to Aiko's left, the entire three-person project team was present and accounted for.

Logan laid a stack of papers on the tabletop and clasped his hands together on top of them. "Good morning, guys. We're a couple of weeks out from demo day at the Ivy First Avenue site, so we've just got a few things to handle before I cut you loose."

"I think things are moving along well," Fiona commented. "The permits are in order and the demolition team from Kirby Construction is ready to get started."

"And the site is prime for the demolition, based on my final surveys," Aiko added, resting her elbows on the table. "Did you get a chance to look over them?"

"I did." Logan smiled. "Excellent work, as always, Holt. I've signed off on the data and turned it over to both Miriam and the head of the demolition department over at Kirby. We're looking good on all fronts to proceed." He paused, his expression turning serious. "Except one."

Aiko felt her eyes widening. *Ah, shit.* She'd spent the last several weeks working on schematics and plans, poring over environmental and safety reports, and completing surveys. "What's the issue?"

Logan pulled out his phone, swiped the screen a few times, and turned it around for them to see. "This."

"Oh, no." Fiona tucked in her lower lip.

When she saw the image on the screen, Aiko cringed. It depicted the very same sign she'd seen Summer hang on the construction fence. "Oh. You mean the preservation society."

He laid his phone on the table. "You don't seem surprised. You knew about this?"

Suddenly, Aiko had two sets of blue eyes locked on her face. She hated being the subject of that type of scrutiny, and she knew better than to lay all her cards on the table. "Yes, I saw it. I went by the site for surveying purposes all last week, remember?"

"Someone texted me the picture this morning, and it wasn't you." Logan ran a hand over his short brown hair. "Aiko, why didn't you tell me about this? Didn't you think I, or Miriam for that matter, would want to know?"

Her job description as the supervisory planner on the project was broad, but as far as she knew, it didn't include any public relations recon. She drew a deep breath, choosing her words carefully. "It's not anything major. Projects like this are bound to draw at least a few opponents."

"True enough, but it's up to the executive team to decide if this is major or not." Logan leaned back in his chair, blowing out a breath. "Aiko, we really need to control the narrative on this project. Ivy is a small, close-knit community, and any opposition could really derail our plans."

Aiko cleared her throat. "I hear you, Logan. But with all due respect, the people in that group have already decided they don't trust us. To them, we're outsiders destroying their idyllic little oasis."

"Aren't you from here?" Fiona asked. "As a local, you could potentially turn the tide of public opinion, if you remind them of the ways the project will benefit the neighborhood."

"I'm a local, yes. I've lived in this city my whole life, and I was born and bred in Ivy." Aiko wrapped her hand around the base of her bun, giving it a squeeze before releasing it. "I'm willing to run point with the preservation group. I'll try to be a voice of reason in support of what we're doing, but I can't promise I can change their minds." She thought of Summer's dogged determination to put the kibosh on the project, and while part of her saw the potential havoc that could bring to the worksite, another, deeper part of her respected Summer's dedication to her cause. Summer obviously had a huge heart—big enough to encompass her family, a classroom full of two-year-olds, and an entire neighborhood filled with working-class people of color. *How could I not be drawn to that?*

"I'm gonna need you to step it up, Aiko. Lean into those personal connections you have. They're more powerful than you might think." Logan turned to Fiona. "I'd like you to talk to marketing and see if they can counter the narrative being pushed by these preservation nuts."

Fiona nodded. "I'm sure they can come up with something. This could also be a good project for the interns to work on." Her thumbs flew as she typed into her phone. "I'll take care of that today, Mr. Warner."

Aiko swallowed the response she wanted to throw out. *I may not agree with what Summer and her people are doing, but I certainly wouldn't call them nuts. But since I just got chastised for not playing tattletale and informing them that yes, there were people who'd rather not have the project go forward, coming to the defense of the preservationists would surely cause more problems than I'm equipped to handle right now.*

Miriam entered the conference room then, and all eyes shifted in her direction. Wearing a bright red wide-legged pantsuit with a black button-down shirt beneath the suit coat, Miriam looked as polished as always. Her springy curls were out today, surrounding her head like a coffee-colored halo. Wearing a confident smile, she walked over and stood behind Logan's chair. "Morning, y'all. How are things going with our multiuse development?"

Logan turned his chair slightly so he could face Miriam. "We're on track, Miriam. We've got a little PR issue, but I'm sure it's nothing that marketing can't handle."

Miriam nodded. "Sounds good. Go ahead and wrap up because we'll need the conference room in about ten minutes. Waterman and Associates is coming in to discuss a national headquarters they want built for their firm." She clapped her hands together. "Y'all have a good day." Aiko smiled and offered a wave as their boss departed. Working in property development could be stressful, especially since it was still a male-dominated field. But working for someone like Miriam, a Black woman from Tuscaloosa who'd turned an idea into a million-dollar company, felt like a privilege.

Logan spun his chair back to its original position. "Miriam is counting on us to make this project a success." He looked pointedly at Aiko. "So, let's do everything we can to make that happen."

Aiko chose to nod rather than open her mouth and say something snarky. She liked Logan and generally enjoyed working with him. But he tended to overblow small issues, and whenever he got into that mode, it tried her patience.

After returning to her office, Aiko dropped onto the soft cushion of the small love seat and sighed. Now that Logan had given her the task of smoothing things over with the preservation group, in addition to her regular duties, she was trapped firmly between her desire to get to know Summer and her desire to get promoted. It was an impossible choice—one she refused to make.

Her mother's years as a Delta flight attendant had left her body in a somewhat fragile condition. She now suffered from peripheral arterial disease in addition to the back and knee problems that had come with two decades of being on her feet in heels at thirty thousand feet.

By the numbers, the situation was far less than ideal. Though only in her late fifties, Janet took four different daily medications to manage her pain and her blood-flow issues. Between her age, her condition, and the drowsiness caused by her medications, she was only months away from needing in-home care. The cost of that care, even part-time, could exceed $400,000 out of Aiko's pocket over the next fifteen to twenty years.

The thought of how she'd pay for her mother's care always loomed large in her mind. And the best way she could see to cover the expense was to continue rising in the ranks at Abernathy. She'd worked hard to get into middle management, and she knew that if she performed well, upper management was just around the corner.

If that means playing both sides of the fence for a while, so be it. She wouldn't lie to Summer, nor would she lie to her boss. But she knew better than to think she could just turn off her attraction to Summer.

Aiko slid open her desk drawer, then took out the turquoise earring and toyed with it absently. In her mind's eye, she could see Summer's beautiful face. Those shimmering brown eyes called to her while full lips tempted her to kiss them.

Tucking the earring away again, she fished around in her garment bag and retrieved the small scrap of paper with Summer's number on it from the pocket of her gym shorts.

CHAPTER SIX

Around eight o'clock on Wednesday morning, Summer rounded the corner from Miramar Boulevard onto First Avenue and pulled her car up to the curb near Sojourner Truth. After she'd parallel parked to the best of her ability, she cut the engine and got out. Popping her trunk, she pulled out the five-gallon red bucket she'd picked up from a home-improvement store, loaded with the items she'd packed for today's activities. She then grabbed her trusty folding camp chair and tucked it beneath her arm before shutting the trunk.

An aged oak occupied the green space between the cracked sidewalk and the curb and had been there since her days as a student. Standing beneath that old tree, she dumped out the bucket. She spilled her portable speaker, a mini-megaphone, and several handmade and printed signs. After unfolding the camp chair, she set the bucket upside-down next to it as a sort of makeshift table, then took a seat, enjoying the cool shade provided by the canopy of leaves overhead.

By twenty minutes after eight o'clock, she'd set up her portable speaker on the bucket and paired it with her phone to play some old-school hip-hop. While the music played, she busied herself unpacking the rest of the signs and spreading them around her.

Crystal arrived a few minutes later, carrying a cooler with two young ladies in tow. "Morning, Summer. I brought along some help.

These are Coach Keys' twin granddaughters, Lynn and Maya. Girls, say hello to Miss Summer." Crystal set the cooler at the base of the tree.

The girls, both dressed in cutoff denim shorts and graphic tees, mumbled their greetings.

Crystal cut them a look, and they repeated themselves, this time more clearly. "I went to see their grandmother a couple of days ago. When I told her what we planned to do, she volunteered them to help out. They're homeschooled, and their mother agreed this would be a great hands-on civics lesson."

Summer chuckled. "Good morning, y'all. I appreciate you coming."

Neither Maya nor Lynn looked excited about being there, but they nodded and smiled anyway.

"Look at you, all dressed to fight the system," Crystal quipped, tucking her straight chestnut-brown hair behind her ear. "That's my baby sis."

Summer glanced at herself: white tee with the classic Black Power–fist logo, black biker shorts, and white sneakers. "I suppose so, but I mostly dressed for comfort."

Crystal spun around, showing off her pink A-line sundress. "I'm cute and comfortable since we might end up on TV today."

Summer's eyes widened. "What are you talking about, Crys?"

"I may have put in a call to a reporter I know down at Channel 7." Crystal leaned in. "She couldn't promise me coverage, but she did say she'd try to sneak away from her desk and give us a little play."

"Is that all you know?"

"She said that if she could make it, it would be during the morning hours. She thinks a local-interest story like this would 'play well' on the noon news." Crystal shrugged. "Hopefully, she can come."

"Looks like we'll just have to wait and see." The breeze picked up, and Summer swiped a hand over her billowing hair, wishing she'd bound it today. Too many ponytails were starting to pull on her edges, though, so she'd opted for a wide black headband instead to hold her somewhat unruly curls out of her face. Gesturing to the signs she'd laid out on the ground, she said, "Lynn, Maya, go ahead and choose a couple of signs to carry, please."

While the girls dutifully followed her instructions, Summer glanced at the screen of her phone. Seeing a text message from an unfamiliar number, she opened it and read it silently.

Hey, Summer. I realized I never asked for your number. Lucky for me you have flyers all over town, giving it away for free. Now you have my number, too. ☺ -Aiko.

Even as she rolled her eyes in response to the cheeky missive, she couldn't hold back her smile.

"Summer?" Crystal eyed her curiously. "What's got you grinning at your phone like that?"

After clearing her screen with a quick swipe, she tucked her phone away. "It's nothing."

Her sister's nose crinkled, her mouth twisting into a half-smile. "I've known you your whole life, so I'm gonna call you on that lie."

Summer cringed. "Come on, Crys. Let me have this. At least for now."

Crystal's brow hitched, but she acquiesced. "All right. But don't think you're gonna keep this a secret from me forever."

Knowing she'd have to field more questions about this later, Summer shooed her away. "Just go pick a sign, Crys."

As nine o'clock in the morning rolled around, a few more people arrived to join the effort, bringing the total number up to nine. It was far less than Summer would have hoped, but seeing some familiar faces, both from the neighborhood and from the preservation group's social media page, made her feel somewhat vindicated. *There may not be many of us here, but at least I know my sister and I aren't alone in our concern for what happens to our former school.*

Summer stood from her seat and looked around to assure herself that everyone had a sign. Then she took the extras, stacked them, and propped them against the cooler. "Okay, folks. First, I want to thank you all for coming. We're all here for the same reason: we care about Sojourner Truth Charter Academy and about this community. Remember that in a world that turns more and more toward individualism and toxic self-interest every day, your commitment to a cause bigger than yourself is commendable."

That comment brought on a smattering of applause. "Let's get started. We'll march this block, go as far up as Miramar, and as far down as Grant. On the back of your sign, I've printed several phrases we'll be chanting. When you hear a key word, use that as a guide to join in if you want. Hold your signs high and let them face the street so people passing by can see them. Any questions?"

"Yeah. How long are we gonna be out here?" The question came from the rear of the assemblage, from the only man who'd shown up.

Summer didn't recognize him but could appreciate his presence, nonetheless. "We'll be out of here by lunchtime, but if you have somewhere to be, you're free to go when you need to." She glanced around in search of other raised hands. "Anyone else?"

The group grew quiet.

"Let's march, then." She handed the bullhorn over to Crystal. "I'll give you first crack at being the ringleader."

Crystal chuckled as she accepted the device. "Great. It'll be like college all over again." Walking to the head of the group, she powered the bullhorn on and shouted, "Legacy over money! History over profits! Abernathy's wrong and we're gonna stop it!" Still chanting, she led the group south toward Grant Boulevard.

Raising her OUR COMMUNITY DESERVES BETTER sign high above her head, Summer walked along at the rear of the group. They marched back and forth, up and down the block, for a good hour before she called for a break. After allowing some time for people to grab drinks from Crystal's cooler and get off their feet, she got them back underway again. This time, Summer carried the bullhorn and led another chant. "Hey hey! Ho ho! Abernathy has got to go!"

A few folks in the houses lining the street watched the proceedings through their windows; some came out onto their porches or stood in their yards. A passing car honked as it zoomed by.

Summer was making the turn at the corner of Grant and First when a *Channel 7 Access News* van rolled by. Leading the group back to the orange construction fence in front of the school, she watched as the female reporter and her cameraman exited the vehicle and approached them.

Crystal elbowed her. "There's Brenda! Looks like we lucked out today."

Mic in hand, the brown-skinned anchor in the mint-green power suit strode toward their group. "Morning, folks. I'm Brenda Willoughby, and this is my cameraman, Latham. We'd like to give you folks a chance to share your message with the greater Austin area." She turned toward Crystal. "I'm guessing you're in charge here?"

"We both are," Crystal insisted, gesturing between herself and Summer. "Thanks for coming, Brenda. I really appreciate it."

"As I said, a local-interest story like this is perfect for the noon broadcast." Brenda winked. Leaning in, she whispered, "This also means I get a jump on the story before those hacks at Channel 3 get ahold of it."

Summer didn't know what to make of that statement, so she decided not to comment on it. "We're happy to chat with you about what we're doing here."

"Great." Brenda turned to Crystal. "Can you round everybody up and have them hold their signs in front of them? I think that will make the most compelling backdrop for the interview."

"Yeah, I can do that."

While Crystal rallied the protestors, Brenda turned to her cameraman. "Frame me up, Latham. Let's get away from the tree a little bit, so we can get better light."

"That's my line," Latham quipped as he set up his tripod and began making adjustments.

"While he's doing that," Brenda said, looking Summer's way, "can you give me a little background on your mission here?"

"Sure." She chatted with the reporter for a few moments until they both felt she had a clear understanding of their efforts and the motivation behind them.

Once everyone was in place, Brenda lifted her mic to her mouth and signaled for recording to begin. "Let's do the bump first." She cleared her throat. "This is Brenda Willoughby with *Channel 7 Access News*. Today, I'll speak with two local women from Austin's historic Ivy neighborhood about their quest to save a beloved local landmark. Stay tuned for more." She paused. "How's that?"

Latham gave her a thumbs-up from his position behind the large camera. "Got it. I'm ready to film the story whenever you are."

"Hello, Austinites. Today, I'm here with Crystal and Summer Graves, both former students of the now-shuttered Sojourner Truth Charter Academy. Together, these sisters have organized a preservation society, with the goal of stopping the planned demolition of the school building and its subsequent transformation into a multiuse commercial development." She held the mic out toward Crystal. "Crystal, what can you tell me about your mission here?"

"Our goal here is to take a stand against the gentrification of our neighborhood. We see more and more of it every day, as families that have lived here for generations are displaced so that the wealthy can tear down their property and move in. Then they raise the rents so high, none of them can afford to come back. It's unconscionable, and if we don't do something about it, who will?"

"Anything you'd like to add, Summer?"

Summer cleared her throat, praying the breeze coming through the area didn't have her head looking like a windswept cornfield. "Yes." She looked directly into the camera. "This school isn't just a part of Ivy history, it's a part of my family's legacy. Our late grandmother Beulah Graves founded it, bringing educational opportunity to this neighborhood in a time when Black people in the South were suffering under the lasting effects of Jim Crow. Sojourner Truth Charter Academy added so much value to the lives of the people in this neighborhood, by preparing two generations of students for success. All we ask is that Abernathy Creative Development, Kirby Construction, and all the other parties involved in this project take a pause and really consider what they are doing."

Brenda offered a nod and a serious yet understanding expression. "I see. According to our research, the project is fully licensed and permitted to proceed. What is your group requesting to be done? Would you like to see the project delayed, altered, or abandoned altogether?"

Summer answered, "For now we'd like to see it delayed so that a more beneficial outcome for the neighborhood can be worked out. We just want this project handled properly, on all sides."

"You heard it here first, folks. More to come on this story, as we'll reach out to Abernathy Creative Development and Kirby Construction for their response. In the meantime, we invite viewers to weigh in on the fate of this property by taking the poll found on the home page of the Channel 7 website. I'm Brenda Willoughby, reporting from the former Sojourner Truth Charter Academy in Ivy, for *Access News*. Back to you in the studio."

Latham gave another thumbs-up, then switched off his camera.

Brenda smiled. "I hate to chat and run, ladies, but we need to get the footage uploaded in time for the noon news." Reaching out, she shook each of their hands. "Thanks a lot for sharing your story."

Crystal opened her arms and gave Brenda a quick hug. "Thanks for getting it out to the masses."

"You're welcome. Good luck with everything, ladies." Brenda joined her cameraman as they got into their news van and drove away.

Once the taillights of the vehicle disappeared, Summer turned to her sister. "Tell me the truth. Does my hair look crazy?"

Crystal laughed. "No. Girl, your hair is fine. I wouldn't let you go out like that."

"Good." She blew out a breath. "Because if I show up on TV looking a mess, Dad will never let me hear the end of it." She pulled out her phone, checking the time. "It's eleven fifteen. What do you say we make a couple more laps, then call it a day?"

"Sounds good." Crystal gestured her charges over. "Let everyone know we're taking two more trips up and down the block."

"Remind them to hold their signs facing the road," Summer added.

While Maya and Lynn informed the protesters, Summer picked up her own sign from her camp chair. As she rejoined the group and started walking toward Miramar, the sound of several approaching vehicles drew her attention to the intersection.

~~

Arriving at the Sojourner Truth site around twenty minutes to noon, Aiko was surprised to see a line of cars already parked in front of the old school. There were also ten or so people loitering near the orange plastic construction fence bordering the front edge of the property.

I haven't seen this many people hanging out here since the day they came to gather keepsakes. What is going on?

Frowning, she glanced in her rearview mirror and saw the two bright orange Kirby Construction trucks rounding the corner behind her. With no other choice, she drove her small SUV down the block and found an open spot near the corner of First Avenue and Grant Boulevard. She parked and watched as the construction trucks took up spots on the opposite side of the street.

She cut the engine and lingered in her car for a few moments to gather herself. She'd anticipated a quick trip to the worksite to check in with the construction company's demolition chief and then a quiet lunch. What she hadn't expected was to show up and find a small crowd gathered in front of the school. She glanced over her shoulder. *I don't know what's going on here, but I have a feeling I know who's behind it.*

She exited her vehicle and headed straight across the street to the first Kirby truck.

Bill Kirby, demolition chief and younger brother to company owner Walter Kirby, rolled down his window as Aiko approached. He ran a hand over his brown hair. His ruddy face was tight, and his blue eyes flashed. "Holt, what the hell is going on over there?"

She shrugged. "I'm not entirely sure, but trust me, I'm just as surprised as you are."

He groused, "We don't have time for this. I've only got until the end of the day to get these fences put up around the site, and I've got no time for foolishness."

"Listen, you and your crew can hang tight in the trucks for a few minutes. I'll go over there and see what I can do to break up the party so you can get to work."

"Great." Bill offered a crooked smile that didn't reach his eyes. "You've got ten minutes."

She walked away to the sound of Bill radioing the rest of his crew and strode up the block toward the gaggle of people who were now moving toward her. At first, there wasn't a familiar face in the group. But as the group separated and one woman cut through, Aiko stopped.

There she was, looking like a decadent dessert and carrying a sign that read simply **STOP GENTRIFICATION**. Her black-and-white attire, while casual, still accentuated the glorious fullness of her figure. Her midthigh-length black shorts hugged the shapely curves of her hips and ass so well, it took Aiko a minute to find her voice. With some effort, she was finally able to say, "Summer? What the hell?"

Summer twisted her full lips into a half-smile. "Good morning, Aiko. And I don't know why you'd ask me that when I think it's pretty clear what we're doing here."

Aiko shook her head. "Okay, whatever. At any rate, y'all gotta go."

"Why? Are you really that eager to destroy our school? We all have some kind of connection or history here, Aiko." She took a step closer, holding eye contact. "You and I, especially."

Aiko swallowed, her tongue involuntarily darting across her lower lip. "So you gonna take it there?" It was a low blow, and they both knew it. Still, the way Summer squared her shoulders and closed the space between them, clearly communicating that she wouldn't back down, had Aiko's brain stalling and clit humming.

"If that's what it takes to get my point across." Summer took another step, coming close enough that if Aiko extended her arm, she could easily get a handful of boob.

A statuesque woman in a pink dress stepped between them, facing Summer. Her presence effectively severed the thick rope of electric desire between them, at least for the moment. "Girl, you mind telling us who this is?"

"This is Aiko Holt," Summer said loudly enough to be heard by more than just her friend. "She works for Abernathy."

A chorus of "boos" rose from the assemblage.

Aiko rolled her eyes. "Sheesh."

"Y'all, go easy. No need for booing." Summer turned her attention back toward Aiko. "This is my big sister, Crystal. She's on my team, in case that's not clear."

"Yikes." Aiko looked into Crystal's face, noting her lemon-sucking expression. "Look. I went to school here, too, and I respect what your grandmother accomplished. But you have to understand, this is business."

Crystal rolled her eyes and snorted. "You really are toeing the corporate line, huh." She turned and walked away without waiting for a response.

Aiko blew out a breath and addressed Summer. "You have to get these people to leave. Kirby Construction has work to do here, and it's not safe for them to stay." Watching Summer's eyes narrow, Aiko added, "They're not tearing anything down today, so chill. All they want to do is put up a fence."

"And what if we don't leave?" Summer asked, her tone defiant.

"Then I'm gonna call the cops and report you folks as trespassers."

Aiko and Summer both turned toward the threat. Bill Kirby stood on the curb, his thick arms folded over his barrel chest, obscuring the Kirby logo on his bright orange shirt. Two of his burly workers were stationed behind him, and none of the men appeared hospitable.

"Excuse me?" Summer waved her hand dismissively. "This is public property, and we have every right to be here, sir."

Beneath the brim of his yellow hard hat, Bill's brow furrowed, his face folding into a scowl. "Well, look at you. You're all mouth, aren't you?"

"Not all. And if you keep talking to me like that, you're gonna see that I got hands, too." Summer's chin jutted out, and her fists clenched at her sides.

Knowing she needed to defuse this before it got out of control, Aiko raised her hands. "Whoa, whoa. Let's not go there." She looked between them, wondering how she always ended up mediating between two hotheads. "Bill, go ahead and tell your crew to start unloading the chain link. Y'all can get started around back. I promise you, by the time you make it around the side of the building, everyone will be gone."

Bill stroked his chin for a moment. "Fair enough. Better that than standing here wasting time." He turned to his workers and made a circling motion above his head. "Let's go, boys!"

After the Kirby workers moved away, Aiko looked at Summer, whose wide stance and tight expression indicated her still-simmering ire. "Can you please, please get your people to clear out of here? As a favor to me?"

She seemed to consider the notion for a few silent moments. Slipping her phone from her pocket, she checked the time, then sighed. "I did tell them we'd be done by now." She clapped her hands together. "Okay, everybody. We're done here."

As folks began to leave, a young girl stopped to ask Summer, "Do you want us to turn in our signs?"

She shook her head. "Keep them. I have tons more at home, and you can use that one again next time."

The girl nodded, tucking her sign under her arm as she walked away.

"Next time?" Aiko shook her head. Cars began to pull away from the curb as the group dispersed, leaving the two of them alone on the sidewalk in front of the worksite. "You really aren't going to let this go, are you?"

"Graves women have never been known to back down. So, nope." She turned her back and strolled to a nearby tree. Bending at the waist, she broke down a folding chair and began gathering up things scattered around the base of the tree.

Aiko tucked her thumbs into the waistband of her slacks and enjoyed the view of Summer's round, upturned ass in appreciative silence. *It really doesn't make any sense for her to be this damn sexy.*

After she placed her stuff in the trunk of her black sedan, Summer came back into Aiko's personal space. "You know I could feel your eyes on my ass, right?"

Aiko gave a one-shouldered shrug. "I'm not gonna lie and say I wasn't looking. That's . . . quite a wagon you draggin'."

A soft, sultry smile lit Summer's face, and she swiped a hand over her hair. "Still talking a good game, I see. Sooner or later, you are gonna have to back up that slick mouth, Aiko."

Letting her eyes travel from the top of her shiny dark curls to her sneaker-clad feet, Aiko then made eye contact. Holding her gaze, she said, "With pleasure. When do you want to get together again?"

Summer twirled a curl around the tip of her index finger. "How about Friday night?"

Surprise lifted her brow, and Aiko smiled. "So you're eager to get some more of what I'm offering, then?"

"You could say that." She sucked her bottom lip. "During work hours, we may not agree. But when you're off the clock . . ." She reached out, placing her hand on Aiko's shoulder and giving it a little squeeze. "I think we can work something out."

"Bet. I'll text you after lunch." Aiko put her hand on top of Summer's and guided it to her lips. She placed a peck on the back of Summer's hand, then let go.

"Later." Summer turned and sashayed to her car. Moments later, she drove away, leaving an outdone Aiko standing on the sidewalk. Once Aiko gathered her senses, she got into her SUV and headed up north, seeking a quick lunch.

She ended up at Stiles Switch BBQ on Lamar Boulevard. Located in the storied 1950s-era Violet Crown Shopping Center, the joint served authentic Texas barbeque in a casual setting, perfect for her appetite today.

Within fifteen minutes of pulling up, she was seated at one of the narrow, pub-height tables in the rear of the restaurant, digging into her lunch. While she enjoyed her spicy brisket sandwich, crisp fries, and a cold glass of lemonade, she watched the television mounted to the wall in the rear corner.

The station was set on Channel 7, and the noon news broadcast was ending. As the anchor ran through a recap of the stories they'd covered, a series of images and video clips accompanied her words. Aiko nearly choked on a fry when she saw Summer's and Crystal's faces flash across the screen. The chyron below them read, "Two Local Women Fight Upcoming Ivy Development."

She closed her eyes for a second, shaking her head. *If Logan wasn't a fan of them hanging signs, he's really not going to like this.* She didn't know which thing was affecting her more right now: the jalapeños piled on her sandwich or what she'd just seen on the television. Either way, she felt stifled and uncomfortable. Opening the second button on her shirt, she drained the rest of her lemonade and went to the fountain for a refill.

She secured the plastic lid on her cup when her phone started ringing. Returning to her seat, she answered the call, fully expecting to hear Logan on the other end, freaking out. "Hello?"

"Aiko, it's Miriam."

She cringed. *Even worse.* "Hi, Miriam. I'm just on my way back from lunch. What can I do for you?"

"I've just seen our business slandered on the noon news."

"Yeah, I saw that, too. It's unfortunate."

"It's more than that. I've already got the public relations officer issuing a statement to Channel 7." She paused. "You have a connection to that school, isn't that right?"

"Yes, I do. I got my high-school diploma there."

"Good. That means you're uniquely positioned to help with this whole mess. I want you to figure out a way to get those protestors to back down. Join the group if you have to."

Aiko inhaled deeply, pressing her fingertips to her temple. Being the Ivy local at Abernathy meant constant pressure to "use her connections." Part of her knew her coworkers were overestimating her power, and the other part of her simply hated being expected to go above and beyond simply because she'd grown up in the neighborhood. "In all honesty, Miriam, I'm not sure how much I can do here. But I'll give it a shot."

"That's all I ask." Miriam chuckled. "In the end, the project is going forward, I'm not worried about that. I just want them to stop bringing negative press on us."

"I understand."

"Wonderful," she answered, her tone bright. "See you back at the office this afternoon." Miriam disconnected the call.

Aiko looked at the two fries left on her plate but couldn't muster the desire to eat them. She was being placed in an odd position, and she hated it.

I'll be careful. I'll do this in a way where nobody gets hurt. All the while, she wondered if that was even possible.

Subtlety and grace would be key. No lies, no going to battle. She'd choose her moves carefully, like a chess master.

She gathered up her garbage, tossed it in the trash, then fired off a quick text to Summer.

Meet me Friday at Cheer Up Charlies. 8 PM.

She was walking to her car when she got Summer's response.

Sounds fun. See you there.

Smiling, despite the looming sense of dread over what the rest of the workday would hold, she tucked her phone away and climbed into her car.

CHAPTER SEVEN

Summer left her apartment building on Third and Brazos around seven thirty Friday evening to be sure she'd make it to her destination on time. She was wearing a cute but comfortable ensemble of lightweight pink slacks, a melon tank top, and a loose-knit crocheted white cardigan, and she'd slipped her feet into a pair of supportive white-jeweled sandals, mindful of the walking she'd be doing. Her hair was loose and curly—she'd known better than to bother straightening it since the day's humidity would turn it to cotton candy within minutes. A pink scarf held her hair out of her face. As she walked down Third Street toward the metro stop at Lacava and Fourth, she felt a tugging near her ear. She reached up and wrestled one of her teardrop citrine dangle earrings free from the scarf, righting it again.

She exited the bus at 805 Trinity and Eighth, then walked up the block and around the corner to Cheer Up Charlies on Red River Street. A glance at her phone showed her she'd made it with ten minutes to spare.

The lesbian-owned bar had been a mainstay of downtown Austin for years, having moved into this location from its former haunt on Sixth Street several years ago. The building, with its stone front and festively painted sides, resembled a rustic cabin and had also previously been home to a lesbian bar called Chances back in the 1990s.

I've passed this place a million times. Now I finally get to see the inside.

She entered the courtyard, passing through the big wooden gate and looking around. There were eclectic seating choices throughout the space, including picnic tables with brightly colored umbrellas, saucer chairs grouped to form a conversation area, and steel chairs positioned around butcher-block-style tables. The rear of the courtyard was occupied by a stage, behind which a glowing smiley face, formed from the business' initials, lit up the rear fence.

Thinking it would be easier for Aiko to find her if she waited outside, she took a seat at a vacant picnic table and pulled out her phone to pass the time.

She was giggling at a silly video of a cat jumping off a desk when she heard a voice call her name. As she glanced up from her phone, her mouth went dry.

Aiko stood over her, a soft smile on her face. She wore a white Texas Longhorns basketball jersey with the number thirty-five, famously worn by NBA-baller Kevin Durant during his college b-ball days, emblazoned on it. Her bared arms were muscled but still slender, indicating that she worked out but wasn't into bodybuilding. She'd paired the jersey with slim, distressed white jeans and orange high-top sneakers. Her hair was piled in a messy bun on top of her head, a large princess-cut fire opal stud glittered in her left ear, and a long silver chain hung from her neck.

Damn. Even in casual clothes, she still fine as hell. "Oh, hey. You really snuck up on me."

She grinned. "I like to make my moves in silence."

Summer laughed, then inhaled. That was a mistake because the intoxicating scent of whatever fragrance Aiko wore flooded her nostrils and nearly rendered her senseless. She tried to pick out the individual notes, and the only two she could identify were something like sandalwood and something tart and fruity, like cherry. "You smell like heaven. What are you wearing?"

Aiko eased closer. "So, you think I smell good?"

"Yes, that's literally what I just said. Now tell me what kind of potion you're wearing, please."

"It's a unisex fragrance by this company called Oakcha." Aiko leaned down, lowering her voice to whisper into her ear. "It's called Sinful."

Sheesh.

"How appropriate." Part of her wanted to tell Aiko all the things she wanted to do to her and how the cologne only made those feelings more intense. But this was the first date, so she decided to play it close to the vest . . . for now. She gestured to the jersey. "Reppin' your alma mater hard today, I see."

Aiko stood back, striking a pose with her arms stretched over her head. "Always. My UT days were some of the best of my life." She let her arms drop to her sides again. "If I get enough top-shelf in my system tonight, I might tell you about some of my shenanigans."

Summer felt her brow arch with interest. "Well, well. I can't wait to see how this evening unfolds, then."

Aiko extended her hand. "Come on. Let's go inside and grab a drink."

Slipping her hand inside Aiko's, Summer smiled and stood.

They entered the small building through the glass-paneled door and approached the bar that stood to the immediate left of the entrance. There were the typical wall-mounted shelves behind the bar, lined with various bottles of spirits. Summer looked around the space, taking in the rustic interior. There were a few other patrons inside, mainly women, keeping to the edges of the space. The cabin aesthetic was even more prevalent inside: everything was wood. From the polished hardwood floor to the paneled walls, painted in rainbow shades, to the thick beams overhead, it was like being in a mountainside lodge. "Wow. Serious ski-chalet vibes."

Aiko chuckled. "I know. It's kinda refreshing. Austin gets so hot and humid, it's nice to imagine you're in Aspen, about to hit the slopes."

"That's easier said than done on a day like this." Summer dashed away a bit of perspiration around her hairline.

"Listen. They have a really good drink here that you can't get anywhere else. Are you willing to give it a shot?"

Glancing at the bright colors of the hand-painted signs with drink descriptions on display above the bar, Summer asked, "Are you gonna tell me which drink it is?"

Aiko shook her head. "Nope. So, are you feeling adventurous?"

In ways you couldn't even imagine. "Sure. I'll bite."

Aiko rested her palms on the top of the bar, which was made of the same polished planks beneath their feet. Gesturing to one of the ladies behind the bar, she said, "Can I get two kale-lime margaritas, made with Patrón, please?"

"Coming right up, honey."

Summer's gaze wandered through the narrow interior, past the small nook that acted as the DJ booth and the alcove where the restrooms were, and all the way down to the opposite end of the building, where a stage occupied the wall. "Have you ever been to a show here?"

"Yeah, a couple of years ago. It's mostly indie bands that play here." Aiko rubbed her hands. "It can get pretty hot in here when there's a sold-out concert."

Summer pictured a show in her mind's eye: the band on the stage, a singer belting out a tune while the music blasted, a mass of dancing bodies moving in a tangle across the floor. She could almost feel the heat radiating off the imaginary crowd. "Yeah, I bet. It's not that big of a place."

The barkeep slid the drinks toward Aiko, along with a bright red paper boat overflowing with popcorn. Aiko paid, then picked up the two glasses. "Wanna sit outside?"

Summer grabbed the popcorn. "As long as we get a table with an umbrella . . . I love those little lights strung inside them." They returned to the courtyard and, luckily, snagged the last table with an umbrella attached. Seated beneath the canopy's shade, Summer placed the popcorn in the middle of the table and accepted her drink. "Thanks."

"No problem. I hope you like it."

She took a tentative sip, first tasting the lime and salt around the rim of the glass. That flavor was immediately followed by the tartness of more lime, the bite of good tequila, and a spicy note she couldn't quite place. "It's pretty good. What's in it, though?"

"Tequila, lime juice, some agave, kale juice, and ginger." Aiko grabbed a handful of popcorn and tossed some into her mouth.

Summer snapped her fingers. "Ginger. That's the spicy thing I taste." She took another sip. "It's different from a regular margarita but in a refreshing way." She smiled. "I'm glad I trusted you."

"Me, too. That means you'll take any other suggestions I make tonight, right?" Aiko raised her glass in tribute, a mischievous gleam in her eyes.

Summer tilted her head to one side. "I'll take them under serious consideration, at least." Shifting her gaze from Aiko's smiling face up to the horizon, she said, "Look at that sunset." The sky was streaked with the soft pastels that heralded the coming night.

Aiko turned her head slightly to take it in. "It's beautiful."

Summer shifted to watch her, drinking in the way the fading light played over her features and the soft yet strong lines of her face in profile. She wouldn't have believed it possible to surpass her powerful teenage feelings for her high-school crush. But sitting with Aiko now, Summer realized that her attractions were only growing stronger.

Rather than dwell too long on that, Summer munched on the popcorn. It was well seasoned with butter, salt, and a few little red flecks she guessed were paprika. It was crisp, tasty, and a perfect complement to their margaritas.

As they finished their drinks and emptied the paper bowl, darkness rose around them. An unseen hand turned on the small bulbs strung up around the courtyard, giving the whole area a soft, dreamy glow.

"I'm gonna grab a water," Aiko said, standing with her glass in hand. "Do you want one? Or would you like a refill?"

"Water, please." The buzz of the first drink had already settled in, and she saw no need to intensify it further.

Aiko grabbed her glass and disappeared inside, returning shortly with waters. "Now that I've got a full drink in me, I think I feel like telling you one of my college tales." She paused, looking at Summer pointedly as she slid back onto the bench. "I'll expect you to do the same, though."

"Fair enough. I'll match you, story for story." Summer leaned in. "Let's hear it."

Aiko shifted her position, resting her back against the edge of the table. A wistful smile came over her face. "Okay. So, junior year. I had a track meet against Texas Tech, and my roommate Peaches had a weekend off from her work-study job at the library. She had family up there, so she tagged along and drove up in her old Toyota when I rode the bus to Lubbock with the team."

Summer frowned. "That's . . . unique. Is Peaches her given name?"

"Nah. Patricia is her government name, but she takes it as a personal offense when anyone calls her that." Aiko chuckled. "Anyway, I took the winning spot in the sixty-meters that day. After the meet, I hung out with the team for a bit of celebrating, then Coach cut me loose to meet up with Peaches. She stayed at the same hotel where the school put the team up, so I went to her room to see what we were getting into that night."

"I'm intrigued," Summer said.

"We ended up going to a bonfire in the wilds of Lubbock County, with Peaches' cousins. There were seven of us altogether, four girls and three guys. We're out there in this clearing behind her aunt's house, blasting music and acting silly, when somebody starts to pass the blunt. Now, I had never smoked before, but I wasn't about to back down in front of my homie, so I joined in."

"And . . . how did that go for you?"

Aiko shook her head, her smile broadening. "The funny part is, I have no memory of that night beyond the second hit I took off the blunt. According to Peaches, who was already a connoisseur of the green at the time, I stood on the picnic table and made an existential speech about the meaning of life, and fell while trying to climb down from said table. Then I ate an entire party-sized bag of Doritos, then passed out in one of her aunt's lawn chairs."

Summer snorted a laugh. "Sheesh."

"Yep. She and one of her male cousins carried me to her car, and she managed to walk me upstairs to my room and tuck me into bed. I woke up the next morning confused as hell, still fully dressed in what I wore to the bonfire, and with maple leaves in my hair."

Summer laughed harder, hard enough that she reached for her glass of water. After taking a sip and collecting herself, she asked, "So . . . do you smoke nowadays?"

"Nope. When I visit my old track buddy that lives in Reno, I might pop an edible. But that was my one and only time smoking." She shrugged. "I'm glad I was with Peaches—she was more experienced and she looked after me."

"As any good friend should. Are you and her still close?"

"I'd say so. She's my best friend to this day." Aiko took a sip from her water glass. "She still lives in Austin, too. Owns a barbershop on the south side of town."

Summer smiled. "That's really sweet, that you two have maintained your friendship all this time. I mean, I keep up with a few girls I went to high school and college with, but I can't say I'm close with any of them."

"Who's your bestie, then? Every woman needs at least one person that's always got her back," Aiko said sagely before draining the rest of the water from her glass.

"My sister, Crystal," she answered without hesitation. "She's two years older, but we've always been thick as thieves, as my dad says."

"I think that's valid." Aiko paused, her gaze locked on the shimmering lights of the city beyond the wooden gate. "I'm an only child, and I think I would really have enjoyed having a sister or brother." She rubbed her hands and watched Summer intently. "Now, about that tale of college foolishness you owe me . . ."

Summer giggled. "I don't know if my story will be as entertaining as yours, but I'll tell it anyway." A catchy tune began to play over the loudspeakers then, and a few occupants of the tables around them rose from their seats to dance in the center of the courtyard. The infectious song had her toe-tapping under the table. "Listen, will you dance with me?"

Aiko narrowed her eyes. "Do you really wanna dance, or are you just stalling? Because you still have to tell me a story."

She stood and grabbed Aiko's hand. "I'm not stalling. I just really wanna dance. I promise I'll talk your ear off after this song." Summer dragged Aiko to her feet and gave her best, most innocent smile. "Deal?"

The skepticism melted from Aiko's face. "Wouldn't want to disappoint you on our first date. Let's dance, baby."

⁓

Aiko let Summer lead her onto the cement slab in front of the stage that served as the dance floor. As the pounding rhythm of the Latin-inspired tune filled the air, she moved in time with it, still loosely holding Summer's hand. Fingertips locked together, they moved around the dance floor, navigating around the other dancers as they shimmied to the beat.

Aiko let her feet move in a way that felt natural while keeping her focus on her date. The sensuous movements of Summer's curvaceous body as she danced were arresting, mesmerizing. The sway of her full hips had Aiko's heart pounding and her pulse racing. She wanted those hips in her hands, wanted to know what it would feel like to knead and massage that soft flesh with her fingertips.

By the time the song ended, Aiko could feel the tiny beads of sweat forming around her hairline from both the humid evening air and the heat generated by her rising desire.

As they started to walk off the floor, a familiar song began to play. Aiko paused, listening for a moment before she picked up the tune: Rihanna's "Love on the Brain." "Wait." She looked into Summer's eyes. "One more dance."

Summer nodded, offering a soft smile as she backed up a few steps.

Aiko closed the distance between them in a single large step, drawing Summer into her arms. Summer placed her arms around Aiko's shoulders, and Aiko felt a tingle go through her as Summer's fingertips grazed the sensitive area at the base of her neck just between her shoulder blades.

The moment their bodies touched, Aiko's entire being was consumed with the intense comfort and rightness of having Summer's soft curves pressed against her. They swayed slowly, rocking in time with the music, and Summer rested her forehead against Aiko's shoulder as they danced.

Aiko closed her eyes and simply enjoyed all the feelings flowing through her. While Rihanna crooned through her impassioned lyrics about untamed desire, she felt them on a whole new level. Though she'd slow-danced countless times since her first school dance in middle school, she couldn't ever remember feeling this level of connection with someone. She tightened her arms around Summer's waist, careful not to squeeze her too tightly but also not wanting her to slip away.

I don't know how she feels right now, but I know I want more of her and I'll take as much as she's willing to give.

As if reading her mind, Summer sighed into her shoulder. "You smell even better up close," she murmured.

An electric charge ran down Aiko's spine, and she whispered in Summer's ear, "Stay as long as you like, baby." She then gave her a gentle squeeze.

The song's final notes faded, and they lingered there for a moment, holding on to each other. People ebbed and flowed around them as another, more up-tempo song started. Only then did Aiko take a step back.

"What's next, Aiko?" Summer looked into her eyes.

"A walk over to Congress, if you're up for it."

"Sure. Sounds fun."

Aiko extended her hand, and Summer slipped hers inside it. They walked out of the courtyard onto Red River Street. At the corner, they turned left onto Tenth.

"So, do we have a particular destination, or are we just taking in the sights?"

"Both. There's a new exhibit up at the Jones Center—I thought we could go take a look. They're staying open late for it." A gallery and multiuse space, the Jones Center was part of the Contemporary Austin art museum and remained one of Aiko's favorite places to take in local artists.

"Awesome. I haven't been there in ages."

"You'll love it. It was remodeled a few years back, and it's really nice." She stopped at the intersection of Tenth and Trinity, waiting at the crossing signal. "So, about that college story you were going to tell me?"

Summer appeared sheepish. "Like I said, it's not as exciting as yours. But here goes. It was sophomore year, spring term. I was really excited because I was being inducted into the campus honor society for maintaining a GPA above three point eight all school year."

"Beauty and brains?" Aiko placed her free hand over her heart as they safely crossed Trinity Avenue. "Be still my heart."

She rolled her eyes, grinning. "Anyway, I got dressed up in a skirt and silk blouse and pressed and curled my hair. My roommate had made it into the honor society as well, so we decided to walk across campus to the induction ceremony together. Along the way, we passed by a dormitory where most of the athletes lived. Just as we went by, some idiots on one of the upper floors started throwing water balloons."

"Oh, no. Not water balloons on the silk blouse and the fresh press."

"Yes." She sighed, shaking her head. "We both got hit, but I got it worse since I was walking closer to the building. I ended up crossing the stage looking like a drowned rat and had to throw away my blouse."

As they continued their stroll, Aiko shook her head. "Damn, Summer. That sucks. You do realize that's more of an embarrassing story than a wild one, right?"

She laughed. "Yeah, I do. But for me, wild and embarrassing are one and the same. I wasn't really doing too much during my college years. I never smoked, and I only drank occasionally. I was the studious, responsible type."

"Nothing wrong with that."

Her brow hitched. "You're about the first one to feel that way. People are always telling me I should have been more adventurous in my college days."

She shrugged. "I think that's a cliché. I think life is meant to be lived on one's own terms. There's no schedule, no time limit, no age by which you have to do something." She looked at Summer pointedly as they paused to let a woman pushing a double stroller pass them. "You're grown, and you can do what you want, when you're good and ready."

Summer's smile was radiant. "Thanks. I really appreciate that perspective, instead of a lecture."

"You'll be getting none of that from me, baby. I don't lecture other adults."

Appearing impressed, Summer started walking again, tugging Aiko's hand gently.

They arrived at the Jones Center. The interior of the space, with its white walls and recessed lighting, echoed with the sounds of footsteps and hushed conversations.

As they perused the new exhibit, which showcased the work of a local artist who created landscapes using mixed media, Summer squeezed Aiko's hand. "These pieces are really amazing."

"I agree." Aiko stared at a particularly large canvas, which showed the Austin skyline at sunset. Reading the description displayed below the image, she shook her head in awe. "It's amazing that someone could depict the city so beautifully and realistically, using only fabric scraps, magazine clippings, and acrylic paint."

"Look at the way the water is shimmering on the lake." Summer gestured to the lower portion of the canvas. "I bet creating that effect took a long time."

"Probably. I definitely applaud their patience."

"You're an artist, too. What gets you inspired?"

"Usually the assignment and the deadline my boss gives me," she joked.

Summer punched her playfully in the arm. "Come on, now. You know you've gotta give me a more artsy answer than that."

"All right, bet," Aiko said, her voice hushed as she steered Summer to the next work, a depiction of the Texas State Capitol created from newsprint and oil pastels. "Honestly, when I get a new assignment, I spend the first day or so just freehand sketching. It lets me bring my ideas to the surface, then I develop them to see which ones will best fit the project at hand." She eyed Summer. "Is that a more 'artsy' answer?"

"Yes, thank you." Summer giggled softly. "Once you've finished that process, how long does it take you to reach the final sketch that gets turned into blueprints?"

"Anywhere from a week to a month, depending on the scope of the project."

She nodded. "I'm impressed. It must be pretty cool to see your art become something tangible and take on a life of its own."

"It's probably the best part of the job." Aiko paused, thinking about what Summer did for a living. "There's a certain art to what you do, as well."

Her eyes grew wide. "You think so?"

"Absolutely. With young kids like that, you've got to know how to reach them and engage with them, or they probably won't absorb a thing you try to teach them. And that's based on my very limited knowledge of kids."

"You're right."

"Then tell me about your art, Summer."

"I suppose there is an art to teaching, though I rarely think of it that way."

Aiko nodded. "There has to be. It takes some special talent to educate kids."

"Well, it all starts with the curriculum—you know, federal, state, and county standards. With that as my basis, I just use my knowledge of child development and teaching theory to create activities for them, exposing them to the information I want them to retain in the most digestible way possible."

Aiko tilted her head, smiling at Summer. "See? That can't be easy. But you get the job done every time, I bet."

She blushed. "I usually get along well with the staff, parents are cooperative, and the students trust me. That's what matters most to me, you know?"

"Sounds like you're doing the work you were put on this earth to do. I think that's beautiful, and those kids are so lucky to have you as their teacher." They reached the end of the exhibit and returned to the lobby to exit the building. Back outside, they spent some time window-shopping a few stores and boutiques along Congress Avenue. Soon after, Summer stifled a yawn.

"It's getting late," Aiko said, glancing up at the darkened sky as they walked up to the parking deck at 701 Congress. It was well past ten o'clock by now. "I want to be respectful of your time, and not keep you out all night. So can I give you a lift home?"

"Yeah, I'm all walked out," she admitted. "I'll let you . . . take me home." She threw Aiko a saucy little wink.

Aiko's tongue darted over her lower lip. "Good." She walked Summer to her black compact SUV, parked near the center of the second level.

As they drove out of the deck and onto the streets, Summer yawned again. "Sorry. I don't want you to think you're boring me, that was a pretty awesome date."

"That's reassuring, I was starting to get worried," Aiko joked. "Next time I won't make you do a mini-marathon. Promise."

She shook her head. "I had a great time. Besides, even though I live downtown now, that was my first time really seeing the sights since I moved back to Austin. And I couldn't have asked for better company."

"I've enjoyed tonight, too," Aiko replied. She'd never had this much fun or felt this comfortable on a first date. She liked the way Summer had been totally open to her somewhat-unconventional way to spend time together and her willingness to open up even though she didn't think of her own experiences as particularly interesting.

Directing Aiko on where to go, Summer said, "Can you pull into the parking deck under the building?"

"Sure." She turned into the garage. "Don't like entering from the street?"

Summer shook her head. "Actually, I wanted you to come upstairs for a little while."

Realization and delight hit Aiko at the same time, and she sucked her lower lip into her mouth in anticipation. Struggling to keep her demeanor calm in spite of her rising arousal, she said casually, "I don't mind."

Soon, Aiko found herself inside the wood-paneled elevator with Summer. They got out on the ninth floor, and Aiko followed Summer's swaying hips down the hallway until she stopped in front of a polished mahogany door. "This is me," Summer announced, producing a key from her purse and opening the door.

Aiko followed her inside, trailing her into her living room. From the polished wood floors to the crown molding and muted beige paint, the place had clean lines and simple details that made it a great canvas for tenants to express their individual style.

Summer's expression consisted of a black microfiber sofa and love seat, accented by black and gray striped pillows, which faced each other in the center of the room. A low oval-shaped black lacquer coffee table sat between them. A granite bar, with four black steel stools with gray cushions underneath it, separated the living room from the kitchen.

Sitting on the love seat, Summer kicked off her shoes and patted the cushion next to her. Aiko joined her and placed an arm around Summer's shoulders.

Summer sighed. "I've gotta say, other than our one sticking point, you're doing a great job of living up to the fantasy I've had of you all these years."

Aiko placed one hand gently against Summer's silken cheek. "I can do so much better."

Desire and mischief mingling in her eyes, Summer whispered, "Prove it."

Aiko pulled Summer closer. Tilting her chin, Aiko looked into Summer's eyes for a heartbeat before pressing their lips together.

Summer released a soft sigh as she yielded to the contact, and the sound spurred Aiko on. Aiko teased her with a series of gentle pecks, then deepened the kiss, letting the tip of her tongue pass over Summer's lips. Summer opened her mouth, and Aiko delved deeper, their tongues swirling and moving against each other. Summer tasted of lime, tequila, and undeniable temptation. Aiko could feel her pulse racing as she tightened her embrace around Summer's waist.

Summer grabbed the back of Aiko's neck, and a growl escaped Aiko's throat in response. The low hum of arousal that had been building inside Aiko since the moment she saw Summer waiting for her at the bar had reached a fever pitch, and she could feel the slickness gathering between her own thighs.

Aiko pulled back, reluctant but resolved. Drawing a deep breath before she spoke, she admitted, "We have to stop."

"What if I don't want to stop?" Summer's tone was innocent enough, but the gleam in her eyes and the slow movement of her hands as she tossed aside her crocheted cardigan were anything but.

Aiko swallowed. "Believe me, I want this. But I can't. Not now, not like this." She stroked Summer's face. "I want to take you beyond your best fantasy. And I will . . . just not yet."

Summer's lower lip extended in a mock pout. "I waited this long . . . I suppose I can wait a little longer." Making no effort to hide her gaze as she raked it up and down Aiko's body, she added, "But you'd better leave now, before I change my mind and drag you into my bedroom."

Aiko's clit pulsed, and she stood. "Yeah . . . let me go. Good night, Summer."

As Aiko jogged toward the door, Summer sultrily replied, "Good night, Aiko."

CHAPTER EIGHT

After Aiko left, Summer slipped out of her clothes and into a hot shower. Refreshed, she put on a thin gown and eased between her covers.

She was clean and tired. But sleep didn't come.

Thoughts of Aiko reigned in her mind, the remnants of desire still humming through her body. Their encounter on her sofa had been so brief yet so impactful. She slipped her hand between her thighs, letting her fingertips play over the aching bud of her clitoris. Eyes closed, she imagined Aiko's slender fingers touching and teasing her, delving inside her, driving her mad with pleasure.

It was only after an orgasm claimed her, and the shivering aftermath subsided, that she finally fell asleep.

As it did most Saturday mornings, the interior of Curly Girls Natural Hair Gallery buzzed with activity. From her spot in the padded leather chair, Summer scrolled through her phone while Natalie, her stylist, detangled her freshly washed and conditioned hair. Natalie had a pleasant manner and genuinely cared about the health of her clients' hair. "You've had a lot of new growth over the last month, honey. Whatever you're doing, keep it up."

Summer smiled. Not much about her routine had changed since returning home to Austin, other than fulfilling her youthful fantasy by attracting Aiko's attention. Surely that couldn't be what was making her hair grow. Could it?

"Beyond that, you're glowing. Your skin is really looking clear and bright." Natalie chuckled. "I'm about to start asking you for your secrets, Summer."

Summer tilted her head slightly so Natalie could begin sectioning her hair for the style she'd chosen. "Just drinking water and staying positive."

"If you say so." Natalie used her rat-tail comb to part a thin section of hair in the front of Summer's head, just above her right ear, and began cornrowing it.

Crystal walked by then, on her return trip from the shampoo bowl. With drops of water trickling down the black vinyl cape she wore over her clothes, she climbed into the chair next to Summer. "Sis, you getting braids?"

"Just in the front. I'm doing two-strand twists in the back."

"Oh, that should look cute. And you won't have to mess for a while."

"That's what I'm hoping," Summer replied. "I'll need that time to handle everything else on my plate, so I figured I'd better tame this head now."

"You should get about two weeks out of it," Natalie added. "And if we get a rare day where the humidity drops, you can switch it up and wear a twist-out."

"I doubt it, but we'll see." One thing she hadn't missed about living in Texas was the oppressive humidity. Often in the summer, the temperature and the humidity percentage matched, and she thought of that as Mother Nature just adding insult to the proverbial injury.

"What were you up to last night?" Crystal posed the question as her stylist, shop owner Dana Reeves, switched out her wet cape for a clean, dry one. Shifting in her chair next to Summer, Crystal added, "I called you like three times, and it went straight to voice mail."

Feeling the grin tugging at the corners of her lips, she admitted, "I was out on a date, and I had my phone on do not disturb."

Crystal's eyes widened, then her lips pursed. "Why didn't you tell me you had a date?"

"Two reasons. One, it was kind of a last-minute thing. And two, you're nosy."

Natalie giggled as she continued braiding.

"Whatever. I'm your sister, so I'm gonna check up on you whether you like it or not." Crystal stifled a yawn. "Anyway, I want to hear all about it." Dana wielded her trusty comb, parting Crystal's hair in four sections.

"I'll tell you after you finish getting blow-dried, so I won't have to shout over that loud noise."

Crystal groaned. "For the sake of my silk press, I'll wait a few minutes. But when she starts flat ironing, tell me everything."

Shaking her head, Summer laughed. "Okay, nosy britches."

Crystal rolled her eyes.

While her sister got her hair blow-dried, Summer sat back in her chair and let Natalie work her magic. The whir of the dryers, the water splashing in the shampoo bowls, and the sounds of conversation in the shop faded into the background as she relaxed, her thoughts returning to last night. She'd had so much fun exploring the city with Aiko, rediscovering some old, familiar places, and seeing so many new things for the first time. Austin still had its essence intact, thank goodness; the populace still seemed to cling to its famed motto of "Keep Austin Weird." The public art, the ever-present music, the eclectic shops—they were all a part of the tapestry of the city, something unique and nearly sacred.

The lines between the old and the new had been blurred significantly. In some cases, Summer couldn't dismiss the newer developments as money-grabs by greedy capitalists. For instance, the updates to the Jones Center had a clear positive impact on the surrounding downtown community, bringing construction jobs to workers and allowing more public exposure for local artists. Being inside the space hadn't changed her overall views, but it had given her some new perspective.

That wasn't even the best part of the date, though. Being with Aiko felt natural. She was stylish, easygoing, and talked a good game.

The moment the dryer shut off, Crystal all but shouted, "Spill it!"

Summer began recounting the date. "Last night, I went out with Aiko Holt."

Crystal looked thoughtful for a moment. "Oh, snap. Is this the woman who showed up at the protest the other day, asking us to leave? The one who works for that company that's tearing down the school?"

"That's her."

"And she's the same one you had a crush on in high school, right?"

"Yeah." She could almost hear the gears turning inside her sister's mind.

"Juicy," Natalie interjected.

Crystal posed a follow-up question. "How did this come about?"

Summer sucked her bottom lip. "Well, after you left, I stayed and talked to her for a minute. She ended up asking me out."

Her brow hitched. "And you said yes."

"I wasn't about to say no."

Crystal frowned, her brow furrowed in obvious disapproval. "Oh, boy. There goes our plan to stop this project moving forward."

"No, Crys. You're assuming I can't separate my feelings for Aiko from my commitment to Ivy. Not only is that not true, but it's also unfair."

"I don't think so, sis. You've only been sweating her for the past decade."

"I'm not denying that."

Crystal leaned forward, only to have her stylist gently ease her back so she could continue flat ironing her hair. "Then you have to be aware of how your emotions could get the better of you."

"I'm not about to listen to a lecture, Crys." Summer sighed, trying to maintain the right position for Natalie, who was now twisting the back sections of her hair. "Do you want to hear about the date, or not?"

She thought for a moment, then said, "Yes. If you had a good time, I still want to hear about it."

"She looked great and smelled even better. We had drinks at Cheer Up Charlies, then took a walk down to Congress Avenue, and . . ."

"That sounds pretty chill," Crystal said, eyeing her intently. "What about later in the date? Did y'all, you know . . ."

Summer balked. "Girl."

"Come on, sis. We all women in here. Just spill the tea." Crystal's gaze took on a wicked glint.

"Things did get a little heated," Summer admitted, thinking back to those passionate moments on the couch. She could still smell Aiko's cologne, still feel her embrace and the way her lips felt against her own. Her whole body had been tingling, begging for more of the intoxicating magic Aiko stirred within her. Her tongue darted out and over her lower lip. *She has no idea what she did to me—how much I wanted her.*

"So what happened?"

Her sister's insistent question drew her out of her fantasy world. The room had grown noticeably quieter, and by now, all the stylists and patrons nearby were listening, if their surreptitious glances were any indication. She swallowed. "If I'd had my way, she would have stayed the night. But she didn't want to rush things, so we stopped."

"That was respectful of her."

"It was." *I also spent half the night tossing and turning because I couldn't stop thinking about her.* She kept that to herself; her sister didn't need to know every detail of her life, especially at a moment like this when they had an audience. "That's pretty much it."

Crystal sucked in her lower lip. "I'm glad to know she treated you well and showed you a good time. So, are you going to see her again?"

"I'd love to, but we haven't made another date yet if that's what you're asking me." She didn't say anything further, hoping that the others in the salon would get bored and go back to whatever had held their attention before. When she felt some of the curious gazes turn elsewhere, she took a deep breath.

"Almost done with your twists, honey. Then you can sit under the dryer for a minute and let them set," Natalie said.

A few minutes later, Summer was sitting under a warm dryer while Crystal and her fresh silk press occupied the chair directly to her left with the dryer's hood up. Crystal grabbed her hand. "I hope I wasn't too harsh on you earlier."

She shrugged. "I'm used to you speaking your mind. It's not a big deal."

"You were right, though. I shouldn't have accused you of losing commitment to our work just because you went out with Aiko."

"I'm glad you realize that." Summer gave her a gentle punch in the shoulder. "Now go get your brows done. You're starting to look a little bushy up there."

Crystal punched her back before getting up from her chair to retreat to the waxing suite in the back of the salon. Left alone with the low hum of the dryer, Summer picked up her phone and unlocked it. A text message, sent about fifteen minutes prior, popped up on her screen. Seeing it was from Aiko, she smiled as she read it.

When can I see you again?

She fired off a quick reply.

Wishing you had stayed last night, I bet. 😏

Summer waited a few moments before an equally cheeky reply came back.

Don't tease me, or you'll pay for it later in moans.

That one took her out of the game for a moment. Thinking about the repercussions of Aiko's rather enticing threat had her pulse racing and her breaths becoming shallow. There was something about the way Aiko carried herself, the easy confidence with which she spoke, that made Summer think she'd turn her whole world inside out.

Her phone buzzed on her lap as another text came in.

You still there? Don't tell me you tapped out already.

She shook her head and swallowed. *The innuendo is killing me. Why does she have to talk so slick?*

I'm still here.

I really want to see you again, baby. The sooner the better.

She smiled at the sweetness in that last message. It seemed more earnest—even a little vulnerable. *Is she weak for me now, the same way she made me weak last night? Maybe her noble self-denial is starting to get to her.*

I'm free tomorrow night. Is that soon enough?

Awesome. I'll meet you in the lobby of your building at seven.

She smiled as she sent off her response.

See you then.

"Oh, she must be texting you, the way you grinning at your phone like that."

Summer looked up to see her sister standing over her, arms folded over her chest, with that know-it-all smirk on her face. She laughed as she tucked her phone back into the pocket of her denim cutoffs. "Yes, for your information, she did text me."

"So when y'all getting together again?" This time the question came from Natalie, who was already applying hair color to her next client.

Unable to hold back her laugh, Summer answered, "Tomorrow night. Sheesh."

"Great. I can't wait to hear if she keeps that same respectful energy on the second date." Crystal winked as she slung her purse strap over her shoulder.

"Girl, I hope not." Summer patted her hair beneath the dryer bonnet. Finding it dry to her liking, she lifted the hood and stood up. "Thanks, Natalie. See you in a couple weeks."

"Bye, honey. Have fun on your date."

After stopping at the front counter to pay, Summer and Crystal left the salon and stepped into the blazing August sunshine.

"Where are we going for lunch? Because I can't be out in this humidity too long, or my hair will be shot to hell." Crystal pulled her trusty satin-lined baseball cap down over her freshly pressed tresses.

"Let's just grab pizza at Via 313. If we go over there now, they shouldn't be too crowded." Summer slipped on her sunglasses as she headed for her car. "Is that cool? We're not too far from the one on Sixth Street."

"Yeah, that sounds good, actually," Crystal answered as they climbed into Summer's car. "I could go for that Stooges pizza they make."

"I was thinking the same thing, so we'll split a twelve-inch." As she started the engine and cranked the air conditioning to full blast, she could almost taste the unique pizza. Topped with spinach, artichokes, shallot, and these crispy little parmesan shavings that just sent the whole thing over the top, it was heavy enough to know you'd eaten pizza but light enough to keep you from needing a nap afterward. And today was simply too hot for a heavy lunch.

"You know I want to hear what happens when you go out with her again, right?"

"Your nosiness knows no bounds," Summer quipped in response. But she also recognized the root of the query. "But don't worry, Crys. I haven't forgotten what we're trying to do, and nothing will make me betray our goals."

~

"You like that?"

"Oh, yes, baby." Summer moaned breathlessly.

Aiko tightened her grip around Summer's waist, altering her movements slightly, wanting even more contact with her slick heat. Summer's thighs opened wider, and the increased friction between their clits made Aiko shiver. Aiko hissed, feeling the insistent throb of an approaching orgasm. "Shit . . ."

An ecstatic growl escaped Aiko's lips as her eyes popped open, the dream still playing out in her mind. Her naked body was spread across her bed diagonally, like a crooked starfish. A thin film of sweat had gathered around her hairline. Her gaze swept over her bed: the covers were strewn about, one of her pillows was on the floor, and the bedsheets were hanging off the side. One hand was clenched around the bunched-up comforter, knuckles white. The other hand was firmly lodged between her splayed-open thighs.

Sheesh. She really got me tripping.

Aiko sat up, tugging the sheet off the floor and around her frame. She shook her head to shake off the lingering remnants of her dream. Taking the high road with Summer had seemed like the right move last night. Now, she was suffering. Because while her mind wanted Summer to know she respected her, her body had wanted nothing more than to give in to the passion flickering between them.

She climbed out of bed, then sought out a hot shower. As the water streamed down her body, she let her fantasies have her head again. She imagined the softness of Summer's flesh beneath her wandering hands, the cries and moans she would draw from her, the way it would feel when their bodies finally met . . .

Freshly showered and ready to satisfy her growling stomach, she dressed in a gray sports bra, matching boxers, and slippers. Then she wrestled her hair into a messy topknot to keep it out of her face and made her way into the kitchen. Stifling a yawn, she started the coffee maker, then opened the fridge.

After a quick meal of a grilled cheese sandwich, a banana, and a tall mug of Italian-roast coffee, Aiko washed the dishes she'd used. By then, she'd had enough of trying to deny her cravings for Summer. Leaning against the counter, she texted, making sure to communicate the way Summer had made her feel. After a night filled with steamy dreams, she thought it only fair to make Summer squirm a bit, too.

Once she and Summer agreed to get together the next day, Aiko headed toward her back double doors. She passed through the dining and family room, then switched from her slippers to a pair of Crocs, opened the glass doors, and stepped out onto her covered patio.

The day was warm and somewhat muggy; the steamy air hit her as soon as she walked outside. Aiko leaned down to the hose reel near her back door, reached inside, and fished until she pulled out the end of it. She twisted the metal knob on the wall of the house to turn on the water, then unraveled the long rubber tube. She walked the short distance across her fenced yard to the small greenhouse in the far-left corner.

Inside, she watered her "babies"—her plants. She had many varieties—mainly ferns and hostas. But the stars of her collection were the exotic orchids she grew. Her mother's work at a plant nursery when she was younger had inspired her passion, and now she sought out orchids in as many unique colors as she could find.

As she adjusted her sprayer to rain and let the water hit her plants, her mind drifted back to thoughts of Summer. What was she doing right now? Shaking her head to bring herself back to reality, she shut off the sprayer to avoid drowning her plants, then replaced the hose in the reel and returned inside. Donning a white tank top and a pair of bright red athletic shorts, she grabbed her keys and went to run errands.

Later, she returned home with a few bags and two suits she'd picked up from the dry cleaners. After putting the items away, she flopped on her couch, grabbed her tablet from the coffee table, and turned it on. Checking the time on-screen, she calculated the time difference between Austin and Fujisawa in her head. *It's four thirty here, so it's seven thirty Sunday morning there.* Knowing her early-riser Pops would be up, she opened the video-call app and dialed him.

Her father answered the call a few seconds later, an image of his aged, bearded face filling the screen. "Good afternoon, Aiko."

"Morning, Pops." Aiko smiled. "How are you?"

"Other than these creaky old bones, I can't complain." He chuckled. "How have you been, dear?" He was sitting on the stone bench in his garden behind the small cottage he lived in; the early dawn glow on his plants and small koi pond was visible behind him.

"You know me. Working, running, gardening. That's pretty much what I do these days."

A slight frown creased his face. "Come on now. No excitement and romance for my dear daughter?"

She laughed, shaking her head. "Well, maybe. But I'm not telling you about any of that until I hear about what you've been up to. Any new inspiration?"

He yawned before speaking again. "Yes. I've been to Enoshima this week. I've been wanting to paint the Sea Candle for some time now, and I finally got over there to do it."

"That's good. How did it go?"

"I went a few times, to see it from various angles in different lights. Sunrise, midday, and sunset, and from the four cardinal directions. Then I picked a good spot in the Cocking Garden and got to work. Took me about four hours but I think it turned out nicely." He reached off-screen for a moment before lifting a twelve-by-twelve-inch canvas into view. "What do you think?"

She smiled as she took in her father's latest work, reveling in the soft, swirling lines of color. "It's awesome. Is it watercolor?"

He nodded. "I outlined a few areas with acrylic, but watercolor was my main medium." He set the painting on the bench beside him.

"Since you went to the island so many times, I'm assuming you did other things besides working on your painting, right?"

He nodded. "Sure, I did. I prayed at the shrine and made an offering to Benzaiten . . ."

"Goddess of the arts and entertainment, right?"

A pleased smile spread over his face. "That's right. You remembered. I sat in the garden to think deeply. And I walked along the beaches and looked out over the Sagami Bay toward the mainland. I could see Mount Fuji in the distance."

Thinking of his earlier plans, she asked, "Are you still going to try and climb it?"

He shook his head. "My doctor says that at my age, it would be a fool's errand. I suppose he's right, so I'll keep my creaky bones to flat land for the time being."

Relieved, Aiko blew out a breath. "I know you're disappointed, but I'm glad I don't have to worry about you taking on something so challenging. People who've attempted the climb say it taxes the body, the mind, and the spirit."

"I know." He offered a small grin.

"I already worry about Mom as it is. You should know she will probably need in-home care within the next several months. And it's not going to be cheap, either."

He looked thoughtful. "I see. I'm sorry to hear that. I can't offer much, but I can send you a little money here and there to help cover some medications, at least."

"I appreciate that."

"Janet and I were like a shooting star. Beautiful, brilliant, and short-lived. I've never forgotten our time together, so I'll do what I can to help out." He paused, then cleared his throat. "Now that I've told you what I've been up to, tell me about your life these days."

She felt the smile tugging her lips. "I went out with the most amazing woman last night."

He snapped his fingers. "Aha! That's where that little sparkle in your eyes is coming from, then."

"I guess so." She chuckled, still heartened about her father's accepting nature in contrast to that of his more conservative countrymen. "Her name is Summer, and we went to high school together. We recently reconnected, and we had a lovely time together." She paused. "There is one complication, though."

His aged brow was crinkled. "What's that?"

She took a deep breath, then gave him a brief rundown of the situation regarding their old school. "I respect her passion, but I'm just trying to do my job."

"I see." He scratched his chin. "That does constitute a complication, I believe."

"So many good things have been happening for me at Abernathy. If I keep moving along this path, and everything goes according to plan, I'm sure Miriam will promote me to senior planner." She stopped short, remembering something. "I'll be right back."

After setting down the tablet, she went into the spare bedroom she used as an office and grabbed her leather-bound portfolio. On returning to the sofa, she opened the portfolio to the finished plans for the Sojourner Truth site. Grabbing the tablet, she held it aloft so he could see them. "Look. Here are the final plans for the site. What do you think?"

"Very nice," he commented. "You've definitely inherited my eye for placement and spatial reasoning."

She cringed, happy her face was hidden behind the portfolio at the moment. Hearing him speak that way, about how much she was like him or how she could credit her talents to him, always bothered her. *How convenient for him to take credit for my accomplishments when he wasn't around for 95 percent of my childhood.*

"Yes, I can see it. The layout has marvelous flow," he continued. "Excellent work, Aiko."

She shut the portfolio and put it aside. "Thanks. I'm pleased with the way the plans turned out. So now, you can see why I can't just tank my project for Summer's sake, right?"

"I suppose."

His answer, pragmatic and noncommittal, irked Aiko. "I could really use advice here. I feel like I'm stuck, having to make a choice between the work I'm passionate about, and the woman I'm falling for."

"Life often presents us with difficult choices, Aiko. You must release yourself from attachment in order to move forward."

She sighed. "Yes, I know. I'm well aware of what the Buddha would advise. I want to know what *you* would advise."

He shrugged. "I'm a humble artist, Aiko. Not a philosopher or a psychic. I can't tell you what path to take. But I can tell you that I trust your judgment, and I know you will choose thoughtfully."

She thought about pressing him further for clearer guidance but thought the better of it. *This is how it's always been between us, and it's never going to change.* It was why she never called him Dad—he never acted like one. To her mind, Pops was a moniker suited to any man who was her elder, so she called him that instead. They were more like old friends than father and daughter. Maybe some people would enjoy a relationship like that with their parent, but it wasn't for her. "Okay. Well, I'm going to try and clean up my place a little bit."

"And I'm going to the kitchen to make myself some breakfast. I'll talk to you later, Aiko. Be well."

"You too, Pops."

He disconnected the call.

Aiko turned off her tablet and returned it to the flat basket on the coffee table. Sinking back into the cushions with a sigh, she tried not to think about how much her relationship with her father frustrated her. Instead, she turned her thoughts and efforts to planning an impressive dinner date for tomorrow night. She wanted to wow Summer with an excellent meal and great conversation. With that in mind, she grabbed her phone and dialed.

Hopefully, there's still time to snag a reservation.

CHAPTER NINE

Summer stood in the lobby of her apartment building Sunday night, keeping near the glass wall at the front so she could see outside. The low hum of conversation and footsteps filled the space, punctuated by the occasional ringing of the phone at the front desk.

She stared through the window as Austinites strolled by on foot and drove down Third Street in various vehicles. The sun hung low in the sky, grazing the horizon.

"Summer."

Summer turned toward the familiar voice, then smiled when she saw Aiko walking toward her, coming from the parking garage entrance on the side of the lobby. She was smartly dressed in a pair of slim-fit navy slacks with a matching jacket emblazoned with gold roses. Beneath the blazer, she wore a crisp sky-blue shirt and a gold bow tie. Her hair was wound in a knot low on her neck. Her dark brown oxfords tapped out a tune as she crossed the polished cement floor in Summer's direction.

"Aiko. You look so good." It wouldn't do to tell her she wanted to peel that suit off her, at least not yet. So Summer kept that bit to herself.

"Thanks. I guess I clean up all right." She stopped just outside Summer's personal bubble, leaning to the side and pretending to dust off her shoulder. "But you look even better. I love the hairdo."

Feeling the smile stretch her lips, Summer did a slow turn, letting Aiko see her mid-thigh-length white dress from all angles. "I'm glad you like it."

Aiko offered her arm, and Summer slipped her hand through. "Let's go. I don't want to be late for our reservation."

"Do I get to know where we're going?"

With a sly smile, Aiko shook her head. "It's a surprise. Don't worry, you'll love it."

They took Aiko's compact SUV on a short drive, and after making it through the late-evening gauntlet of traffic, arrived at a familiar white bungalow on Fifth Street. The small neon sign by the roadside—the only clue to the uninitiated about what was inside—was lit, its red-and-yellow letters glowing in the dusky dimness.

Summer turned Aiko's way. "You got us reservations at Justine's?"

She grinned. "See? I did say you'd like it."

"I'll never doubt you again."

Aiko drove a few yards past the building to find a free spot along the curb, then swung her car into the space. After cutting the engine, she walked around to the passenger side and opened the door, helping Summer out onto the sidewalk.

Summer smiled as they stepped inside the small courtyard in front of Justine's. The abundance of potted plants surrounding the area, along with the white umbrellas and the white bulbs strung above them like a canopy of fairy lights, made it seem like an enchanted woodland glen. Soft instrumental jazz played from unseen speakers, adding to the ethereal atmosphere.

The hostess spoke briefly with Aiko, then led them to one of the round marble-topped tables near the side of the building. The little nook was out of the way of the other diners, as the two closest tables were unoccupied.

Summer eased into the cushioned wicker chair. "Looks like we got lucky and came on a Sunday that wasn't so busy."

"Either that or I tipped the hostess enough that she won't seat any-body near us." Aiko winked.

Summer smiled with delight. "Trying to spoil me good, eh?"

"Real good."

Summer watched her date with interest, following the graceful movements of her long-boned fingers as she adjusted her tie, then reached for her menu. She couldn't help imagining what talents those fingers might possess. Swiping her tongue across her bottom lip, she turned her attention to the menu.

When their waitress approached with two full glasses of water, Aiko deferred to Summer to order first. "I'll have the soup à l'oignon and the ratatouille, please."

"I'd like the salade de crabe and the bolognaise." Aiko handed off her menu. "And a bottle of Justine's favorite champagne, if you have it."

"I'll have that right out." The waitress disappeared inside the building.

Alone again, Summer turned her attention back to Aiko. "So. What's on our agenda tonight, other than a great meal?"

"Great conversation, a little adventure on Ladybird Lake, and then . . ." Aiko shrugged, letting her gaze linger on Summer's face. "After that, it's all on you what we do next."

Summer swallowed. There was an unveiled mischief in Aiko's eyes, an open invitation to finish what they'd started on her sofa the other night. "Oh, I definitely have something in mind."

She smiled. "I bet you do. But for now, I just want to listen to you." She leaned back in her chair, tenting her fingers. "Tell me something about your life that you think I should know. Something that colors who you are."

"That's intense for a first question, but I'll bite." Summer tilted her head slightly to the right, thinking about how she would respond. Considering the circumstance between them, she settled on some-thing pretty quickly. "I'll tell you more about my relationship with my grandmother. Because if any one person has had the most influence on the person I am today, it was her."

"I'm listening." Aiko's eyes were clear and focused on Summer's face.

"When I was a kid, I spent a lot of time with Grandma Beulah. Whenever my parents had something going on or wanted to get away, she looked after Crystal and me. We spent so many weekends and summers at her place up in Cedar Park."

The waitress returned with two crystal flutes and a chilled bottle of champagne, nestled in a steel bucket of ice. After skillfully popping the cork and letting the foamy head ooze for a moment, she poured them each a glass and set the steel bucket in the center of the table.

Aiko picked up her champagne and took a sip. "Sounds like y'all were pretty close."

Summer smiled at the memories as she grabbed her own bubbly. "She spoiled us. I remember trips to the zoo, the planetarium, the amusement parks. But I think the best times were when we were just together at her house." She grew silent for a moment, trying not to let the pain of missing her grandmother drown out the joy of the time they'd shared. She sipped the golden liquid, picking up the bright citrus notes and the slightly sweet bite.

"What memory stands out most for you when it comes to your grandmother?"

"When I was thirteen, Crystal and I were in our cousin's wedding. Grandma took us to get manicures and pedicures. Crystal refused the latter because her feet were too ticklish. Anyway, Grandma and I were sitting next to each other in the pedicure chairs. The nail techs had left us alone for the soaking part. She asked me if there was anyone at school that I liked. And I admitted that there was, but the person was a girl."

Aiko rubbed her hands. "That must have been hard."

"That's just it. It wasn't hard at all. She made it easy by being completely and totally accepting." She paused. "I didn't hesitate to answer her question truthfully, because she'd always accepted me, no matter what. So that day when I told her about my crush was my very first coming-out."

Aiko gave a slow nod. "I see. That's really meaningful, and I'm glad you felt safe enough to be honest with her."

"I'm close with my dad, too, but I didn't feel comfortable enough to come out to him until a few years later. Grandma Beulah gave me a safe space to be who I was before I even understood the real value of that."

"I don't know that we had the language back then to identify that feeling, you know. People were so concerned with appearances and putting on airs, and I think that concern sits at the apex of cultural, regional, and generational norms." Aiko sipped from her water glass. "I'm just glad things are changing for the better. It's nice to see that kids today feel so much freer to be themselves."

"That's a really astute observation, and I definitely agree." Summer quieted as their plates were delivered, then spooned up some of the steaming soup and enjoyed the warmth of the flavorful broth as it slid down her throat. "This soup is heavenly."

"The food here never misses. The crab on this salad is super fresh." Aiko ate a second forkful and nodded her approval.

They ate in congenial silence for a short time. After finishing her soup, Summer savored the well-seasoned ratatouille. She could smell the heady aroma of the herbes de Provence, which combined nicely with the spicy tomato sauce.

"Go on with what you were saying. I'm listening." Aiko laid her fork and knife across the plate, having finished her bolognaise.

By now, Summer was full, having downed most of the first glass of champagne along with the delectable meal. She took a deep breath before speaking again. "Honestly, the role she played in my life can't be overstated. I can remember listening to her talk about the school and the students she'd worked with, even though she retired when I was in high school. Her passion for education was obvious and infectious, and it's why I chose to teach as my career."

"Wow." Aiko smiled. "It sounds like she was an amazing woman." She held her champagne glass just above the tabletop, staring down into it as if she were counting the bubbles. She remained silent for a few long moments.

Summer watched her intently. *What is she contemplating over there?*

"This is really valuable information, Summer. It helps me understand why you acted the way you did when you first found out about my involvement with the redevelopment project."

"I know I came off pretty harshly, but I'm glad you understand where I'm coming from now." She cringed, remembering how snarky she'd been. "My grandmother's vision lives on through my sister and me. Even though Crystal didn't choose education as a career path, we're both very cognizant of what our grandmother believed, what she stood for. Now that she's gone, it's so important for us to preserve that."

After draining the glass, Aiko set it down again. "How long has it been since she passed?"

"Nine years. There are moments when it seems like just yesterday." Summer could feel the tears gathering in her eyes, and she did her best to blink them back. She hadn't spoken to anyone at length about her grandmother in several years; the bittersweet reality of having loved and lost her rose to the surface. It occurred to her that the very fact that she'd spent this time talking about Grandma Beulah with Aiko indicated that a level of trust and comfort existed between them.

Aiko reached across the table, taking Summer's hand and giving it a gentle squeeze. "I'm sorry for your loss. I've heard people say it's possible to bounce back from these things, but honestly, there's no time limit on grief. When you lose someone you love, I'm not sure it's something you're meant to ever fully get over."

Dashing away an errant tear, Summer offered a small smile. "I appreciate you saying that, Aiko."

"And please don't think you have to hide your tears from me. Not about this, or anything else." Aiko reached into her suit coat with her free hand, extracted a clean handkerchief, and handed it to Summer. "Your feelings are valid, love."

"Thank you." Summer took the handkerchief and used it to dry her eyes. Aiko's empathetic, nonjudgmental response felt both endearing and refreshing. In the past, Summer had encountered people who either attempted to downplay her grief or who simply went into an awkward silence when she brought it up. *It's nice to know she cares, and that she isn't uncomfortable with letting me feel my emotions.*

"Thank you for trusting me with everything you've told me." Aiko worked the pad of her thumb slowly over the back of Summer's hand. "I wanted you to open up to me tonight, but I didn't expect you to do so on such a deep level."

"I didn't, either," Summer admitted with a chuckle. "Maybe it's the champagne, or the atmosphere, or just your vibe." She shook her head. "I can't really explain it."

"Some things defy explanation." Aiko continued lazily caressing Summer's hand with her thumb. "I feel it, too, though. There's this really light, positive energy flowing between us."

"That sounds about right. So, you're a spiritualist?"

She shrugged. "I was raised in the Bible Belt by a woman who valued the social and communal aspects of church more than anything else, and my absentee father is Buddhist. I was bound to become spiritual, don't you think?"

Summer laughed. "Attractive, empathetic, and witty. You're just full of surprises."

"I got a few more up my sleeve." She chuckled. "Do you want to take a look at the dessert menu?"

She shook her head. "I couldn't, I'm stuffed. Besides that, I'm ready to get on with whatever other adventures you have planned for us tonight."

Her smile broadened. "That's the spirit." She raised her hand to signal the waitress and paid for the meal.

Summer laid some cash on the table for the tip.

"I already . . ."

She gave Aiko a look that quickly silenced her protest.

A few minutes later, they left, with the remains of the bottle of champagne wrapped and placed in a narrow bag.

As Aiko pulled away from the curb, Summer said, "I'm having such a good time with you, Aiko. I'm glad we're spending tonight together."

Aiko smiled, reaching over to place a hand on Summer's thigh, just beneath the hem of her dress.

Summer smiled, too, as she reveled in the firm yet gentle pressure of Aiko's hand against her skin. The warmth of Aiko's touch radiated through her entire body, reminding her of the other night and how badly she'd wanted more. She regarded Aiko's profile as she drove, anxious to know what this night would hold.

Maybe tonight, I'll get my wish.

—

Aiko drove her SUV down Springdale Road, very aware of her beautiful companion in the passenger seat. She kept her eyes on the road as she navigated onto Cesar Chavez, then shortly after, turned onto North Pleasant Valley.

Summer asked, "Any reason why you didn't just take Chavez straight to Congress?"

Aiko chuckled. "Yep. This route takes about the same amount of time, but I've found it's far more scenic." She gestured out the window.

"You're right. The river looks so pretty at night," Summer commented, her gaze fixed on the sights they passed.

Aiko had to agree as she glanced out the driver's side window and caught a glimpse of the city lights dancing on the surface of the Colorado River. Night had fallen, but one could scarcely tell among the brightly lit, still-bustling surroundings of Austin after sunset.

It was just after nine o'clock when Aiko pulled into an empty spot at the Austin American-Statesman. After she cut the engine, she got out. Standing in the open door, she shrugged out of her blazer and bow tie, then tossed them into the back seat. She loosened the first two buttons near her throat, rolled up her shirtsleeves, and went around to help Summer out of the car.

"Heat starting to get to you?"

"You know what they say," Aiko quipped as she shut the passenger door. "It's not the heat, it's the humidity."

Summer walked just a bit ahead of Aiko as they headed down the dirt trail, their fingertips laced together. Aiko's position afforded her an unencumbered view of Summer's full, round ass swaying from side to side beneath her white A-line dress. It was all she could do to hold on to Summer's hand when what she really wanted was to grab a handful of that bounty. *Whatever the bats do tonight, there's no way they could beat this visual.*

After making their way to the broad swath of summer-brown grass in the shadow of Congress Avenue Bridge, they stopped beneath a tree. There were a good twenty or thirty other people there, talking, laughing, and enjoying the evening.

"I didn't think there would be so many people down here on a Sunday night," Aiko said, draping her arm over Summer's shoulder. "I purposefully didn't take you on a bat cruise because I knew that would be crowded, and I want you all to myself."

Summer chuckled. "That's actually fortunate, because I've been on those cruises several times, and I always seem to get seasick." She shook her head. "It definitely wouldn't have been pretty after such a nice, filling meal."

Aiko whistled. "I made the right decision, then."

A rustling sound drew Aiko's gaze up toward the bridge. A group of about twenty or thirty bats flitted out from beneath the structure, a mixture of fully grown bats and pups. Within a few moments, they were floating away, their black wings beating and stirring the night air.

"I'm guessing we probably missed the big exodus around sunset," Summer remarked.

"The conversation was so good, it was worth it." Looking around at the gaggle of folks, Aiko asked, "Do you want to hang here, or would you rather walk a bit further down the trail, so we can have some privacy?"

"I'm up for a walk." Summer looked at her feet for a moment. "These heels are actually pretty comfortable."

Aiko glanced at the bejeweled black straps crossing over the top of Summer's feet and wrapping around her ankles, struck by how nicely they framed and presented her slender feet and bright orange toenails. "They certainly look good on you." Aiko dragged her gaze slowly up Summer's body, from her ankles to her calves to her thick thighs and magnificent hips beneath the thin white fabric of her dress. Her eyes traveled on to the tops of Summer's full breasts, lingering for a moment before moving to the line of her collarbone and shoulders, revealed by the dress's thin straps and sweetheart neckline. Meeting her eyes again, Aiko said, "This seems like a good time to remind you how beautiful you look tonight."

Summer's soft smile and sidelong glance gave her away. "I'm flattered. But you didn't really have to say it aloud, since you're looking at me . . . like that."

"Like what?" Aiko asked teasingly.

"Like a little kid looks at an ice-cream cone on a hot day."

Aiko chuckled, drawing Summer closer as she started to walk. "You'd be surprised just how many licks I have in me . . . if the treat is sweet enough."

Summer pinched her hip. "You naughty girl."

"You don't know the half of it." Aiko squeezed Summer's hand as they left the observation area and headed back onto the trail. Passing beneath Congress Avenue Bridge, they walked along the river's shore. They passed the big hotel and the launch points for two of the companies that offered river cruises, then crossed beneath the First Street Bridge.

They circled the small pond at Grulke Plaza to the tree-shrouded spot where the Fannie Davis Town Lake Gazebo sat near the water's edge. Aiko glanced around. It was significantly less crowded—only three other people in the area.

"I haven't been down here in years," Summer commented as they entered the gazebo.

They were the only two people inside the old stone structure. Aiko let Summer lead her to the bench running along the inner wall. Taking a seat in the center, where they had the best view of the city, Aiko slipped her arm around Summer's waist and pulled her close. "Look at that skyline."

"It's amazing. It reminds me of everything I love about Austin."

"Me, too. That's why I run this trail so often." Aiko sighed, looking out over the glassy surface of the river, the city lights dancing over it. On the opposite side, she could see a good portion of the Cesar Chavez corridor, from Austin Central Library to City Hall to the Wells Fargo building, and so many illuminated points between. "Indulge me a little bit while I get nerdy with you."

Summer chuckled, cozying up to her side. "I'm listening."

"This gazebo is a midcentury structure, built in the late sixties. The style is called Googie; it was supposed to represent space-age architecture—think *The Jetsons*."

"I can definitely see that influence here. Even when I came here as a kid, I thought it looked kind of like a spaceship."

"Right. The coolest thing, though, is the roof. It's said that the architect was inspired by looking at a morning glory bloom, so he inverted it to create the roof's shape."

"So, we're sitting under a big, upside-down metal flower right now?" She laughed. "That is kind of a cool fact." She paused before she spoke again. "Now tell me something more personal."

"What do you wanna know?" Aiko inhaled, taking in the sweet scent of Summer. She was wearing perfume or used some deliciously fruity-smelling shampoo or shower gel. Either way, her aroma was as tantalizing as her appearance.

"Your coming-out story. You've already heard mine."

She shrugged. "I can't say I really have an official coming-out story. My mom just seemed to know. In fact, she asked me about it when I was fifteen."

"Yikes. What did she say, exactly?"

"We were in the kitchen doing dishes. I was washing, she was drying. Out of nowhere, she said, 'Aiko, do you like girls instead of boys? Or do you like both?' I was so shocked that it took me a minute to answer her." She shook her head. "But when I did, I told her I was only into girls. She just nodded and told me she loved me no matter what and I should tell my father when I felt ready. Then we finished the dishes, and she didn't bring it up again."

"Did you tell your father?"

She nodded. "A week or so later, the next time I talked to him. His reaction was pretty much the same as my mom's, only a bit more zen. He told me to 'follow my bliss.'"

Summer looked at her, her eyes full of curiosity. "How did that make you feel? It's hard to tell just listening to your description."

"I'm not sure. They were both so ambivalent . . . I guess you could say I was underwhelmed." She sighed. "Don't get me wrong. I've heard plenty of coming-out horror stories, and I'm glad I didn't have to go through anything traumatic. But their reaction still didn't sit right with me."

Summer tilted her head slightly to the right. "Maybe you wanted to be celebrated instead of just accepted?"

"Maybe." *How would that even have looked, though? If they'd have thrown me a party or something like that, I would have been mortified.* "It's all good, though. I'm all grown-up. I know who I am, and what I want." She held Summer's gaze. "And right now, what I really want is you."

With a sly smile, Summer raised herself into Aiko's lap. "Oh, really."

Aiko groaned at the delicious pressure of Summer's ass against her thighs. "Absolutely." Aiko stared at Summer's full lips, aching to kiss them. "In fact, we need to get to your apartment, before things get indecent." She could hear her own breaths speeding up.

Summer leaned in, pecking her on the forehead before sliding off her lap and standing. "Let's go, then."

They all but ran back to the parking lot, and Aiko got them back to Summer's apartment as quickly as she could without getting a speeding ticket. All the while, the delicious tension rose within Aiko's body, a steadily intensifying craving for Summer and for whatever this night would hold.

Once they were inside, Summer pushed her down on her sofa and straddled her lap. "I can't wait to get you out of these clothes."

Aiko groaned, her nipples tightening inside her bra as she pulled Summer's sassy mouth against hers. While she kissed Summer, gripping her shapely hips, Summer worked the buttons of Aiko's shirt free of their holes. One pearl button popped off, and Aiko couldn't have cared less. Summer continued to kiss her while caressing Aiko's shirt down her shoulders. Aiko eased her hands beneath the hem of Summer's dress, rucking the gauzy fabric as she went. Breaking the kiss, Aiko stared into Summer's eyes. Slowly, she began to move her touch to Summer's thighs. "I know we have all night, but I just want to see you cum. Let's get this first one right quick."

Summer sucked on her lower lip, offering a slow nod.

Aiko dragged her fingertips between Summer's thighs, licking her lips as her hands made contact with Summer's damp panties. Finding the edge, Aiko pushed the garment aside and slipped her index and middle fingers beneath it. Aiko's own clit pulsed when she felt how hot and wet Summer's pussy was.

Summer shuddered on her lap as Aiko stroked her warm, slippery flesh. "Yes . . ."

Aiko swirled her fingertips around Summer's clit, feeling it swell. Summer's soft, crooning moans rose in the silence as Aiko continued to stroke and play. Summer's hips began to circle, and Aiko found herself moving against them, her hips rising to meet Summer's rhythm.

Summer slid the thin straps of her dress down, and her heavy breasts fell into view inches from Aiko's face, brown nipples hard and straining. Leaning forward, Aiko took one into her mouth and sucked while her free hand rested on Summer's soft, pliable ass, giving it a firm squeeze.

Summer's head dropped back, and Aiko kept up her motions as the pitch of Summer's moans rose an octave. When Aiko slipped her middle finger inside Summer's slick opening while rubbing her clit with her thumb, Summer made a sound that could only be described as a squeal. Moments later, Summer gritted her teeth and cursed aloud. *"Fuck!"* A trickle of liquid ran down Aiko's hand as she eased her finger from inside Summer's body.

Summer collapsed against Aiko, resting her head in the crook of her shoulder, her heavy breathing echoing in Aiko's ear.

After taking a moment to tuck her own thumb into her mouth and suck off the sweetness Summer had left, Aiko watched Summer with hooded eyes. Stroking her hair, she spoke into Summer's ear. "You suffer beautifully. Good girl." Her phone buzzed, and she ignored it.

She felt Summer's body shudder against her. "Shit."

"I'm just getting started, baby." But the insistent buzzing of her phone in the pocket of her slacks tugged Aiko's attention away from Summer. Reluctantly, she slid the phone out and answered it. "Hello?"

"Hello, am I speaking with Aiko Holt?"

"Yes, it is," she said, frowning. "Who is this?"

"My name is Louise Richards, I'm a nurse practitioner at St. David's Medical Center. Your mother, Janet, asked me to call you."

Aiko sat straighter, her arm still clasped around Summer's waist. "What's going on? What happened with my mother?"

Summer stiffened in her arms.

"She's taken a pretty bad fall. We're getting ready to move her to the orthopedic floor, and she'd like you to be here to discuss next steps."

Aiko cursed under her breath. "Yes, I understand. I'll be there as soon as I can." She ended the call and tucked her phone away again.

Summer sat up then, tugging her dress straps over her shoulders. "Seems like our parade just got rained on."

Aiko kissed her on the lips. "It did. I'm sorry, baby. I have to go to the hospital to see about my mom."

Summer waved a hand as she scooted off Aiko's lap. "No, don't apologize. I wouldn't stop you from looking after your mother. Go on, do what you need to do."

"Thanks for being so understanding." Aiko stood, rebuttoning her shirt. Fortunately, the button that had popped off was near the top, so it didn't look too bad. Her still-throbbing clit protested the end of her lovemaking with Summer, but responsibility took precedence at the moment. *I'm an only child, so who else would Mama call on?* "Trust me, we are going to continue this the first chance I get."

"I'm gonna hold you to that." Summer stood, sucking on her bottom lip. "If that was just the prelude, I can't wait to see what else develops between us."

Aiko drew a deep, cleansing breath, trying to shift her thoughts away from all the nasty things she wanted to do to Summer so she could focus on what she had to do. She returned to the front door, with Summer close behind her. "I'll reach out once I've got my mother squared away, okay?"

Summer tossed her arms around Aiko's neck, pulling her in for another lingering kiss on the lips. "I'll be waiting. Call me as soon as you know something, no matter how late it is."

Feeling her heart squeeze at the concern in Summer's voice, Aiko opened the door and stepped out into the corridor.

Just before one o'clock in the morning, Aiko slipped into the nearly empty hallway near her mother's room. Taking a few steps away from the door, she found a bench, then sat down, slipping her phone from her pocket to dial Summer.

"Hello?" Summer's sleep-heavy voice answered. "Is your mother okay?"

Feeling the smile tilt her lips, Aiko said, "Yes, she'll be fine. She's a little bruised, but still intact. Now that she's finally asleep and stable, I'm just gonna hang out here the rest of the night, in case she needs me."

"Like any good daughter would," Summer replied before yawning. "I'm glad to hear she's all right, though."

"You and me both. I'm exhausted, but relieved." Aiko let her head rest against the wall behind her.

"I've been in and out of sleep since you left." Summer yawned again. "You got me open, Aiko."

"Don't worry, I'm gonna take care of that very soon."

"Oh, really? It's like that?" Summer chuckled. "I'm getting serious top vibes from you right now."

"Switch, actually. For you, it's whatever." Aiko swiped her tongue over her lower lip.

"Good. I've got my toys here, so when you come back, bring your harness."

Aiko jerked her head up. She heard Summer's sultry laugh, and it took her a moment to formulate a response. "Bet. Are you just taking, or are you dishing out?"

"I'll do a little of both, if you want."

"Ease me into it and we'll see," Aiko quipped.

"And on that note, good night, Aiko." With a laugh, Summer hung up.

Aiko's eyes widened, and she shook her head as she stood and stretched, then returned to her mother's room.

Gotta love a woman who isn't afraid to ask for what she wants.

CHAPTER TEN

Summer grabbed the open halves of her charcoal-gray cardigan and buttoned it to guard her upper body against the chill in the air. The interior of the teachers' lounge at Young Scholars Academy seemed to be perpetually refrigerator-cold. She stifled a sneeze, worried the droplets might freeze midair if she released them.

Summer didn't know if she was anemic or just cold-natured; either way, she wore pants to the building most of the time, despite the high temperatures outside. Today was no exception, and as she brushed a few Danish crumbs from the thigh of her dark denim jeans, she wondered if she'd ever get used to the chilly conditions at her job.

It was Monday morning, and she was still coming down from the high she'd experienced last night with Aiko. Those torrid moments on Aiko's lap, when Aiko had kissed and stroked her right over the edge into orgasmic bliss, still haunted her thoughts. Summer raised her travel mug for another sip of dark roast, knowing it wouldn't banish thoughts of Aiko but would at least help her stay alert after a less than restful night.

"Okay, everyone. We'll begin our orientation at two o'clock this afternoon. So I'll need you all to finalize your classroom organization and any other odds and ends before that time." Scarlet Goodwin, director and headmistress of the school, stood near the window as she spoke.

"I'm going to go ahead and release you so you'll have some time to wrap things up."

The ten other teachers and the front-desk staff all rose and began to file out of the room. Knowing she had a one-on-one meeting with Scarlet, Summer lingered in her seat at the round table near the kitchenette.

Scarlet strode over and sat down as the room emptied. Her brown skin, accentuated by light makeup and dark pink lipstick, held kind brown eyes. She wore a close-trimmed hairstyle, shaved on the sides and the back with blond-highlighted spiral curls on top. Her attire, a pair of black slacks and black loafers with a flowing bright green tunic, looked comfortable and professional. A black-and-white lanyard with her faculty badge hung from her neck. "So, how are you feeling, Summer? You're our newest teacher, so I just wanted to take a few moments and see how things are going for you."

"Honestly, I'm really excited. I can't wait to meet my students."

Scarlet smiled. "You've certainly got the right attitude; I love the enthusiasm. Do you feel comfortable with the classroom setup and your materials?"

She nodded. "Yes, I do. I really think the curriculum here is effective, especially for students this young. It will be interesting to see how they take to it, and how they perform academically and socially."

"I'm glad to hear you've got an analytical approach. I'd like you to make use of that today." Scarlet leaned back in her seat. "Take notes during the orientation today. When you interact with parents and students, gather as much data as you can about them. Family life, their background, parental philosophies. You can usually pick up on some of the child's personality quirks and idiosyncrasies if you pay close attention."

Summer eyed the school-issued laptop peeking out of her tote bag. "I'll do that."

"I'd recommend you write up a couple of paragraphs in each student's chart, just for your own reference. It will make things easier on Wednesday, trust me. When you encounter the inevitable meltdown, your files will have some information to help you determine the proper response."

She nodded. "That's pretty similar to what I've always done. Those first couple of weeks of school are where the rubber meets the road for us teachers." Summer was completely confident in her knowledge of child development, her teacher training, and her patience, but having information that let her see each child's individual needs would only make her a more effective educator. "Is there anything else I need to know?"

"I don't think so. You're a skilled educator, and I know you're pretty well versed on school policies by now." Scarlet stood. "If you should have any questions, just buzz my office and either I or Paula will come down to the classroom, okay?" From what Summer had heard, Paula Wilkins was the school's rarely seen co-director.

"Sounds great. Thank you, Scarlet."

"That's what I'm here for. I'll catch up with you after orientation." The director left the room, leaving the lounge door open as she departed.

A few moments later, Summer gathered her things and left the lounge, heading down the hallway toward her classroom. She smiled when she arrived at the door, which she'd festooned with colorful balloon cutouts bearing each of her students' names. In the center, next to the rectangular window that allowed a peek into her room, was her name in big sparkly bubble letters: Ms. Graves.

She was about to turn the doorknob when her phone chimed. Taking it out of her pocket, she read the text on the screen.

Hey beautiful. How's your day going?

She grinned as she tapped out a response.

Good so far. You?

Pretty good. Can't figure out what I want for lunch tho. What are you gonna have?

Summer leaned against the wall and thought for a moment before replying.

I'm gonna have a two-piece dark plate from Gus's Fried Chicken.

Ooh. Sounds good. TTYL baby.

She tucked the phone away again and entered her classroom, shutting the door behind her. After setting her tote bag down on her desk, she took off her cardigan and hung it over the back of her chair, knowing she'd get hot once she started moving around. She still had a short list of tasks to complete before her lunch break, so she walked over to her manipulatives corner to start there.

Once she took the huge plastic case out of the cabinet, she dumped the pile of small manipulatives onto the colorful carpet. Legs tucked beneath her, she began the process of separating them. There were plastic animal figurines, small flat discs used as counters for mathematics, gram cubes, tangrams, and various magnets. As she went through the items, she set them on the colored squares of the carpet by type, forming piles of like objects all around her.

The sound of gentle but insistent knocking made her glance at her door. "Come in," she called.

The door opened, and Olivia Cook, who taught three-year-olds in the classroom next to hers, stuck her curly head in. "Sorry to bug you, honey. Do you have any tape I can use?"

"Sure. What do you need? Masking, clear, or painter's?" She gestured to the clear plastic shoebox on her desk, full of various kinds of tape.

"Wow, looks like I've hit the mother lode," Olivia quipped as she went to the desk to rifle through the bin. She wore her usual colorful scrub top and black scrub pants. Olivia was petite and slender. Her curly red hair framed her friendly, heart-shaped face, which featured a sprinkling of freckles scattered beneath her blue eyes. "I'm finishing up my bulletin board where I'll display the children's artwork. What do you think . . . masking tape?"

"Yeah, if it's going on the back of something." Summer's eyes scanned the carpet for a missing goat from her pile of animal figurines. "If the tape will be visible, use the clear one."

"I'm not sure yet, so do you mind if I borrow both? I'll have 'em back to you in a jiffy."

Summer waved her off. "Go ahead. I've got some stuff to hang but I'm using poster tack, so it's all good."

"Thanks, honey." Olivia grabbed the two rolls of tape from the bin. "That looks like quite the job there," she remarked, gesturing to the large pile of stuff Summer was sitting in.

She chuckled. "It is. Part scavenger hunt, part organization."

"Good luck with that. I'll bring the tape back shortly." With a wave, Olivia slipped from the room.

Shifting a bit, Summer felt something sharp jab her in the hip. She reached beneath her, then shook her head as she wrapped her fingers around the missing figurine. "Okay, Mr. Billy Goat. Time for you to go into the farm pile."

She stood and walked to the stack of smaller plastic bins from behind her desk, grabbing them along with a roll of stick-on labels and a permanent marker. Returning to her spot on the carpet, she began putting the manipulatives into the smaller containers and marking them with the contents. Once she'd cleared the floor and labeled all the bins, she slid them into place on the open shelves above the lower cabinet. Their positioning placed them around the eye level of her students for easy reach.

Standing again, she stretched her arms above her head and did a few squats, working out the stiffness that had developed during her time on the floor. She headed to the closet in the corner behind her desk, where she found the rolled-up posters she'd purchased for her science station. Grabbing the tall, narrow cardboard box holding them, as well as the small package of poster tack, she carried them across the classroom.

By the time she'd finished hanging the posters and sat back down at her desk, her growling stomach was cutting through her thoughts. Checking her phone for the time, she saw that it was ten to one. *Let me go get something to eat before I start doing something else.*

She reached into her tote bag and fished around for her wallet. Before she could find it, the intercom system sounded in her room. "Ms. Graves, please come to the reception desk for a delivery."

Delivery? Frowning, she left her room and walked down the hallway to the reception desk. There, she was surprised to find a uniformed driver for one of the local food-delivery services holding a paper sack from Gus's Fried Chicken. Her stomach growled again in response to the delicious aroma emanating from it.

"Ms. Graves?"

"Yes, that's me."

"Here you go, ma'am. And thanks for the generous tip." He handed over the food along with a bottle of water and tipped his hat before leaving.

"Why didn't you tell me you were ordering lunch?" Beverly, the receptionist, eyed her. "I would have added something on."

"I didn't order this," Summer said, feeling the smile tug her lips. "Someone very thoughtful ordered it for me." She headed down the hall, returned to her classroom, and then set the bag on her desk. Reaching inside, she pulled out the lunch she'd been craving: a leg and thigh, crisply fried, baked beans, coleslaw, and the customary slice of white bread. She picked up the leg and took a bite, sending her taste buds straight to Valhalla. After wiping her mouth and fingers with a napkin, she fired off a text to Aiko.

If you are trying to win me over, you're doing a great job.

So you got the delivery.

She smiled as she replied.

I did. Thank you.

You're welcome.

Setting her phone down, she savored her lunch in peaceful silence. Once she'd finished eating, she drained the bottled water and tossed her trash. She used her tiny broom and dustpan to clean the crumbs off her desktop and ducked out of the room for a quick bathroom break before the orientation began.

A few minutes after two o'clock, the first family of the day came into the classroom. A tall, dark-skinned man with a beard entered the room, holding the hand of a little girl whose hair was done up in two haphazard ponytails. Standing from her seat behind the desk, Summer went to greet them. "Hi, I'm Ms. Graves. Welcome to my classroom. And you are?"

"I'm Alton Johnson, and this is my daughter, Ella." He gave Ella's small shoulder a gentle squeeze. "Ella, say hello to your teacher."

Little Ella, whose eyes were fixed on her tiny Mary Jane shoes, mumbled a greeting.

Alton sighed. "Ella."

Summer waved it off. "It's not a problem. It's only natural for little ones to be nervous around new people, and I'm no exception. Don't worry, Mr. Johnson. I'm sure we'll be fast friends." Summer squatted, bringing herself to eye level with Ella. "I'm very glad to meet you, Ella. Why don't you go and have a look around the classroom while I talk to your dad? How does that sound?"

She didn't speak, but her head bobbed affirmatively.

"Okay. Go ahead."

As Ella ran off to the manipulatives center, Summer stood to her full height again. "Let's head over to my desk so we can chat." There, she gestured Alton to a chair, and she sat, then opened her laptop. "According to what I have, Miss Ella has never been to school or day care before."

He nodded. "That's right. I'm expanding my landscaping business, and I'd rather she have this kind of immersive learning versus being home with the nanny. It will also give me more flexibility in working from home if she's here."

She nodded. "I see. Can you give me a brief rundown of her personality? You know, her likes and dislikes, just to review what I have on her intake form." While Alton spoke, she entered key phrases into the notes field of Ella's student file. By the time he'd finished, she'd added a good two paragraphs. "Thanks for that. This will be very helpful in working with your daughter."

Another family entered the room, and Summer got to her feet. "Excuse me, Mr. Johnson. Feel free to stay and look around as long as you like." Walking across the room, she went to greet the next family who'd be entrusting her with their child.

∼

Sitting at her mother's bedside at St. David's Medical Center, Aiko contemplated her next move in the game on her screen, hoping that if she engaged her brain, she'd be able to stay awake. She'd spent the entire night in that chair to keep an eye on her mother, and now her back protested that decision. Even in its fully flat position, the chair could be described as lumpy at best. She'd slept maybe three hours and was now trying to fight off the post-lunch nap she felt creeping up. *Why hasn't someone engineered one of these things to be comfortable yet?*

She glanced in her mother's direction and found her in the same position she'd been in since she'd finished picking over her hospital-provided lunch tray.

Janet, for her part, reclined in the bed, paying rapt attention to an episode of *Judge Judy* playing on the wall-mounted television. Perpetually cold, she had the white hospital blankets pulled to her chin, leaving her face and the pink floral satin bonnet covering her head visible.

Aiko let her gaze shift back to her phone and the game of solitaire in progress. As she stacked a two of diamonds on a three of clubs, she heard her mother grouse, "How long is it gonna take them to spring me? They said I could go home today."

Aiko chuckled. "Chill, Mama. I'm sure they'll let you go soon. Besides, I need to talk to the doctor before we leave."

She sighed. "I already told you, I'm fine. I was working in the front garden yesterday evening, got a bad cramp, lost my balance, and fell. My neighbor was outside and saw the whole thing, and she decided to call me an ambulance."

"I'm glad Ms. Mabel was outside," Aiko responded. "I already sent her some thank-you flowers."

"I suppose it was a good thing," Janet admitted, seeming none too pleased to do so. "Who knows how long I would have been laid out in the grass if she didn't make that call."

A short, stocky man in a white lab coat and wire-rimmed glasses entered the room then. As he picked up Janet's chart from the clear plastic pocket on the wall and looked it over, he said, "I'm Dr. Marberry. How are you feeling, Mrs. Holt?"

"That's Miss." Janet offered a wry smile, gesturing toward Aiko. "Her daddy could've made an honest woman out of me, but he decided against it."

Dr. Marberry cleared his throat. "My . . . uh . . . apologies." He walked over and sat down on a low stool next to Aiko. "You're the daughter, correct?"

"Yes." She stuck her hand out. "Aiko Holt. Nice to meet you, Doctor."

"Firm grip," he commented as they shook. "So, Ms. Holt, your mother has suffered from a simple twisted ankle, along with a sprained wrist from instinctively catching herself during her fall." Sliding his stool nearer to the bed, he tugged back the blankets. "As you can see, the team put her wrist in a splint last night. She'll need to wear that for about a week. As for the ankle, apply ice to keep the swelling and bruising down, and make sure she takes the anti-inflammatory I prescribed."

"Got it. Anything else I should know?"

"Excuse me," Janet interjected as she sat up, her tone sharp. "I'm not an infant, and I'm not senile, either. I've still got enough sense to be involved in my own care."

Dr. Marberry rotated to face her. "My apologies. I didn't mean to make you feel left out in my attempts to inform your daughter. As I said, you'll need to take your meds, wear the splint for at least a week, and get plenty of rest."

Janet's back and shoulders stiffened visibly. "I can do the first two things. But when you say rest, does that mean I can't work in the yard?"

The doctor slowly turned and looked at Aiko, who merely shrugged. "Welcome to my world, Doc."

Returning his attention to Janet, Dr. Marberry shook his head. "I'm sorry, Ms. Holt. You'll need to stay off your feet and limit the use of your right hand to just the bare necessities."

"I'm only partly done with putting my bulbs in the front." Janet stared at him, chin raised, as if her withering gaze might make him change his mind. "If I don't get them in the ground, they won't bloom next month. Aside from that, my yard is a mess. I've still got mulch to spread, and . . ."

Aiko swallowed a sigh. "Mama, I'll do that stuff for you." *Yard work at Mom's house will probably be far more time-consuming and physically demanding than taking care of my own orchids. But if that's what it's gonna take to keep her from hurting herself even more, then so be it.* "I took the day off from work, and I'll get it done right after we leave here."

"Thank you." The doctor appeared relieved. "And please see that your mother doesn't do anything more strenuous than supervising from a comfortably seated position." He eyed his patient. "Can you agree to that, Janet?"

She gave him a nod as she acquiesced. "I suppose."

Thirty minutes later, they were in Aiko's SUV, driving away from the hospital.

"We need to stop by the pharmacy and pick up your prescription." Aiko pulled up to a stoplight and glanced at her mother sitting in the passenger seat. "Is there anything else you wanna stop and get before I take you home?"

"Yeah. You can take me to get some real food."

Pulling off as the light turned green, Aiko shook her head. "I thought you weren't hungry. At least that's how it looked based on the way you turned your nose up at your trays at breakfast and lunch."

She snorted. "Girl, come on. That was hospital food. I've got a bowl of wax fruit at the house that looks more appetizing."

Aiko laughed. "Okay, I hear you. But since you have to mind your blood sugar, it's only so much I can do."

"I know, I know." Janet let her head fall back against the seat's headrest. "Just let me get a salad and a bottled water, and that'll do."

"Deal." Aiko drove her mother to the pharmacy, then to a local fast-food place for her salad, and then home to her cottage on Desmond Place.

Pulling into the driveway, Aiko cringed. Her mother hadn't exaggerated about the state of the front yard or the amount of work that needed doing. The bags of mulch, the rake, her mother's favorite gardening gloves, the wheelbarrow, and all manner of garden implements were scattered across the small patch of grass. "Yikes, Mama. Why didn't you just call me to help you do all this in the first place?"

"I know you're busy with work, Aiko. I don't want to bother you for every little thing."

Aiko sighed. Her mother's dogged desire to stay out of her hair was both endearing and concerning. "I'd rather you just call me and ask before you take on so much. Promise me you'll ask next time, okay?"

"I promise, sugar."

Aiko helped her mother out of the car and got her into one of the two old rockers on the front porch. Once Janet was settled onto the floral cushion, Aiko handed over her mom's food, water, and pill. "Go ahead and take some now, while you're eating."

Janet begrudgingly accepted the pill, washing it down with a swig from her water bottle. "Okay. Now I'm gonna eat, and after we chat, I want you to get started on this work."

"I will. Because if I don't, I'll probably have to take another day off." Taking a sip of the strawberry shake she'd ordered for herself, Aiko sat down in the rocker next to her. Aiko rocked slowly, enjoying the cold sweetness of her shake and the quiet familiarity of the old neighborhood.

"So, what's going on with you?" Janet asked as she set aside her empty plastic bowl. "Anything new?"

"Just trying to get the new development over on First Avenue off to a proper start."

"You say that like I don't know you're talking about your old school." She chuckled. "I saw on the news that there are some folks around here that aren't too fond of the project. They'd rather do away with the whole enterprise."

Aiko had been trying to forget that day, but her mother's words brought the memory of seeing the news story flooding back, along with the accompanying annoyance and frustration. "I know. It's like that with every project, to some degree. Some people just don't like change, no matter how beneficial it might be."

"Hmm." Janet snatched off her bonnet and ran a hand over her chin-length salt-and-pepper dreadlocks. Hanging the bonnet on the back of her rocker, she quipped, "Getting hot under there."

She could tell by her mother's expression and that telltale humming sound that she had something more to say. "What is it, Mama?"

"Y'all tearing down the school and putting up a fancy new office park might benefit some folks. But it isn't necessarily gonna be people from Ivy that reap those benefits."

She sighed. "I know, Mama."

"I'm sure you know what you're doing, Aiko. I raised you with good sense, and you were born with a good heart."

Thinking about the project, about Summer, and about how they stood on opposite sides of the divide made Aiko wonder if things could ever be solid between them. "You know, I saw that news story, too. And I've been on two dates with one of the protestors."

Janet's eyes widened. "You're kidding. Which one?"

"Her name is Summer. We graduated from Sojourner Truth the same year."

"I remember her. The fiery one." Janet's slow nod and sly smile accompanied her words. "If she's as outspoken in real life as she was on camera, you've got your hands full, daughter dear."

Aiko chuckled. "Yeah, she's something else. But I'm really starting to care about her, even though we don't necessarily agree on the project."

"And when are you going to see her again?"

"Tonight, if she's free." She paused, careful not to admit too much with her next sentence. "I was with her last night when I got the call from the hospital."

"Aha," Janet said with a raised brow. "And I'm assuming you have unfinished business with her, then."

"Mama!" Aiko could feel her face getting hot. "We are not about to go down that path."

She laughed. "I'm just teasing you, sugar! I'm not trying to get in your personal affairs. Not on that level, at least." She reached over and squeezed Aiko's shoulder. "Sorry. I know my little spill was inopportune."

"Don't apologize, Mama. I'm just glad you're all right." Aiko stood and stretched her arms above her head. She'd changed out of her date clothes and into the spare workout clothes she kept in her trunk before retiring to the hospital chair last night. Considering the amount of work ahead of her and the high humidity, she was glad for the gray basketball shorts and black tank top. "Let me go ahead and get this stuff done. After I clean up, what else do you want me to do?"

"I need eight snapdragon bulbs buried, then I need you to roll out that landscaping fabric and mulch the flower beds. You'll have to cut out some holes for the snapdragons, of course."

Aiko whistled, then clapped her hands together. The physical labor would definitely be taking the place of her daily workout. As she took the two steps back down to the yard and grabbed the rake, a vision of Summer's smiling face popped into her mind.

It was quickly replaced by an image of Summer's O face, eyes rolled back, mouth wide as she rode the waves of pleasure atop Aiko's lap. Aiko wanted both those faces in her life: the easy, relaxed smile and the look of passion at its peak.

I just need to focus on what I feel and what's happening between us. It's not about the project or what anyone else thinks.

It's all about the two of us.

CHAPTER ELEVEN

"This is a really unconventional date." Summer undid her seat belt as Aiko pulled them into a spot at the Blue Starlite in Round Rock. The boutique theater, located just north of Austin, was part of a dying breed of old-fashioned drive-ins.

"Not really. It's a drive-in movie—a classic place to make out." Aiko winked.

"Maybe, but not when it's a team-building event and all your coworkers are there." Summer gestured to the other cars they'd passed on the way to their somewhat secluded spot. "Are all these cars occupied by people from your job?"

Aiko glanced around for a moment. "Yeah. I saw Miriam, the owner, and Logan, my supervisor. This was his idea. Then there was Tricia, and Fiona, and Calvin from accounting . . ."

"The gang's all here, then." Summer chuckled. "I must have really wanted to see you, or else I wouldn't have agreed to this. It also helps that we're all in cars and not sitting next to each other in a regular theater."

"Well, we're not the only ones on a date; Calvin brought his wife." Summer eyed her.

Aiko laughed. "At least it's a good movie. *The Magnificent Seven* is a classic. Besides, part of the reason I was able to get the day off on such short notice was that I agreed to show up for this." She blew out a breath. "It's been a long day. I slept terribly in one of those hospital chairs last night, then my mom had me doing yard work. I'm honestly just glad to be off my feet."

Summer sank into the leather seat, casting her gaze out the window. Darkness blanketed the parking lot, save for the orange beacons carried around by the theater employees and the soft glow of a commercial playing on the big inflatable screen.

Summer turned her gaze to Aiko, who was watching the advertisement—or at least looking in that general direction. Aiko wore a pair of denim shorts and a white short-sleeved button-down with a green tropical print. The halves of the button-down were open, a green tank visible underneath. A spicy, enticing aroma floated from her body to Summer's nostrils, and Summer could tell it was the same fragrance she'd worn last time, some heady mix of citrus and sandalwood. *It's her signature scent . . . I think it's called Sinful. She always smells so good.* "How long before the movie starts?"

Aiko glanced at her phone. "It's supposed to start at eight, so about fifteen minutes."

"That gives us a little time to talk, then." Summer drew a deep breath, knowing her topic of choice might not go over well. But if there were any *real* chance they could build their very *real* connection into something more, they'd have to address it. "I don't want you to think I'm unreasonable, or just looking for problems when it comes to the Sojourner Truth project."

"Everyone else here calls it the Ivy First Avenue project. But go ahead, I'm listening."

Quashing her slight annoyance at what felt like a correction, Summer cleared her throat. "At any rate, I'm just trying to clarify my perspective. I haven't spent a lot of time at home since I left for college, and it really pained me to see some of the changes when I finally did return. Ivy is so different from how I remember it, how it used to be."

"How so? I've heard you say that before, but you haven't given me concrete examples." Aiko shifted in her seat, turning her body toward Summer. "I really want to get a clearer understanding of what you mean."

Summer laced her fingers together and laid them across her lap. "When I first moved back to town, I went over to the Shoppes at Ivy, to get a cake from Swingin' Sweets. When I got there, I found two of the old stalwart businesses were gone. Wong's Chinese is now some generic chain restaurant. Mr. Wong made the best egg rolls I've ever tasted, bar none. Now I've got to settle for the same chicken tenders I can get at a thousand other places."

Aiko's lips stretched and thinned. "I know how it is when you fix your mouth for something and you can't get it."

"Yes, that's a thing. But it's deeper than that. Also missing was Mary Ellen's Tea Room. When I was very young, my mother used to take my sister and me there for high tea." She could clearly envision those Saturday afternoons, back before things became complex and she'd lost that special bond with her mother. "Picture little four-year-old me, wearing my grandmother's pearls and this straw hat with silk flowers that was way too big for my head, sipping tea with my mom and Crystal."

Aiko chuckled. "Did y'all hold your pinkies up when you held the cups?"

"Always." Summer laughed, remembering the silliness and joy of those moments. "We were using fine china, after all."

"Yeah, I'm picturing it, and it sounds absolutely precious." She sobered a bit. "Those memories must be very valuable."

"They are, especially considering how strained my relationship is with my mother now." Summer sighed. "To see that Mary Ellen's was gone was bad enough. But then to know that they just tore it down, and replaced it with parking spaces, instead of letting another small business move into that space? That made it so much worse."

Aiko offered a solemn nod but didn't say anything.

"I see these changes as personally painful. But I also see them as hurting the neighborhood. Those small, mom-and-pop businesses, the ones passed down from generation to generation, and the people that run them, comprise the soul of Ivy. They're what make it home, a place unlike anywhere else. I just don't want to see something so unique and special sacrificed on the altar of profit and convenience, you know?"

Resting her chin on her hand, Aiko appeared to be weighing Summer's words. "Thank you for telling me. I feel like I understand you better now."

"Good." Summer fixed her with a penetrating stare. "Does that mean you're going to switch sides and help me stop the project going forward?"

Aiko frowned. "Summer, you know I can't do that without putting my career in serious jeopardy. I've worked hard to get where I am, and I can't take that kind of risk. Not at this stage in the game."

Part of Summer wanted to start yelling because maybe raising her voice would make Aiko truly see where she was coming from. *But that's not gonna work inside a vehicle, with all her coworkers surrounding us.* Swallowing her frustration, Summer said, "You've listened to me explain my point of view. Now I want to hear yours. Tell me why you're so invested in seeing our old school, and my grandmother's legacy, turned into yet another corporate development?"

Aiko sucked in her bottom lip briefly before responding. "Okay. As I said, trying to stop a project that's already so far into the process could end up getting me fired. That would look terrible on my résumé, which affects my ability to get another job. So I'm serious when I say my career would be hindered." She paused. "But, like you, I have multiple reasons. Philosophically, I simply don't agree that all change is bad change. I like to look beyond Ivy because it's just one neighborhood. Look at the Jones Center, where we went the other night. That remodel greatly improved the museum space, allowing more access and potential exposure for local artists."

"That's true." Having seen it firsthand, Summer couldn't dispute that.

"Let's look deeper still. There have been quite a few new affordable housing developments put up in the last decade, all around Austin. In a lot of those cases, developers came in, razed existing buildings that were in various states of disrepair and dilapidation, and built brand new units. And yes, that meant displacing residents, but look at the overall picture. Once construction was complete, the city stepped in and ensured the rents were controlled. So in the end, people who were living in poor conditions, sometimes under slumlords, now have safer, more modern housing."

"I can see where you're coming from. But you do know that a lot of the people who were displaced from those neighborhoods weren't able to get back in, don't you? It sounds like you're wearing your rose-colored glasses here, Aiko."

Aiko made a sound between a scoff and a snicker. "Maybe so, but you can't deny there's been a real positive impact in this city that can be traced directly back to urban renewal and development." She tapped her index finger against her chin. "And here's something I need to know. If you're as invested in the community as you claim, then what made you take on the teaching position at a private school?"

Summer balked, pursing her lips. "Why would you ask me that? Don't you think I looked?"

"Or what about the public schools in East Austin? It's right next door and there's a district-wide teacher shortage. A lot of kids from Ivy get bussed to schools there."

"How do you know all that? You don't even have any kids." Her tone was terse.

"No, but Peaches has three nieces in the area." Aiko folded her arms over her chest. "I don't need to have kids in the public schools to care about them." Aiko eyed Summer expectantly. "You didn't answer me about East Austin."

Summer sighed. "I did look there, as well. YSA has a better curriculum, a better learning environment." She paused. "I went where I thought I could do the most good. I'm not gonna sit here and let you insult where I choose to work. I had to make a decision that was right for me."

Aiko's eyes widened, and her lips pursed. "I don't know if we'll ever be able to agree on this."

"Not beyond agreeing to disagree, I'm thinking." Summer settled back against her seat and blew out a breath, her lips vibrating in time.

The opening theme for the film began to play over the car speakers, effectively putting an end to the conversation, at least for the time being. Summer turned her attention to the big screen, hoping two hours of protracted western drama might take her mind off their ever-persistent differences.

It had been years since Summer had seen the 1960 classic, an old favorite of her father's. Yul Brynner as Chris Adams, leader of the ragtag band of gunslingers, stood out to Summer as one of his more impressive performances. During scenes when Brynner and costar Steve McQueen were on screen together, she remembered the discussion she'd had with her father about the two actors' purported on-set feud. She could see signs of the tension between them when they were in the same scene, and it made her shake her head. *Nothing more than your typical pissing contest between two men trying to outdo each other.*

During the scene where Petra made her declaration of love to Chico, Aiko eased her hand across the center console, letting her palm rest on Summer's thigh. Summer immediately felt the charge emanating from the point of contact between Aiko's hand and her skin, which was bared by the pink denim miniskirt she'd worn for their date. Summer didn't flinch or move away from the contact because, despite their ongoing disagreement, she couldn't deny the attraction crackling between them like lightning.

Aiko's hand remained there for the rest of the movie, occasionally giving a soft squeeze. Each time, a new jolt of desire snaked its way through Summer's body, reminding her of how long it had been since she'd been properly made love to and of the promise of fulfillment she sensed rolling off Aiko.

After the movie ended, Aiko drew her hand away. "I'll be right back. I'm going to talk to Logan for a sec." She opened the door and got out, leaving Summer alone in the car.

Summer looked at the spot where Aiko's hand had been, still feeling the heat radiating there. Now that the film was over, they had the rest of the night ahead of them, and she knew exactly how she wanted to spend it.

Aiko returned, buckled, and started the car. "I don't wanna keep you out too late on a school night, teach." She winked. "So let's get you home."

Summer smiled, then nodded.

As they traversed the route back to her downtown apartment, they conversed about the movie.

"I guess I can see why Logan thought of it as a movie about team-work," Aiko commented. "Those guys really did stick together through a whole lot of mess."

"Yeah, that's definitely true." Summer chuckled. "And not all of them made it out alive."

"Let's hope things at the office never get quite so intense." Aiko shook her head with a short laugh. "I like my coworkers but I ain't taking a bullet for any of them."

Summer snorted. "Big facts. It was very short on emotional scenes, though. That little subplot between Chico and Petra was basically it. I think there coulda been a little less gunfighting and little more romance."

"If it's romance you want, I got you covered, baby." Aiko glanced at Summer long enough to wink, then turned her eyes back to the road.

"You're something else."

"Entirely." Aiko stopped at a red light. "Follow me on this, though. The movie is about teamwork, friendship, courage, and all that good shit. But I took another meaning from it."

Intrigued, Summer asked, "What's that?"

"The core theme of the film is risking it all for what you think is right. Even though it could all go bad, and you could lose big, you take the risk anyway. You follow your heart even though you have no real control over the outcome."

Summer sucked on her bottom lip, feeling her body temperature climb a degree. "Really."

"Really. If you look at it that way, it could be about love." Aiko drove through the intersection as the light turned green. "Any time you open your heart, let someone see the real you, you're taking the risk of getting hurt." She paused. "But if you truly feel it's right, you let yourself fall anyway. Because if you're right, it's gonna be worth the risk, and more."

Watching Aiko's profile, Summer felt her heart do an Olympic gymnastics–level flip.

"Obviously, our views on certain things are very different, and I don't know if that will ever change. What I do know is how much I enjoy your company, and how good you make me feel." Aiko's words were soft but spoken with conviction.

Summer's pulse quickened. "I feel it, too, Aiko. Being with you just feels natural."

As Aiko turned the vehicle onto Brazos, she said, "It's getting late, and we both have to work tomorrow. If you want me to just drop you off, I won't be offended. I don't want to monopolize your whole night."

Summer reached over the console, then rested her hand against Aiko's forearm. "I can't think of any better use of my time than for you to park this car in the garage and bring your fine ass upstairs with me."

A grin spread over Aiko's face. "Oh, so it's like that?"

"It absolutely is." Summer turned her head to surreptitiously glance behind her. "Did you bring what I asked you to bring?"

"Yeah. I didn't know when I'd see you again, so I wanted to be prepared." She held up her thumb and jerked it backward. "It's in the back."

Now it was Summer's turn to smile as Aiko stopped, then made a quick turn into the garage beneath the building.

—

Aiko parked the car in Summer's secondary space, then got out and went around to help her out, as usual.

As soon as Summer's sandals hit the pavement, Summer whispered, "Grab your backpack or whatever."

"In a hurry, baby?"

Shifting her weight from one foot to the other, Summer sucked on her lower lip again and nodded.

Needing nothing beyond her silent affirmative, Aiko opened the rear passenger door and grabbed her crossbody bag from the floorboard.

Summer eyed Aiko curiously.

Aiko shrugged. "The backpack's kinda stereotypical, isn't it?"

Summer answered with a giggle, her eyes sultry. "I really don't care what you carry it around in. I'm far more interested in what you can do with it."

Using the plastic buckle to clip the bag around her body and letting the pouch rest on her right hip, she smiled. "Don't worry. You about to find out."

While they walked into the building through the garage entrance, Aiko purposely fell back a few steps to watch Summer walk. Summer's outfit—a light-pink camisole, hot-pink denim miniskirt, and that cute little white crocheted shrug she favored—complemented her curvy frame nicely. On the way to the elevator, Aiko took full advantage of her position, enjoying the sexy sway of Summer's hips beneath her closely fitted skirt and the sight of Summer's long brown legs—legs that Aiko had every intention of throwing over her shoulders at the first reasonable opportunity.

Inside the confines of the apartment building's elevator, Aiko pulled Summer into her arms. Summer's big brown eyes connected with hers, and with a groan, Aiko brought Summer's chin up so their lips could meet.

What began as a series of brief, sweet kisses quickly morphed into longer, hungrier ones. Their mouths stayed fused as the elevator ascended toward the ninth floor, though Aiko didn't recall it taking this long before. Urgency and heat seemed to charge the very air around them, filling the elevator car with invisible yet perceptible steam. Aiko swept her tongue through the cavern of Summer's mouth, again and again, drawing a moan from her throat.

As the car finally, mercifully halted, the bell dinged to herald their arrival on the proper floor, and the doors parted. Aiko reluctantly dragged her lips away from Summer's and let herself be pulled along by the hand out of the elevator and into the corridor. The glazed cement floors echoed their footsteps as they jogged to Summer's door, where she pulled her keys out of her skirt pocket and unlocked the door.

They fumbled their way inside, a tangle of lips and limbs as Summer reached around Aiko to close and lock the door behind them. The motion briefly broke the contact between their mouths until Summer grabbed the front of Aiko's tank top, dragged her face closer, and captured her lips again. The small show of aggression sent Aiko's desire soaring another ten notches, and she slid her hands down Summer's body, grasping handfuls of her pillow-soft ass.

Bodies fused, they moved down the hallway to the back of the apartment, where Summer shifted to the right and maneuvered them into her bedroom. They came to a stop as Summer backed up to the foot of the bed and lowered herself into a sitting position there.

Standing above her, Aiko ran her hand over the rich, dark tresses of Summer's twists, giving the ends a gentle tug.

Gazing at Aiko, eyes simmering with heat, Summer tugged off the open halves of Aiko's button-down.

After unclipping her bag, Aiko removed it, set it next to Summer on the bed, and then slipped her arms out of the shirt. Summer took Aiko's shirt and tossed it unceremoniously to the floor. Then she reached into her skirt pocket, slipped out her phone, and swiped her finger across the screen.

Aiko's impatience was rising. *What is she doing? I don't know how much longer I can wait.* Tonight, nothing would disturb this groove; nothing would come between her and her determination to turn Summer's world inside out.

When the first notes of Corinne Bailey Rae's sensual tune "Closer" filled the room, Aiko smiled. "Setting the mood, I see. I was about to get restless."

"Can't have that." Summer dropped her phone on the pink shag rug near the bed, then slid a black chest from beneath the bed. She opened the latch, reached inside, and produced a sparkly blue dildo. After returning the chest to its hiding spot, Summer showed the toy to Aiko, then crawled over the silver brocade bedspread and slid it beneath the pile of silver-and-cream-colored pillows.

Making note of yet another silent hint, Aiko couldn't help licking her lips at the thought of what she wanted to do to Summer.

From her perch in the center of the bed, Summer beckoned to Aiko with a finger. "Come here."

Aiko moved next to her and began reveling in the soft kisses Summer placed against her forehead, her eyes, her cheeks, and then her lips. Pulling away, Summer caressed Aiko's arms and guided them up, then reached down to slip Aiko's tank top off. A bit thrown by Summer's take-charge manner, Aiko asked, "What are you about to do?"

"You said you had a long day. Let me help you release some tension, Aiko." Summer held Aiko's gaze as she reached around Aiko to undo the clasp of her soft-cup bra, then ease it away from her body.

Naked from the waist up, Aiko followed Summer's unspoken guidance and lay on her stomach across the fluffy bedding. She heard a bit of rustling around behind her, then shuddered when Summer's hands began to glide across her back with a skilled and smooth certainty she hadn't been prepared for.

Aiko felt a slight wetness in Summer's palms, and the aroma of rose and lavender filled her nostrils as the massage continued, melting away the lingering aches and tension in her back and shoulders. An involuntary groan of pleasure escaped Aiko as Summer leaned in, increasing the pressure as she moved the heels of her hands down Aiko's spine. That familiar warmth pulsed between Aiko's thighs, bringing with it the dewy slickness of awakened desire. Summer kept up her motions until something popped, and Aiko groaned again. "Oh, shit, girl."

"You like that?"

"Yes," she half-said, half-sighed. Summer's ministrations had relieved her of an ailment she hadn't known she had until it miraculously disappeared.

Summer chuckled. "Good. Because I have talents you can't even fathom."

Aiko rolled over onto her back, noting the way Summer's gaze drifted down to her bare breasts. "You've got good hands. Now let me show you mine." Aiko grabbed the back of Summer's neck and pulled her down for a kiss. When Aiko released her, she smiled at the slow, panting breaths Summer took.

Getting off the bed, Aiko tugged Summer's hand until Summer stood before her. With a slow and deliberate touch, Aiko caressed her out of her clothing, from her shrug, camisole, and skirt, then stripped off her yellow lacy balconette bra and matching thong. Then Aiko paused, her hand lingering at the base of Summer's throat, and simply looked at Summer. The beauty of her naked body arrested and captivated Aiko. The fullness of her breasts, the slight swell of her belly, the flare of her hips, the roundness of her ass, and the thickness of her thighs capped by a triangle of black curls—the sight of her was nothing less than glorious.

Aiko closed her hand slightly, applying the tiniest bit of pressure to the area where Summer's throat met her shoulders. "Do you like this?"

Summer's eyelids drooped, and her head lolled to the side as she hissed, "Yes."

Using her free hand, Aiko gently pushed Summer back until she fell across the bed. She ran worshipping hands over her body, enjoying the softness of her. When Summer's soft croons rose in the silence, Aiko felt confident Summer knew how talented her hands were, so she let her mouth take over. She started by kissing Summer's lips, then moved down the side of her neck and flicked her tongue over the sensitive nook of her collarbone.

Summer's moans stretched and expanded as Aiko took one dark nipple into her mouth, then the other. Aiko's arousal grew in tandem with Summer's—each cry or sharply drawn breath pushing Aiko further and further toward the apex of need.

After kissing her way down the plane of Summer's belly, Aiko smiled as she draped Summer's juicy thighs over her shoulders at long last. Aiko leaned in, hovering over her pussy, inhaling the intoxicating aroma. She stroked the tip of her finger through Summer's wet folds, smiling at the strangled sound Summer made. A breath later, Aiko dragged her tongue over her pussy, and Summer uttered a low curse.

"Fuck!"

That's what I'm gonna do, baby. Aiko thrilled at the taste of Summer as she took her time exploring every peak and valley of her pussy with her tongue. Beneath Aiko's impassioned feasting, Summer trembled, her thighs shaking. The tremors intensified, as did Summer's moans, until a deep, full-body shudder overtook her, and she screamed. Aiko remained at work until Summer clamped her thighs down, threatening to crush her head. Wriggling free, Aiko sat up and let Summer's legs drop. She smiled as she took in the sight of Summer, spread open, back arched, like a sensual work of art.

Stripping out of her shorts and panties, Aiko reached beneath the pillows, then fitted the dildo into her harness before donning it. Once she was properly attired, she knelt between Summer's splayed legs and bent low to kiss her lips. "Are you ready for me to come inside, love?"

Summer crooned the response against her ear. "Please."

Aiko adjusted herself, then tilted her hips forward ever so slowly. She could feel the tight grip of Summer's pussy on the strap, and she let Summer reposition herself, moving accordingly. Summer had other notions, however, because she grabbed Aiko's hips and yanked until their pelvises touched and the strap was completely buried.

Seeing how ready Summer was, Aiko began the ride with slow strokes. She rested one hand on Summer's breast and gripped her hip with the other, providing leverage for her thrusts. Summer's throaty moans, and the way she alternated between squeezing Aiko's hips and digging her acrylics into Aiko's back, indicated her rising pleasure.

Aiko's pussy grew wetter by the moment from the combination of Summer's cries and the pressure of the base of the dildo against her own clit. Soon Aiko started to hear two sets of moans, and she knew she didn't have long before she came.

Aiko shifted her pelvis a bit, changing the angle of penetration.

"Right there," Summer whispered. "Oh, God, right there."

The new angle proved beneficial to them both because Aiko felt her inner walls begin to flex. "Shit." Orgasm caught hold of her before she could take her next breath, and she cursed again. "Fuck."

Aiko's sounds were overshadowed by Summer, who called her name as she dug her nails into the sides of Aiko's waist, clinging to her as if she were the last lifeboat in a storm.

Aiko moved to ease out of Summer's body, inadvertently kneeling in a damp spot on the comforter as she did so. *So there was a flood . . . and we probably both contributed to it.* Rolling onto her side, she faced Summer and drew Summer's still-shaking form into her arms. Making love to her had been even more amazing than she could have imagined. Holding her close in the silent aftermath didn't rank far behind.

In the silence, Aiko simply held her and listened to her rapid breaths, aware of the way they matched with her own. She was tired, sweaty, and satisfied, and if Summer's manner were any indication, Summer felt similarly. "You okay?"

Face pressed against Aiko's chest, Summer nodded and murmured, "Yeah." A moment later, their eyes met in the darkness. "You're amazing."

"You definitely gave me the proper inspiration." Aiko squeezed Summer's ass. "A body like yours deserves nothing less."

Summer made a sound low in her throat as she slipped from Aiko's grasp and slid down her body. "You know I gotta get you back, right?"

Aiko sucked in a breath as Summer rolled her onto her back, then nudged her thighs apart. "Girl . . ."

"Shhh." Summer laid herself between Aiko's legs, moving the harness aside. "Time for payback, boo."

A moment later, at the first deep, thorough pass of Summer's tongue, Aiko's eyes rolled back.

CHAPTER TWELVE

Summer awakened with a start, blinking her eyes to allow them to adjust to the predawn glow flowing through her sheer curtains. She shifted a bit, releasing herself from the sheet she'd rolled herself in during the night. Aiko, sprawled on her back like a starfish, snored next to her, comforter draped over her body from the waist down.

For a moment, Summer simply watched Aiko sleep. Aiko's face held an expression of restful peace, her features relaxed and open. Her round breasts rose and fell in time with her breath, nipples standing like dark jewels against her skin, begging to be tasted. Summer licked her lips but decided against awakening Aiko since she'd been tired the night before.

She reached toward the nightstand for her phone. *Six thirty-four . . . early enough to beat the breakfast rush.*

Still nude from last night's erotic encounter, Summer turned over and scooted toward the edge of the bed. She stood, stretched, and tiptoed to the bathroom. After washing up and getting dressed in a pair of khaki pants and a green polo with the Young Scholars logo on it, she wrestled her slightly frizzy twists into a low ponytail, then stepped into a pair of gold ballet flats. Grabbing her purse and keys, she glanced again at Aiko's sleeping form before heading downstairs to the parking garage.

Summer took the short drive to satisfy her early-morning craving, traveling down Brazos to Cesar Chavez. Soon, she pulled up to the familiar melon-colored cement exterior of Juan in a Million. The local family-owned eatery was one of her favorite spots for breakfast. Knowing the restaurant still thrived now, having been a staple of East Austin since 1980, did her heart good.

She pulled into a parking spot, then got out of the car to join the short line of other early birds like her who'd come to enjoy the signature breakfast offerings. She stood in line for about ten minutes before making it inside the small building. Stepping to the counter just to the right of the door, she inhaled the heavenly aroma and smiled. She could smell spices, fresh jalapeños, and the smoky evidence of grilled meats. Looking to the wall of framed family photos and newspaper clippings behind the counter, she was filled with an altogether comforting sense of place.

She placed an order for two chorizo-and-potato breakfast tacos, with sides of chips and guac, then stepped aside and sat at the empty two-top table near the coin-operated candy machines to wait. Within ten minutes, she was out the door, still-warm paper bag in hand.

While driving back home, her stomach growled loudly in response to the delectable smell filling the cabin of her car. Turning on the radio, she heard the familiar notes of the classic Zhané ballad "Crush." Normally, she wouldn't be so moved by an old tune from the late '90s, randomly played by a DJ on the local throwback station. But considering that very song had been playing over her wireless speaker last night when Aiko first entered her, her reaction was much more pronounced.

Summer's pulse quickened as the memories flooded her mind, and she suddenly felt warm all over. She recalled the searing heat she'd felt, the girth of the dildo as its veined surface touched her walls, and the delicious friction of Aiko's skillful stroking.

The encounter had been steamy, soul-shaking, and amazingly pleasurable. It had been over a year since she'd last had a full sexual encounter, but much longer since she'd made love with someone on Aiko's level. That one-night stand during her junior year of college felt like ancient history, even more so now that Aiko had shown her everything she'd been missing out on. Even her hormone-fueled teenage fantasies of Aiko couldn't have lived up to the torrid reality. Aiko wore her intellectuality and charm on her sleeve, and she was something of a flirt. Aiko had warned Summer what to expect—in that overconfident, almost braggadocious way she'd responded to her offer to come upstairs. Still, Summer hadn't fully taken her seriously.

Who knew she could talk all that shit and back it up, too?

Summer returned to her apartment, shifting things around at the door so she'd have a free hand to unlock it. Once inside, she kicked off her shoes, set the bag on the bar between her kitchen and living room, and went back to her bedroom to see if Aiko was still asleep.

Peeking inside the room, Summer found Aiko sitting on the side of the bed, her back to Summer. She was fully dressed except for the button-down shirt, and she busied herself by scrolling through her phone.

"Good morning." Summer walked around to that side of the bed, smiling. "How long have you been up?"

Aiko smiled back, stifling a yawn before she answered. "My alarm went off like five minutes ago." She pocketed her phone and stood. "Where did you go?"

"Over to Juan in a Million, to grab some breakfast. Are you hungry?"

"Yeah, I could definitely eat."

Summer started walking to the kitchen, Aiko close behind. "Go ahead and sit, and I'll grab us a couple of waters. I'll put on some coffee, too."

Aiko waved her hand as she sat on one of the tall stools. "I'll just take a water. I've got to go by my house before going to work, and I don't want to be late."

Summer nodded, retrieving two bottles of water from the bottom shelf of her fridge. Joining Aiko at the bar, she took out the wrapped tacos, chips, and guacamole and set them out on the granite surface. "I got chorizo-and-potato, I hope that's okay."

"I haven't tried that one," Aiko admitted. "But I've never had a bad taco from Juan in a Million, so I'm game."

Summer dug into her taco, her taste buds rejoicing. She loved the combination of flavors and textures: the snap of spicy chorizo and crisp potato, surrounded by the subtle sweetness of the soft tortilla. "What do you think?"

"Pretty good," Aiko replied between bites.

They finished their food in silence, and Summer couldn't help wondering what was on Aiko's mind. *She seems pretty quiet . . . maybe it's been a while for her, too.*

As Summer cleared their trash and threw it away, she said, "I really enjoyed last night. I'm glad you decided to stay."

Aiko drained the last of her water, then showed her a slight smile. "So am I. I think we really connected well."

"Me, too. I haven't been fucked like that in . . . well, ever. No one's even come close in the last several years." Summer walked back around to the side of the bar in the living room and stepped behind Aiko's stool, draping her arms over her shoulders.

She noticed that while Aiko didn't shun her embrace, she didn't lean into it either.

Aiko chuckled. "That's quite a compliment."

Summer moved to Aiko's side, bringing her hand to cup Aiko's chin. After placing a soft kiss on her lips, she whispered, "I can't wait to experience you again."

"I'd love to give you the full tour again right now." Aiko's eyes changed, momentarily displaying the same heated desire Summer had seen in them last night. Their gazes caught and held for several long, silent beats, and Summer seriously considered calling in sick today so she could stay home and discover all the new ways she and Aiko could make each other scream.

"I . . . feel like I can be honest with you." Part of Summer felt like an absolute fool for letting her feelings get to this level, but maybe this was destiny. Aiko had been her crush way back when, and she thought she'd put that youthful obsession aside. Seeing her again had shown her just how wrong that assumption was. Now that she'd gotten to know Aiko and seen how far she exceeded her fantasies, how could she not fall for her? "I think . . . I mean, I'm pretty sure . . ."

Then Aiko blinked, and the fire in her gaze seemed to disappear—extinguished in an instant. "I'm sorry to rush off, but I need to go so I won't be late for work."

Swallowing the emotional speech she'd been building to, Summer gave her best nonchalant chuckle instead. "Perils of gettin' busy on a weeknight, I suppose." She gave Aiko one more kiss, then backed away to allow Aiko space to get down from the stool. "I won't hold you up."

Aiko went to the bedroom, leaving Summer to her own thoughts. *What just happened? Is she really in a hurry? Or did she anticipate what I was about to say and cut me off to keep me from saying it?*

Summer didn't have long to ponder because Aiko soon returned with her button-down and sneakers back on. Summer's eyes drifted to the crossbody bag on her hip, and when she looked up again, she found Aiko wearing a Cheshire-cat smile. "Don't worry. Me and my equipment will be back."

Summer laughed despite the tangle of feelings inside; amusement and desire overrode all else. "Go on to work before I pin you to the sofa and make you pay for that smart mouth."

Aiko threw her an exaggerated wink, kissed her on the cheek, and headed for the door, tossing a quick goodbye over her shoulder as she departed.

Summer stood there for a few moments, wondering how she'd be able to focus on finalizing her lesson plans today. *I don't have a choice but to get it together; tomorrow is the first day of school.*

She brewed herself a cup of coffee to go, then grabbed her tote bag. Throwing her small purse and phone inside, she set out for work.

Once she was behind her desk in her classroom, she took her lesson-plan book out of the top drawer, opened it, and laid it out in front of her. The school's curriculum incentivized curiosity and emphasized exploration and hands-on learning as its main tenets, setting it apart from teaching models that required children to be docile and passive.

She was reading over one of her lesson plans when she heard someone enter the room through the door she'd left open.

"Hey, Summer." Olivia approached the desk, holding the two rolls of tape she'd borrowed. She was dressed in another festive scrub top, this one with the planets of the solar system as the print. "Sorry it took me so long to bring these back, I kept forgetting."

"Let me guess. Beginning of the year overwhelm?"

"Big time." Olivia laughed. "I just keep looking over my lesson plans and pacing around the classroom, worried that I forgot something."

"I definitely understand where you're coming from," Summer said with a chuckle. "But remember what the school philosophy is. Child-centered learning."

"Logically, I know that. It's just a holdover habit from when I taught traditional school, I guess."

Summer stuck her pencil into the base of her ponytail. "I'm not sure what brought you to Young Scholars. But I know I chose to take a position in this school because I honestly think it's a superior learning environment, especially for very young children."

Olivia nodded. "Then we're basically here for the same reason."

"So that means our main jobs are to be the best facilitators for their natural curiosity about the world as we can and to keep them safe while they learn."

"You're right." Olivia's brow rose. "How many years have you been teaching again?"

"Nine, but this is my first year in a private school."

"Well, you talk like a seasoned vet." Olivia returned the tape to the box on the corner of the desk. "If I get overwhelmed tomorrow, I'm gonna come find you."

"I'm sure you'll be fine, O." She laughed. "And if not, we can always rendezvous in the lounge for a pep talk."

"Thanks, Summer." Olivia left the room.

Alone again, Summer returned her attention to her lesson-plan book. She reached back for the pencil she'd tucked in her hair, then erased some of her earlier notes and rewrote them more legibly. *I'll have enough to do tomorrow without having to decipher my own terrible handwriting.*

She was still writing when an image of Aiko entered her mind. She smiled but tucked thoughts of her away for later. For the moment, she had serious work to do.

Aiko took a seat on an empty barstool at Halcyon in the Warehouse District just after six o'clock on Tuesday evening. She let her eyes sweep over the open shelves displaying the finest liquor and the staff moving back and forth behind the bar.

All around her, the place teemed with activity. It wasn't wall-to-wall packed as it would be on a Friday, but it was still a sizable crowd for a Tuesday. The coffee bar and lounge served breakfast and light bites and featured a number of unique cocktails, including recipes that combined coffee and spirits. It seemed the idea of mixing caffeine with alcohol was a hit with the locals. Any weekday between the hours of four and eight o'clock, Halcyon was the spot of choice for many young professionals working in and around Austin looking to blow off some steam after a long day.

The interior was reminiscent of a barn, its beige brick walls rising toward a high ceiling that featured exposed wooden beams and a huge, crimped steel pipe that extended across it. The floors, bar, and tables were all fashioned from different varieties of wood, adding to the rustic yet modern feel.

There was one empty stool to her left, so Aiko placed her work portfolio on the white plastic seat. A bartender approached, and she ordered a glass of water, wanting to hold off on ordering more until Peaches arrived.

Peaches came in about ten minutes after Aiko, wearing a navy-blue short-sleeved polo and matching baseball cap with slightly baggy dark denim jeans and a pair of gray Timberland boots. She grinned when she saw Aiko and quickly found the empty stool. "Sorry, I'm late. Traffic getting over here was a bitch." Peaches reached out and gave Aiko a half-hug around the shoulder. "You looking mighty sharp, playa."

"It's cool, I haven't been here long." Aiko grabbed her portfolio before Peaches sat down. "And thanks for the compliment." She'd come here straight from work and was still attired in the burgundy slacks, pale pink button-down, and burgundy vest she'd worn into the office. She'd forgone her tie today in favor of leaving a few buttons loose at her throat. She gestured to Peaches' feet perched on the lower bar of the stool. "I like the Timbs, very stylish. I see you."

"Please. Look at you with the fine brown leather oxfords." Peaches held up one hand, extending her pinkie. "I'm tryna get on your level!"

"Now we both know that ain't likely." Aiko laughed. "But I applaud your efforts, though."

Peaches rolled her eyes, but the smile remained on her face. "Did you order yet?" She reached for one of the laminated menus and brought it closer to her.

"Nah, I waited for your ass." Aiko gave her a playful punch on the shoulder.

The bartender returned. "What can I get you?"

"I'll have a Queen Bee and the grilled cheese sandy bites," Aiko said.

Peaches glanced at the laminated menu for a few moments before speaking. "Let me have an Ibuprofen and a chicken quesadilla."

After the bartender left, Aiko asked, "Peaches, why the hell do you do that every time we come here?"

"Do what?"

"Look at the menu, then order the same thing you order literally every time?"

Peaches laughed. "I do it just to piss you off, my G."

Aiko cringed but found herself laughing anyway. Ever since that first semester at UT, their relationship had always had its basis in goofy jokes and shit-talking. When it came right down to it, though, they always had each other's back.

Peaches turned her way while they waited for their orders. "So. Give me the details on what went down last night between you and Lil' Miss Activist."

Aiko shook her head. "First of all, I'm sure she'd hate that nickname. But anyway, we went to the Blue Starlite up in Round Rock."

Peaches touched her shoulder. "A, I'm gon' have to stop you right there. When I said I wanted to hear about your night, that ain't what I meant."

Aiko rolled her eyes. "Really, Peaches?"

"You already know the deal." Peaches squeezed Aiko's shoulder. "Come on, now. Give me the good stuff."

Aiko gestured to the bustling crowd filling Halcyon's interior for the popular happy hour. "We're not exactly in a private place. I'm not about to give you all the details while we sitting in here."

"Damn, you right. Streets is watching." Peaches released a long, dramatic sigh. "All right, I guess you can give me the PG version of events. At least until we're somewhere more private."

Their orders arrived then, and Aiko took a quick sip of her drink. The signature drink, made with gin, honey-ginger syrup, and fresh-squeezed lime juice, had a refreshing sweetness along with an intriguing spicy kick. Aiko popped a cheesy bite into her mouth and groaned. The drink and the snack complemented each other well.

"Don't get quiet on me now," Peaches insisted between mouthfuls of her quesadilla. "Tell me what happened."

Rubbing her hands together, Aiko shifted slightly in her seat, so she faced her friend. "All right. So I'm driving her home from the movie. We'd had this intense conversation about the changes in Austin before it started, but afterward, she seemed pretty chill. We were just discussing the movie and its themes . . ."

"Wait, what movie?"

"*The Magnificent Seven.*"

"Yul Brynner or Denzel Washington? You know I love my westerns."

"You're such a trip." Aiko scoffed as she took another sip from her glass. "A minute ago you were rushing me past this part."

"Whatever. Which version was it? I need to know, for contextual purposes."

Aiko chuckled. "Yul Brynner."

"Bet. Go ahead."

She eyed her friend for a moment before continuing. "Anyway, we're talking, and I'm like, it's late, I'm gonna take you home because we both have to work in the morning. And she's like, bring your fine ass upstairs."

Peaches' head tilted to the right, and a half-smile twisted her lips. "Oh, word?"

"Yeah, she wasn't trying to get dropped off. So I said, cool. She asked me if I had my bag with me . . ."

Peaches whistled. "Aw, shit. Please tell me you had it, A."

"Of course I did. You know I roll prepared. Anyway, grabbed my bag, we went up to her apartment and . . ." She threw up her hands. "Soon as we hit the door, it was on."

"And did you emerge victoriously?"

"Of course I did. More than once." Aiko laughed. "But then again, so did she."

Peaches shook her head with an expression of mock solemnity. "Gotta pour out a little liquor for the homie that got slutted out."

Aiko's laugh morphed into a cackle. "Hush, dummy."

"I'm just playing. You know I'm not about to waste no liquor." To emphasize her point, Peaches lifted her glass and drained the rest of the contents. "But honestly, though. Overall, how was it?"

Aiko felt the smile tugging her lips as she recalled last night's lovemaking with Summer. "She was amazing. Her body is so soft, she's a little freaky, and she wasn't too shy to vocalize and let me know when I got it right." She finished her own drink. "Definitely one of the best I ever had."

"That's what's up. I'm happy you had a good night, playa." Peaches gave Aiko's upper arm a supportive slap. "So, does this mean she's gonna stop protesting and carrying on around your jobsite?"

Aiko sighed. "Unfortunately, I don't think so."

Peaches sucked in a breath. "Then you got a problem. Sis is gonna get you fired if she keeps this up." Peaches raised her hand, signaling for a refill on her drink. "How in the world is this thing between you two gonna work out?"

Aiko shrugged. "I honestly don't know. Don't you think I've been asking myself that same question, ever since we went on the first date?"

"Maybe you have, but it hasn't kept you from seeing her." Peaches thanked the bartender as she accepted her second drink. "You do know that pretending there's not a problem won't make it go away, right?"

"I know." Aiko sighed, then took a drink of water as she resisted the temptation to order a refill. "We've talked about it, but we keep going back and forth without either of us really changing the way we approach the situation. We've got this agree-to-disagree arrangement right now."

"The question is whether that's sustainable long-term." Peaches appeared thoughtful as she took another bite of her quesadilla and chewed. "I really don't think it is."

"As much as I hate to admit it, you're probably right." She'd spent most of her downtime at work today thinking about Summer and how much she enjoyed being with her, at least until the topic of the First Avenue project came up, which it inevitably did. "I'm really torn because I know there's a pretty good chance this won't end well."

"So why do you keep going back?"

"My feelings are too wrapped up in her to just walk away."

"Oh, snap. Pimp down." Peaches shook her head grimly. "She must really be something special. It's been a minute since I seen you this pressed over anyone."

"She is special." As she said the words, an image of Summer's radiant smile flashed across her mind. *I'd do just about anything to keep that smile on her face, and that's precisely the problem.* "And I think she's just as invested in being with me."

Peaches' brow arched. "What makes you say that?"

"This morning before I left, I feel like she was about to make some kind of declaration."

"What you mean, 'about to'? You cut sis off or something?"

"Basically." Aiko cringed when she thought back on the moment and how she'd reacted. "She caught me off guard. I was already late for work, and I just didn't have time to have that level of conversation right then."

"Aiko, if you weren't ready to hear what she was trying to tell you, just say that! Sheesh." Peaches leaned against the barstool's backrest, feigning exhaustion. "You're killing me, you know that?"

"I'm the one whose life is really on the line here. I might have to choose between a woman and my career. Who the hell wants to be in that position?"

Peaches patted her on the back. "I don't know what to tell you. Except this. I'm here for you either way."

"Thanks, Peaches." Aiko offered a small smile. Their friendship had gotten her through many rough patches and sticky situations over the years, and she was glad she had Peaches' crazy yet consistent presence to fall back on should things go left.

CHAPTER THIRTEEN

As Summer shepherded her six pupils outside through the classroom's rear door Wednesday, she could feel the exhaustion beginning to creep up on her. She expected four more students to join the class within the next week after returning from their various summer vacations. Wiping the back of her hand over her brow, she did the same quick head count she did whenever she escorted the children from one space to another.

As each child passed by her, she silently recited their names.

Ella, Samantha, Max, Imani, Madison, and Jeffrey. Four girls, two boys.

The moment they cleared the small cement patio, the kids took off running, scrambling around the fenced-in play area. She stood back for a few minutes, letting them release some of their pent-up energy under her watchful gaze. She smiled at the exuberant and carefree way they played. Adulthood would come soon enough to steal away their innocence and unbridled joy, but for now, the world was theirs to explore.

After they'd had a chance to run around a bit, she gathered them all around the small raised garden bed set aside for her class. She'd constructed it herself, with a little help from Olivia, when she'd come into work a couple of weeks ago. It was a simple structure consisting of four thick wooden rails nailed together and placed over the landscaping fabric they'd pinned to the ground. "Okay, students. Let's get started with our class garden." She walked to the fence and took the lid off the big plastic tote she'd filled with garden soil. "Who wants to start getting our dirt inside the bed?"

The response was enthusiastic and immediate, and within moments, all six children were using the various pails and scoops she gave them to fill the bed with soil. As time went on and their interest waned, she hoisted the tote and poured the rest of the dirt in.

Kneeling in the grass, she clapped her hands together. "Okay. Now, we're going to spread the soil out. I'll show you how, it's like frosting a cake." Using the back of a plastic shovel, she started flattening out the top of the soil.

She spent the next half hour working with the children to dig holes, place sweet pea plants in them, and form small mounds of dirt around their young roots.

Her eyes flitted between the kids, mindful of their every move as they worked together on the class garden. She gently reached out and stayed one of her students' hands, keeping him from pounding his seedling into mush. "Gently, Jeffrey. Put in the seed, then gently pack the dirt, honey."

He laughed in response. "Okay, lady."

She shook her head, doing her best to keep her expression neutral despite the laughter bubbling inside. "My name is Miss Graves, remember?"

His head bobbed vigorously in the affirmative.

She then gathered her collection of small watering pails, filled them partway, and distributed them to the children. She watched as they watered the plants, glad she'd anticipated the potential of overwatering before passing out the pails. The children had different approaches to the task: Madison, Ella, and Imani gently rained water over the seedlings through the spout, while Jeffrey, Max, and Samantha chose the quicker, slightly more aggressive method of turning the pail upside down and dumping the contents on their plants.

Remembering to tie their task to a practical fact, she said, "It gets very hot this time of the year, so we'll have to come out here and check on our plants every day, to see if they're thirsty."

"Thirsty plants," Madison parroted with a giggle.

Summer laughed. *They're so stinking precious at this age.* "That's right, Maddy."

She took them back inside then, shutting the door behind them. "Okay, everyone. Let's use the restroom." She assisted as the children took bathroom breaks one by one, shepherding them in turn to the low wall-mounted sink to wash their hands. When they'd finished, she guided them to the bright blue carpet in the reading center. "Let's sit on our dots, please." Once each small bottom was firmly placed on a corresponding dot, she went to the shelf and pulled out the book she'd planned to read today.

After taking a seat in her glider rocker, she held the book for everyone to see. "Today, we're going to read *Chicka Chicka Boom Boom*, by Bill Martin Jr. and John Archambault." The book was a classic and a favorite among early-childhood teachers because of the clever way it helped students begin to recognize and retain the letters of the alphabet. The brightly colored illustrations were also a hit and very effective at capturing and holding the attention of young children.

When the story was done, and she and the children had lunch, Summer tucked them into their individual cots and switched off the overhead lights. Setting the sound machine to play a nature track that included chirping crickets and a soft breeze, she pulled her chair to her desk and took a long, deep inhale.

After reaching into her tote, she pulled out her phone. She kept it on silent during the school day to cut down on possible distractions. Swiping through all the random emails and app notifications, she frowned. *Aiko hasn't texted me today.* She knew it would be immature to pout, but she couldn't shake the disappointment of knowing Aiko hadn't reached out.

Maybe she's just busy. Or maybe she's avoiding me . . .

Seeing no benefit in dwelling on that line of thought, she pushed it away and instead tapped out a quick text to Crystal.

Are we still on for coffee?

Yeah. I'll meet you at the Starbucks by the school at 2.

After reading her sister's response, she set a timer and put the phone on her desk. She quietly handled a few odds and ends around the classroom, careful not to disturb the children.

While she worked, her mind strayed to Aiko. Summer remembered how hot Aiko had been, how the wetness had gathered between her thighs when Aiko kissed her, how it felt to have Aiko's slow hands gliding over her skin.

When the alarm went off, she silenced it, then roused the children and got them to the science center. As the afternoon continued, the children went to the cubbies to gather their things for dismissal. Parents began arriving to pick up the children, and by a quarter till two, she was alone in the room, reflecting on a busy but pleasant first day. She took time to straighten things in preparation for the next day, then left.

Just after two o'clock, she was sitting at a two-top table near the back of the coffee shop, with Crystal across from her. Crystal wore the royal-blue shirt, black blazer, and black slacks that comprised her uniform as front desk manager at Hotel Azure, a boutique hotel situated on the banks of the Colorado River, near Lake Austin Marina.

"So," Crystal asked as she took a sip of her cold brew, "tell me all about your first day of school."

Summer smiled. "You make it sound like I'm a kid and you're my mom. Anyway, it was great. I only had two of my kids cry this morning at drop-off, and nothing in my classroom is broken beyond repair, so I'd call that a win."

Crystal laughed. "What did you do with them all day? I can't imagine keeping up with that many toddlers for several hours at a stretch."

"I'm not gonna lie, it's kinda like herding cats. But more fun, I think." She tasted her iced green tea, grimacing at the slight bitterness. Stirring it with her straw to better distribute the sweetener, she continued, "Today was mostly about introducing them to me, and to the classroom. New environment, new person. But we did get the class garden off to a solid start."

"Aw, that sounds so cute." A sort of goofy grin came over Crystal's face. "I can picture them playing in the dirt." Crystal chuckled. "What did you plant?"

"Sweet pea seedlings. They're hardy, relatively easy to take care of, and the kids can eat them once they're fully grown. They get a science lesson, and hopefully a willingness to eat vegetables. Two birds, you know."

"See? That kind of thinking is what makes you such a good teacher." Crystal nodded. "Yeah. By the end of the year, those kids will be ready for college."

"Not quite, but I appreciate your faith in me." She sipped the tea again, finding it much better this time around. She snapped her fingers, recalling something. "I was going to ask you if you heard anything else from the Travis County Historical Commission about our case."

Crystal nodded, but her expression turned grim. "I did, but it wasn't the news we wanted to hear. They basically said that if the city wouldn't intervene, they weren't inclined to do so, either."

Summer didn't bother holding back her sigh. "Yikes. Well, next stop, Texas State Historical Association."

"Yeah. And since I dealt with the city and the county, it's your turn this time."

Summer nodded. "Fair enough. The school day is short enough that I should be able to handle it tomorrow afternoon. That will give me enough time to build a strong case."

"Hopefully." Crystal shook her cup, and the ice rattled around inside. "Lay it on real thick. Give them the guilt trip; play the minority card. Do what you have to do to make them see how important this is. Grandma Beulah's accomplishments demand nothing less."

"I know, and I'll do my best to convince them to put a stop to this thing."

"What about you? Any news on your end?"

Summer shook her head. "As far as I know, the demolition is still scheduled to begin in earnest next week."

"You mean to tell me that's all you know, even though you've been spending time with one of the project architects?"

Summer cringed. "Yes, Crys. That's all I know. What do you think I've been doing, going out with her for the sole purpose of pumping her for information?"

She shrugged. "Maybe not the sole purpose, but I assumed that was part of it."

"Sheesh." Summer struggled to find the words that would effectively convey her frustration with her sister's assumption. Finally, she said, "Me dating Aiko isn't some kind of recon mission to get dirt on Abernathy. I care about her."

"Sorry, Summer. I didn't mean for it to sound like that." Crystal reached across the table and grabbed Summer's hand. Then Crystal shifted her gaze until their eyes met, observing Summer for a few silent moments. "Something's different, I can tell. It's written all over your face that something has changed."

Summer swallowed. "It's a little disconcerting to have someone stare at you and read your mind, Crys."

"What can I say? It's what big sisters do." She gave Summer's hand a gentle squeeze. "Now tell me what happened."

Summer sucked her lower lip, then took a deep breath. "Aiko and I went out Monday night."

"On a school night?" She sounded a bit incredulous.

"Oh, hush. I'm grown." Summer rolled her eyes. "Anyway, we went to the drive-in, then she took me home. She offered to drop me off since it was late and we both had work. I . . . asked her to come upstairs."

Crystal's eyes widened. "Oh. I think I see where this is going."

"Yeah, and you'd be right. We had sex, and it was the most amazing sex of my life." Summer kept her voice low because, while she didn't mind sharing with her sister, she didn't want to share with everyone else in the coffee shop. "You say something changed, and I can tell you exactly what that is. I've fallen in love with her, Crys." She sighed again. "Being with her in real life exceeded my fantasies by leaps and bounds, and I wasn't ready for it. I lost my heart, maybe on the first date. Either way, it's too late for me."

Crystal's expression morphed from a look of concerned curiosity into a soft smile. "I'm happy that you get to experience what love feels like, Summer. Honestly, I am. I just don't know what this means for Sojourner Truth."

Summer felt the emotion building and the tears welling in her throat. "It doesn't mean anything when it comes to that. Or at least, it doesn't have to."

Crystal answered with a slow shake of her head. "That's not true, sis. You have to choose. If Aiko isn't willing to intervene somehow in this project, how can you think she truly cares about you?"

"I never said she loved me back. But I do know she cares about me. She's said as much, and she's treated me with kindness and respect." One of Summer's deepest fears about this whole thing was the very real possibility that she was in love alone.

"I don't want to see you get hurt, Summer. So I'm going to say something that might sound harsh." Crystal gave Summer's hand another squeeze. "Get out now, before your feelings get any deeper."

An errant tear slid down Summer's cheek before she dashed it away. Needing a distraction, she picked up her phone and swiped the screen.

There was a text from Aiko.

Hi. I hope you had a good first day. 😍

It was cute but somehow rang hollow.

Unable to respond, she tucked the phone into her pocket and reached for a napkin to blot her eyes.

What if my sister is right?

⌒

Aiko took the last empty seat at the conference table Thursday morning and tucked her leather portfolio case into her lap. Sliding her chair closer to the table, she greeted architects Bill Talbot and Shirley Moore, who occupied the seats on either side of her. Bill, an older white man with a windswept brown comb-over, offered a wide grin reminiscent of a car salesman. Shirley, a Black woman around Miriam's age, offered a "Good morning" so quiet, Aiko could barely hear it.

Logan Warner, Aiko's direct supervisor, sat across the table from her, amusing himself with something on his phone. His occasional snorts indicated his consumption of something comedic. Next to him sat Zach Ames, another senior planner. He had a baby face, even though he was over thirty, and looked perpetually nervous. Zach ceased the rapid drumming of the end of his pen on the polished tabletop long enough to wave at Aiko, then started again. Nancy Drake, the young planner with curly red hair who worked with Bill, sat beside Zach. Pushing her glasses up on the bridge of her nose, she waggled her fingers in Aiko's direction.

At the head of the table sat company owner Miriam Abernathy. Miriam was wearing a smart yellow pantsuit, black top, and black pumps, her hair in a french roll with tendril curls at either temple. Miriam stood, then clapped her hands together as she often did to get people's attention. "Good morning, everyone. I'd like to get some updates on each of your team projects today. Let's start with the Kelsey Hotel Remodel team."

Bill stood. "The Kelsey Hotel remodel is moving along a little slower than we anticipated, due to supply shortages with our materials distributor. Thankfully, those issues have been resolved. We expect to catch back up to our original completion timeline within the next two to three weeks."

Miriam nodded. "Do you anticipate any further delays?"

"No, I don't," Bill answered. "The distributor already sent the materials to our construction partner, and I convinced them to give us a percentage off our next project as a way to make up for the delay."

Aiko couldn't help noticing the slight bluster in Bill's tone. It was something she'd come to expect whenever he spoke about his accomplishments; these meetings were his favorite place to brag about how great a worker he was. *He never holds back. I don't think he's got a humble bone in his body.*

"Excellent work, Bill." Miriam's smile indicated she was genuinely pleased. "All right. Shirley, what do you and Zach have for me on the North Austin Ambulatory Care Center project?"

Shirley nodded to Zach, who straightened his tie as he stood. "Shirley's a bit hoarse today, so I'll give the update. We've moved into the second phase of interior structural work and are now fine-tuning the details: putting in windows, outfitting plumbing, and running electrical wiring."

"And how long do you think it will be before Ulrich Interiors can get into the building?" Miriam asked.

"We should be ready for the interior designers to come in about twenty to thirty days. I'll be in contact with Ms. Ulrich today to update her to that effect."

"Sounds good." Miriam turned her gaze, glancing between Logan and Aiko. "I definitely need to hear what's going on with Ivy First Avenue."

Logan cleared his throat. "We're all good. Kirby Construction has completed the installation of the safety fencing around the property, and we plan to start the demolition by the beginning of next week."

Miriam eyed Aiko pointedly. "Aiko, do you have anything to add?"

Aiko swallowed. "No, I don't think so. We're moving ahead as scheduled."

"Really? Because we have three major projects at various stages of completion here, but only one of them has drawn any negative attention from the local press." Miriam opened the case on her tablet and swiped the screen. "Like this headline in yesterday's paper from the *American-Statesman*. 'Local women battle against urban renewal.'" She flipped the tablet around so the others could see.

Aiko cringed. "I . . . forgive me, I wasn't aware of that story."

"That much I can understand; reading the local paper isn't something younger folks tend to do." Miriam closed the tablet and set it on the table in front of her. "But we've all seen the news coverage and the social media chatter, right?"

Most of the staff nodded or indicated agreement in some way.

Logan cleared his throat. "That's true, Miriam. The buzz around the Ivy First Avenue project hasn't been ideal. But that protest was an isolated incident, and we believe that as we continue the project, the tide of public opinion will inevitably turn in our favor."

"I agree with Logan," Aiko added. "Things are progressing well, and on schedule. I think the best way to combat any negative attention is to show the press, and the local citizenry, what a safe, efficient, and ultimately beneficial project this is going to be."

"I hear you, Aiko. But how do you plan on doing that?" Miriam leaned back in her chair, arms folded over her chest.

Aiko launched into her answer. "I've been thinking about this. If we want to build community trust, we have to spend time with Ivy residents. I propose we throw a simple, yet engaging community-outreach event."

Logan's brow hitched. "What exactly do you have in mind, Aiko?"

"They need a chance to meet us and see that we're average Austinites, just like them. It should be a town hall. Part of the reason they don't trust us is because we haven't given them a forum to voice their concerns directly." She paused. "So far, everything they know about us is based on what they got secondhand, from the press, or from social media. They deserve a chance at real dialogue with Abernathy employees about our plans for the site."

"It's brilliant. I love it." Miriam straightened and let her arms drop, placing her palms on the table. "How soon can you do it?"

"Sunday," Aiko blurted before she could stop herself. "Ivy First Baptist is having an anniversary service this weekend, so there will already be a lot of locals in the immediate area."

"And how will they know about our event?" Logan posed the question.

Aiko rubbed her hands. "I'll use a three-pronged approach. Social media, word-of-mouth through my mother and her social circle, and letting the church members know that this event will happen immediately following the service, at Ivy Park. It's right across the street from the church and about two blocks up from the project site." Aiko shrugged. "It's short notice, but with all those strategies in place, I can get at least fifty to a hundred people there."

A buzz of conversation went around the table, and Aiko leaned back in her chair, observing. *The office gossip really doesn't matter. If Miriam's on board, then I'm good and I still have a shot at that promotion.*

"All right, Aiko. Hold your event. I'll expect an impressive turnaround in local sentiment when this is all over, understood?" Miriam fixed her with a penetrating gaze. "And I need you to understand how important this is."

"Crystal clear. I've got it," Aiko assured her.

"Great. Then, this meeting is dismissed." Miriam was on her feet and out the door within a few moments, followed closely by most of the other staff.

When only the two of them remained in the room, Logan turned to Aiko. "That was a pretty bold thing to do."

"I know. But I don't see how we have another choice." She shrugged. "Something has to be done, so I'm just gonna do it." *Isn't that the mantra of every Black woman ever?*

"Well, I'm glad you stepped up. But I did want to ask you something. Are you truly using *all* your connections to the neighborhood?" He ran a hand over his hair. "Because I get the distinct feeling that you could be doing more. Don't you know anyone in this group of protestors?"

"Yes, I know a few of them."

"And do you know any of them particularly well?" he pressed.

Aiko nodded. "Yes, I do." She didn't give more details because, despite whatever point Logan was currently driving at, what she did in her personal time was none of his business.

"Am I right in thinking she's one of the same women from the news?"

Aiko felt her jaw tighten. *How does he know that? He got me lojacked or something?* "Yes, she was with the group that day. What are you getting at, Logan?"

"You know I'm not one to get involved in my colleagues' personal lives, but I can definitely see how your involvement with her could benefit Abernathy." He paused. "That is, as long as you stay on her good side."

Aiko frowned. Though she couldn't quite identify what, there was something unsavory about his words and his tone. "I don't know where you're going with this. But I would strongly suggest you stick to your normal policy of not meddling in your coworkers' business."

Logan appeared taken aback. "Fair enough. All I'm saying is if you're dating her, that puts you at a strategic advantage here." He stood, gathering his briefcase and gold-plated pen. "Maybe you can get her to come around to our side, even recant her earlier statements and become a vocal supporter of the project."

She narrowed her eyes. "Logan."

He offered a crooked grin, backing toward the door. "Don't mind me. I'm sure you've got the situation well in hand, Aiko." With a knowing smirk, he turned and left the conference room.

Sitting alone at the table under the glow of the fluorescent lights, Aiko blew out a breath. If she dwelled too long on the things Logan had said to her—or worse yet, implied—she'd likely fly off the handle. There were parts of her that wanted to go to his office and take his ass to the proverbial woodshed, but she had better sense than to actually do it. There was simply too much at stake for her, and she knew Logan would likely come out of the situation relatively unscathed.

Her ire at her supervisor was the least of her worries. *I just volunteered to perform a miracle. Yikes.* She'd told Miriam she could pull off a successful event in three days. And no matter how absurd it seemed now, she knew her boss would expect her to do as she'd promised.

Having no time to waste, Aiko left the conference room and headed to her office to begin the process of pulling a full-scale event out of thin air.

CHAPTER FOURTEEN

Summer pulled into a parking spot at Melted Memories Creamery around seven o'clock Friday evening and shut off her engine. The small parlor, which had opened during her years living away from home, sat on the corner of Wilder Road and Green Street, on the cusp of Ivy and East Austin.

Melted Memories was in a cute little one-story building whose coloring mimicked the inside of a ripe lime. Inside, there was only room for the counter and the back area where the ice cream was made, so the seating consisted of several bright green picnic tables positioned outside the parlor.

Summer glanced around the tables, seeing a few people enjoying their frozen treats. Content to remain in her car until Aiko arrived, she unbuckled her seat belt and laid her head against the headrest.

She'd been somewhat excited to get the text from Aiko earlier today asking her to meet for ice cream.

She was still contemplating what flavor she wanted when she saw Aiko's SUV pull in a few spots away. Getting out of her car, Summer straightened the bottom of her pale yellow maxi dress, leaned against her car, and waited.

Aiko strode toward her, wearing khaki shorts, a bright red polo, and red sneakers. A red baseball cap, turned slightly sideways, was atop her head. Dark sunglasses obscured her eyes. As she got closer, Summer could see that she'd fed her low ponytail through the opening at the back of her hat. "Hey, Summer."

"Hey." Summer pointed to the sunglasses. "Those things don't look like they let any light in."

Aiko chuckled as she slipped them off, hooking them to her collar with one of the arms. "Sorry. So, what are you going to get?"

"The first thing I'm getting is an answer," Summer quipped. "You wanna tell me why we haven't had a real conversation from the time you left my apartment Tuesday?"

Aiko cleared her throat. "I . . . just didn't want to bother you. I know you were busy with your first couple of days of class." Snapping her fingers, she asked, "How has that been going, by the way?"

Summer noticed the swift change of subject but decided not to address it for now. "Pretty well. I have six students at the moment, and they are a joy."

Aiko nodded. "Glad to hear it. So . . . I've never been here before. What are their best flavors?"

"I like the brownie batter and the berry blast." Summer paused. "And they have really good waffle cones, too. I never bother with the paper bowls; the cones are too good to miss." She led the way to the entrance, and Aiko held the door open for her to enter.

The interior of the ice cream parlor felt cozy and smelled of the familiar sweetness of freshly baked waffle cones. Inhaling deeply, Summer stepped up to the counter.

The teenaged girl behind the register, wearing a bright green T-shirt and a matching ribbon around her high ponytail, smiled in her direction. "Welcome to Melted Memories, what can I get you today?"

"Hi. Can I have a double scoop of brownie batter in a waffle cone, please?"

"Sure thing. And you, ma'am?" She turned to Aiko.

Still studying the twenty flavors handwritten on the chalkboard above the counter, Aiko tapped her chin. After a short period of debate, she said, "Let me have one scoop of berry blast and one scoop of orange cream soda in a waffle cone." She reached into a pocket on her shorts and pulled out her wallet, then gestured between Summer and herself. "I'll be paying for both."

A few minutes later, they sat beside each other at one of the empty picnic tables outside, facing outward. Summer savored each sweet mouthful of rich chocolate flavor along with the crunch of the mixed-in dark chocolate chunks and salted walnuts.

Between bites, Aiko asked, "Tell me the funniest thing that happened in your classroom this week. I hear kids that age are hilarious."

Summer thought for a moment before answering. "Let's see. There has been quite a lot of silliness during these first few days of school, and I wouldn't have it any other way. I guess the funniest thing so far happened yesterday."

"Do tell," Aiko insisted, leaning forward.

Summer smiled as she recalled the incident. "We were finger painting in the art center. I'd put their little smocks on to protect their clothes and set them up with easels outfitted with these really big pieces of paper. I gave them each five colors: red, blue, yellow, green, and orange."

"I'm assuming all these colors were washable."

"And non-toxic; the brand the school uses is derived from food coloring. Now, because of space, I had to arrange the easels in a circle. I sort of stepped back and allowed them to do their own thing; that's the basis of the school's curriculum."

"You left them?" Aiko shook her head. "This must be where the funny thing happened."

She sucked her bottom lip. "No. But I did glance down at my notebook, the one I use to keep up with their daily activities. That was long enough for little Max to smear his face with blue paint. He looked like a Smurf."

Aiko hummed a few bars to the theme song of the classic '80s cartoon, and soon they were both laughing uproariously.

When Summer finally composed herself, she said, "I'm sure that's just the beginning. They'll be pulling stunts like that all year long."

Aiko polished off her first scoop. "Teaching sounds like quite the adventure."

"It is." Summer snapped off a piece of waffle cone and chewed it. "What about you, Aiko? Anything interesting happen at your job this week?"

Aiko swallowed and gave Summer a sidelong glance. "Nice segue. I know you're talking about the First Avenue project, but nothing noteworthy happened in terms of the building itself."

"But it sounds like something related did happen," Summer said, "so tell me about that."

"Abernathy is planning to hold a community town hall this Sunday. The idea came up in a meeting yesterday, and I'll be handling the logistics of it."

Summer paused mid-lick, feeling her brow arch. "This Sunday? As in, day after tomorrow?"

Aiko nodded.

Summer thought about that for a moment. "Seems odd to be putting something like this together on such short notice." She paused, then frowned as she remembered. "You're trying to take advantage of the church anniversary crowd?"

Aiko pursed her lips for a moment before sticking her tongue back into her ice cream.

"I see there's no low your company won't sink to for this project, huh." She scoffed. "Whose idea was this?"

"Does it matter? It seems like you don't approve, and I don't think knowing who came up with it will change your mind." Aiko started nibbling on her waffle cone. "Nothing ever seems to."

Summer felt her frown deepen because, despite Aiko's neutrality, she had a very real suspicion that she'd been the one to suggest this outreach event. "Fair enough. Are you sure nothing has happened with the project itself?"

Aiko shook her head. "No. Demolition is going to start by next week, but that's been on the calendar since the beginning. I'm not sure what else you want me to say."

Summer sighed under the weight of her growing exasperation. "So, it seems like you haven't said anything to your higher-ups about moving the timeline or changing the scope of the project."

"Why would I do that?" Aiko's expression conveyed genuine bewilderment. "This project has been planned for months, almost a year. By the time I saw you sitting on the bleachers that day, the wheels had long since been in motion. Why would I put my job in danger to change it, this late in the game?"

Shaking her head, Summer finished off the last of her waffle cone. "You just don't get it, do you? I can work with the other members of the preservation society to create plans for the new development. But I need an in."

"Okay, but why does it have to be me?"

Summer stared, twisting her lips into a frown. "Who else at Abernathy is going to listen to me? Why would anyone else working there have any reason to care about what I think, or how I feel about what's happening to my old school, my old neighborhood?"

Aiko quieted for a moment. "I can't speak for anyone else at the company, Summer. I can only speak for myself, and I think you're being unfair."

"How so?" She genuinely wanted to know why Aiko felt that way when it was so obvious she was acting out of concern for the community.

"You're essentially equating me doing what you want with proving I care about you. You're making it seem like it's impossible for me to care about you because I won't risk my job to do what you think is right." Aiko shook her head.

Summer leaned her back against the table, turning over Aiko's words in her mind. "Is that really how I'm coming across?"

"Yes, it is."

Summer blew out a slow breath. "I don't mean to sound that way, and I'm sorry if you think I'm placing you in an awkward position. But you're not the only one taking a risk here, Aiko."

Aiko eyed Summer expectantly.

"This thing is important to my sister and me, and to my whole family, because it's about Grandma Beulah's legacy." Summer clasped her hands together, trying to still them so she wouldn't start wringing them. "Then there's the larger community. I'm well aware of what the school meant to us, but I have no indication of any benefits for the people of Ivy coming from the new building being constructed on the site."

"You do understand that's not up to me, don't you?"

"I know that. But you're the closest person I know to the action." Summer paused, feeling the weight of her responsibility sitting on her chest like a bowling ball. "I don't know what Ivy might gain from this project. But I'm very clear on what Ivy will lose." She stood, knowing that if she kept sitting there, chances were good that Aiko would see her cry.

As Summer started to walk toward her car, Aiko got up, then placed her hand on Summer's shoulder. It was gentle, not aggressive, but the touch still stopped Summer in her tracks.

"Look at me, Summer. Please."

She turned to face Aiko.

Aiko used that opportunity to close the space between them. In an instant, their lips met, and that familiar heat started to build low in Summer's belly. Aiko placed her free hand on Summer's waist, then brought her body closer with a subtle yet insistent tug. Their tongues tangled and mated until Summer finally backed away, hoping to recapture her breath.

Still maintaining her hold on Summer, Aiko stared into her eyes. "Did that feel like the kiss of someone who doesn't care about you, Summer?"

Summer swallowed and shook her head. "No, it didn't. But you can't kiss me senseless and think I'll forget what's important to me."

"I don't expect you to do that. I just wanted to kiss you." Aiko's tone was soft, earnest.

Summer leaned in and gave Aiko a peck on the cheek. "Thank you for the ice cream. I really have to go."

"So soon?" Aiko called as she walked away.

"I'm sorry." It was the only response Summer could formulate that wouldn't start up the waterworks. Aware of Aiko's gaze on her, she climbed into her car, started the engine, and drove away.

∼

"Thanks for agreeing to help out with this," Aiko said as she opened the front door of her childhood home and stepped aside.

Peaches came in, wearing a broad grin and a black-and-red striped tee, jeans, a red baseball cap, and black sneakers. "You know I got your back, A. You're just lucky I took this weekend off at the barbershop."

Aiko chuckled and closed the door. "I can't promise you excitement, but I'm sure Mama will be glad to see you."

"Where is Ms. Janet, anyway?" Peaches moved farther into the house, glancing around.

"Right here." Aiko's mother appeared in the short hallway beyond the living room. She slowly ambled their way using the cane her doctor had required. "Hey, Peaches. It's so good to see you."

"Good to see you, too, Ms. Janet." Peaches came in for a hug.

Janet held up her hand and pointed at Peaches' head. "Not till you take off that hat in my house."

"Oh, snap." A sheepish-looking Peaches snatched off her hat. "Sorry 'bout that."

Janet laughed and opened her arms. "Come here and give me some love."

After they'd embraced for a few moments, Aiko called out with feigned jealousy, "All right, Peaches. Don't go taking all my mama's hugs, leave some for me." Aiko was joking, and they both knew it. Nothing warmed her heart as much as seeing the way her mother and her best friend got along.

Leaving Janet's embrace, Peaches clapped her hands together. "All right, Ms. Janet. I'm ready to work. What you got for me?"

"That's what I like to hear," Janet said as she shuffled past them into the kitchen.

They gathered around the small island in the center of the kitchen, and Aiko admired the white quartz surface her mother had chosen during last year's kitchen remodeling. "I really like these countertops, Mama. They're a big improvement over that old yellow linoleum."

Janet chuckled. "Thanks, sugar. But don't you slander those old counters. They were original to this house, and I made you many a meal on those hideous old things." She shook her head, her expression a bit wistful. "I don't know what was worse, the cracks or the stains. Either way, I finally got sick of it, and had these put on."

"So, what's first?" Peaches asked.

"The first thing I need y'all to do is make these finger sandwiches. I'd do it myself but my wrist is still bothering me." Janet pointed to the fridge. "Aiko, go in there and get the cucumbers, the pimento cheese, cream cheese, and that little plastic pack of fresh dill. Oh, and grab that bread off the top of the icebox."

"Gotcha." She gathered all the supplies and brought them to the island.

Peaches fished around in the silverware drawer for a butter knife. "About how many whole sandwiches should we make?"

"Three pimentos, three cucumbers, and cut 'em up in four triangles." Janet eased her way toward the sofa as she spoke. "After that, turn on the crockpot to heat up my meatballs, and then you can set everything out." She grunted as she sank into the sofa cushion. "Don't forget that crudités-and-cheese plate in the icebox."

While they washed up and set about the task of preparing the food, Peaches commented, "Your mama sure puts out a nice spread for her book club."

Aiko nodded. "Yep. She only gets to host once or twice a year. I tried to get her to cancel since she's not completely healed yet, but . . ."

"It would've messed up the rotation," Janet interjected, glancing up from the pages of the open book on her lap.

Peaches laughed. "I hear you, Ms. Janet." Spreading a thin layer of cream cheese on a slice of bread, she asked, "So. Anything new happen between you and Ms. Fight the Power?"

Aiko shook her head. "Peaches, you call her a different smart-ass nickname every time you mention her." She sliced into a crisp cucumber. "I don't even know what to say about her, honestly. We did go out for ice cream yesterday, but that didn't really go the way I'd hoped."

Frowning, Peaches asked, "What happened?"

Aiko briefly recapped the ill-fated conversation she'd had with Summer. "It's the same old disagreement, but it only seems to be getting more intense."

"Damn. Sorry to hear that, A." Peaches shook her head solemnly. "I don't wanna be a killjoy, but I still don't see how this is gonna work out between y'all."

Aiko shrugged. "Me, either. I care about Summer, I really do. But I don't know how many more times I can rehash the same argument with her."

"Pick up the pace, you two. The girls will be here soon." Janet continued to leaf through her book as she made her decree. "Go ahead and take that bottle of prosecco out, too."

"I will. And I'm gonna set up the paper plates, plastic utensils, and napkins, too," Peaches promised.

"You're such a good girl, Peaches." Janet blew her surrogate daughter a kiss.

Peaches elbowed Aiko, speaking in a low voice for her ears only. "Now there's something I say way more than I hear."

Aiko snorted a laugh and elbowed her friend back. "Just help me get the rest of this food set up, crazy."

By the time Janet's "girls"—members of the Seasoned Ladies Book Club—began arriving, all the food was on platters on the countertop bar between the kitchen and the dining room. The bottle of wine Janet had mentioned sat in a bucket of ice next to a set of six of her crystal wineglasses.

As the members filed in, Aiko and Peaches greeted them. Aiko, having sat in on a few meetings before, recognized the four women who made up the core contingent of the club. There were other members, but these were the ladies who most often attended meetings, and for whom an absence usually indicated an urgent situation of some kind.

They were Myrtle; Theresa, who went by Reesie; Debra; and Zinnia. All the women knew Janet through membership at Ivy First Baptist Church or from Janet's days as a flight attendant.

Aiko and Peaches served the women food and wine after they were settled into the cushions of the brown leather sectional, then retired to the dining room table with plates of their own. "I didn't read the book, but I like to observe them from a safe distance," Aiko joked.

Peaches chuckled around a mouthful of crudités.

They listened quietly while the ladies discussed their book selection, a cozy mystery about a murder at a fancy ski resort. Based on Aiko's observation, the consensus seemed to be that the ski instructor did it, and the club members thought the mystery was too easily solved.

Soon, the discussion changed directions, the ladies drawing parallels between the book and real life.

"I just thought the lady working at the pro shop was too much of a pushover," Myrtle commented. "It's how that nasty ski instructor was able to make her an accomplice to his crimes."

Reesie nodded solemnly. "I know that's right. I put aside far too many of my principles for my first husband, and I regret it to this day."

Aiko watched Reesie take a long, contemplative sip from her wineglass. She couldn't help thinking about Reesie's words and how they might tie into her situation with Summer. If Peaches' pointed stare was any indication, she was thinking the same thing.

"Don't be too hard on yourself, Reesie," Zinnia offered. "Lord knows we've all done something foolish in the name of love."

Aiko cringed. *Here's hoping I don't open up that can of worms.* Having her heart trampled on was one rite of passage she wouldn't mind missing out on. *Recently, I've been able to keep my romantic connections casual. But this thing with Summer is more intense than anything I've ever dealt with. That made this little liaison ripe for disaster.*

"You know what, though?" Debra spoke up after being silent through the last portion of the discussion. "Janet, I gotta say something about your daughter and her friend."

Peaches stilled midchew, shifting her gaze toward the living room without turning her head.

Aiko felt her shoulder muscles tense. *Oh, shit. What is she about to say?*

Janet scooted up to the edge of her seat and said, "What is it, Debra?"

While Janet's expression appeared calm, Aiko knew her mother's ways. *I hope Debra doesn't say anything sideways because my mama will slap her in the name of Jesus.*

After a few long seconds, Debra said, "Seeing them makes me sad sometimes. But only because of what I missed when I was coming of age. I think it's wonderful, that the younger generations now feel so free and comfortable, that they can be just who they are."

Janet's expression morphed into a soft smile. "So do I. I raised Aiko to think for herself, and to listen to her heart." Janet looked Aiko's way. "And I tell you, she makes me proud every single day."

Aiko smiled at her mother. "I love you too, Mama."

Debra sighed. "I wish our mothers had been so evolved." She looked off into the distance, wearing the weight of unspoken memories on her face. "I was plumb smitten with a girl who grew up down the street from me, and I'm pretty sure she felt the same. Times being what they were, nothing ever came of it."

"She still living?" Myrtle asked.

Debra nodded. "She lives in one of those fancy senior-condo developments in Houston."

"Well, no disrespect to Harvey, may his soul rest in peace," Janet began, "but you've been a widow for three years now. And if she's still living . . ."

"There's still a chance," Zinnia added.

Debra didn't say anything, but the small smile that played over her face spoke volumes.

After the ladies left, Aiko stood on the front porch with Peaches. "What a meeting."

"And to think you said it wouldn't be entertaining." Peaches chuckled with a shake of her head. "That was like an episode of a '90s talk show."

"Yeah. Trust me, I'm just as surprised as you are. I definitely didn't see that coming." Aiko stared ahead, watching as Mr. Rollins across the street carried shopping bags into his house. "I hope Ms. Debra can make that love connection with her friend up in Houston."

"Me, too. My mama's always using that saying about there being snow on the roof, but still a fire in the furnace." Peaches started down the steps, tossing over her shoulder, "I'll send up a prayer for Ms. Debra's pilot light."

Peaches got into her car, and Aiko waved as her friend drove off. Going back inside to tidy up, she couldn't help dwelling on the two cautionary tales she'd heard today.

And it was the shorter, less complex one that stood out the most. Reesie hadn't said much, but her words held a great deal of regret, making them stand out in Aiko's mind.

Never trade your principles for love.

CHAPTER FIFTEEN

When Summer pulled into the driveway of her parents' modest brick ranch Saturday evening, she slid into the remaining space. With her father's old '90s-model pickup truck parked in the carport and her mother's red sedan right behind it, Summer's car was the last vehicle that would fit.

Rodney sat on the front porch, reading. He rocked back and forth on the old steel swing and looked up from his newspaper as Summer got out of her car.

"Hey, Dad," Summer said as she climbed the steps.

He smiled. "Hey, honeybun." As she came closer, he reached out and grabbed her hand. "I want to thank you for being big enough to say yes to this. I know your mother hasn't made things easy for you. All I ask is that you hear her out because I really think she's come around."

Summer nodded, swallowing the lump of nervous energy sitting in her throat. "Crystal's still coming, right?"

"Yeah. She texted me that she's running late."

Summer sat down on the swing and snuggled up to her father's side. "I think I'll sit out here with you and wait for her." She didn't really want to go in and see her mother yet, at least not without both of her biggest supporters close behind her.

"How are you doing, Dad? Haven't talked to you in a few days."

"Pretty good." Rodney's gaze was settled on the horizon. "Just your usual aches and pains, but that just means I'm still living, right, kiddo?"

"Right." She drew a deep breath, filling her lungs with the humid air that carried the fragrant scent of the magnolia trees and white bush honeysuckle blooming in the front yard. Her thoughts drifted to Aiko, as they always seemed to do lately, but she pushed them away. She'd need all the bandwidth she could muster to deal with whatever this family dinner might bring.

Crystal's black coupe pulled up to the curb in front of the house. After cutting the engine, Crystal climbed out. She wore the dark slacks and blouse she'd worn to work. She walked around to the passenger side to get something out, then turned and started walking up the driveway beside the line of cars.

As she got closer, Summer smiled, recognizing the brightly colored box in her sister's hand. "Ooh, Crys. What did you get from Swingin' Sweets?"

"Hello to you, too, sis," Crystal replied with a laugh. "It's a marble cake with caramel-vanilla glaze."

Summer's mouth watered at the very thought. "Sounds amazing. I wish we could have dessert first."

Rodney chuckled. "You know your mama will never go for that."

"Did you come straight from work?" Summer asked.

"Nah, I got off at three. I just didn't have time to go home and change."

Rodney stood, and that was Summer's cue to get up.

"All right, girls. Let's go on in before my dinner gets cold." He held open the screen door.

Crystal went in, but Summer found herself hesitating.

"It's gonna be okay, sis." Crystal stood in the living room, just beyond the little square of linoleum at the door. "Dad and I have your back."

Taking a deep breath, Summer entered the house. As soon as she was inside, the familiarity of home washed over her. The interior, largely unchanged from her childhood, reflected her mother's love of all things yellow. From the framed images of canaries on the walls to the curtains to the throw pillows on the gray sofa that was at least as old as Summer, Meadow Graves had used shades of her favorite color at every opportunity.

Beyond the living room lay the kitchen. The lemon-print wallpaper lent a sunny quality to the room, and white appliances coordinated with the oak butcher-block countertops and beige cabinetry. As they filed into the kitchen, Summer noted that her mother wasn't in the room. Summer took her usual seat at the round oak table at the center of the room while Crystal sat to her left, and father went to the stove to look in on his pots.

The heavenly aroma of the meal made Summer's stomach growl. She could smell the savory scent of roasted meat as well as the onions and garlic her father seasoned most of his dishes with.

After a few moments, Meadow emerged into the kitchen from the short hallway that led to the three bedrooms in the rear of the house. The sight of her was jarring for Summer since she hadn't seen her mother in person in over a year. Her mother was dressed in a white tee and a pair of royal-blue track pants with white piping down the sides of the legs, and she'd tied a blue scarf around her head to hold her shoulder-length silver curls out of her face.

Meadow's eyes met Summer's as she sat down across from her. "Hello, Summer. Thank you for coming."

"Hi, Mama." Summer offered a smile because it was the polite thing to do. She had no idea what to expect from this encounter, but she held out hope for a positive outcome.

Rodney soon began placing plates in front of them, loaded with thick slices of ham, baked macaroni and cheese, and green beans seasoned with slivered sweet onions. After adding tall glasses of sweet tea, he finally sat. His deep voice echoed in the silence as he said a brief grace. When he finished, he said, "Y'all dig in."

Summer cut off a piece of the tender ham, then groaned as she chewed it. "Wow, Dad. This is so good."

"Thank you." He grinned, never one to tire of folks complimenting his cooking. "It's hickory-smoked, and I added a little bit of flair to it." He took a sip from his glass. "I got it from Marvin. Y'all remember him? He plays in my poker league, but he owns that butchery and smoke shop over in Georgetown."

"I remember him." Crystal nodded. "The one that always wears that straw fedora, whether it matches his clothes or not."

Rodney laughed. "That's him. He's had that thing thirty years or more, and the dang straw is starting to unravel, but nobody can convince him to get rid of it or replace it."

"You mean nobody in the poker league can convince him," Crystal insisted. "Let a nice-looking lady friend ask him to lose it."

Summer giggled at the banter between her father and older sister, noting her mother's relative silence. She shrugged it off. *I've waited years for Mama to come around; I can wait a few minutes longer. She'll speak up when she's ready.*

As if Meadow had somehow heard her younger daughter's thoughts, she asked, "How have you been, Summer? New job going well?"

"It is, thanks for asking." Summer washed down a bite of macaroni with a swig of ice-cold tea, appreciating the hint of lemon she detected. "The kids have a lot of mischief in them, but I love seeing them learn and explore. It's what makes teaching worthwhile."

A smile spread over Rodney's face. "You've got a lot of Beulah in you. That passion for education is flowing through your veins just like it flowed through hers."

Hearing that made Summer's heart swell with pride. "Thanks, Dad."

"Mama would certainly be proud of your work, both with your students and with the old Sojourner Truth site. I know I am."

All eyes at the table turned to Meadow, who'd broken her silence to comment.

While Meadow had everyone's attention, she segued smoothly to another topic. "Ivy First Baptist's is having a ninetieth-anniversary service tomorrow. I'm gonna sing with the senior choir." She speared a few green beans. "Y'all welcome to come by and hear me warble." She uttered a soft chuckle and looked pointedly at Summer.

Summer regarded her mother, sensing that she was extending the tiniest of olive branches. "I could probably swing by."

Meadow took a deep breath. "Before you decide if you want to come or not, there's something I need to say to you, Summer."

Oh, boy. Tension entered her neck and shoulders. *Here it comes.*

"I want to apologize to you. For so long, I've been unfairly judging you and pushing you out of my life. I see the way you and your father and Crystal get along, and I'm left out of that relationship. But I know it's my own doing, and it's time I did right by you."

Summer nodded but didn't say anything. *No way I'm interrupting her while she's feeling apologetic.*

Laying her silverware down across her empty plate, Meadow continued, "At work the other day, one of my coworkers came to me to talk about the guest list for my retirement party. It's coming up in a few months. As we were going over the guest list, I realized that you probably weren't gonna be there." She paused, tears gathering in her eyes. "And honestly, I wouldn't blame you. It made me realize how much I miss having you in my life, and how much I miss the relationship we used to share. I've been acting so silly for so long." She laughed bitterly. "I can't get that time back with you. But there's still so much time ahead of us, Lord willing. I just hope and pray you'll give me a chance to earn back my place in your life."

Dashing away her own tears, Summer nodded again. "I really appreciate everything you've said, Mama. And I'm willing to give you a chance, as long as you understand that full forgiveness is gonna take some time."

"I do understand, baby." Meadow reached across the table to clasp her daughter's hand and squeeze it. "I accept you, and whoever you choose to love. I supposed I could've festooned this whole place in rainbows, but that seems a little cliché."

Summer laughed through her tears. "It kinda is."

"In light of that, I came up with my own way of making amends, something I thought was more meaningful and personal to the women in this household." She released Summer's hand and stood. Walking across the kitchen, she opened one of the upper cabinets and pulled down what looked like an oversized shoebox. Returning to the table with an almost-reverent look in her eyes, she touched the box's lid. "I've been saving these for a while, and I think it's time."

Rodney gave his wife's shoulder a loving squeeze. "It most certainly is, Meadow."

Her mother slowly lifted the lid off the box, then reached inside. After a brief rustling that sounded like crinkling tissue paper, she lifted a beautiful, familiar-looking item into view. "When Mary Ellen's was about to close a few years back, I went and talked to her. I was able to convince her to part with three of her best teapots if I promised they'd be well taken care of. It cost me more than I care to admit, but considering the memories we made there, they were worth every cent." She turned the first pot around, showing off the glistening jade color and the elephant's trunk that made up the teapot's handle. Smiling, she passed it to Crystal.

Crystal accepted it, her free hand flying to her mouth. Her eyes wet, she whispered, "Mama. It's my favorite one."

"I know. I remember she used to keep her most valuable, unique teapots on display in a glass case by the cash register. We'd look inside of it every time we went in there for high tea, and each of us had a favorite." She took out a second one; it was a pale shade of pink and featured a peacock's curved neck as its handle. "This was mine." Setting that one beside herself, she reached into the box again.

Summer's heart climbed into her throat like one of her students scaling a jungle gym.

"And this one is yours, Summer." Meadow lifted the teapot and held it out to her.

Tears ran down Summer's face as she took it and turned it over in her hands, admiring the shimmering lavender color and the hand-painted floral design. The memories of all those Saturday afternoons, eating pastries and drinking tea with her mother and sister while she peered from beneath that big-ass hat, came flooding back. Gripping the braided handle that was fashioned to look like a section of wisteria vine, she released a muffled sob. "Thank you, Mama. Thank you so, so much."

"You're welcome. It's very literally the least I can do, to show you I meant what I said." Meadow wiped her face with a napkin. "We're gonna start over from this moment forward. And I'm gonna do whatever it takes to do right by you, to get back that closeness we once had."

Still clutching her teapot, Summer nodded. There wasn't a dry eye around the table at this point, but she didn't care. Receiving a gesture like this from her mother, after over a year of fractured relations with her, was overwhelming and shocking, but in the best possible way. For the first time in a long time, she felt there was a real chance to mend their bond.

⌒

Looking over the bustling green grounds of Ivy Park Sunday afternoon, Aiko breathed a sigh of relief. Her position on the small temporary stage that had been erected a few hours ago gave her an excellent view of the space, and from where she stood, it seemed everything had all come together.

In only two days, and with a small four-figure budget, she managed to plan what she considered a pretty impressive event. There were bounce houses, face painting, and a snow-cone cart, sure to be a hit with the kids. Several informational booths, stocked with Abernathy-themed giveaways for the adults, had been set up around the park's perimeter. The centerpiece of the gathering was the stage and the one hundred chairs set up in two sections of neat rows, with an aisle dividing them. A microphone was positioned near the stage to allow citizens to voice their concerns.

Hours of shopping, filling out online forms, and a lucky find of several hundred pieces of merchandise left over from a conference had made it all possible. And while she was thrilled to have pulled it off, she had no desire of ever doing anything like this again.

"It's pretty amazing what you managed to do here, on such short notice," Fiona commented. Wearing a simple pair of jeans and a blue tee with the Abernathy logo, she was as casually dressed as Aiko had ever seen her.

"Thanks. I'm glad you're impressed because my event-planning days are officially over. I've experienced levels of stress and exhaustion over the past few days that I never want to revisit." Aiko shook her head.

Fiona chuckled. "Well, at least you've done the hard part of your work already. Now I have to go up there and make a speech." She shuddered. "I'd rather have a root canal than engage in public speaking. But my therapist says it's important to face my fear. Exposure therapy and all that jazz."

"So, you volunteered to do this?" Aiko asked.

Fiona nodded. "Yes. I'm having serious regrets, but there's nothing to be done about it now." With that said, Fiona stepped down from the stage and wandered off across the grass.

Left alone with her thoughts, Aiko fought the urge to pace. Rather than wear a dent in the stage, she visited the four booths, making sure each one was properly outfitted and attended. Interns staffed them, and she checked with each to ensure they had what they needed. Three booths were informational, and the fourth was the food tent, where attendees could enjoy free hot dogs, individually packaged snacks, and cold sodas. As she left each booth, she did so with the same parting words. "Be polite and engaging. And make sure you direct any questions you don't understand or are unsure how to answer to either me or Fiona."

She was walking toward the stage when her phone vibrated in the pocket of her tan slacks. Checking the screen before she answered, she said, "Hi, Miriam."

"How are things going at the park, Aiko?"

"We're about an hour from starting the event, and everything is in place."

"Good. I'll expect great news later today, then."

Aiko cleared her throat. "I only have one concern. Fiona seems . . . a little uncomfortable about her speech."

"Yes, I know. We had a long chat about her stage fright, and how she's going to tap into her personal power to overcome it. I think she'll be fine."

Miriam has far more confidence in Fiona than I do. What am I missing? "I hope so."

"If you're genuinely concerned, you could always make the speech," Miriam suggested.

Glad her boss couldn't see her cringe, Aiko replied, "No, I'll leave it to Fiona. Frankly, I'm too tapped from the planning to say anything coherent."

"Don't sell yourself short." Miriam laughed. "At any rate, be sure to let me know how it goes."

"I'll check in with you after we wrap up here."

"I look forward to it." Miriam disconnected the call.

Putting her phone away, Aiko glanced around until she saw Fiona. She was back onstage, sitting in one of the two folding chairs behind the small podium. While shuffling through a handful of index cards, she appeared to be mouthing the words she planned to say.

Around three o'clock, the first few attendees began filtering into the park through the open gates. Aiko had used her knowledge of her mother's faithful church attendance to determine the best time to start, about thirty minutes after service ended. As a youngster, she'd attended services with her mother; she stopped going around the age of twelve. She'd won her freedom after a spirited debate with her mother about the role Black women played in their church. Twenty minutes of anecdotal evidence pointing to an unequal balance of power between male and female congregants had been enough for Janet to cave and agree not to force Aiko to attend service.

Just as they had all those years ago, parishioners lingered on the church steps and lawn for a while after service to greet the pastor and to socialize with one another. And due to the park's position across the street from the front doors of Ivy First Baptist and the brightly colored signage and activities, even people who weren't aware of the event were bound to wander over out of sheer curiosity.

Aiko made her way to the gate, welcoming people as they entered. "Thanks for coming. Please, help yourself to some refreshments." She gestured toward the food tent near the stage. She'd ushered in twenty or so people when her mother appeared with her friend Myrtle. Both were decked out in their Sunday finery: Myrtle wore a jacket-and-skirt ensemble in a pale shade of pink, while Janet's outfit, a soft mint green, had a contrasting darker green border on the hem. Each woman wore a large flowered hat that coordinated with her outfit. Aiko greeted them both with hugs.

"This is a nice little setup." Janet glanced around from beneath her hat brim. "You're not bad at this organizing thing."

"Thanks, Mama." Aiko noted the hint of teasing in her tone. "How was service?"

"It was good. The pastor was on a roll today."

"Too much of a roll," Myrtle complained. "We gotta be back over there at six for the evening service and the dinner. I don't know why he was so long-winded; our pastor never talks that long."

"You know how he gets when he thinks he's being profound." Janet chuckled.

The two women went to investigate the happenings inside the park, so Aiko made a quick circle around the area, shaking hands and chatting with folks, encouraging them to come to the mic if they had concerns or questions. After checking the time, she returned to the stage, where Fiona still sat, clutching her index cards with trembling hands.

Sitting down in the chair next to her, Aiko asked, "Are you ready for this, Fiona?"

Fiona nodded, yet her wide-eyed stare told a contradictory story. "I'm going to do this. I have to."

Aiko tried to keep her face neutral so she wouldn't spook the already-fragile woman any further. "Why don't you just run through your main points with me? Maybe that will help you feel more confident and prepared?"

Fiona's head bobbed again. "Yeah, yeah. That's a great idea. Okay, so here are my points. I'm gonna talk about progress, and growth, and how those two things might seem frightening, but really, they're good."

Aiko stared. She knew that wouldn't be enough to appease the citizenry of this neighborhood. But five minutes before Fiona was due to speak—there wasn't anything Aiko could do to save her now. "Okay. Well, good luck, champ." Aiko patted her on the shoulder. *I've already taken on too much for this event. I don't have the strength or the energy to bail her out.*

Fiona took the podium a short while later, leaning into the microphone. Her eyes were still wide, but she appeared composed. "Good afternoon, citizens of Ivy. My name is Fiona Dawson, and I'm a junior designer with Abernathy Creative Development. I want to talk to you about two things: change, and growth."

"Boo!"

Aiko saw the teenaged boy who was the source of the heckling, and she also saw the exact moment an older woman next to the boy, potentially his grandmother, caught hold of his ear and led him away.

Clearing her throat, Fiona continued. "If we break down those two terms to their basic components, we can come to an understanding of why they are necessary to a fulfilling life."

Aiko tuned Fiona out as she segued into giving dictionary definitions of change and growth, and from the looks of it, most of the people in attendance were tuning her out as well. Fiona's speech was going about as well as Aiko had expected, and Aiko could barely contain the wry laugh building inside her.

Scanning the assemblage, she spotted Summer entering through the gate. Accompanying Summer were her sister and an older couple Aiko assumed to be her parents. Trailing behind the Graves family were three others whom Aiko didn't recognize. Among them was an elderly woman in church garb ambling along with the aid of a walker.

Aiko watched as the group quietly took seats in the third row of the section on the left. While she felt some relief that Summer and her companions had shown up without protest signs or chants, she still couldn't help wondering what would happen next.

Fiona continued struggling through her speech until finally, mercifully, she finished. A smattering of applause went across the seating area, and Aiko chalked that up to politeness more than anything. As Fiona rushed to her seat, Aiko stood and approached the podium. "My name is Aiko Holt, supervisory planner with Abernathy. I'd like to thank my colleague, Ms. Dawson, for that informative talk. Now, though, we'd like to hear from you, the citizens of Ivy. We welcome you to bring any questions or concerns you might have to the microphone." She gestured to the other mic, positioned on a flat paver on the grass.

Scanning the crowd, Aiko observed a small line of four people form in front of the mic. *This is a good sign—they seem willing to talk.*

Over the next few minutes, Aiko answered their queries to the best of her knowledge, all the while mindful of Summer's presence. Three of the four citizens voiced common concerns about construction noise, road closures, and whether locals would be included in the work crews. In response to the fourth person's question about leasing space in the new development, she referred the asker to the folks at Yates. Yates Properties, who'd purchased the old school and hired both Abernathy and Kirby, hadn't yet revealed the totality of their plans for it. After reading out the contact information, the last person sat down, seemingly satisfied. "Is there anyone else who wants to speak?"

Summer stood then, as did the elderly woman in her group. With a steadying hand on the older woman's arm, Summer escorted her as she shuffled slowly to the mic.

Aiko swallowed, feeling the nervousness rise within her. *I'm not surprised Summer would have something to say. I just hope it's not too outrageous.*

After taking a moment to lower the mic to better suit the woman's short stature, Summer stepped back.

Aiko felt her brow rise in surprise.

The older woman leaned toward the mic, then spoke in a wavering voice. "Hello. My name is Melba Keys. Most folks around here know me as Coach Keys. I taught physical education at Sojourner Truth for twenty-three years."

Coach Keys paused at the boisterous applause that answered her simple statement, a smile curling her lips. "I see many of my former students here, and I'm proud to have been a part of their educational journey. That's why I came here today."

"You're obviously a beloved member of this community," Aiko said. "I'm eager to hear your thoughts, Coach."

"Good, 'cause I'm gon' give 'em." Coach Keys chuckled. "Anyhow, I don't much care what gets built on the site of the old school. I only care about one thing: Ivy's youth. They need a safe place, where they can learn and grow, and even play some." She paused and cleared her throat. "We need to invest in them, for the future of this neighborhood, this city, and heck, this world. All I'm asking is that you developers take your minds off the bottom line long enough to ask yourselves how this place can benefit the children. These babies need grown folks to look out for them." She adjusted her hat. "That's all I got to say."

Summer leaned into the mic. "And I think that's all that needs to be said."

Nodding her head, Coach Keys stepped back from the mic and let Summer escort her back to her seat to the sound of another rousing round of applause.

Aiko felt herself smiling. It seemed Summer had finally found a way to approach the subject with a soft touch. Still, Aiko knew Summer's stance probably hadn't changed.

She's taking it light for now, but she's not gonna go easy on me.

CHAPTER SIXTEEN

Pacing her apartment, Summer turned over the facts in her mind.

"If you keep doing that, you're gonna ruin your floors," Crystal insisted from her seat on the couch. "You've been at that for ten minutes now. Talk to me, Summer."

She stopped midstep, releasing a loud sigh. "Did you see Aiko? The way she was watching me come to the mic with Coach Keys?" She recalled Aiko's curious, guarded gaze. "It seemed like she was waiting for me to say something out of line."

Crystal scoffed. "I gotta admit, I wasn't looking at her. My focus was on the blonde who gave that shallow-ass speech." She shook her head. "It was utter crap. Just a bunch of company talking points and empty rhetoric. 'Change is good' this and 'You can't stop progress' that. It was insulting."

"At any rate, now that some of us have spoken, Abernathy knows exactly where we stand." She flopped down on the sofa next to her sister. "Coach Keys was amazing, wasn't she?"

Crys smiled. "Yeah. Your idea of making her our spokeswoman was brilliant."

"Thanks, sis." Summer let herself be buoyed by her sister's praise, even though she knew this development issue was far from over. "I don't know how much difference this will make, but I feel like Aiko really listened to the people who spoke. Or at least, she looked interested."

"I guess we'll have to wait and see if anything changes, now that Abernathy knows people living in the neighborhood are truly concerned about their plans."

Summer sighed. "I can't believe I let myself get so tangled up in my feelings for Aiko. I was so concerned with getting to know her, and trying to satisfy my fantasies of her, that I couldn't see that we'd end up clashing like this."

"I don't think you should blame yourself. You had an epic crush on her. In that situation, most people do the same thing you did. Accentuate the positive qualities and downplay the negative."

"Still. I should have known better." They weren't schoolgirls any longer; the lanky, athletic girl she'd been enamored with all those years ago was now a career woman, bent on success—even if that success came at the expense of the very neighborhood that nurtured them during their formative years.

"I'm sorry, sis."

"Nah. This is my fault." Summer touched her fingertips to her temples. "What's worse, I don't even know if I accomplished much of anything today, you know? I didn't really stay long enough to talk to anyone in the crowd. They were just hanging out in the park, eating hot dogs and snow cones."

"I don't know if you're giving them enough credit, sis. We've already been on the news once, talking about this. Plus the stuff on social media, and just word of mouth." Crystal reached up, stretching her arms above her head. "I think they know more than you might assume. I don't think they can be won over with free snacks and empty words."

"You're probably right. Sometimes, I worry no one else cares what happens to our old school."

"That's not necessarily true. What's probably true is that no one cares about it as much as we do. Me, you, Mom, and Dad. We're the ones who are most closely affected because the school is a big part of the Graves family legacy."

Summer's eyes filled with tears of frustration that threatened to spill. "I just hate feeling like this, like I got distracted and didn't do everything I should have."

"You're putting way too much pressure on yourself to fix this. It's not as if you're alone." Crystal put her arm around her sister's shoulders and gave them a gentle squeeze. "I'm with you. And so is the entire Sojourner Truth Preservation Society, which is your brainchild, by the way. Give yourself a little grace. You've done plenty."

Laying her head on her big sister's chest, she asked, "Then why do I feel so crappy?"

"I think the way you feel is less about the project and more about you and Aiko." Crystal delivered her answer with that sage wisdom Summer had come to love and depend on. "You already know what you have to do to fix that, don't you?"

Summer drew a deep, shaky breath and nodded. "I can't keep seeing her. I always feel like I'm choosing between her and my family's legacy."

"All right. So we can consider that part handled." Crystal gently helped Summer sit up straight again. "Now, we need to figure out the next step when it comes to the project. What's the most impactful thing you can think of? Because that should be the next action you take."

"I don't really know. The Texas State Historical Association is so backlogged with applications, they won't be able to address our concerns any time soon." She sighed. "So that's a non-starter."

"Okay. Time to dig a little deeper, then," Crystal insisted.

Summer tilted her head, letting her gaze settle on a single spot just above her framed print of Audre Lorde's poem "Who Said It Was Simple." It had been a favorite of hers since she'd discovered Lorde's work as a teen. She'd had an artist she met at the Ivy Community Market make the print for her. She stood, then walked across the room until she paused in front of the image, reading the first stanza in her mind.

*There are so many roots to the tree of anger
that sometimes the branches shatter
before they bear.*

I'm angry. Perhaps that is the emotion that forms the roots of my entire crusade. "I'm angry," she said, turning to her sister. "I'm angry that the school closed. I'm angry that it's grown dilapidated and is being torn down like common blight. I'm angry that none of the people involved seem to care about how we feel." She paused as realization hit hard. "Mostly, I'm angry that Grandma isn't here." The pain of missing her was heavy, palpable. It sat like a weight in her chest, pressing against her heart, making it hurt.

Crystal inhaled deeply. "I miss her, too, Summer. It's been years since she left us, but sometimes, it feels like it just happened yesterday."

For a moment, they were both silent, and Summer knew they were each wrestling with their own personal grief over a woman whose life had shaped their very existence. *Grandma deserves so much more. Where's the respect for all she accomplished? For all the lives she impacted? I can't let them disrespect her this way.*

Summer's mind wandered as she debated what she could do, with help from the other members of the preservation society, that might finally turn the tide in their favor. A few moments later, she snapped her fingers. "Remember that day we protested, and you had Brenda from the news station come down and interview us?"

"Of course I do. What are you getting at, exactly?"

"That got the company's attention. I'm pretty sure there were no plans for 'community outreach' or whatever they call that event at the park until after the news coverage." She tapped her chin. "Why not take what we already know is effective, and just do it bigger?"

"And how are we going to do that? I can call on Brenda again but beyond that?" Crystal shrugged. "I'm not sure. Her showing up the first time was kind of a fluke; it all depends on what's going on around the newsroom when I reach out to her."

"I know. But they're starting demolition this week. So if we can get more people together we can make a bigger impact. We need all hands on deck. More folks to carry signs. More coverage—television and radio this time. Social media. Word of mouth. Everything." Summer started walking toward her office. "We need to make this protest so big, Abernathy and Kirby Construction won't be able to just ignore us or send us home."

Crystal followed her into the room. "Okay. Do you know what day?"

Summer shook her head as she sat down and pulled her chair up to her desk, then switched on her computer. "Not yet, but it should be easy enough to find out. Between the two companies' websites and social accounts, there's bound to be some kind of announcement about it."

With Crystal stationed behind her chair, Summer opened her browser. On the website for Kirby Construction, she clicked a link that read "Current and Upcoming Projects." The link downloaded a file to her computer, and she opened it, revealing a chart containing the names of their job sites and pertinent dates. She touched the screen. "Look, Crys. Ivy First Avenue. That's it, it's the same name Aiko referred to it by." Reading the date column next to the name, she could feel her eyes widening. "They're starting demo on Tuesday. Seven a.m."

"I work at three that day, so I'm good." Crystal paused. "What about you? I know you have school."

"I do, but class is from nine to two. If we do this right, I should be able to get to work in plenty of time."

"What about the rest of the squad? They have jobs, families, all of that. Plus, it's short notice . . ."

"You asked me to come up with a plan, and I did. I'm telling you, if we execute this right, it's going to change things." She turned and looked at her sister. "Are you with me, or nah?"

Crystal gave Summer a crooked smile. "Of course I am. What do you need me to do?"

"Reach out to Brenda, and then look up contacts for at least two other TV stations broadcasting news in Austin, so we can have three networks covered. Then try to get ahold of somebody at 100.5 WTRV 'The Groove.'"

"You mean that hip-hop station that plays twerking music all week and then gospel on Sundays?"

Chuckling, Summer nodded. "Tip them all off that they need to send someone to the school site at 6:45 Tuesday morning, ready to film or record."

Crystal shrugged. "All right. Let me grab my phone, and I'm on it."

The two of them worked in tandem for the next hour, Summer reaching out to as many people as she could think of who might show up to carry signs while Crystal worked on drumming up media attention.

Crystal's phone pinged, and she checked it. "Oh, shoot. I almost forgot I'm meeting Hector for dinner."

"Give me a status report, and then you can go. I don't want to hold you up."

"It's Sunday, so it was a bit of crapshoot reaching folks. Still, I was able to get five different reps from television stations and two radio broadcasters to say they'd try to send someone."

"That's a start. I've got a list of twenty people who might be able to come." She genuinely appreciated their willingness to rearrange their schedules, and she'd made sure to tell them that. While none of the media personalities were very committal, their tentative agreements were enough to give her hope that she might just be able to pull this off.

Summer gave her sister a tight hug, then walked her to the front door as she left. Sitting alone at her counter, Summer sighed. Now that her sister had gone, and she'd done what she could to set about disrupting demolition, her thoughts drifted back to Aiko. She had to end it.

There was no way around it. Knowing that, even on such a deep level, didn't make her feel any better about it.

She swiveled on the stool to look at her couch. Not too long ago, Aiko had been on that couch with her, kissing her, caressing her, making her senseless with passion. But that was all over now, or at least, it would be soon.

For now, she thought it best not to talk to Aiko. She'd avoid her calls and text messages and generally stay away from her until the first day of demolition came.

The less contact I have with Aiko, the less I have to worry about my feelings getting in the way of what I have to do.

I've made my choice.

Now Aiko has to do the same.

At six thirty on Tuesday morning, Aiko pulled her SUV into an empty spot along the curb across the street from the First Avenue worksite. Yawning as she shut off her engine, she reached for her travel mug. When she lifted it and took a swig, a single drop of tepid coffee slid past her lips, and she groaned.

One cup ain't gonna do. It's too damn early to be up, let alone working. She'd slept like crap the last two nights, thanks to her rising stress levels. Part of that could be attributed to Summer, who seemed to be ignoring her existence all of a sudden. Her calls went unanswered, and her texts unread. Thinking it too invasive to just show up at her apartment, she'd simply given up on reaching out.

For now, though, she needed a pick-me-up to get through the rest of the day. Certain her friends at Kirby Construction would have a coffee maker in their trailer, she got out of her car and inhaled a deep breath of fresh morning air. The temperature was warm, but in the predawn light, the humidity hadn't yet taken hold.

There were orange Kirby trucks parked farther down the road, closer to the corner of First and Grant and the site's entrance.

After crossing the road, she went around the side of the building, then entered through the security fence's gate and shut it behind her. She passed a few employees in bright orange Kirby shirts, vests, and yellow safety helmets. She also saw the diggers, a wrecking ball, and other large equipment parked around the side. "Everything good out here, guys?"

"Right as rain," the foreman, identifiable by his blue vest, called out.

She walked the short distance to the small white trailer sitting in the rear corner of the property, then climbed the four wooden stairs and opened the door.

The interior of the trailer featured a simple setup. A table sat near the door, with extra vests and helmets piled high. Beyond that, there were two more tables. One was set aside with chairs around it in a way that seemed to form a makeshift break room. The other rested against the back wall and had a coffee maker, cups, and all the drink supplies, as well as a basket of snacks. Across from the coffee maker sat a desk, its surface littered with papers, pens, and various tools. Aiko assumed the lone desk belonged to construction manager Bill Kirby. She made a beeline for the coffee station and grabbed a foam cup.

She was still fiddling with the settings on the single-serve coffee maker when she heard the door open and close. Turning her head, she said, "Morning, Bill."

"Morning, Ms. Holt." The big man's voice and manner were jovial despite the early hour. "Helping yourself to a cup of joe?"

"Yeah, I'm trying to. Problem is, I think I might be too tired to figure out how to operate the machine."

He chuckled as he joined her at the coffee station. "That's the one problem with coffee. When you're really zonked, just making a cup becomes an ordeal."

Aiko stepped aside, gratefully observing as he put the small pod into the coffee maker, positioned the cup beneath the spout, and started it up. "Thanks."

"No problem. Today's a big day, and we all need to have our heads in the game." He made himself a cup, and the two of them stood side by side for a few moments, adding cream and sugar to their liking.

Caffeine in hand, they sat across from each other at Bill's desk.

Aiko took a long sip of the dark brew and sighed contentedly. For a few minutes, they simply enjoyed their coffee in amiable silence.

"I'm glad this day has finally come," she admitted. "Seems like we've been building up to it for a really long time."

"Same here. This is one of our more involved projects, considering all the new building materials we'll be using."

She nodded. "It's a good thing, though. I'm glad Yates decided to use green materials; I think it sets a good precedent for others who may want to develop this area further. It'll be nice to finally see what they do with it, too."

"Yep. Once we finish this place up in a few months' time, I'm sure they'll do great things with the site." Bill drained his cup and crushed it before tossing it into the plastic waste bin near the desk. "We'd better get out there. The fun's about to begin."

Aiko finished her coffee, discarded the cup, and followed Bill to the trailer's door. As they descended the steps, Aiko's eye was drawn to First Avenue by a set of flashing lights.

Bill approached his foreman, who stood among a group of workers standing and pointing toward the road. "Tommy, what the hell's going on over there?"

The foreman shrugged. "Not a clue. Just seems to be a whole lot of vehicles pulling up."

"But why?" Bill demanded.

"Beats me." The foreman's face displayed his bewilderment. "Do you want me to go over there and check it out?"

"No, I'll do it. You all get to your stations while I take care of it." Bill was already on the move by the time he finished his statement.

The sun was up higher now, though full daylight had yet to show itself. The site's work lights provided most of the illumination. While Aiko strode across the grass beside the construction manager, her gears started to turn, coffee kicking in. When they stepped through the gate and onto the sidewalk, she was annoyed but not surprised by what she saw.

All along both sides of First Avenue, for the length of the entire block between Grant and Miramar, were vehicles taking up every spot. Scanning the scene, Aiko saw cars, trucks, and, worst of all, vans from various media outlets. There were news vans from both Channel 7 and Channel 10, the tricked-out SUV belonging to local hip-hop radio station 100.5, and a tamer van belonging to the sister station of 100.5 "The Groove," 96.3 WRNB. A white station wagon bearing the logo of Austin's independent newspaper, the *Chronicle*, sat nearest the gate.

One word came to mind, and Aiko uttered it a moment later. "Yikes." She watched as people began to climb out of their conveyances. The media folks hauled out their various equipment; the others carried their brightly colored signs.

"Holy shit," Bill groused. "These folks just won't quit!"

Aiko began to notice that all the people with signs were converging at the same point, an old willow tree on the other side of the street. She knew if she watched that spot long enough, she'd catch a glimpse of their ringleader.

"What on earth are they doing over there?" Bill seemed to have noticed them congregating as well. "Whatever it is, I bet it means trouble for us."

"You're not wrong." Aiko shook her head. *I haven't seen her yet, but I know she's behind this. After all, she's pulled this stunt before.*

Bill stomped out into the road. "Well, I'm going over there, and letting them know they can't be here."

Aiko went with him, but before reaching the tree, the group fanned out and began marching north toward Miramar Boulevard, carrying their signs and chanting. Aiko cringed when she heard what they were saying.

"Hey hey, ho ho! Abernathy has got to go! Hey hey, ho ho! Kirby Construction has got to go!"

As the line moved and flexed, Aiko finally caught a glimpse of Summer. She wasn't marching; instead, she was standing beneath the tree, talking into a microphone held aloft by one of the radio DJs. She could hear Summer's words as they got closer.

"Our main mission for the preservation society is to get people to see the evils of gentrification. We won't stand by and have our neighborhood stripped of its character, or see it slowly destroyed."

Aiko shook her head. *How dramatic can she be?* As Aiko stepped up on the sidewalk, the DJ turned the mic her way.

"All right, listeners, we have someone here that's part of this demolition project. What's your name and affiliation, ma'am?"

"My name is Aiko Holt, I'm a supervisory planner from Abernathy Creative Development, and I have no comment."

The DJ shook his head and drew his mic away. With a chuckle, he announced, "You heard the lady, folks. She's not trying to talk to us."

"I am." Bill's gruff voice cut through the clutter of sound in the area. "I'm Bill Kirby, construction manager. All I want to say is that if all of you people don't get away from my site, I'm having you escorted off the premises. We've got work to do."

Summer narrowed her eyes. "Now, Mr. Kirby, I'm sure you're aware that as long as we stay outside that security fence, we're not trespassing and you can't use the police to get rid of us."

Bill's eyes flashed. "I anticipated as much, little lady. That's why we hired a private security firm, who will gladly do whatever we ask." He folded his arms over his chest.

Summer tensed visibly. For a moment, she looked to Aiko as if waiting for her to say something or intervene somehow. Their eyes connected and held for one long moment, but Aiko remained silent. *I'm not about to stick my neck out for someone who can't be bothered to answer my calls.*

"Sorry," Summer told the DJ, "I'm gonna have to cut this short."

"I feel you, sis. Fight the power." The DJ raised his fist in solidarity.

As Summer stalked away, Aiko trailed behind her. Once they reached the corner at Miramar Boulevard, Summer stopped and spun around to face her. "I can't believe you stood there and let that man threaten me."

Fighting hard not to roll her eyes, Aiko said, "I'm glad you can acknowledge me. But I didn't even know about this paid security until just now. Besides, what was I supposed to say?"

"I don't know. But anything would have been better than nothing."

"I haven't heard anything from you for the last two days. The last time we saw each other before that, you were participating in an effort to ruin my career, which you continued on an even larger scale today. And yet, you expect me to rush to your defense."

Summer's gaze lowered until she was looking at the pavement.

"Why, Summer? Why do you keep doing these things to me when you know my hands are tied?" She tried but failed to keep the hurt and exasperation out of her voice.

"Stop making this about you. This is about so much more."

Aiko threw up her hands. "Whatever it's about, I'm done trying to appease you. You act as if you're some kind of martyr for the cause, but you chose a private school over one in the community when it came time to take a job. I guess only my decisions get scrutinized, though."

Summer looked up again, staring Aiko right in the face. "How could you say that?"

Aiko shrugged. "It is what it is. You could have taken a job here, but you wanted something different. You sold out, Summer. You just won't admit it to yourself."

Summer's lip trembled. "We both made choices, and those choices can't coexist. Tell that guy not to bother calling his guard dogs, we're leaving."

"Good. Because the less of you I see from now on, the better." Aiko paused. "Goodbye, Summer." With that, she turned around and walked away, without so much as a backward glance.

CHAPTER SEVENTEEN

Thursday morning, Summer left the parking garage beneath her building and drove in the opposite direction of the way she normally did. Headed toward her childhood home, she felt the rightness of her decision to take a few days off work.

Yesterday, I went to work and I pushed through it. But I just can't give my students what they need right now, so it's better to let the substitute teacher take over.

When she'd entered Scarlet's office yesterday afternoon, the headmistress took one look at her face and asked how much time off she needed. Gratefully accepting the offer, she'd taken two days off, though Scarlet was willing to give her more. Scarlet kept a cadre of substitutes on hand to make sure her classrooms were always covered. Summer didn't want to waste too much of her PTO, and by Monday, she expected to have sufficiently recovered from the absolute fuckery of the last few days.

Her first step toward recovery, at least in her mind, was a good old-fashioned distraction. To that end, she'd volunteered to drive her parents to the port in Galveston, where they'd embark on a week-long Western Caribbean cruise to celebrate their upcoming thirty-fifth wedding anniversary.

When Summer pulled into the driveway, her parents were already on the porch. While her mother sat on the old swing, her father appeared to be wrestling the last of their bags through the creaky old screen door. They were both decked out in leisure couture, her mother in a butterfly-print maxi dress and a wide-brimmed sun hat, and her father in a Harry Belafonte–esque ensemble of white sneakers, cargo shorts, and a white shirt imprinted with palm fronds and hibiscus blooms. Getting out of the car, she called, "Good morning, lovebirds."

Meadow smiled. "Morning, sugar. Thanks again for volunteering to drive us. You know neither of us likes to drive that long."

"I know." Summer came onto the porch and held the door open for her father. "Dad, let me help with that."

He passed her the handle of the large rolling suitcase. "Have at it. That's your mama's stuff, and you know she packs for every trip like she's going on an extended overseas mission."

Meadow blew a raspberry in her husband's direction. "You won't be complaining when I'm the best-dressed woman at the captain's dinner."

"I'm not complaining now, just saying." He leaned down and pecked Meadow on the forehead. "And you're right. I'll be proud to have you on my arm, and all the other fellas will be jealous of my good fortune."

Meadow blushed. "Rodney, you sweet-talker, you."

"Ewww," Summer teased. "Save it for the stateroom, you two." After helping her parents move their luggage into the trunk of her car and putting one last bag belonging to her mother on the floor behind the driver's seat, she asked, "Who's sitting where?"

"Shotgun!" Meadow climbed into the passenger seat.

Rodney shrugged. "Whatever the lady wants." He ducked into the back seat behind his wife, then closed the door behind him.

With a shake of her head, Summer got into her car, then buckled up. After switching on the radio, she put on a jazz station, keeping the volume low. Driving out of the old neighborhood and through the southeastern fringe of Austin, she glanced surreptitiously at her mother, who quietly flipped through the glossy pages of a travel magazine. It almost felt odd to have her in such close physical proximity after they'd spent so much time avoiding each other. Still, she believed in the veracity of her mother's words and her gesture of giving her the teapot from Mary Ellen's. So while she felt strange at this moment, she didn't feel unsafe.

That's good because I'm already too fragile to add any more complicated feelings to the mix. As she merged into eastbound traffic on State Highway 71, she wondered how long she'd be able to keep her mind off the tragic state of things between herself and her long-held crush.

Her father's voice came from behind her, the depth of it seeming to fill the entire car. "So when are you gonna tell us what's wrong with you?"

She exhaled long and slow. "Dad, I . . ."

"Don't you dare say you're fine, because your face has already told on you." Meadow reached across the center console and touched her daughter's shoulder. "You took time off work, and we know how much you love your students. Something's going on."

"We watch the Channel 10 news, sugar. We know it's got something to do with your grandma's school and that Holt woman." His tone held both sympathy and curiosity. "Just go on and tell us."

"I know I haven't always done right by you," Meadow added. "But I want to try now. I'm ready to listen."

Keeping her slightly watery eyes on the road, Summer unburdened herself by giving her parents a condensed recap of the events of Tuesday morning, ending with her street-corner conversation with Aiko. "I guess I expected her to be upset, but not like that. The whole thing just blew up in my face."

Silence reigned in the car for a few moments before Meadow spoke, "First of all, I'm sorry you're hurting, Summer. It sounds like you're in a tough situation here."

"I am." Summer sniffled, then brushed away the tears that threatened to cloud her vision. "Now I'm beginning to understand all the ways I pushed her away. I don't know what's worse: missing her, or the feelings of regret."

"Goodness." Glancing in the rearview, Summer could see her father shaking his head. He pointed toward a road sign. "We're headed into Columbus. I think we ought to find a place to grab some lunch and talk this out a little more."

Summer exited the highway shortly after that. After finding a fast-food place that wasn't too far off their route, she pulled into the parking lot. Once they were seated in a booth with burgers, fries, and sodas, the conversation continued.

"I'm sure your grandmother would be proud of your commitment." Rodney dunked a fry in a pool of ketchup. "Still, there is such a thing as taking it too far."

Summer released an embittered scoff. "Yeah. I'm not sure where the line is but it seems I've crossed it." She took a long drink from her soda and let the cool bubbly liquid wash down her throat. "I want two things, and I don't see a way to have them both. I loved Grandma, and her legacy is so important to me." She paused. "But I love Aiko, too."

Rodney smiled. "So, she's got your heart, then."

Summer nodded. She'd thought her feelings were intense for Aiko when they were younger. But nothing could have prepared her for the way she felt now, after experiencing Aiko's company, her smile, the comfort of her arms, and the power of her lovemaking.

"Well, that complicates it," her father added. "But it's not insurmountable. Not by a long shot."

Meadow offered a soft smile. "Things have been crazy for you lately. Moving back home after being away for so long, seeing all the things that changed while you were gone, starting a new job. I think you should take some time. Really think about what you need, and what's important to you."

"I thought I knew what was important to me. Saving the world, or at least my little corner of it."

"It's a noble cause, to be sure. But you can't be so single-minded, sugar. Look at things from a wider perspective, and your heart will tell you how to proceed."

Summer reached across the table to grasp her mother's hand and squeezed it. "I can't tell you how much I've missed talking to you like this."

Meadow's smile broadened, and her eyes turned misty. "I've missed it, too. So we won't be going back down that path ever again."

After getting back on the road, they reached the port at Galveston around two o'clock, in plenty of time to make the cruise's four o'clock departure. After taking the exit at Twenty-Second Street and Harborside Drive, Summer followed the signs to the terminal drop-off area. There, she helped her parents get their bags to the porter, hugged and kissed them, and sent them off to enjoy their trip, one that would take them to the shores of both Honduras and Mexico.

After leaving the port, she stopped for gas and then sat in the parking lot, trying to decide where to go next. Going back home was out of the question; everything within a ten-block radius of both her apartment and her childhood home seemed to remind her of Aiko. She pulled out her phone and did a quick search of the attractions in the surrounding area. That helped her settle on her next destination: the historical landmark known as the 1892 Bishop's Palace.

The sprawling Victorian-era mansion, with an interior space of over nineteen thousand square feet, sat on Broadway Avenue like a castle towering over its surroundings. Wandering inside the nineteenth-century grandeur of the structure while reading all the interesting facts posted around during her self-guided tour took a good hour. The mansion was beyond impressive. She soon learned the name of the architect who had built it, a Nicholas J. Clayton.

Has Aiko ever worked on a project of this scale? Has she ever had a hand in building a structure so massive, so sturdily constructed, that it will be around for people to tour two hundred years from now?

They were questions she'd never gotten to ask Aiko, and now, it seemed they would go unanswered. With a shake of her head, Summer left the mansion and its manicured grounds behind.

Still not ready to return to Austin, Summer drove to Galveston Island Historic Pleasure Pier next. The amusement park sat right on the Gulf of Mexico and bustled with a late-summer crowd of folks out enjoying the warm weather. The breeze coming off the water did much to cool her body as she roamed the grounds, taking in the sights and sounds.

The children's laughter and the upbeat music flowing from the rides and games on the midway faded periodically, drowned out by her thoughts of Aiko and the impact of losing her presence in her life. The tears came again, and she didn't bother to brush them away this time, choosing to let them fall, knowing the soft breeze would dry them soon enough.

She stayed long enough to play a few midway games and ride the Galaxy Wheel. At the top of the wheel, she looked over the colorful lights of the park and to the shimmering blue water beyond. The view, spectacular though it was, did little to distract from her very real inner turmoil. When she disembarked from the ride, she saw no further point in remaining on the island. It became clear that no matter how long she lingered here, pain would remain her constant companion.

So she climbed in her car to make the drive back home.

⁓

"Aiko! Don't you hear me calling you?"

Snapped back to reality by Peaches' insistent tone, Aiko shook her head. "Sorry, P. What did you say?"

Gesturing around them to the bustling interior of Austin Beerworks, Peaches said, "I asked what brew you're gonna start with?" Peaches shook her head. "You really bringing down my birthday mood, homie."

Aiko cringed. "My bad. I promise to have my game face on by the time everybody else gets here." It was an empty promise since she'd had very little luck controlling either her emotions or her facial expressions over the past few days. But with the alternative being disappointing her best friend on her birthday, she made the promise, nonetheless. Glancing up at the menu board posted behind the counter, she debated for a moment before answering. "Probably a Galactic Lawnchair, I think." The brew, described by brewery staff as a "low-gravity IPA," was a favorite of hers.

Peaches nodded. "That's more like it. I'm definitely about to have a few, but I might start with the Sun Shovel since I never tried it before."

Glad she'd appeased her friend for the moment, Aiko did her best to channel her mind in the right direction. She'd been haunted day and night by thoughts of Summer. Even though she felt she'd done the right thing by walking away from Summer, that did little to soothe the ache in her chest. Despite all the times and the ways Summer had managed to frustrate her and push her buttons, she still held on to a modicum of guilt about the way things had ended.

The interior of the Beerworks, an Austin institution for two decades, was filled with clean lines fashioned from wood and steel. The polished tables and benches were positioned across the cement floor in a manner both practical and aesthetic. The exposed framework of the building allowed a good view of the brewery equipment. There were never fewer than eight distinct beers on tap, and most of them were exclusives that couldn't be found anywhere else.

Joining Peaches and Aiko was their immediate circle of close friends. Claudia, a self-proclaimed stem, showed up in black shorts, a Hawaiian shirt, an upside-down visor, and black sneakers, her bone-straight hair grazing her shoulders. As she slid onto the bench next to Peaches, she proclaimed, "Party up, bitches!"

Next came Taylor, their nonbinary buddy who worked the shampoo bowl at Fresh Cutz and loved to refer to themself as a "genderless enigma." With them was Jamie, the only high femme in their group. They were dressed alike, in skinny jeans and bedazzled UT Austin jerseys. Taylor's close-trimmed bright red hair contrasted Jamie's chin-length black two-strand twists.

"Well, look at you two, dressed alike. Y'all cute, though." Peaches stood with a laugh, then greeted them with hugs. Their party of five was complete—allowing Peaches' birthday celebration to begin in earnest. "Thank y'all for coming."

They headed out to the CAN-tina, the permanent in-house food truck, and loaded up on tacos, burritos, and nachos. Back at their table, they each got their first brew of the evening, except for Taylor, who ordered a seltzer.

"So, what you got us doing tonight, birthday girl?" Taylor asked before tucking a cheese-laden nacho into their mouth.

"It's gone be very low-key and laid-back, really." Peaches turned up her can of Sun Shovel. "I thought a lot about how I wanted to bring in this new era. I decided I want to just assemble my squad, get fucked up, and chill."

"That's what's up," Jamie commented, raising her 13 Leaf Clover high.

Aiko couldn't help noticing Claudia's sly smirk. *What the hell is she up to? She got that sneaky-ass look on her face.*

Elbow-deep in cheese and salsa, they ate, drank, and talked shit as they always did when they got together. "What's going on with that nail shop you've been trying to open, Jamie?" Aiko asked between bites of her burrito. "Any more progress?"

"I think I found a place I like, but I'm gonna have to talk them down a lil' bit on that lease." Jamie shook her head. "I mean, it's a good space in a nice area, but I think they asking too much."

"Where is it?" The question came from Claudia.

"Buda."

A collective groan went up around the table.

"I looked over there when I was seeking out a spot for the barbershop." Peaches wiped salsa verde from her mouth with a napkin. "You see I ended up in Cannon Oaks. See if you can talk them down, but if not, you can always come over on my side of town."

"You got some pull over there?" Jamie asked.

"I got a good Realtor that knows the area. Just let me know what you need, and I got you." Peaches reached across the table to fist-bump her.

"See?" Claudia clapped her hands together. "This what I'm talking 'bout. We always got each other's backs, and that's what makes our squad the best squad."

Deep into her second beer, Aiko had to agree. The first hint of buzz was upon her, and it helped with dulling her pain. She missed Summer, missed the softness of her body and that sweet smile, but she set that aside.

Tonight's not about me or Summer. It's about making sure Peaches has a kick-ass birthday.

After they'd had their fill of eats and brews, designated-driver Taylor drove them out to Peaches' house in Crestview. The two-story condo in a swanky development featured two bedrooms and two baths, with plenty of space for Peaches and her collection of vintage '80s memorabilia. The group settled onto the sofa and love seat in Peaches' living room while the birthday girl held court in the center of it all. "A, can you set out the snacks and drinks."

"Yeah, I got you." In the kitchen, Aiko pulled out the cheese tray and set it on the dark granite countertop along with a sleeve of red plastic cups, a bowl of chips, some dip, and a dish filled with Peaches' favorite candy, Skittles.

"Gift bag time!" Claudia went to Peaches' coat closet and returned with five blue gift bags. She distributed them, giving the largest one to the birthday girl before scooting off to the kitchen. "What else we drinking?" she asked as she crossed the room and opened the fridge, sticking her head inside.

"Whatever you see in there that you like." Peaches stretched her arms, then placed them behind her head. "Bring me a cup of that Patrón while you in there."

"I see some margarita mix in here, too." Claudia whistled. "I'll bring a round of margaritas and a ginger ale for Taylor."

"Thanks, girl." Taylor glanced up from their phone long enough to grin before returning their attention to the screen.

While absently rooting around in her bag, Aiko felt something semihard and very familiar brush against her hand. After peeking inside at the contents, she snorted. "Claudia, you gave me a dildo?"

"No, bitch. I gave everybody one." Busy making the drinks, she added, "We all use 'em, and I always say the best gift is the practical one. It's some toy cleaner in there, too, so play safe, y'all."

"Nothing practical about this dragon dick you gave me," Peaches quipped as she looked inside her own bag. "But whatever you say, girl."

Aiko could only shake her head. *All my friends are wild, but I swear I love them.*

Nightfall found them all clustered on Peaches' sofa, telling jokes and laughing uproariously. Aiko, having finished up Claudia's rather tequila-heavy margarita, felt herself starting to lean. Her head drooped onto Jamie's shoulder. "Shit, Claudia. That liquor hittin'."

"I make a hell of a drink, don't I?" Claudia giggled. "But the fun's just beginning, y'all."

Through the haze of her tipsiness, Aiko realized she was finally about to find out what Claudia was up to.

A knock sounded at the front door, capturing everybody's attention.

"Who invited extra people?" Peaches groused. "Y'all know I don't like everybody in my house."

Everyone watched as the grinning Claudia bounced off to answer the door. When she returned moments later, Aiko's bottom jaw hit her thigh, and she was sure she wasn't the only one.

Claudia marched proudly into the center of the room, flanked by three fine-ass women who were clad in next to nothing.

"Oh, shit," Peaches whispered. "You got me strippers?"

"Burlesque dancers," Claudia corrected. "We keep it nasty, but classy on tonight."

The three dancers each wore the same costume in different colors. A petite one wore hers in orange, while the most statuesque one wore blue, Peaches' favorite color. Aiko couldn't peel her eyes away from the third—the thickest among the women. She had hazel eyes, just visible above a purple mask, and long waves of dark hair parted in the center and hanging down her back. Her cocoa skin shone. Her shapely body was adorned in sheer, crystal-encrusted purple fabric, with strategically placed satin covering her areolae and the place where her plump thighs met. Be it shapewear or just good genes, every full-bodied inch of her was tucked and tight.

Aiko swallowed, then licked her lips. *I know my eyes big as hell right now.* Yet she was just drunk enough not to care.

"You all right, Aiko?" Taylor laughed as they stood, walking across the room to turn on Peaches' sound system. "'Cause the party just getting started. Don't fall out on us yet, boo."

Aiko straightened up, not wanting to miss whatever show the ladies were about to put on. Peaches, obviously of a similar mind, clapped her hands together. "All right then. How y'all ladies plan on helping me celebrate my birthday?"

The music started then, and Taylor and Claudia returned to the couch as the dancers went into a coordinated routine. Aiko felt her mood improving by leaps and bounds as she enjoyed the sights and sounds of bouncing breasts and clapping cheeks with her closest friends.

A few songs in, the dancers separated from one another. Each of them chose a target then, the shorty in orange tugging Claudia into a standing position and the tall one in blue taking a demure seat on Peaches' lap.

Aiko felt her mouth go dry as Ms. Purple sidled over to her. Before she could draw her next breath, her dark brown breasts were placed squarely in her face. "Wanna party, sugar?"

The sounds of her friends whooping and hollering became muffled as Aiko leaned into the bounty.

Fuck.

Aiko opened her eyes, then immediately squinted against the bright sunlight flowing through the window. Shifting her gaze around, she found herself sprawled across Peaches' sofa. She sat up, regretting the speed of her action since it only caused the pounding in her head to increase. Now that her field of view was changed, she could see the state of the room. Throw pillows, empty red cups, and crumpled napkins were scattered on the soft beige carpet, a sign of the wild night they'd had.

Aiko inhaled, taking in a breath of fresh oxygen accentuated by the scent of frying bacon. Turning her head toward the kitchen, she could see Taylor at the stove. As Taylor turned around, too, they said, "Good morning, sleepyhead."

"Damn." Aiko rubbed her eyes. "What the fuck went on here last night?"

"You don't remember?" Taylor laughed as they cracked eggs into a bowl. "That's why I like being the sober one. Don't worry, I got a lot of it on video."

Aiko swung her legs off the sofa, then looked down as her foot hit something soft. There, between the couch and the coffee table, Claudia lay face down on the floor, snoring softly.

Sheesh. Aiko carefully stepped around Claudia and went to the kitchen. "Where's Jamie and Peaches?"

"Peaches in the bed. Jamie passed out in the coat closet, so Peaches and I threw a blanket over her and let her sleep." Taylor beat the bowl of eggs with a fork. "Y'all was really clowning last night. It was something to see."

"The coat closet?"

"I mean, she went in there with that dancer in orange, and . . ."

"Say no more, fam." Aiko laughed, then cursed as her head pounded. "Oh, shit. Listen, T, tell me the truth. How handsy did I get with that dancer in purple?"

"It wasn't too bad. You stayed in her cleavage for a while, felt on her booty, then she moved on." Taylor poured the eggs into the skillet.

For some reason, Aiko felt relieved to know she hadn't done more with the dancer. But there was still the matter of Summer and what to do about her. Something had to give because she was learning that she didn't do well with heartache.

CHAPTER EIGHTEEN

Thunder rumbled above as Summer drove through the pouring rain on Saturday afternoon, but the weather did nothing to deter her. She'd reached the stage of her sadness where only copious amounts of cake could help. With that in mind, Summer was on her way to the place that had the best baked goods she'd ever tasted outside of those baked by her own sainted grandmother.

Parking in front of Swingin' Sweets, she decided to forgo her umbrella. The distance between the curb and the door was so short. Grabbing her purse, she bolted through the sheets of rain and pushed her way through the glass doors.

She entered to find the place empty except for its proprietors. Kat, posted behind the counter, was leaning over the countertop, flipping through the pages of a book. Nellie sat at a table just inside the door, quietly dozing.

The sounds of the steadily falling rain, swirling wind, and distant thunder were muffled but still very identifiable. For a moment, Summer looked out on the streets, watching as water rushed over the curb to fill the gutters and as windswept trees waved their branches, dancing beneath the gray sky.

Kat looked up as Summer approached. "Summer. It's good to see you again, though you might be the only one willing to come out in this weather."

Summer chuckled. "Hey, Kat. Channel 7 said the storm would probably last a few more hours, and I just couldn't wait that long. I need cake, stat."

Kat laughed, and the sound echoed through the store and woke Nellie from her impromptu nap.

"Summer. What are you doing out in this weather?" Nellie stifled a yawn as she straightened in her chair.

"What can I say? I'm having a cake emergency."

Nellie stood, then walked behind the counter. "We gotta take care of our girl, Kat."

"I agree, my love." Kat's smile was accompanied by a giggle as Nellie wrapped an arm around her waist and nuzzled her neck.

Summer's heart squeezed in her chest. *I love seeing them together, but right now, it hurts like hell.* She turned away for a moment, feeling the involuntary grimace taking over her face. When she turned back, she found both of the bakers watching her with unveiled concern in their eyes.

"I know you said you had a cake emergency, but it looks pretty serious, based on your expression." Nellie continued to watch Summer as she spoke. "Tell me your order, and I'll decide based on that."

Summer swallowed. "I want a marble pound cake and a triple-chocolate Bundt. Extra ganache."

Nellie and Kat looked at each other, then back at Summer.

"Girl." Kat whistled. "Extra ganache? Honey, we gone have to sit down and talk about whatever's bothering you before we serve you."

Summer folded her lips into a mock pout. "Can't I just take my cakes and go home? Find some solace in your confections?"

Nellie shook her head so vigorously, a few of her dreadlocks fell free of the high bun she'd styled them in. "Maybe if you were just any random off the street, we'd let you buy your stuff and go. But one of our best customers, who's been coming here since she was knee-high to a piano bench?" She shook her head again. "Nope. Gone over there to that table and sit your butt down."

Summer looked to Kat for help, only to have her point to a table. "I'll get us some tea and be over there in a minute."

While Kat disappeared into the kitchen, Nellie escorted Summer to a four-top table in the front corner of the bakery, letting her sit first. Nellie sat across from her, closest to the window. "You can decide the best way to tell your story while Kat makes the tea."

Summer turned the offer over in her mind. *How do I describe my utter heartbreak? My disappointment and sadness at how I acted, and the way things turned out?* Maybe there was no eloquent way to express such deep, unsettling emotions. She only hoped they'd understand where she was coming from and perhaps offer some new insight.

Kat came then with a small tray holding three steaming ceramic cups. After setting one in front of each of them, she took the last cup, then propped the tray up in the windowsill beside Nellie.

"What kind of tea is this? It smells amazing," Summer said.

"It's jasmine-and-citrus green tea, with a dollop of honey." Kat took a small sip from her cup. "Try it, it's good."

Summer took a tentative sip, then let the warm, sweet, and slightly floral brew flood her mouth. Swallowing, she nodded. "It is pretty good." She took another sip and enjoyed the way the tea seemed to warm her entire body, helping shake off the slight chill of her damp clothes against her skin.

"Glad you like it. Now, tell us what's going on." Nellie wrapped her hands around her cup. "We're all ears."

Summer drew a deep breath, then began her tale. Nellie and Kat paid rapt attention to her as she told them everything, going back to her days as a teen carrying a torch for Aiko and then up to their recent time together, ending with their breakup a few days ago. "I'm not sure where things went off the rails, and now, the whole train has crashed and burned."

Kat's eyes held sympathy. Her mouth twisted into a frown edged with sadness, then she said, "Oh, honey. I'm so sorry."

"I appreciate that." Summer drank more of the tea. "These last few days have been absolute misery. I took Thursday and Friday off of work, and the only productive thing I've done since then was to take my parents to the port for their anniversary cruise."

"Come on. You've done other things since then, right?" Nellie asked.

"Sure, I have. I've wandered aimlessly around Galveston, stared out the window, listened to sad songs, and cried into my cereal. Today, I finally got so desperate to drown my sorrows in cake that I left my apartment in a damn monsoon." Summer shrugged. "Believe me now?"

"Yikes." Nellie stared at Summer. "You got it bad, girl."

"Yeah. And when I get here and see the two of you together, somehow that makes the pain even worse, which I didn't think was possible." Summer paused. "Don't get me wrong. I love the way you two love each other. Seeing you show that love, openly and shamelessly, was a balm to my little queer soul as a young woman. But now, your happiness only reminds me of all the wonderful things I'm missing out on."

The sympathy in Kat's face dialed up to level ten, and Kat pressed her palm to her chest. "That's so sweet. I'm touched to hear you looked up to us, and you want what we have. The real question is, do you want it with her?"

The tears came then, spilling over Summer's cheeks without warning. As Nellie handed her a napkin from the tabletop dispenser, Summer offered a slow nod. "Yes. I want a life with her. I fell in love with her, and I never even got the chance to tell her."

"I've been thinking about the things you said, how you described your actions." Nellie tapped her chin. "My question is, why? What made you so hell-bent on stopping that project going forward, and why now?" She tilted her head to the right. "No offense, but change has been happening in Ivy, and in Austin at large, for a while now. You just haven't been around to witness it."

A sob rose in Summer's throat then, and the sound rose over the pounding of the rain hitting the roof.

Kat elbowed Nellie. "That did it."

"I didn't mean to upset her. I said no offense," Nellie explained.

As Summer recovered from her burst of emotion, she had a moment of intense clarity. "That's why. That's precisely why." She wiped her tears with the crumpled napkin. "I wasn't here for the changes, I wasn't there to intervene, or to do anything meaningful to preserve all the magic of my home, of this place I love so much." She sniffled. "And then, when I finally do come home, I take a job at a private school."

"And now you feel guilty." Kat stated it as fact.

She nodded. "Yes. And I let that guilt take over my entire being and drive all my actions since the day I moved home." She sighed. "How could I not have seen this before? How could I have let things get so bad that they blew up in my face?"

"Sometimes we can't see what we're doing to the people we love until after it's over." Nellie stood. "You know what they say about hindsight."

"I have to fix this. I have to do something to get her back." Summer was on her feet in a flash. "I'd like to change my order. Just the triple-chocolate, no extra ganache."

Kat smiled. "Looks like another crisis averted, Nel."

Arriving home a short time later with her freshly baked cake, Summer cut herself a big slice. With the cake and glass of milk in hand, she went into her office, sat at her desk, and brought her computer out of its sleep state.

Inhaling the rich scent of the cake, she thought about her favorite bakers and the way they took the same basic recipe and remixed it. *One foundation, many variations, each one unique and delicious. But it was all still cake. The same approach Kat and Nellie applied to their cakes could be applied to my life.*

Between forkfuls of cake, Summer crawled the internet, gathering all the information she'd need to make a real difference as it pertained to the Sojourner Truth project. Then she compiled her statistics, data, and sources into a document and backed it up to her personal cloud.

When done, Summer left her computer and returned to the kitchen to wash and put away the dishes she'd used. Heading into her bedroom, she flicked on the light in her closet and reached toward the back of the single shelf that spanned its length. She dragged down the small wooden chest, then took it with her and sat on her bed.

She opened it and dumped its contents onto her comforter. The chest, which had belonged to her grandmother and been left to her by the stipulations of her grandmother's will, contained a plethora of mementos. There were aged, sepia-toned photographs, letters exchanged between her grandparents, and a small leather-bound journal her grandmother had kept when she was younger.

Picking up the journal from the pile, Summer ran her hand lovingly over the slightly cracked cover. She opened it and flipped through the pages, looking at the dates in the upper-right corner of each page. Stopping on one dated in the mid-2000s, she read the entry. She was a few lines in before she realized its significance: it had been written on her grandmother's last day at school—the day she retired.

Today, I step away from my work, from the school I founded so many years ago, and from the students I love. Part of me would remain in this position until the Lord calls me home, but I know there are younger, equally capable people to fill this role. Now is their time to do the work. And for me, the time has come to spend more time with my family. I look forward to the years with my children, and my grandchildren. But most of all, I look forward to quiet evenings spent in the arms of the one I love.

Wiping a tear from her eyes, Summer closed the journal, then returned it and the rest of the items to the chest. After she'd replaced the chest in its special spot, she sat on her bed, thinking about what she'd read. In the silent apartment, with the rain still falling outside her window, she came to know what her grandmother had known all those years ago.

There is joy in the work.

And love only makes that joy more complete.

～

Arms laden with plastic grocery bags, a soggy Aiko rang her mother's doorbell just before six o'clock Saturday evening. Aiko had been at home, recuperating from a night of alcohol-fueled foolishness, when she'd gotten a call from her mother, who asked her to go out into the rain to pick up a few things. So, like any good daughter, she'd thrown on her sweats and a hoodie.

Meanwhile, the list she texted me had way more than a few items on it.

Thankfully, the thunder and flashes of lightning from earlier in the day had passed by the time she'd left her house, leaving behind only a softly falling drizzle. Still, it had been raining most of the day with no signs of stopping, and the dampness in the atmosphere caused an unseasonable chill in the air.

Aiko was contemplating ringing the bell again when her mother swung the front door open. "There you are. Just bring that stuff in and set it on the counter."

Aiko walked through the door as her mother held it open, then jogged to the kitchen and set the armload of bags down. "Mama, you do know grocery delivery is a thing now, right? You just go online or use an app."

Janet pursed her lips and rested one hand on her housecoat-clad hip. "I know that. I'm old, not out of touch. I just don't trust strangers to pick my meat and produce. You, on the other hand, know my standards." Janet sidled past Aiko into the kitchen, then grabbed Aiko's cheek and gave it a pinch. "Now come on and help me put this stuff away."

They worked together to put away most of the groceries, leaving some ingredients out to prepare dinner.

"It's been ages since I had your Cajun chicken Alfredo," Aiko commented.

"Then you're due for a dose," Janet joked. She set her cast-iron skillet on the stove to heat up. Drizzling olive oil into it, she said, "Pound out that chicken breast for me. And while you do, tell me all about Peaches' birthday party. Did you gays and theys have a good time?"

Aiko stopped midstep, holding the pack of chicken breast. Brow arched, she stared at her mother and gave a single, slow blink.

"As I said, I'm old, but not out of touch. So tell me what happened." Janet pulled out her stockpot from a lower cabinet, filled it with water, and set it on a burner to boil.

Aiko placed the chicken inside a gallon-sized resealable bag, then put it on the designated poultry cutting board and laid into it with her mother's old stainless-steel meat mallet. Speaking loudly enough to be heard over the steady thud of her pulverizing the chicken, Aiko recapped the night—or at least the parts she thought her mother could bear to hear. "I definitely drank too much. I don't remember all of it, and it took me most of the day to shake that hangover headache." She shrugged. "At least Taylor got some good footage of it."

Janet shook her head. "Y'all are a whole mess. What about Peaches? Have you talked to her today?"

"I did, she called while I was driving here from the store." Aiko slid the cutting board over the counter toward her mother, who began seasoning the chicken. "She said she had a great time, and that thirty-three suits her quite nicely."

"That's good to hear." Finished with seasoning, Janet laid the chicken in the hot skillet. The sounds of sizzling rose to accompany the bubbling emanating from the stockpot. "I'm glad my bonus daughter had a good birthday. But as for you, we need to talk, missy."

Aiko dropped her gaze. *Damn. I didn't even tell her the most scandalous thing I did last night, and I'm still in trouble?* She'd left out her time spent getting friendly with the burlesque dancer, partly because she didn't remember most of it and partly so she wouldn't offend her mother's tender sensibilities. Doing her best to keep her expression and tone neutral, Aiko said, "Okay, Mama, what is it?"

"I just want to point out something about you that I think you may not realize." Janet tore open a box of penne pasta and added it, along with a few stems of basil and some chicken bouillon, to the boiling water.

"What's that?" Aiko was almost afraid to ask, but her curiosity demanded satisfaction.

"Whenever you get into a negative emotional state, you drown yourself in bad decisions. You only ever behave in that way when you're running from something." Janet stirred the pasta with a wooden spoon. "So, based on that story you just told me about Patricia's birthday party, I know two things."

Oh, snap. She used Peaches' government name. That means she's about to drag me, and maybe all of us.

"One, you're leaving out some details of what happened last night, so you won't offend me."

Aiko cringed. It wasn't easy being read like a book, let alone by the woman who'd given her life. She started to respond but thought better of it.

"And two," Janet continued as she used a spatula to flip the chicken breast, "something has happened between you and Summer, and you haven't told me about that, either."

By now, Aiko was sweating, more from her mother's scrutiny than the heat rising from the stovetop. "What makes you say that?"

"I thought you might ask that, so I have two examples. I'll give 'em to you at the table, though. I need to focus on finishing my Alfredo."

Aiko nodded, then busied herself by taking out two china plates and sets of silverware along with two glasses. She filled the glasses with lemonade and carried everything to the table while her mother put the final touches on her signature dish.

Soon, they were seated at the table—plates piled high with pasta. Janet had added spinach and sun-dried tomatoes toward the end and drizzled the dishes with balsamic vinegar and parmesan. As she ate, Aiko reveled in the fireworks that the spicy chicken set off in her taste buds, loving the way it combined with the smoothness of the Alfredo sauce.

After she'd finished eating, Janet picked up right where she'd left off. "So, I promised you some examples. I can think of two good ones. Remember when you dated that girl in college? Your first serious girlfriend?"

Aiko frowned. *How could I forget that shit show?* "Yes, Mama. I remember Laquita."

"Then you'll recall that when she broke things off with you, you suddenly lost interest in going to class or turning in your assignments. You'd had a near-perfect GPA all freshman year, but after that girl was through with you, you dropped down to a C average."

After drinking from her glass, Aiko said, "Okay, that's more time than I wanted to spend thinking about that incident."

"I know. But there's still one more." Janet tilted her head. "This time, it involves Sharon, that woman you dated at the first architecture job you got after graduation. What was that firm called again?"

"Landon and Vincent."

"Right, right. Anyway, you broke company policy to date her, which I told you was a bad idea. Then you found out she was taking credit for your ideas and using you to get a promotion. And after you broke up with her, what did you do next?"

Aiko felt her shoulders droop. "I quit."

"That's right. You quit your very first job in your field, after less than eight months working, without another job lined up." Janet blew out a breath. "Bad feelings, bad decisions."

"Is that it, Mama? Please tell me those are your only examples."

"They are. I rest my case." Janet leaned back in her chair, stretching. "Now it's your turn to talk. Tell me what happened with Summer, beyond what I heard on the radio and through the neighborhood gossip mill."

"What did you hear?"

"That she and a bunch of protestors crashed your site on demolition day."

"That's true. I pulled her aside after all that, and we ended up arguing. I told her I didn't want to see her anymore."

"I see." Janet was quiet for a few moments as if thinking over her daughter's words. "Let me tell you something about your father and me. I haven't really spoken about it with you before, and I think you need to hear it now."

"I'm listening."

"I never pressured Kosuke. I told him I was pregnant because he had a right to know. But I never tried to force him to marry me, or to be in your life. I let him know, in no uncertain terms, that I would do whatever it took to ensure you had a good life. And then I left the choice up to him as to what he would do next."

"And he went back home."

"Yes. Because he and I weren't a love match. We were never meant to be, just two people who turned to each other for a little excitement, a little warmth." She smiled. "But look what he did. He supported you from day one, financially anyway. And now you and him have a relationship I was afraid you'd never have."

"There's still plenty of room for growth there, but I think I see what you're getting at."

"The point I'm trying to make is, what's meant to be, will be. You can't shape and mold someone into who you want them to be; they're a person, not a lump of clay. You just have to trust that if you leave it up to them, and let them choose, things will work out as they should."

"So, you're saying you don't regret not marrying Pops?"

Janet shook her head. "Heavens, no. I've enjoyed the freedom of being single all these years, and so has Kosuke. We're both free to pursue our passions; plus, being single doesn't mean being alone."

Aiko thought for a moment about the connotations of that before shaking her head. "Cool, cool. But let's not travel too far down that road."

Her mother laughed. "Just let Summer be who she is. And if you two are truly meant to be together, she'll find her way back to you."

Aiko sighed. "It's not what I want to hear, but it makes a whole lot of sense."

"Of course it does." Janet stood and gathered the dishes. When she returned from putting them in the dishwasher, she said, "Why don't you sleep in your old room tonight?"

"I think I will. Sounds way better than going back out in the rain."

"Good. I'm going to read in bed for a little while." She kissed Aiko's forehead, then disappeared down the hall.

Later, Aiko lay in bed in her childhood room, her gaze resting on the glow-in-the-dark stars stuck to the ceiling above her. The stars still had a bit of their phosphorescence and cast a mottled-green glow onto her comforter.

Aiko thought about her mother's advice to essentially leave things be and allow Summer to decide.

It's not going to be easy. But I think I'm going to try it anyway.

Either she'll come back to me, or I'll have to learn to live without her.

CHAPTER NINETEEN

Monday afternoon, Summer tossed her things into her tote bag and left school as quickly as possible. It was just after two o'clock when she merged onto MOPAC going north. Around thirty minutes later, she arrived at Research Park Place, one of the newer, swankier office complexes in the greater Austin area. While she'd never been there before, today, she had a very good reason to make her first visit.

Pulling into a parking spot, she glanced at the bright red folder hanging out of her tote bag. The folder contained several hours' worth of her research, notes, and carefully drawn conclusions on tearstained paper. Summer tucked the folder fully inside her bag to cut the risk of dropping it or any of its precious contents along the way, grabbed the tote, and got out of her car.

After crossing the massive parking lot to what appeared to be the main entrance, she grabbed the polished steel handle and used it to pull the heavy glass door open. Inside, she looked around the cavernous interior in awe. The lacquered concrete floors and soft gray walls made the place appear professional and elegant. *It's certainly a far cry from the little brick building I work in. No bulletin boards, laughing kids, or primary colors here. I don't think I could work in a place like this. Too quiet.*

There was a long counter running along a good portion of the length of the eastern wall, fashioned of steel and glass, just like the building itself. She assumed it to be a reception area for the whole building. No one was there at the moment, so she decided to find her own way rather than waiting for help to appear.

She made a beeline through the cavernous lobby to the large black lacquer directory on the wall between the two elevator banks. She got close enough to read the text, engraved on small individual plaques, each corresponding to a suite inside the building. Scanning through the dozen or so businesses that occupied office space there, her gaze finally settled on the one she was looking for.

ABERNATHY CREATIVE DEVELOPMENT. SUITE 201. 2F, WEST.

She pressed the up button for the elevator and waited. A car arrived shortly and whisked her to the second floor. When she exited, she looked to her left.

Suite 201 lay directly in front of her. A large blue-and-gold logo was printed on the glass doors displaying the company name and the phrase "Since 1996." Seventy-five percent or more of the wall was made of glass, allowing her to see some of the goings-on inside the suite. She could see the reception area, and behind it, part of an empty conference room and another small room where a young man stood over a machine making copies of something.

Coming closer to the door, she saw the decals posted in a line beneath the logo. Among them were the distinctive ribbon logo of the Greater Austin Chamber of Commerce, a square-shaped one for Texas Women in Business Austin, and another that simply read Proudly Black-Owned.

Hmm. Seems Mrs. Abernathy is very much tied into the community. That gives me hope.

Summer pushed the door open, then entered the suite and approached the reception desk. A young, pretty Black woman with box braids, wearing a white blouse and navy skirt, smiled as Summer came near. "Welcome to Abernathy Creative Development. How can I help you?"

"Hi. I'd like to see Aiko Holt please."

"Do you have an appointment?"

Summer shook her head. "I don't, but I'm hoping she can squeeze me in."

"I can certainly ask her." After picking up the phone, she used her shoulder to hold the handset to her ear. "What's your name?"

"Summer Graves."

"Okay. Just give me one moment and I'll check with her. You can have a seat right there." She gestured to the black Queen-Anne style chairs positioned around a low black lacquer table.

"Thank you." Summer went to the chair in the far corner and sat down, then placed her tote bag on her lap. In her mind, one of two things was about to happen. Either Aiko would soon appear before her, or the nice lady behind the desk would ask her to leave. Either way, at least she could say she'd given it a shot.

I have so much to say to her, and it needs to be said in person, not over the phone or by text.

Summer remained in the chair, doing her best not to stare at the receptionist while she waited. While nervously crossing and uncrossing her legs, she stared at the pattern on the Persian rug beneath the furniture grouping.

"Summer?"

Summer slowly looked up, her gaze traveling from a pair of stylish black loafers to slim black trousers with a dark leather belt encircling the waist. Aiko also wore a crisp pink shirt, black vest, and pink-and-black striped bow tie. Aiko's hair was wrapped in that sleek low bun again, and her lips were slightly parted. When Summer's gaze finally met Aiko's, Summer struggled to hold back her tears.

Aiko's brow creased as if she sensed Summer's emotions threatening to bubble over. Grabbing Summer's arm, she helped her stand. "Here. Let's go talk outside." As they left, Aiko said to the receptionist, "Hold my calls for about fifteen minutes, Tricia."

"You got it," Aiko heard the young woman respond as she ushered Summer out the door.

Aiko led Summer past the suite and down a short corridor to what appeared to be an out-of-the-way common area. The area sat on an extended balcony of sorts—one that jutted out over the cavernous lobby below. Two tan leather love seats faced a low marble-topped table between them.

They each took a seat on one of the love seats; Summer left a bit of distance between them, unsure how Aiko would react if she got too close.

"Thank you for seeing me." Summer kept her voice low. "I would have understood if you didn't want to."

Aiko cleared her throat. "You caught me off guard, that's for sure. But out of all the times you've done that, this time is the most low-key."

Summer closed her eyes against the guilt attached to her previous actions and steeled herself with a deep breath. When she opened her eyes again, she found Aiko watching her. "I don't want to take too much of your time, I know you're working. But there are some things I have to say to you, and they had to be said in person."

"I'm listening."

"The first thing you need to know is that I was wrong, and I'm sorry. I was doing way too much, and now that I'm looking back on it, I can see that clearly."

Aiko's brow arched. "Wow."

"I need you to understand that I'm not apologizing for my dedication to my grandmother's legacy, or for being concerned about what happens to my old neighborhood. But I'm deeply sorry for the way I expressed those concerns. I should not have done so much to make your job difficult, nor should I have tried to force you to do things that may have put your job at risk."

"Wow."

"Can I ask why you keep saying that?"

Aiko chuckled. "I'd tell you, but I doubt you'd believe me."

Summer frowned, somewhat confused by the cryptic statement.

"It's like I've always said. I respect your dedication to what you believe in. And I'm sorry if it seemed like I was trying to talk you out of pursuing the things that were important to you, or if my attitude came off as condescending or dismissive."

Summer felt the smile tugging her lips. "You had your moments. But I was so much worse, and I hope you can forgive me, even if you can't do it right now." She paused, taking a deep breath. "There's something else I need to say."

Aiko inched closer to her. "Go ahead."

"I love you. I've known for a little while now, and you should know it, too." Summer let her gaze rest on her lap, too afraid to look into Aiko's eyes right then.

Aiko chuckled softly, then responded, "I guess that's fair, since I love you, too."

Summer blinked back tears as she lifted her head, and their eyes met. "Really? You wouldn't joke about this, would you?"

Aiko shook her head. "No. I'm serious. I do love you, and I'll gladly tell you as many times as you need to hear it, so you'll believe it."

Summer fell into Aiko's arms and let herself be enfolded. She was unable to stop the tears coursing down her face.

Aiko nuzzled against her, burying her face in Summer's hair. "I missed you so much."

"Don't worry." Summer dabbed at her eyes. "You'll never have that problem again."

Aiko laughed and loosened her grip just a bit. "You're too much, Summer."

"Not for you, I'm not." Summer winked. Glancing at Aiko's shoulder and seeing the wet spot there, she cringed. "Oh, no. I messed up your shirt."

"No worries. I keep a couple of spares in my office." Aiko wriggled her tie. "With coordinating ties, of course."

Shaking her head, Summer reveled in the lightness she felt in that moment, a feeling that had seemed lost to her just hours ago. Now that she and Aiko had made amends, they could move toward their dreams and goals together. "Of course."

"Since that's out of the way, what brought you to my office? You could have just asked me to meet you somewhere." Aiko eyed her. "Were you trying to corner me?"

Summer laughed. "Yes, and no. I came here because I have a proposal involving the site."

Aiko pursed her lips.

"No, really. I just need you to hear me out. I promise it doesn't involve any further interruption to your work over there. I even disbanded the preservation society. Took down the page and everything."

"Really?"

"Sure. Have a look." Summer waited while Aiko ran an internet search for the name of her group.

"I clicked the link, and it says 'Page not found.'"

"See? It's time I change my approach. Less protesting, more working within the confines of the project."

Aiko stood, clapping her hands. "Then let's go to my office."

⌒

Aiko let Summer into her private office and closed the door behind them. "All right, let me hear this grand plan of yours. And please tell me you have something written up about it."

"Of course I do." Summer gestured to Aiko's desk. "I'll lay it all out here if that's okay."

Walking around her desk, Aiko opened the top drawer and swept her stapler, pen cup, and a few other odds and ends into it. "Go ahead. I'm gonna change shirts."

While Aiko grabbed a clean shirt in a bright shade of melon, along with a coordinating tie, from her lower drawer, Summer pulled out a red folder. She opened it and fanned the papers across the desktop, displaying them to face Aiko. Then, she took a seat in the guest chair.

Aiko undid her vest, then turned her back to Summer as she removed it and the damp shirt, which had a hint of black mascara on the shoulder. She put on the clean shirt, buttoned it, and donned the vest again. She turned around as she secured her tie and noticed Summer staring at her with wide eyes. "What is it?"

Summer licked her lips, and her brown eyes smoldered with heat. "I just . . . really want to . . . well, you know."

Aiko smiled, tucking the tail of her shirt into her trousers. "I know, *koibito*. But we need to take care of this first."

Summer's lips twisted into a pout that Aiko found precious. "What was that word you just called me?"

"*Koibito*. It's Japanese for lover . . . or girlfriend." She chuckled. "If we're ever in Japan, though, just know I won't be saying that word out loud. Culturally, pet names aren't really a thing over there."

A soft smile replaced Summer's pout. "Fair enough."

"And as for . . . you know what, trust me, it's gonna get handled." Aiko held Summer's gaze. "When we get this taken care of, I'm leaving for the day. We're gonna make up for the lost time." Aiko winked, then sat down in her chair. "Where should I begin?"

Summer swallowed, then pointed to one of the pages. "Start here and read to the right. They're basically in order."

Aiko read over the data. Charts and tables pulled from scholarly sites online, showing various statistical data about Ivy, East Austin, and the Austin metro area. "Okay. What I'm seeing here is a lot of statistics about people of color in this area. Graduation rates versus dropout rates. Unemployment for young people. Health statistics."

"Right. I did my research, and just like I suspected, there's a disparity. On the whole, people living in our old neighborhood near East

Austin and the surrounding areas have it a lot harder than others in the broader city." She pointed to one of the pages. "For example, see how Ivy's graduation rates compare to those of other, wealthier areas like Zilker, or Rosedale, or Barton Hills?"

"Yeah, I can see that in the figures, and I can see it anecdotally." Aiko leaned back in her chair. "Just a quick drive around the city will show you the difference between those areas. Wealthy areas also tend to have better schools, which leads to higher student-retention rates. What are you getting at?"

"It's not just better schools that set those ritzy areas apart. It's community resources. There are far more fitness centers, after-school-care programs, safe places for young people to socialize, job opportunities, you name it."

"Right. People in those areas usually demand as much."

"And their money speaks on their behalf." Summer shook her head. "Anyway, people in my old neighborhood aren't any less worthy of such resources than families living in Barton Hills." Her eyes were alight with excitement. "If the development going up at the Sojourner Truth site is really going to be so large and modern, why can't we use some of the space to bring some much-needed resources to the community?"

Aiko tapped her chin. "Yates has been pretty noncommittal about how they'll use the space. I know they have some tenants lined up, but as far as I know, there are still some empty suites, as well."

"Good. Then that space could be potentially used in a way that actually benefits the neighborhood." Summer smiled. "We just have to convince the developer."

Aiko nodded and rubbed her hands. "You've already done most of the legwork here, but I can't really interrupt Miriam with this right now."

Summer's lips twisted slightly. "How are we going to handle this, then?"

"I'll talk to Miriam and to the folks at Yates, and see if I can set up a meeting. Do you have any free days coming up?"

Summer's expression relaxed. "Actually, I do. I've already taken this Friday off of work. It's my mother's birthday."

"What time do the festivities start?"

"Oh, not until lunchtime," Summer replied. "Mama's not much of a morning person these days."

"I'll see if I can set something up for Friday morning. Maybe we can convince Peter Yates to commit to a tangible plan, one that will benefit the community."

"Awesome." Summer stood, then rounded the desk. "Now, about that makeup sex . . ." Her voice trailed off as she fixed Aiko with her sultriest stare.

Aiko's hand shot to her own neck. As she loosened the knot of her tie, she all but growled, "As soon as I tie up my work for the day, that ass is mine."

Summer licked her lips. "I'm counting on it. Just remember that turnabout is fair play, baby."

CHAPTER TWENTY

Summer stepped over the threshold into Aiko's house, then moved aside so Aiko could close the door behind them. "You've got a nice place."

"Thanks." Aiko locked the door, then tossed her keys in a nearby wooden tray. "I'd like to show you the rest of it since it's your first time being here."

"Great." Summer followed Aiko around her home, viewing the living and dining rooms, the spare bedroom Aiko used as an office, and the other bedroom set aside for guests.

Walking toward the back door, Aiko said, "I feel like I should leave my bedroom for last."

"Why?" Summer teased.

"You know if we go in there, that's gonna be the end of the tour." Aiko chuckled, sliding open the glass door. "Come outside with me. There's something I want to show you."

Summer's eyes widened when she got outside and saw the small steel-framed structure sitting in the corner of the backyard. "You have a greenhouse? I had no idea you were such a hard-core gardener."

Aiko shook her head. "Nah. My mama's the hard-core gardener. I have a few types of plants, but I have a lot of the one I love the most." She untied a canvas rope, then lifted the see-through flap. "Come on in and take a look."

Summer entered, amazed at the sight of so many colorful plastic pots holding tall, regal blooms. "Are these orchids?"

"Yes. I collect them and grow them. I particularly like rare or cross-bred orchids, and I've been known to breed a few myself."

Summer stopped in front of a shelf filled with orchids with snow-white petals and bordered in a deep, rich shade of purple. "What's this one called?"

"This variety is called *Vanda coerulescens*. It's native to China, India, and Thailand, and it cost me a mint to get it here. I like it because not only does it have this awesome coloring, but it's hardy and very easy to divide and get a bunch of new blooms from. That's why I have so many."

"I see. They're really beautiful, I can see why you like them." Summer inhaled the subtly sweet fragrance. "How did you get into growing orchids in the first place?"

"Not only is my mother an avid gardener, but she worked at a plant nursery when I was younger. I saw the orchids on display there and thought they were so neat. That's how this whole thing got started."

"It's definitely not your average hobby," Summer commented as they left the greenhouse.

Aiko retied the flap, and they headed to the house. Once they were inside, Summer grabbed Aiko's hand. "I really want to see your bedroom now."

Aiko smiled. "I was just about to offer you some food. You're not hungry?"

"Oh, I'm hungry." Summer locked eyes with Aiko. "Just not for food."

Aiko's tongue darted across her lower lip. Silently, she tugged Summer through the family room into a short corridor leading to her room. The room was of a good size and sparsely furnished with only a dresser doubling as a TV stand, two nightstands, and the king-sized bed outfitted with plush white bedding. Two pillow shams featured a black fleur-de-lis emblem, providing the only bit of color in the hotel-like color scheme. Light-filtering curtains on the windows made the space dim but not totally dark.

Aiko draped her arms around Summer's waist and moved her toward the bed. Stepping out of her loafers, she asked, "What do you think of my room?"

"I like what I see." Kicking off her sandals, Summer reached up to undo the bow tie around Aiko's neck. Her voice barely a whisper, Summer added, "What I really want to do, though, is test the acoustics of the space . . . and the springs on this bed." She tossed the tie aside and began working on Aiko's vest buttons.

Summer took her time, moving in a slow, deliberate fashion as she undressed Aiko, stripping away her business attire to reveal the lithe, athletic body beneath. When Summer pushed off Aiko's shirt, she placed a series of soft kisses along the column of Aiko's throat.

"Mmmm." A low, rumbling groan left Aiko's throat.

Aiko's shirt landed on the pile of clothes on the floor, which was soon joined by Aiko's trousers, sports bra, and boxer briefs. Fully nude, Aiko stood there in all her glory while Summer placed soft kisses and slow licks in every nook and cranny she could access. Aiko's strangled moans only urged her on, a sound like music of the most erotic kind.

Summer took off her sundress and undergarments and tossed them on the floor among Aiko's scattered clothing. Lowering herself to her knees between the foot of the bed and her lover, Summer ran a hand along Aiko's hip. "Prop your foot up on the bed for me, boo."

"What you doing?" Aiko whispered.

"You know what I'm doing." Summer applied gentle upward pressure to the back of Aiko's thigh. "Now put that leg up and let me do my work."

Aiko exhaled and did as Summer asked, resting her foot on the end of the mattress.

Summer trailed kisses along Aiko's lower belly, then leaned in and placed another kiss in the dark curls crowning the V of Aiko's thighs. Then Summer moved lower and swiped the tip of her tongue over Aiko's clit before leaning in fully.

Aiko's knees buckled a bit, and Summer clamped an arm around her waist to steady her. *Stopping is not an option. Not now, not when I'm just getting started tasting Aiko's sweetness—a delicacy I was almost cut off from forever.* Summer remained there, alternating between worshipping Aiko's clit and dipping her tongue inside her until Aiko's rising moans morphed into a long, guttural cry. Then Summer stayed a few moments longer, enjoying the warm honey flowing from Aiko until Aiko finally caught hold of the back of her neck and dragged her up.

"Damn, Summer." She breathed the words into the side of Summer's neck as she pulled her into her arms.

They fell onto the bed then, a tangle of limbs kissing, caressing, and enjoying each other. Summer felt a persistent throbbing deep in her pussy, a desperate need that only Aiko could fill. But she'd been so unsure Aiko would forgive her or even see her that she'd left her toy chest and all its contents at home. She turned Aiko onto her back, straddling her but leaving a gap between their bodies. Then she moved her hand between Aiko's thighs, thumbing her engorged clit and reveling in the silky wetness.

Aiko purred.

Hovering over Aiko, Summer made a scissoring motion with her middle and index fingers and asked, "Can I?"

Aiko's tongue swiped over her lower lips as she nodded.

Summer positioned her legs to create maximum access, then eased her clit against Aiko's and began circling her hips.

"Ah shit." Aiko's eyes rolled back.

Summer kept up the slow grinding motion as long as she could, but only a few minutes passed before she came, shaking and cursing as it happened. She then leaned down on Aiko. Enjoying the way their breasts smashed together, she whispered, "Please tell me you got a dick around here somewhere."

"No, baby, I . . ." Aiko stopped as if just remembering something. "Wait a minute, yes I do." Aiko gently moved Summer aside, stood, and crossed to her closet.

Lying across the bed, nude and horny, Summer listened to the sounds of Aiko rustling around until Aiko returned to the bed. Aiko was wearing her harness and carrying a blue bag.

"I went to a party the other night, and I just remembered this was in the gift bag." Aiko reached inside and pulled out a brand-new fluorescent-yellow dildo still encased in its plastic clamshell packaging. "Damn. I didn't know it glowed in the dark."

Summer giggled. "Be sure to communicate my thanks to whoever put that together."

"Oh, I will." Aiko used scissors from her nightstand to free the member from its plastic prison.

Summer swallowed. "That's an inch or two bigger than I usually take . . ." She let her voice trail off.

"I'll be as gentle as you need me to be," Aiko assured her, standing up to secure the dildo in the harness.

"I know you will," Summer answered softly.

With a smile, Aiko rejoined Summer on the bed, kneeling between her open thighs. After reaching the nightstand again, she squirted some lube on her palm. Summer felt her pussy flutter with anticipation as Aiko worked her hand up and down to spread the lube around.

An instant later, Aiko found Summer's opening. Aiko rocked her hips forward in a long, slow stroke. Summer swore she'd died and ascended to heaven as the girth slid inside her, touching every wall, every cavern, of her pussy. "Fuck, yes."

Aiko leaned in to kiss Summer's lips, bringing their bodies flush, their breasts brushing against each other in time with her rhythmic stroking. "You like that, love?"

"Yes . . ." It was all Summer could say as the searing-hot pleasure of Aiko's skillful thrusts melted her brain into ecstatic ooze. Summer wrapped her arms around Aiko's neck, clinging to Aiko, her only port in the storm of orgasmic bliss.

Aiko rocked faster, increasing the speed and friction of her strokes, all while continuing to kiss Summer's lips, her eyes, her throat. Aiko gripped Summer's ass with one hand while lifting her breast with the other. She closed her lips around Summer's nipple, and Summer screamed.

A second later, Summer screamed again and felt a gush of fluid pooling beneath her as her pussy flexed around Aiko's strap. A sweet, delicious agony built inside her as Aiko continued to stroke, apparently undeterred by that initial orgasm. Before Summer knew it, she came again, her body releasing another torrent.

Lying in Aiko's arms, sweating and breathing heavily, Summer sucked on her bottom lip. "I might have ruined your comforter."

"If you did, it was well worth it." Aiko pecked Summer on the cheek. "You can feel free to destroy my bedding whenever you like."

"Keep destroying my pussy, and I'm gonna do just that." Summer laughed. She couldn't pinpoint why, but she felt a little wired. Maybe it was the emotional roller coaster of a day she'd had, but for some reason, the post-fuck nap wasn't calling her. Her stomach rumbled loudly, and she cringed.

"All right. Now I'm not asking if you're hungry, I'm telling you to eat something. I love you too much to let you starve."

Summer's heart turned a flip. "Say that again."

Aiko grabbed Summer's ass with both hands, then gave it a firm squeeze. "I said, I love you too much to let you starve."

Summer kissed Aiko on the lips. "I love you, too. Now what you got in your refrigerator?"

"Let's go find out." Aiko stood, grabbed Summer's hand, and pulled her toward the kitchen.

Friday morning, Summer followed Aiko into the conference room inside Abernathy's offices. At Summer's suggestion, they'd coordinated their clothes to give the "visual cue of a united front." Aiko wore a yellow button-down shirt, charcoal slacks with a matching vest, and a gray paisley tie—Summer, a yellow midi dress with a charcoal cardigan and matching peep-toe pumps.

Three of the other four attendees were already present. Miriam sat at the head of the table, wearing a cream-colored jacket and skirt. Summer recognized her from the pictures on the company website. Next to her sat a brown-haired man in a smart navy suit whom she vaguely remembered but didn't know. Her gaze then swung to the tersely set face of Bill Kirby, the burly construction chief. *It appears our time apart hasn't softened his feelings toward me.*

As Summer and Aiko took their seats, Miriam spoke. "Good morning, ladies. Aiko, would you make the introductions while we wait for Mr. Yates?"

"Sure." Aiko gestured with her hands as she spoke. "Everyone, this is Summer Graves. Summer, this is Miriam Abernathy, our company founder, and Logan Warner, my direct supervisor." She paused. "I'm sure you remember Bill Kirby."

"I do." Everyone said hello to Summer, though Bill's was noticeably the least enthused.

Another man walked in then and took a seat at the opposite end of the table from Miriam. He was tall, tan, and dressed in a tailored suit that mimicked the color of his brown eyes. He had a full blond beard, which contrasted his shaved head. "Morning, all. Sorry I'm late."

"Think nothing of it, Peter. We're glad you could join us," Miriam said. "Everyone, this is Peter Yates, chief executive of Yates Property Management."

"I'm excited to hear these suggestions," Peter said, settling into his chair and removing a slender stylus from a compartment in his phone case.

Summer straightened in her chair, making direct eye contact with the developer. "Mr. Yates, let me start by apologizing for all the disruption I've caused at your site. That old, dilapidated school building was once a storied learning institution, founded by my late grandmother. I let my passion for preserving her legacy cloud my judgment, and I won't be acting in that way going forward."

"That's good to know, and I respect the guts it must have taken to come here and say that to me, face-to-face." Peter offered a soft smile.

"I agree." Miriam rested her elbows on the table, then tented her fingers. "Honestly, I can respect your reasoning, too. Legacy is a very important thing." She opened up an image on her phone, then turned it around so they could see it.

"This is my granddaughter, Mimi. She's almost two." Miriam's face showed a smile radiating with that special brand of grandma love. "Everything I've built here will belong to my daughter Ryan when I'm gone, but someday, it will all be Mimi's."

"She's beautiful." Summer grinned. "Is she your only grandchild?"

Miriam nodded. "At least until I can convince Ryan and her husband to have another one." She laughed, then turned off her phone display and set it down. "Anyway, I can see you and your grandmother had a great relationship, and I can see the impact she left on you as well."

"I appreciate that," Summer admitted.

"I've got four children at home, myself. The things we leave behind for our families are so important," Peter said.

"So, from a legacy keeper to legacy makers, are you willing to hear me out?" Summer asked.

"I'm all ears." Peter tapped his stylus on the screen of his phone.

"Wait a minute." Logan spoke for the first time since the meeting had begun. "Are we really going to sit and listen to this woman, after the amount of disruption she's caused?"

"She's already had her say," Bill groused. "I've heard her mouth firsthand and watched her gum up my worksite."

Summer swallowed the snappy retort that came to mind. "True enough. But you threatened me and my companions, and I think that was way over the line."

Miriam's eyes widened. "What? Bill, is that true?"

Bill looked flustered for a moment. "I only said I'd have that security team remove them from the premises. It's what Logan told me to say! He was the one who had me hire them. He said 'concrete consequences' would keep her and her ilk from making any more trouble."

Silence fell, and all eyes turned to Logan.

Miriam's eyes narrowed. "Logan, what do you have to say about that?"

His face reddening, Logan stammered, "I did say that, but I didn't mean . . ."

Miriam raised her hand. "Save it. You and I can talk about that later." She looked back in Summer's direction. "You've won even more of my respect now that I know you faced such a threat."

"That definitely isn't how YPM does business," Peter added, tossing a displeased glance toward Logan and Bill before returning his attention to Summer. "Let's hear your ideas."

Taking her cue, Summer opened her red folder. "I'm glad you asked."

For the better part of the next twenty minutes, Summer talked about the data she'd gathered, the correlations she'd drawn, and her best ideas for solutions. Summer ran point, Aiko filling in when Summer needed but mostly observing. The more Summer talked, and the more Miriam and Peter engaged with her, the more passion and conviction took hold.

"Aside from everything I've said, I can tell you're plugged into the community, Miriam. The chamber of commerce, Texas Women in Business. I know you graduated cum laude from your architecture program, and that you built this place from the ground up, much as my grandmother did with Sojourner Truth." Summer gathered her papers and closed her folders. "And Peter, you were top of your class at Duke, you've won awards for client satisfaction, and you've had great success with similar projects to this one. So, what do you think?"

"I think I'd like to know what you do for a living," Miriam joked. "You'd make a hell of a lawyer."

Summer laughed. "Actually, I teach at a private preschool."

"Wow. Those kids are getting some impressive education, then," Peter interjected. "I think you've presented a very convincing case for setting aside space in the new development to be used for more community-minded purposes."

"Awesome." She imagined Aiko could feel the excitement rolling off her body. "I'm glad you agree. So, how do we proceed?"

"We'll have the team here draw up some detailed plans for the interior of the building," Peter replied, "and talk with our prospective tenants about the changes to see if we're all on the same page. I think we can reach a compromise that's both profitable and beneficial to the community."

"Thank you, Mr. Yates, Mrs. Abernathy." Summer stood and went to shake their hands. "I'm happy to help along the way."

"Sounds good. I'm glad we could come to an understanding." Peter offered a hearty handshake.

"I think we can consider this meeting complete." Miriam rose from her seat. "Good chatting with you, Peter." She eyed the other two men. "I'll expect you two in my office in twenty minutes. Aiko, you, too."

Logan and Bill offered quiet affirmative replies.

Aiko nodded. "I'll be there."

As everyone filed out of the conference room, Summer and Aiko walked to the lobby. Summer commented, "I still need to stop off to pick up Mama's gift."

Aiko wrapped her arm around Summer's waist and kissed her softly on the lips. "You were amazing in there. They really had no choice but to agree to your ideas, you presented them so well."

"Thank you." Summer felt her cheeks warm at the praise.

"Go celebrate Mama Graves. And give her this for me." Aiko took a small envelope out of her vest pocket. "It's a gift card for a spa day."

"How sweet." Summer grinned. "I'll see you later, baby."

With a parting wave, Summer was out the door.

Shortly after Summer left, Aiko joined Bill and Logan in Miriam's office, claiming a seat on the comfy, overstuffed red sofa in the sitting area.

Seated behind her desk, Miriam addressed the two men sitting in front of her, side by side. "Bill, your work for me is as a contractor, so I can only place so much blame at your feet. Suffice it to say that I won't stand for anyone, least of all a group of women and teens, to be threatened by grown men. Not on this project, or any project that I'm associated with."

Bill swallowed. "I understand."

"Good. Then you're free to go on with your day. I sense we won't have to have another conversation like this." Her tone was polite yet just slightly venomous.

Bill nodded, then exited in a hurry.

As soon as Bill left, Miriam turned to Logan. "I can't believe you would encourage such behavior from a contractor. This calls into question every other project you've ever led with this company, Logan."

Logan stuttered. "I . . . uh, listen. Miriam. It was definitely bad judgment on my part, and I apologize. Really. It won't happen again."

Aiko held back a snort. *He's only sorry he got caught.*

"I wish you'd said that to Ms. Graves while she was here. She's owed an apology for what transpired." Miriam paused. "I can't trust you with authority, not after you've behaved like this. So I'll give you two choices. You can either take a pay cut and a demotion to junior planner, or you can clean out your office and find a position elsewhere."

Logan slid to the edge of his chair. "Miriam, I . . . but . . . you can't . . ."

"As long as my name's on the door, I absolutely can." Miriam leaned back in her chair. "And I just did. Now make your choice."

Logan's head drooped, and he released a defeated sigh. "I'll take the junior-planner position."

"Fine. You can clean out your office and move into the empty cubicle in the commons, with the other juniors."

Aiko cringed. She could easily recall how difficult it was working in the commons. There were ten cubicles in the space as well as the copier, the employee mailboxes, and the vending machines. There was constant noise and foot traffic, making it difficult to concentrate on design work.

Logan's head snapped up. His eyes were wide and his mouth agape.

Unable to resist, Aiko called out, "Pick ya jaw up off the floor, my guy."

With his voice laced with frustration, he said, "I have to give up my office, too? This is insane!"

"Think so? Take it up with your new boss." Miriam pointed toward Aiko.

Aiko stared. "Miriam, are you saying . . ."

Miriam nodded. "The senior-planner position Logan just vacated is yours."

Feeling the smile tugging at her lips, Aiko said the only words that came to mind. "Wow. Thank you."

"You're welcome. You've done excellent work here; you earned it."

An outdone Logan rose from his seat and trudged from the room, eyes cast downward.

Aiko spent a few more moments chatting with Miriam before returning to her own office. Seated behind her desk, she thought about all that had transpired. It was definitely one of the most eventful days she'd had since she began working at Abernathy.

This isn't how I pictured getting promoted, but Logan really fumbled the bag. I just happened to be there to catch what he dropped. Shaking her head, she opened her laptop and began the day's tasks.

When she left shortly after four, she paused to grab the earring from her desk on her way out.

A short drive back into the city led her to Carmella's Fine Jewelry. The shop was Black- and woman-owned; Peaches had told her about it once when Aiko complimented her custom-made watch.

After walking inside, Aiko approached the glass-fronted counter filled with sparkling gems. The woman herself, Carmella Radford, was behind it, wearing a fitted black dress with pearl earrings. "What can I do for you?"

Aiko took the earring out of her pocket and handed it over. "Well, Carmella, I've got a little project for you."

CHAPTER TWENTY-ONE

Seven Months Later

On a beautiful spring day, Aiko escorted Summer across the grassy expanse in front of the brand-new Sunrise on First Multiuse Center. Aiko couldn't help admiring the landscaping as they walked; after all, she'd agonized over the placement of every tree and shrub. Seeing it all come to fruition now made all her efforts feel worthwhile.

Aiko glanced at the woman on her arm, the love of her life, and felt her smile broaden. Summer looked gorgeous in the aqua-colored strapless dress she'd chosen for the ribbon-cutting ceremony. Her loose waves framed her face, and long, teardrop-shaped aquamarines dangled from her ears. Aiko loved how well Summer's dress coordinated with her own ensemble of a tan vest and trousers, brown oxfords, and a teal shirt.

They found their seats on the lawn in front of the main entrance and sat, waiting for the festivities to kick off. About thirty others were expected at the event, and most of them were already seated in the grove when Aiko and Summer took their seats near the front.

Aiko waved to Miriam and her coworkers, who were already present. All of them waved back except Logan. He sat near the rear of the grouping of chairs, wearing dark sunglasses that obscured his eyes. His thin lips were pursed so tight they'd basically disappeared.

"This is so exciting," Summer said, a broad grin on her face. "The outside is so nice, I can't wait to see what the inside looks like."

Aiko squeezed her hand. "As soon as the ceremony ends, we're going in for a private tour."

Once the ceremony began, they listened to speeches given by various dignitaries, including Austin's mayor and the city councilman. They represented the district containing Ivy and a portion of East Austin. The most moving speech, however, came from Peter Yates.

"When I purchased this property last year, my main goal was profit. I saw a prime piece of land occupied by a dilapidated building and immediately thought of the potential revenue it could bring in. I told myself that, by buying the property, I'd be doing a good thing. I'd remove blight, I'd bring jobs to the community. And for a long time, I was content to proceed that way." He paused. "But then, I met a remarkable woman. She helped me see that profit and community uplift do not have to be mutually exclusive. In fact, they can coexist rather nicely, with the right planning. So, I'd like to thank Summer Graves for inspiring me to think more broadly about Sunrise on First, and what it could be."

At Aiko's urging, Summer stood for a hot second and got an enthusiastic round of applause. Ending his speech, Peter came over to shake her hand before moving on.

The end of the ceremony came when Peter and the mayor used a giant pair of scissors to sever the blue ribbon wrapped around the front of the building, which drew more applause. Aiko walked hand in hand with Summer through the entrance, nodding to the person who held the door open as they passed.

"The center is three separate single-story buildings, linked together by glass-enclosed breezeways." Aiko turned to the left. "I'm going to show you the west wing first. It's the commerce side."

Inside the western end of the complex was an open layout that resembled a town square. Skylights allowed natural light to flood the space, and unique storefronts gave each of the five retail shops a distinctive look.

"This is really nice," Summer commented. "I see three of the storefronts are already leased, so that's good."

Aiko nodded. "Yeah. Two of them are boutiques, and the other is a confectionary."

"I love this. Let's take a look at the main building next."

Aiko smiled. "We will. Right after you see the east wing."

Summer poked her lips out in an exaggerated mock pout but followed Aiko across the complex to the east wing anyway. There, they perused the empty room that would soon host private offices and a communal break room and conference room.

Summer sighed. "I wish I needed an office. These spaces are so nice."

"Top-notch everything. Energy-efficient, green building materials all throughout the place." Aiko linked arms with Summer and steered her back toward the center's nucleus. "Okay. Now you can see the main building."

Summer excitedly giggled as they returned to the main building, passing through the double doors that separated the entryway from the interior. She'd only glanced at this space earlier, and it was even more impressive close-up. Inside, there was a large circular lobby featuring black plush-looking furniture situated around a soothing fountain built into the floor. Plants adorned the fountain's border, creating a lush, tropical look.

"Are these real plants?" Summer touched one large frond.

Aiko shook her head. "Nah, but they're made to look like they are. Pretty good, right?"

"Right." Summer still had her hand on the leaf. "It's amazing. The surface feels waxy, just like it would on a real plant." She walked on, going around the fountain and into the corridor beyond. "Hey, babe? What's back here?"

"Just keep going and you can take a look." Aiko deliberately slowed. Unable to keep the smile off her face, she added, "I think you're really going to love it." Aiko came around the fountain just in time to watch Summer push through the double doors into the next room. Since it would be Aiko's first time seeing it finished, she entered behind Summer but stood back to allow her to experience it on her own.

"Oh, my God." Summer stood in the center of the room, staring up at the three-dimensional all-capital letters attached to a ridge along the roofline: **Beulah Graves Community Outreach Center**. Her hand flew to her mouth, and she turned around, tears standing in her eyes. "Aiko! Did you do this?"

Aiko smiled. "You haven't even seen it all yet. Keep exploring."

The room was circular, like the last, allowing two-way foot traffic without the bottlenecks common in more traditional spaces. Summer took slow steps around the area, moving to the right, announcing every new thing she found. "Oh, there's a fitness room. A youth game room. Oh, is that a computer lab? It has a computer lab?"

Trailing behind Summer, Aiko nodded. "Keep going, love."

Summer made her way to the leftmost side of the circle, where the reception desk was located, and stopped. Staring at the wall behind the desk, she covered her mouth again as a new wave of tears came. Aiko followed Summer's gaze and smiled when she saw it. *They did such a good job with that.*

There, high on the wall, hung a portrait of Beulah Graves. Not just any picture, but the one that used to hang in the entryway of Sojourner Truth Charter Academy. Just beneath the image of the Graves matriarch hung a large, framed photograph of the school, as it had appeared shortly after its founding—a photograph Summer's father, Rodney, had provided.

Aiko knelt, waiting for Summer to finish looking around and notice her.

Summer spun slowly around, tears streaming down her face. She glanced around . . . until she finally saw Aiko, kneeling at her feet.

Holding out the black velvet ring box, Aiko opened it to reveal a custom-made turquoise-and-diamond engagement ring. "You've taught me so much about passion, and about the importance of legacy. Your love for this community has impressed me at every turn, but it's your love for me that's truly amazing. And I hope you know how much I love you right back. I don't know what the future might hold, and what I might leave behind when I'm gone. But I do know that I want to build my legacy with you." Aiko cleared her throat, struggling to finish against the tide of tears she felt rising inside her chest. "Summer Monique Graves, will you be my wife?"

Summer sobbed in earnest as she joined Aiko on the floor. Pressing her hands to the sides of Aiko's face, Summer nodded. In a tearstained voice, she whispered, "Yes, Aiko."

Aiko felt a grin stretch her lips as she slipped the ring onto Summer's finger.

Summer's eyes widened. "Is that my earring in the center?"

Aiko nodded. "I couldn't think of a better way to return it to you than this."

"Omigosh." Summer sobbed anew. "I just . . . love you so much!"

Tears spilled down Aiko's cheeks as she caught hold of Summer and tugged her into her arms. "I love you, too."

There they were, two women deeply in love, crying all over each other on the cold tile floor of a community center deep in the heart of Texas.

As Aiko held Summer's body close to hers, she knew she wouldn't want it any other way.

On the last Saturday of spring, as the blooming flowers began to give way to the heat of summer, Summer donned a white tea-length A-line gown. White sequins adorned the sweetheart neckline, and sheer white tulle formed the off-the-shoulder sleeves. She smiled at her reflection in the mirror as her mother placed a silver chain with a teardrop diamond pendant around her neck. "I can't believe this day is finally here."

"Me either," Meadow replied as she placed the crystal-encrusted tiara atop Summer's upswept hair. Brushing a bit of lint from the jacket of her turquoise skirt suit, Meadow added, "You know what they say, time flies when you're having fun."

Crystal entered then, already dressed in the simple teal strapless cocktail dress she'd chosen to wear as her sister's maid of honor and sole attendant. A broad grin came over her face as she caught sight of Summer. "Wow. You look beautiful, baby sis."

"Thanks." Summer swallowed the lump of emotion in her throat, determined to keep her carefully applied makeup in place for as long as possible. Stepping into the clear acrylic pumps, "glass slippers" she'd chosen as a nod to her and Aiko's encounter all those years ago, she smiled. *I'm ready.*

When there were three knocks on the door from Aiko's friend Jamie, they went to the entrance of the multipurpose room to await their cue.

Summer peered around her sister's shoulder to get another look at the decorations. The atrium of the community center had been transformed into a chapel of sorts, with loads of crepe-paper streamers and other festive decors in shades of silver and turquoise. Thirty-five guests were seated in artfully arranged chairs, and a balloon arch had been set up to function as an altar. Taylor, Aiko's friend who'd gotten ordained so they could officiate, was already positioned there.

Above it all, her grandmother's face looked down on the scene.

"Girl, get back before somebody sees you." Crystal gently nudged her sister.

Stepping back, Summer sighed. "I just wanted to see it again. When I go back out there, my eyes will be on Aiko."

"As they should be," Crystal quipped.

When the time came, Crystal exited to make her walk toward the altar. Shortly after that, Rodney appeared at the door in his gray suit, arm extended. "Let's get you hitched, sugarplum."

They linked arms, and Meadow joined them, tears standing in her eyes.

With her parents flanking her, Summer moved slowly down the makeshift aisle toward Aiko, who stood next to her suit-clad best friend, Peaches. True to her word, Summer couldn't take her eyes off of the love of her life. Aiko wore a silver-and-turquoise brocade jacket and white slacks with turquoise loafers. Hair piled atop her head in a neat bun, Aiko looked more regal than any prince Summer had ever seen in a storybook. As their gazes met, Aiko offered Summer a broad grin.

I'm a lucky woman.

Summer reached the altar and, after her parents gave her away and took their seats, joined hands with Aiko.

Aiko leaned close and touched her forehead to Summer's, bringing with her the scent of her cologne. "You're so gorgeous."

Summer smiled with all the love she felt. "So are you."

Taylor cleared their throat, and as they read the predetermined words from a scroll, Summer and Aiko exchanged their solemn promises of forever. Summer soon lost the battle with the tears she'd been holding back but managed to keep her voice clear and loud as she endeavored to put her love for Aiko into words. When Aiko answered with vows of her own, Summer's tears increased.

Taylor grinned. "The deal is sealed, y'all. I now pronounce you married!"

Aiko drew Summer into her arms, dipped her low, and kissed her lips so slowly, so sweetly, that Summer knew she'd melt into a puddle, leaving nothing but a pile of clothing and a pair of "glass slippers" behind.

Hoots, whistling, and applause filled the room as the kiss dragged on. When they came up for air, Summer and Aiko paraded from the atrium into the larger multipurpose room in a shower of confetti thrown by the guests.

A bit later, Aiko and Summer sat at the head table, and Summer leaned her head against Aiko's shoulder. "Babe, who is that absolutely adorable older couple sitting at table four?"

Aiko glanced at the table in question. "Oh, that's Debra and Irene. Debra's in my mom's book club, and she and Irene actually have a really sweet origin story."

Summer listened, her eyes on the two gray-haired women as Aiko told the tale. Watching the way they gazed into each other's eyes, she could easily see the love radiating off them. "Wow. I'm glad they finally got together."

"Me, too." Aiko put her arm around Summer's shoulder and squeezed it. "And I'm doubly glad I didn't have to wait that long for you."

"Nah, I'm not *that* patient." Summer laughed, resting her head on Aiko's shoulder again and enjoying the feeling of peace that came with having her near. "Besides, how can you keep a girl waiting like that when you can't resist her?"

ABOUT THE AUTHOR

Photo © 2021 Kianna Alexander

Kianna Alexander has always been something of a dreamer. Raised among the Carolina pines, she routinely read fifteen or more books a week and was always thirsty for more. Her vivid imagination eventually led her to spin tales of her own. Kianna published her first novel in 2009 and has been publishing steadily ever since. Her passion for building empathy through fiction shows in her writing, and she truly believes literature can have a profound and positive impact on people's lives.

Kianna is also a mother of two; a dabbler in various crafts; and a lover of random trivia, music, white wine, and sunrises on the beach. She lives in the western US with her children, her partner, the world's highest-maintenance cat, and a precocious pup. For more information visit www.authorkiannaalexander.com.